S0-AAC-847

A LOVE OUT OF TIME

Their eyes locked for a brief, devastating moment, sapphire-blue clashing with hazel, as something treacherous flitted between them, touching Rebecca's heart. The sensation was like an old key turning the rusty tumblers of an ancient lock. The relinking of lost souls, Rebecca thought, drawing back as if shocked.

"This is stupid!" Rebecca gasped.

"Why?" Alexander asked, stunned by the feeling that had overtaken him.

Rebecca wanted to say, "Because I'm not of your world. Because in *my* time, you're already dead and buried, and in yours, *I* haven't been born yet."

Instead, her practical concern overrode her passion for an instant as she fought the rapturous fate threatening her more rational side.

"Because I'll hurt you."

PASSION'S TIMELESS HOUR

VIVIAN KNIGHT-JENKINS

LEISURE BOOKS NEW YORK CITY

A LEISURE BOOK®

July 1992

Published by

Dorchester Publishing Co., Inc.
276 Fifth Avenue
New York, NY 10001

If you purchased this book without a cover you should be aware
that this book is stolen property. It was reported as "unsold and
destroyed" to the publisher and neither the author nor the publisher
has received any payment for this "stripped book."

Copyright © 1992 by Vivian Knight-Jenkins

All rights reserved. No part of this book may be reproduced or
transmitted in any form or by any electronic or mechanical means,
including photocopying, recording or by any information storage
and retrieval system, without the written permission of the Publisher,
except where permitted by law.

The name "Leisure Books" and the stylized "L" with design are
trademarks of Dorchester Publishing Co., Inc.

Printed in the United States of America.

This book is dedicated to:
My brother, Richard, and father, Ganson Lloyd, the true historians in the family.
My sons, Gerald and Marc, and my husband.
Peg, who stood staunchly behind me all the way (mainly so I'd have no recourse, but to move forward).
Alicia Condon and Lydia Paglio — the reality behind the dream.
And to all American servicemen and women throughout history who have sacrificed so much for their country.

You have been mine before—
  How long ago I may not know;
But just when at that swallow's soar
  Your neck turned so,
Some veil did fall, —I knew it all of yore.

Has this been thus before?
  And shall not thus time's eddying flight
Still with our lives our love restore
  In death's despite,
And day and night yield one delight once more?
                Dante Gabriel Rossetti
                English Poet & Painter
                1828-1882
                from "Sudden Light"

PASSION'S TIMELESS HOUR

Prologue

Vietnam
January 2, 1968

God, she was burned out on the intricacies of war.

Rebecca Ann Warren and the other members of the Mobile Army Surgical Hospital were in the mess hall, rallied around the popcorn-strung bamboo tree—a poor, spindly stand-in for a Scotch Pine—singing carols. But Rebecca craved solitude to enjoy her package from home. So she stole away from the company party, scooting across the compound toward her bunk in a makeshift dormitory, better known as the nurses' hooch.

Halfway across the inner perimeter, Rebecca waved a casual salute to an M.P. standing guard near the motor pool.

Vivian Knight-Jenkins

"You aren't staying for the festivities, Lieutenant?" he asked as she passed him.

"Not this time. Seems I've lost my taste for rice wine and spicy finger foods."

"I can't believe the mail finally made it through the lines!"

"I know what you mean," Rebecca responded, continuing on without a break in stride.

"I bet they've postponed the holiday bash three times, waiting on those packages," the M.P. called after her.

"More like four," she said over her shoulder.

The rain-warped hooch door proved no match for Rebecca. One expert kick and it swung open obligingly. Once inside, she collapsed on her bunk, her package cradled in her lap.

The Christmas present was over a week late. The postal service was atrocious in the backwater MASH unit, but Rebecca couldn't have cared less. It was the thought behind her parents' gift, mailed from Atlanta, Georgia, in the good old U.S. of A., that counted.

Beneath the stark electric sheen of an overhead bulb, Rebecca removed the crushed satin bow and laid it aside. Sliding a surgical knife along the tape line, she unwrapped the package, careful not to tear the festive Currier-and-Ives gift wrap.

Rebecca folded back the tissue paper to discover a nightgown with a pleated yoke, high collar, and long sleeves, trimmed in delicate openwork embroidery. The gown reflected the traditional cameolike charm her mother, an antique collector, prized.

"Oh, Mom, Dad, how lovely—irresistible," Rebecca whispered, her eyes tearing as she laid aside the dress box to caress the gown. Rising, she held the white creation against her asexual Army fatigues, gazing down appreciatively at the luxurious yards of pure femininity.

Her sapphire eyes sparkling, she turned in a waltz step and the skirt belled gracefully.

Her full lips creasing into a smile that emphasized the dimple in her chin, Rebecca spread the gown across her bunk. Unable to resist the impulse to try it on, she stripped out of her T-shirt, and her dog tags swayed and jingled from her hurried movements.

"Hardly appropriate, Mother," she chided, as if her mother could hear her over the miles that separated them. "Where in the world will I wear it?" she questioned aloud, the rusty sound of down-home happiness creeping into her voice for the first time in months.

Rebecca unlaced her combat boots and kicked them under the bunk, then shimmied out of the fatigues and tossed the pants across the foot of the bed. Relieved of the olive drabs, she donned the nightgown.

Sliding the sensuous folds over her head, tugging her auburn braid from beneath the collar, Rebecca allowed the material to glide across her breasts and down her torso. It cascaded against her body, conforming to the slender curves of her five-foot-seven figure to fall in a whisper about her ankles.

She thrilled to the texture of the fabric as she

buttoned the bodice, so different from her seemingly indestructible uniform. The gown, a size seven, fit perfectly—and why wouldn't it? The food was awful—canned, hashed, mashed, overcooked, underdone yuck! She didn't have to worry about her figure while dining on Army rations.

Daintily, she stepped into the slippers her mother had included. Relishing the comfort of padded satin against the soles of her feet, she danced a quick two-step to test their softness.

A card was enclosed in the gift box. Rebecca had saved the handwritten treasure for last.

Bending at the knees, she retrieved the envelope. Rebecca kissed it, preparing to read the mail-belated Christmas wish when the sirens sounded, and the loud speaker blared.

"In-coming wounded! The cease-fire is over, ladies and gents. It's high noon, the cavalry's landing, and you're all invited to the tea party."

Reacting instantly, Rebecca dropped the card into the zippered side pouch of her first-aid satchel. Clamping her stethoscope around her neck, she flung the leather field bag over her shoulder, grabbed her helmet stuffed with rolled bandages, and headed for the door. Her cotton nightgown gathered above her knees, she burst from the hooch at a dead run.

Gazing skyward, Rebecca watched the helicopter swing drunkenly, its red-and-white insignia a dizzy blur. The pilot was in trouble—a medevac mission gone wild. That he would miss the metal helipad plate was inevitable.

The Huey steadied for a moment, hovered overhead, then dipped toward the red dirt field to the left of the official landing mark. Her heart pounding, Rebecca veered diagonally in that direction.

Another nurse, in a blue surgical suit, ran neck and neck with Rebecca toward the casualty-evacuation machine. "Our radioman says the bird sustained ground fire. Rice-paddy assault," Janet, Rebecca's friend, panted.

"Serious?"

"Pilot injured, possible chest wound. Co-pilot, dead. Crew-chief/medic—inexperienced kid—caught it in the arm. Scared as hell...and flying the thing. Pilot's lucid. Trying to talk the boy down safely."

"How many others?" Rebecca, now the efficient nurse, asked.

"Full load, I think. No info on their conditions."

"Damn!"

The copter hung twenty feet above the ground—almost safe. A gritty cloud of crimson dust rose as it descended, and trash spiraled like a tornado from a dump at the end of the field. Sucked up in the chopper blades and flung outward, dangerous airborne debris scattered helter-skelter.

An empty ration can whizzed past, barely missing Janet. Two corpsmen, stretcher bearers, close on the women's heels, yelled, "Duck!" just as a heavy object hit Rebecca squarely in the temple.

She felt herself falling, her knees striking the ground with jarring force as her helmet slid off her arm and tumbled out of reach. Rebecca clutched her first-aid satchel like a lifeline, as the red haze enveloped her and blackness descended.

* * *

"For pity's sake, get up!" Fingers tugged at Rebecca's hand, encouraging her to her feet. "The watch says we've got stragglers comin' in from Stones River. More wounded, no doubt. I thought we'd gotten the last of them on a train bound for the hospital, but I suppose I was mistaken. Wishful thinkin'. Lordy, Lordy! I swear, the unpleasantness of this war just goes on and on, doesn't it?"

"Seems that way," Rebecca agreed faintly, rising to her feet. What was Janet talking about—Stones River? She remembered nothing by that name in the Central Highlands of Vietnam.

"Brings to mind a piece of poetry I once read by an English gent, Thomas Hood. 'But why do I talk of Death? That Phantom of grisly bone, I hardly fear his terrible shape, It seems so like my own—It seems so like my own, Because of the fasts I keep; O God! that bread should be so dear, And flesh and blood so cheap!' But that's neither here nor there, seein' as how the poem was about stitchin' shirts, not war."

The petite woman paused to catch her breath, clucked her tongue at Rebecca, then once again grasped her hand. "Come on now, Rebecca Ann. Dust off your knees and roll up your sleeves, suga'. I know you're bone-weary. I am, too, but they'll be arrivin' any minute," drawled the woman with a deep, Southern accent.

Southern? Janet was from New York, wasn't she? And as for Rebecca Ann, only her brother, a gung-ho Marine, had ever used her full name—

14

and he'd been killed by a sniper near the DMZ prior to her enlistment.

"I'm coming."

Rebecca shook her hand free, groping for her first-aid satchel. It rested on its side, beneath the hem of her gown. She snatched it up, squeezing it tightly in agitation as she found her feet, and her stainless steel stethoscope swayed like a necklace draped around her throat.

"Have they landed in one piece?"

"Landed! Where is your mind? You must be sleepwalkin'. Sakes alive, they're not on a ship! They're in a wagon—ambulance, I presume—and Mrs. Amehurst, our matron, isn't going to like you traipsin' about outside in your night things, even if you are an honorary captain."

"A lieutenant," Rebecca corrected automatically.

"Whatever. Anyway, we knew you were exhausted from your trip, so she just left a uniform on the foot of your bed . . . had no idea you'd sleep the afternoon through."

"A uniform?"

"Naturally, like mine. You should have dressed properly before answerin' the yard bell. Decorum is a necessity with soldiers nigh. We must never forget the golden rule, Rebecca Ann. 'We are ladies first, nurses second,'" she quoted. "Besides, you'll catch your death, prancin' around with neither cape nor shawl to cover yourself. Not to mention what notions the healthy men might get if they see you in that . . . elegant sleepin' gown."

The woman's voice sounded faintly envious. Rebecca couldn't fathom why. Janet had received a nice care package from home, too—pancake and pizza mixes, a tin of homemade cookies, a utility light—useful gifts.

An uncomfortable thought struck Rebecca. Maybe this wasn't Janet.

Rebecca peered around. It was dark, *cold*. She could feel the dampness of the frosty earth through the thin soles of her slippers. An owl hooted, drafting a pattern against the mellow light of a pale winter moon as it glided across the clearing in search of prey. Rebecca shivered, confused.

It had been broad daylight, sweltering due to the humidity. The temperature was never under seventy-eight degrees. Now, through the distorted darkness, she could discern the flicker of campfires ringed with men hunkered in bulky bedrolls, and the ghostly glow of whale-oil lanterns suspended from yard posts. A lone harmonica moaned hauntingly somewhere in the bowels of the camp a sad refrain of "Dixie."

The buildings of Rebecca's MASH unit had vanished, swallowed by the shadows of the cedar forest sheltering the bivouac. In their place stood unbleached canvas tents and tarps beneath which crude tables and ladder-back chairs rested. An oddly dressed soldier played cards at one of the tables, puffing on a pipe as he dealt hands to his eager compatriots.

A weary, yet vigilant sentry with a bayonet-tipped musket shuffled in and out of the campfires' wavering lights, glancing over at the card players wistfully. Stomping periodically to awaken leaden limbs, he stopped, shifted his rifle into the crook of his arm to blow on his cupped hands, then resumed his patrol with the same methodical precision of a wind-up toy.

A ramshackle farmhouse painted with a white cross loomed ahead. *An EVAC hospital? Triage?* Rebecca wondered.

No chopper blades whirred, scattering red dust and trash. Instead, horses and mules, tied on long rope lines, whinnied to one another; harness leather creaked. Wood smoke mingled with the mouth-watering aroma of meat sizzling over open tripod spits. Why were there no aviation fumes from the helicopter's exhaust?

Rebecca's stomach twisted in alarm, and her skin tingled as the hair on her arms stood to attention. Dazed, she turned to the woman in the muslin cap and scarlet cloak. Not exactly the indomitable Janet she knew, but a reasonable facsimile of her blond friend, Rebecca thought, gauging the woman's facial features through the play of light and shadow.

"What the *hell's* going on here?" she demanded, conquering her fear in true military style. Had she broken under the stress of the last few months? Her tour of duty was almost up. Good nurses were so desperately needed that she'd entertained the idea of re-upping for another year. Maybe she should say farewell to the service after all and make her parents happy.

"Rebecca Ann Warren! Matron doesn't cotton to foul language, nor, I might add, the consumption of spirits either. She'd be monstrous unhappy to learn you're not a teetotaler."

Rebecca sniffed. She smelled alcohol. Had the antiseptic bottle in her satchel broken during her fall?

"An upright woman herself, Matron expects us to be above reproach. But, you'll learn the regulations soon enough, I daresay, and a wee nip of cordial never hurt a body. 'Specially in these tryin' times," the blonde added more kindly, removing her cloak to display an indigo dress and bib apron. Deftly, she fastened the outer garment around Rebecca's shoulders, adjusting the hood over her hair and tying it snugly beneath her chin in a motherly fashion.

"There, modest enough for a Bluelight at Sunday service, I'd say. Now you needn't take the time to change till later on."

Rebecca snuggled into the cloak's warmth, glad for the comfort of the rough wool against the chill seeping into her bones.

The woman rattled on. "The war has changed us all, I fear, made us harder than the genteel Southern women we once were. The gaiety has ceased, and we are at war for our very livelihood."

Warming to her subject, the young woman climbed aboard an imaginary soapbox. Rebecca stared, amazed by her fervor.

"We must do our part for the cause, support our menfolk as best we can. I am proud to wear my cornhusk hat rather than a more expensive bonnet, though I must admit I do miss my coffee... so costly these days. Dried, ground sweet potatoes just can't hold a candle to the real thing..." Her voice trailed off. "But you've heard all this before, haven't you, my brave dear, an Atlanta-born gal such as yourself?"

"Atlanta?" Rebecca questioned distractedly, shaking her head to clear it. To save her life, she couldn't make heads or tails of the woman's gibberish; however, "Atlanta" did ring a bell.

A vivid picture of her hometown flashed through Rebecca's mind—highrise buildings, four-lane parkways, cars. Now she had proof she was dreaming, Rebecca reasoned, her mind in a turmoil. Georgia—home—was a lifetime away, the Pacific Ocean separating it and the crude MASH unit where she was stationed.

"Yes, Atlanta. That's where you said you hailed from, wasn't it, though you couldn't tell it by your accent?"

"O–rig–i–nal–ly," Rebecca agreed, pronouncing each syllable as if she were speaking to an alien from Mars.

She hadn't been home since finishing her two-year stint at Johns Hopkins Nursing School in Maryland. Her tour of duty in the armed forces hadn't allowed it. She'd been shipped overseas the week following graduation.

In less than a day, the twenty-four-year-old Rebecca had found herself plopped into the stench of an intensive-care burn unit near the South China Sea. Another month, and she'd replaced a health-broken nurse in a MASH unit in Timbuctoo. The years away from Georgia had modified her accent, taken the edge off her Southern drawl and given a new value to her pronunciation of certain words. Rebecca readily admitted that sometimes her tongue twisted over those words, making them sound contrived.

"I thought that fall only skinned your knees. I think it addled your wits, too. Now, come along, no more time for idle chitchat. We must hurry... Don't want to be late," Rebecca's companion offered impatiently. "The wounded are in dire need of medical attention, whether we find Yankee blue, Cadet gray or butternut."

"What?" Rebecca asked, dumbfounded. The Huey was in trouble, something had hit her in the head. She remembered that much. Her knees hurt, but, otherwise, she was uninjured—breathless, overwhelmed, confused, but basically A–OK. Perhaps she had sustained a concussion... was delirious. Or, heaven forbid, maybe she was *dead?* Could that be why her body seemed so buoyant, why she remained relatively calm amid such strange surroundings?

"We'll be late. The wounded don't wait."

I feel like Alice in Wonderland, Rebecca thought woozily. *I've met the verse-spouting White Rabbit,* she reasoned, looking to the restive nurse hopping around beside her. *All I need now is a grinning Cheshire Cat to complete the picture.*

"I do declare! Try to pull yourself together, you hear. They say you're the best field assistant this side of the Mason-Dixon line, Rebecca Ann... your credentials impeccable. Havin' studied with Florence Nightingale at St. Thomas's Hospital in London, I don't doubt it. Now's your chance to show off some of that fancy education. Rumor has it we've got a chest wound comin' in. A cavalry officer of some status. I'm anxious to see how you handle it."

"Me?"

"To be sure. Our only surgeon, Major Gibbs, passed on this morning."

"A casualty!"

"Not dead. He and Matron accompanied the wounded on the train—the Nashville and Chattanooga—to oversee their welfare durin' transit to the base hospital further along the line, deeper south where it is safer. I told you before, we didn't realize there were more wounded. Looks like it's up to you to do your best in his place."

"But I'm not a doctor!" Rebecca blurted, thinking, *Chattanooga*. Was this woman trying to convince her they were in Tennessee . . . U.S.A.? She knew Tennessee—The Great Smokey National Park; Sunday picnics with fried chicken, potato salad, and canned pork-n-beans; lazy, autumn drives to see the leaves turn. These primitive shadows weren't from the Volunteer State she knew.

Maybe she'd been captured by the enemy and drugged out of her gourd. Rebecca pondered the possibility and rejected it as absurd. It just didn't add up.

"Surely there's someone else. Someone better qualified? I'm an O.R. scrub nurse," Rebecca gulped, fending off panic.

"A what? Never mind. Jargon from that English school, I'll warrant. Look, you're the only professional nurse we've got, Rebecca Ann. I'm a worker bee—you know, read war bulletins and write let-

21

ters for those who can't, or don't know how; bathe a face here and there. Now, come along, please," the woman urged, her words ending on a pleading note. "That's what you were sent for, isn't it?"

"Yeah. Sure, I guess so. Lead on," Rebecca conceded hesitantly, a frown creasing her arched brow. After all, she'd been trained to give aid to the sick and wounded, hadn't she? And two could play at this weird mind game—whatever it was.

"By the way, we're mighty proud you chose to join our unit when you did. I've never been so happy to see anyone in my life, as I was when I saw you ridin' bareback into camp this mornin', saddlebags filled with precious medical supplies ...The best New Year's gift I can imagine. Beats me how you got through the Yankee patrols, but it was a prayer answered."

"Bareback?" Rebecca whispered under her breath. She hadn't ridden a horse since her summer-camp days, though she could drive a jeep as well as any man—better than most.

"Sure and certain. All I've got to say is, I'm glad you're here. Thank heaven for small miracles."

Losing one's mind could hardly be termed a miracle, Rebecca thought. Undoubtedly, the reality of war had been too much, and she'd mercifully crossed the fine line into insanity. "And I considered myself a tough nut, too hard to crack," Rebecca muttered introspectively, fighting off her rising hysteria.

As she blindly followed the flaky blonde toward a bonfire on the far side of the entrenched encampment, Rebecca reminded herself that she'd been trained not to blow her cool under extreme conditions. And she didn't intend to cop out at this late date, especially when these people—whoever they were—seemed to need her so badly. But, if she wasn't crazy, where in the heck was she?

Chapter One

January 2, 1863
Tennessee

In the still watches of the night, the coolness of a soothing hand gently caressed Lieutenant Colonel William Alexander Ransom's feverish forehead, brushing back the dark curls plastered there by dried perspiration. The flutter of a benevolent angel's wings touching his brow? he wondered fleetingly. An insidious grayness hovered around him, obscuring everything else except the pinpointed light of her haloed presence.

"Hold the lantern higher, for God's sake. I can't see to take a pulse, much less examine the wound." The angel bent over him, her warm breath fanning his face as she added in a muttered whisper, "What

I wouldn't give for a hundred-watt bulb and an hour's worth of electricity right now!"

Her halo grew, the stethoscope around her neck reflecting the expanded light. The bell, as shiny as a newly minted coin, dazzled Alexander with its unique brilliance.

He could feel the cold disk weighing on his chest as the angel pressed the bell to his heart. Sharp talons tore at his burning shoulder when his linen shirt shifted beneath his coat and fangs pricked his skin to suck at his immortal soul. The encroaching shadows seemed determined to draw him under their spell as, painfully, the ravaged flesh diagonal to his heart was probed, stealing his breath away.

With a feeling of suffocation, Alexander lashed out. Someone caught his hands, forcing them to his sides.

"Please, Rebecca Ann, help him," Cordelia implored as the beam of light fell across the officer's face. "This man's my cousin! I had no idea he'd be our chest wound. I'd word his brigade was outside Tennessee—foolish prattle."

"Your *cousin? How ironic.*"

"Yes. William Alexander's the only Ransom left of three vibrant brothers. We call him Alexander. Well, his brothers, Beau and Edward, fell at bloody Sharpsburg in a single day of fightin', September last. Our family will be crushed, purely crushed, if we lose him as well!"

"I'll do my best, but you're going to have to be still. I feel as if there's a jitterbug dancing under my elbow."

"All this while he lay wounded near the cedar grove! It sends cold chills up my spine to think of his fate if those volunteer corpsmen hadn't stumbled upon him ... Divine Providence, I'm certain."

"Probably so, now, stay *still*. It's your job to direct the light. I've got my hands full with this wild man."

The conversation going on around him jogged Alexander's memory. Dusk. He had been on a reconnaissance mission, scouting the Federal lines to determine whether the Army of the Cumberland—the enemy—showed any signs of retreat. They had not. Before he could get the information back to his superior officer, he'd been wounded.

"A Yankee sharpshooter spotted me," he mumbled as if in report, reliving the incident in his feverish mind as if it were a dream.

The whiplike crack of a carbine had split the morning in two as the sniper's first shot plowed into Alexander's mount. He'd felt his faithful steed's knees buckle under him.

Vaguely, Alexander recalled gathering strength to shift his weight in the saddle so he could spring clear of the horse as it dropped to the ground, but the second bullet, hot on the tail of the first, had hit him squarely in the shoulder. The force of the lead ball ripping painfully through muscle had momentarily stunned him. In that instant, the animal had gone down, and his left leg had been trapped beneath the horse's massive body.

The earth, softened by the previous days of rain, cushioned his leg, but the horse's dead weight was so much that Alexander couldn't drag himself from beneath it. The rowel of his starred riding spur, digging deeply into the ground, only compounded the problem, fixing his foot at an awkward angle as if toenailed into position.

Hand on the Colt Dragon revolver tucked into his waist belt, Alexander had waited for the sharpshooter to climb down from the trees and finish the job. But the enemy had never materialized.

There was more, something vital yet elusive. But as the pain in his shoulder increased, Alexander's thoughts seesawed back to the moment at hand. His square jaw taut, he tried to concentrate on something other than his wound.

He realized someone, perhaps the young corpsman, had already divested him of his caped greatcoat and knee-high riding boots, leaving his buff-colored corduroy trousers for modesty's sake. Alexander fixed his eyes on the angel's freckled face, grabbing her hand in a bone-crushing grip when she attempted to cut off his yellow-trimmed, gray frock coat with a pair of gleaming scissors retrieved from her medical satchel. The shears were fashioned from the same unusual metal as her stethoscope. Obscure memory suggested that the coat was a link to his mission prior to his injury. Consequently, he was stubbornly loath to see it damaged.

Barely lucid, he cautioned the angel hoarsely, "Don't cut the coat." Then, with an inbred civility that defied even the most unlikely situations, Alexander tried to rise to his feet in the presence of a lady.

"Stay down, you nitwit! Do you want to rip open

what little tissue is still intact?" Rebecca spat, shoving the gallant Southern gentleman flat against the makeshift operating table—a thick pine door stretched between two chairs—situated in the farmhouse's large front room.

"I'm not sure about *this* place, but cutting off a garment is standard medical procedure where I come from, GI Joe. I need to cleanse the wound, there are bits of thread inside. I can't get to it through the coat," she stated flatly.

"Best try, ma'am," Alexander said, frowning at the angel's outlandish speech.

"The hell I will, soldier! I don't care if you are an officer," Rebecca countered. "The coat is hardly worth your life," she explained stubbornly.

Alexander scanned the angel's face, stopping briefly when he had reached her fantastic eyes—long dark lashes shading irises the color of wild, mountain bluebells. His gaze panned lower, and his groggy mind forgot why the coat was so important. He could only stare at the column of her throat as delicate as any swallow's.

Rebecca's heart skipped a beat.

"If you honestly believe your men will fare better in the field without your leadership, I'll let you ease out of this world in full regalia, without a fight," she snapped, more disturbed by the draining assessment of her patient's gaze than she cared to admit.

Beneath the dirt, spattered blood, and shadowy beard, Rebecca could detail the features of an extremely handsome man. It would be a pity to deliver such a hunk into fate's stickly fingers, she thought, excusing her reaction to Cordelia's cousin by submerging it in concern.

"Make your choice but make it double quick. Time's wastin'," she prompted, bent on breaking direct eye contact with the lieutenant colonel, preferring instead to remain as detached as possible.

The whole situation was ludicrous, Rebecca thought as she awaited his answer. She felt as if she was trapped in a bizarre Civil War battle reinactment. She had no idea who these people were, and yet, she was compelled by instinct to utilize her superior medical knowledge to save a life. Once she had wrestled her obstinate patient into submission, she realized she was going to have to figure out what the hell had happened to her!

Alexander squeezed his hazel eyes shut a moment, clenching his fingers into a fist against the blunt edge of his garnet-eyed serpentine ring. He found comfort in the heavy gold Ransom family heirloom worn on his right ring finger—a snake with its tail in its mouth, the symbol of eternal life.

The ministering angel was blunt, but she exuded a quiet confidence that broke through the haze clouding Alexander's befuddled mind. The throbbing in his shoulder had already begun to lessen. Without a doubt, she seemed to know her business, although her luminescent medical tools were strange indeed.

The shadows were advancing again, like relentless troop companies. Alexander shuddered, pondering, should his own will fail, whether the angel at his side possessed the skill to pull him back from death's door. He prayed that she did; he had far more important tasks to fulfill than the Grim Reaper's stagnant assignment.

White-faced, Cordelia asked, "Rebecca Ann, how does it look?"

"Cordelia?" Alexander heard the familiar, beseeching voice chime in a second time. He'd discredited her first plea as a hallucination.

"Yes, it is I, in the flesh."

"What are you doing here, on the fringes of Hell's Half Acre? You should be safe away . . ."

"Less talk and more action," Rebecca admonished, cutting abruptly into the family *tête-a-tête*, her patient's welfare uppermost in her mind. "There'll be time for conversation later. For now, hold the lantern *behind* my head so I can see to work, Cordelia! You swing it in front again, you'll blind me for sure—if your cousin doesn't give me a black eye first."

Cordelia drew herself up to her full height, her eyes wide and round. "A Ransom would never strike a woman, Rebecca Ann! It wouldn't be seemly."

"I never intended to cast aspersions on your family honor. I was just stating a fact, Cordelia. He's already tried to sock me once! Loosen up."

The angel's attention rounded gracefully back to Alexander as she placed her hand at his nape and lifted his head to press a canteen to his lips.

"Listen, if your coat is that important to you, I won't cut if off. I'll just snip out a swatch around the wound, and you can slip the darned thing off and use it for a pillow, A—OK?" Rebecca relented in a soft voice, strangely touched by the close ca-maraderie between the dashing cousins—one small, fair, and feminine; the other dark and de-cidely masculine.

Alexander swallowed obediently and coughed as the invigorating sip burned a pleasant path down his throat toward his empty stomach. It had been a long time since he'd enjoyed fine brandy.

"A–OK?" Alexander mimicked, confused by the unfamiliar term, still tasting the strong drink as he licked his parched lips.

Rebecca searched her vocabulary for a moment. "If that's all right with you?" she elaborated.

"Done," Alexander consented with a slight grin, his wry sense of humor and genuine native spirit shining courageously through the unmistakable pain.

So, the Cheshire Cat finally makes his appearance, Rebecca thought as she responded in gruff repar-tee, "Well, now that that's settled, let's get the ball rolling. We haven't got all night," she added, roll-ing up her sleeves.

Rebecca had been harsh with Alexander Ran-som, but then, it was because she knew she could save him if he let her and her technique had worked like a charm.

A masterful angel, with a cocky disposition and a peculiar way of expressing herself, Alexander thought, intrigued. He was twenty-eight years old, and he'd never heard a female use such unortho-dox language. But then celestial beings couldn't be expected to follow the linguistics of English. After all, they weren't of this world, he decided before the gray shadows once again claimed him, tugging him into unconsciousness.

Rebecca was thankful when Alexander passed out. It allowed her to proceed unhindered without filling him to the gills with morphine—such an addictive drug.

Using her surgical scalpel, she cut away the dead tissue to avoid gangrene, swabbed the area with iodine, then applied a sterile dressing, leaving the wound open.

"You aren't going to stitch it shut before you bind it? The surgeon always does," Cordelia observed with surprise.

"Trust me, Cordelia. I may not be a doctor, but I know what I'm doing. I'll suture the bullet hole closed in a few days' time. That way the tissue will have a chance to heal from the inside out without festering."

At the word "festering," Cordelia blanched.

"If you'll excuse me for a moment, I find myself in sudden need of a bit of fresh air," Cordelia said, her hand over her mouth as she scurried outside.

"What in the world set *her* off at this late date?" Rebecca wondered aloud, turning back to her sleeping patient.

As the grand finale, while Cordelia was otherwise occupied, Rebecca administered a hefty dose of antibiotics via syringe, pronouncing Alexander Ransom a lucky man. Even without X-rays, she could tell the gunshot had gone clean through. The lead ball miraculously passed through the shoulder muscle, then out his back without lodging inside a bone or puncturing a lung.

"Between the coldness and the padding created by his heavy woolen clothing, your cousin's loss of blood was effectively reduced," Rebecca told Cordelia when she returned. "His respiration appears normal for his condition and he's resting easy enough. I think the prognosis for recovery is favorable," she predicted.

Rebecca glanced around her at the carnage postured on the stretchers, men who had been brought in with Alexander Ransom. Her hands balled into fists at her sides. "I wish I could say the same for these other poor wretches." The majority had sustained injuries far too severe for treatment with the limited medical means available.

What she'd yearned for to kick off the New Year, Rebecca thought, was some small measure of peace. What she'd gotton was a repetition of the same old junk in daguerreotype!

Composure, under the circumstances, was hard won; the reality succinct. Rebecca had an overwhelming desire to burrow into a secluded corner and to tear her hair out at the brutal fatality of war. To counteract insanity, an abiding numbness set in. She glided among the poorly clothed, frostbitten unfortunates almost as if she really did sport a pair of fragile wings.

"Lady," a leathered farmer swathed in body bandages cried out, clutching at her skirts. "My eyes are afire! I can't see nothin'."

Rebecca checked his wounds, burns that covered eighty percent of his body, then flipped open her satchel.

"That's only because it's night, black as pitch outside. I'm going to give you something to make you more comfortable. Before you know it, you'll be resting like a baby and the darkness will feel like a blanket, snug and warm around you," she said soothingly, a tear gathering in her eye.

Rebecca had no idea what year syringes were invented, but she knew the soldier required something for pain. Did she have the guts to stand by and allow him to blindly wallow in his torment? she asked herself. Or was she going to give him something to ease it?

No one around her was in any shape to question her methods, Rebecca reasoned. The corpsmen were outside; Cordelia was once again cooperating, her eyes closed, facing heavenward as if in earnest prayer.

Glancing around furtively like a paroled convict bent on robbing a bank, Rebecca made her decision. Filling a hypodermic with morphine, Rebecca injected the sedative.

The man seemed not to have even noticed the prick. "Hate to admit it, lady, but I'm plumb scared," he confessed groggily as the shot began to take immediate effect. "Will yuh...sit by me ...till I drop off?"

Rebecca cleared her throat and blinked several times. "I've got rounds to make, but this pretty blonde beside me will be glad to join you, won't you, Cordelia?" she stated chipperly, pulling Cordelia back to earth.

"Y—yes, if you really think it necessary," Cordelia stammered. She usually made it a practice to steer clear of the really awful cases whenever possible, particularly those that pertained to rednecks recruited from the general working populace.

"I do," Rebecca confirmed, her words threaded with steel.

Leaving Cordelia to hold the soldier's limp hand, Rebecca stopped to trail her palm over Alexander's brow. He was already cooler to the touch. "You make a very good nurse, angel mine," he commented, surprising her. His hazel eyes tightly closed, she'd thought he still slept.

"It's my job, Lieutenant Colonel Ransom," Rebecca replied, shrugging off his praise as she moved on, though she couldn't curb the tingle of pleasure that welled inside her at his words.

A gangly youth had gone into shock. Rebecca covered him with a blanket made from a braided rag rug. It was the most she could do for the once-proud Johnny Reb without typed, bottled blood.

"I'm so thirsty," someone else moaned. Rebecca dallied only long enough to retrieve a tepid pail of water and dipper from beneath the operating table, then quenched the soldier's thirst much as she had Alexander Ransom's earlier.

"They say a camel can go weeks without water. What do you think?" Rebecca asked him in low tones as he sipped from the tinware dipper.

"Can't say . . . as I know, ma'am. I reckon I ain't never seen . . . no camel."

"I saw one in a circus once. Ugly fellow with

35

buckteeth, cloven hooves, and a hump the size of a mountain. Saw a llama, too. They spit at you, you know."

"Naw!"

"So help me. Now, swallow this pill for me, and I'll tell you all about it."

And so the night passed, a solemn vigil as the women worked side by side. Sunday morning broke through the moist fog then waned. Rebecca barely acknowledged high noon's approach and demise. Catching only cat naps, she diligently worked through until evening. It was Cordelia, wrung out and dragging, who drew her attention to the Sabbath's blood-red sunset.

"The fightin' is over, Rebecca. They'll be no more casualities. Word's been passed that General Bragg's made the decision to begin evacuation of the lines tonight. The Army is headin' south, for Tullocoma in Coffee county, to set up winter quarters near the railroad depot. Rosecrans's bluecoats will, of a certainty, occupy Murfreesboro, three miles southwest, until spring. There is little left for me, but to return to Oak Mont, the Ransom family plantation in the Nashville basin. I'm goin' to obtain permission to take Alexander back with me."

"But Nashville is north, isn't it?" Rebecca asked, punchy from lack of sleep.

"In enemy hands to be exact," Cordelia informed Rebecca, "but there are no Yankees billeted at Oak Mont, and my conscience insists I see Alexander home. As a volunteer, I already have the passes necessary to accomplish the deed . . . and he would have wanted it that way."

"Your cousin is doing well, all things considered. You talk as if the man's death is a foregone conclusion!"

"Isn't it? What life you've given him will be sapped by the wagon journey," Cordelia lamented sadly, resigned to her cousin's fate like that of so many others before him. "But I appreciate your resourcefulness and your kindness, Rebecca Ann. Perhaps your patchin' will see Alexander home," she stated in an emotion-filled voice.

Rebecca hadn't considered travel. A wagon. Imagine that! The rough trip *might* kill him, if she didn't accompany them to give medical supervision and to forestall any hemorrhaging that could occur from the jostling.

Besides, sending her boys off had always been one of the hardest parts of nursing. She'd stabilize them then they'd ship out as fast as possible. When the medevac copters flew off toward hospital facilities on the South China Sea, she never knew if her patients survived and were sent back to the world—the States—or not.

Their fates weighed on her mind, became personal. Sometimes she saw their nameless faces in her dreams. Now was her chance to follow a case through to the end, never to wonder how he'd fared—or whether he'd recovered.

Plus, what if she really had been thrown back in time and the Ransoms were her link to the future? If they were lost to her, would she be stuck in the past forever? As unlikely as that was, she couldn't completely dismiss that it was a possibility.

And after all was said and done, Rebecca thought, *she* certainly wasn't going into winter camp with a bunch of strange men—Confederate patriots or not. What recourse did she have, but to tag along with Cordelia, and her injured cousin, Lieutenant Colonel Alexander Ransom?

Now she knew what her mother's favorite phrase, "Stuck between a rock and a hard place," really meant. She was living it!

"You won't change your plans, Cordelia? Go to another town in unoccupied territory, take the train farther south to the hospital you spoke of earlier . . . something less drastic?"

"I can't. Besides, there will be no train passin' through with that Yankee Rosecrans hoverin' over the tracks like a vulture."

"Pigheadedness must be a Ransom family trait!"

"Rest assured."

"Well, some of it runs in my family, too. I'm going with you. A woman alone, a wounded Confederate officer, crossing enemy lines . . . You can't do it by yourself. It's far too dangerous. The entire state is a potential combat zone!"

Unbidden, bits and pieces of Rebecca's elementary school education in Southern history came seeping through the leaky dam of memory. In fact, wasn't Tennessee the largest contender for Civil War battles next to the champion, Virginia? Rebecca asked herself, wracking her brain. Yes, yes it was!

Disgusted, Rebecca clamped her satchel shut with a decisive snap. Just her luck! She'd landed in the red-hot middle of another disturbing conflict. No nice, cool, normal R & R in Hawaii for her. No sirree. What in the world had she done to deserve this? Life was a paradox. She'd been rescued from one hellhole and dropped smack dab into the middle of another.

Rebecca had never contemplated history repeating itself, folding over into some sort of fifth dimension like cake batter, but she did so now. Did such wacky things like time warps, really exist, other than on TV? This dream seemed real enough—the wounded, the chilling winter darkness, Cordelia and, last but not least, Alexander Ransom.

If I keep thinking about stuff along those lines, I'm sure to blow a gasket, if I haven't already, Rebecca silently cautioned herself, shifting her mind into cruise control to keep from hyperventilating.

"I so wanted you to join me, care for Alexander, but I wasn't sure what you might say to such a forward invitation with your work and all, and the brevity of our acquaintance...Feel as if we've known each other far longer. So pleased...Forever in your debt...Alexander, too...Won't be sorry. Oak Mont is a wonderful place to catch up on your rest. Really quite beautiful, Becky."

Cordelia's relieved chatter brought Rebecca back from her reverie, her attention centering on the final word of her last long line. She'd never cared for being called by the diminutive version of her name.

39

As if she'd read Rebecca's mind, Cordelia said, "I hope you won't be terribly offended if I call you Becky. Rebecca Ann seems so formal between travelin' companions. Quite a mouthful really."

Rebecca sighed. Anything to be accepted, she thought, feeling suddenly drained and in dire need of the respite Cordelia spoke of.

"Whatever makes you comfortable, Cordelia."

"Good. Now, if you will make yourself present-able and gather your things, I will have the picket bring up your horse directly. Meanwhile, I'll col-lect the necessary supplies, and have Alexander settled into the wagon. I'd like to be on our way while we have the cover of darkness to skirt the Federal lines. Though its only thirty or so miles as the crow flies, it will take quite awhile along the Nashville Turnpike, even if we're lucky."

My horse? So, the plot thickens, Rebecca thought, looking down at her blood-spattered gown peeping from beneath the scarlet cloak, then back at Cor-delia.

"Pity you people haven't heard of gas-powered engines, airplanes, hot, *running* water," Rebecca grumbled in a low voice, wondering how in the world she'd catch a ride back to reality if she left the bus stop where fate had dropped her off by mistake.

"What?"

"I said your cape. I'm still wearing your cape over my nightgown."

"That's all right. I'll get it later."

"Fine. Where can I change?"

"In your quarters, over there, of course." Cordelia frowned, pointing out the canvas tent to the left of the infirmary. "As I explained yester eve, there is a uniform waitin' for you."

Troubled by Rebecca's forgetfulness, she added, "Don't act so . . . Oh, I don't know—daft. I understand what the harsh sights of war can do, what you've suffered travelin' back and forth through the enemy lines, but they're like to put you up in one of those horrible old lunatic asylums, if you continue on so befogged."

Don't panic. Just do . . . not . . . panic, Rebecca told herself. She didn't know who they might be or where the ambiguous nineteenth-century asylum Cordelia spoke of was located, but she wasn't taking any chances. She didn't intend to end up in an institution if she could help it.

Rebecca Warren decided then and there, to take Cordelia up on her suggestion. She would try and appear relatively normal until she discovered the trap door back to her own time frame and she would tell no one her fantastic story. That she was a reluctant traveler from the future, caught in a time warp which had snatched her from a medevac mission gone haywire, and projected her into the past—into the role of a Civil War nurse in Tennessee—would remain her own secret psychosis for the time being.

Chapter Two

The musty, rain-dampened tent to which Cordelia had directed Rebecca proved to be more pleasant on the inside than out. Candlelight filtered out of a tin-punch lantern hanging from a strap in the ceiling, spattering the canvas walls with shimmering dots of light.

The tent contained a cot spread with a slightly rumpled hand-stitched patchwork quilt, and a chicken crate table dressed up with writing paraphernalia and a chipped china washbasin. For an instant, however, Rebecca thought the tent already occupied. A cloaked figure stood in the back in a far corner, glaring at her from beneath the broad brim of a battered felt hat.

"Pardon the intrusion. Miss Ransom told me..." Rebecca began, backing away, then stopped. There was something odd about the rigidity of the shadowy form.

On closer inspection, Rebecca was relieved to find her "someone" to be a cloak-draped wooden valet crowned in a black slouch hat.

"Well, what did you expect, to be accosted along with everything else? Cordelia *said* this was your tent. Getting awful skittish here. Calm down," Rebecca cautioned herself aloud as she moved further into the tent.

Not quite home, but passable in most respects Rebecca granted. It was as good as the nurses' hooch she shared with three other women.

The uniform Cordelia had spoken of—a pristine gown with fichu collar and button-down sleeves, sporting a snowy apron with huge Captain Kangaroo hip pockets—lay spread out on the cot. Rebecca wrinkled her nose in distaste. Hardly her style of clothing. Cordelia looked cute in the uniform, but she'd look more like Raggedy Ann than a competent nurse.

Rebecca flicked the uniform aside, pulled off Cordelia's cloak, and sagged gratefully onto the shaky cot. She felt drained, still uncertain how in the heck she'd gotten into her present predicament. Was Janet, head nurse of the modern-day MASH unit, searching for her? she wondered. Had the Red Cross informed her parents she was missing in action? Her mother would be heartbroken; her father would retreat into that ominous silence he'd hidden behind following her brother's death.

Then again, maybe they'd be saved the grief. Perhaps she wasn't missing at all but here, and there, too, at the same time. Sweet Jesus! Was such a thing possible?

Rebecca felt a thread of fear course through her for the first time since her arrival. She never allowed herself the luxury when working with her patients. Now all of a sudden, her head ached; her teeth were chattering. She was afraid! *What am I going to do?*

Rebecca squeezed her eyes shut, fighting back the tears. "Hold on now," she said aloud, giving herself a much-needed pep talk. "You deceived yourself in Vietnam that everything would be all right. You can do it here, too. No difference. A piece of cake. Self-control and discipline are the key words. They're *everything*, when you exist amidst madness." And nothing could get any crazier than this!

"Humph," Rebecca said, opening her eyes as she took a swig from the canteen Cordelia had provided, hoping to bolster her flagging spirits. "I doubt there's enough brandy in the entire state of Tennessee to make sense out of this mess!"

Leaning back, Rebecca closed her eyes to savor the flavor of the warm brandy when the cot, tilting precariously, collapsed under her weight, tossing her on her derriere. Her eyes wide with surprise, Rebecca laughed aloud at the absurdity of her plight. Here she was, dressed in a bloodstained cotton nightgown, sprawled on a lumpy cot in a Confederate-issue tent, swilling century-old brandy, in the middle of her great-grandfather's war. She'd like to see the guys in the MASH unit top this one.

Rallying her wits, Rebecca sobered. *Stop dwelling on the statistics*, she advised herself. As surely as she'd come here, she'd return to her own time. She'd just have to be patient. Time would right itself—but when?

There were no easy answers. And no telling how long she'd be trapped in the nineteenth century, Rebecca decided, her eye catching a valise she hadn't spotted in her earlier surveillance. There was one thing for sure, though. It was high time she stopped acting like a baby and moved on, made the best of her dilemma. Cordelia...and Alexander Ransom were waiting for her.

Stretching, Rebecca drew the bag onto the cot beside her. She delved into the luggage, discovering undergarments—a camisole and drawers, corset, unstiffened flannel petticoat, and striped cotton stockings with garters—as well as a forest-green walking skirt, a twilled woolen jacket with taffeta-covered buttons, and a stylish yellow satin neckcloth topped with a beribboned lace bag of honeysuckle sachet.

"Aha, success at last," she proclaimed, well pleased with the acquisitions, the fragrance of dried flowers wafting up as she sorted the clothes. Wouldn't her mother have a fit over these?

Searching further, Rebecca figured out why the cot was so lumpy. She'd landed on a pair of low-heeled leather boots that had been placed beneath the bed. Inside one boot was tucked a pair of soft kid gloves which Rebecca would once have termed "driving gloves." In this day and age, she assumed they must be referred to as riding gear, used to steer the horse Cordelia had mentioned earlier.

She seemed to have everything she needed to clothe herself properly. "Now, if only these things are the right size," Rebecca said, shaking out the fitted jacket and holding it to her breast.

To Rebecca's astonishment, they were. Fleetingly, she wondered if it was possible to revert back to a previous life. At least that would explain the clothes.

Rebecca shrugged into the underwear, pulling it over her own synthetic bra and panties. Fumbling with the drawstrings, she was reminded of a favorite off-the-shoulder cotton blouse she'd used as a bikini cover-up the summer after high-school graduation. The blouse had been made along the same lines as the camisole. Fondly, Rebecca recalled she'd played the beach bum through August that year until fall and college entrance exams forced her to trade in the fun in the sun for a stack of medical books as high as Mount Everest.

As for the drawers, she'd seen enough black-and-white snapshots of her mother during the 50s to recognize pedal pushers when she saw them. But these fit rather oddly—baggy in the front, tight across the buttocks. Rebecca frowned, then snickered at her mistake. She'd put them on backwards. Turning them around and trying them, she fingered the lace rosettes at the knees, deciding the drawers quaintly acceptable.

Rebecca reached for the whalebone corset, stepped in, cinched it, then balked. Stays biting into her ribs, she clawed at the shoe-like lacings, then tore off the uncomfortable garment and flung it aside. No way! She was not wearing that museum piece, thank you very much. Talk about taking authenticity a bit far. How did women stand those damn things. You couldn't breathe in it.

The soft petticoat passed inspection well enough as Rebecca's body warmed with each added layer of clothing. The unadorned tailored outfit proved a class act, the color complimentary to her auburn hair and freckles. Last came the elastic-topped leather ankle boots, also a perfect fit.

She repacked the tapestried valise with the uniform and apron, as they were her only other change of clothes. Then, saddened and disappointed that her parents' beautiful Christmas gift had been ruined, Rebecca carefully folded the nightgown, placing it in the first-aid satchel for possible use later on as strip bandages.

Quickly, Rebecca splashed her cheeks with cold water from the basin, dried her face and hands with a rough towel, then using a silver-backed brush from the valise, she smoothed her bangs and rebraided her rich auburn tresses. Thus fortified, she gathered up the valise, canteen, and satchel, donned the cloak and slouch hat off the valet, threw the scarlet cloak over her arm, and vacated the tent to locate her new-found friend, Cordelia Ransom.

Rebecca didn't have far to look. Cordelia, her pretty face illuminated by the yellow flame of a crude, hand-held flambeau, stood just outside the tent flap at the rear of a straw-filled wagon, her head bowed. To her right stamped a bobtailed, dapple-gray horse held steady by a sentry, and on her left, a robed chaplain clutched a pitchpine torch and spoke in a low, earnest voice. A hasty "Amen" ended the Lord's Prayer as Rebecca stepped within the circle of light.

Opening their eyes, the trio parted slightly, and Rebecca realized what had been taking place. Alexander, stretched out in the wagon bed, sound asleep and oblivious to their concern for his mortal soul, was being given a form of last rites.

Rebecca cleared her throat. "Can you do that, when someone's, uh...dead to the world so to speak?" she asked, attempting to project a lightness she was far from feeling.

"Ah, there you are, Becky," Cordelia said, then stopped and stared at her friend. "I declare! You are such an eccentric. I never know what you'll do next."

"What? Is my slip showing?" Rebecca asked, glancing down at her clothes. She saw nothing out of place. No petticoat on the outside, though she must admit, walking in the long skirts was reminiscent of Senior Prom night. She hadn't worn an ankle-length gown since then. Mini skirts and bell-bottomed jeans were all the rage. She'd forgotten how cumbersome yards of material could be.

"It's just that, well..." Cordelia, for once, seemed at a loss for words.

"Spit it out. I thought *I* was the only one who 'took a nip' now and again," Rebecca joked.

"Becky! Whatever will these dear men on either side of me think. I haven't been d—drinkin'," Cordelia stuttered, mortified. "It's just that you resemble nothin' so much as an old black raven in that masculine slouch hat and gutta-percha clasp military cloak. Most women wouldn't be caught dead in those dusty old things."

"The better to steal through Yankee lines at night," Rebecca explained with her best Bela Lugosi accent, flapping her cloak like bats' wings as she threw herself into the part of a vampire. Might as well enjoy the stir she had created.

"I believe you are one of the most entertainin' females I've ever met," Cordelia confessed thoughtfully, a smile on her lips as she noted the mens' similar interest in Rebecca.

War certainly had made a mishmash of decorum. It wasn't seemly, but Cordelia did enjoy Rebecca's outlandish company, and was thoroughly enchanted by her offbeat, spontaneous personality as well as her complete competence in action. For her, Rebecca was a rare jewel. But what would prudish Jubadessa have to say when she walked into Oak Mont with her unusual find? Oh, well, best not put the cart before the horse.

The sentry, eager to make the attractive redhead's acquaintance, spoke up. "Ma'am," he said, doffing his kepi, "I hope you don't mind. I saddled your mare with Lieutenant Colonel Ransom's horse furniture, seein' as how you're short on gear yourself."

"Thank you," Rebecca remarked, eyeing the mount uncertainly. She had never seen such a *big* horse—a hunter, solid, deep-chested, and with the longest legs. The "horse furniture" the sentry spoke of included a hand-tooled leather saddle with heavy brass stirrups, a booted musket and scabbarded saber fixed to one side of the saddle-horn, a canteen with a detachable mug, a bedroll and gum blanket, and a compact knapsack of personal items.

"Vedette's an out–n–out dilly. You're right lucky to have her, if you don't mind me sayin' so. Sound, bridlewise, and good square trotter that she is. She took the weight of the officer's accoutrements without a blink," the sentry added.

So, the horse's name was Vedette, Rebecca thought, watching the mare roll her big brown eyes and bat her lashes flirtatiously, as if she understood her handler's compliments. Strangely enough, Rebecca was familiar with the unusual term. Her father, an avid outdoorsman and sailor, had taught her the meaning. For him, a vedette was a small scouting boat used to watch the enemy, taken from the Latin word *vigilare*, to watch through the night. An appropriate companion for a nurse traversing Yankee lines, Rebecca mused.

"Vedette, pretty lady," Rebecca cooed gently, reaching a tentative hand out to pat the mare's velvet nose. At first the animal shied from her touch, ears laid back, but then, as if she suddenly caught her mistress's scent, she emitted a guttural whinny and nuzzled Rebecca's hand familiarly, looking for a treat.

We're old friends, are we? Rebecca marveled, so on impulse, she reached into the side pocket of her cloak and pulled out several lumps of crystallized fruit. She wasn't surprised to find the candy there. She'd instinctively known where to look. When she was a child, she'd owned a golden retriever with a tongue long enough to lick your whole face in one clean swipe. The dog had been addicted to chocolate-chip cookies and Rebecca had made it a policy to keep them on hand. Her mother had always fussed that her coat pockets stayed crusted with crumbs throughout the winter.

"The lieutenant colonel asked tuh keep his pistol and coat in the wagon with him," the sentry informed her.

Rebecca's attention was drawn back to the private. "He would," she remarked flatly.

What was it about that blasted frock coat that made it so precious? Rebecca wondered as she glanced over the side of the wagon to check on Alexander Ransom. Surely, a simple coat couldn't be all *that* important, even if material was scarce.

When she'd put the coat under Lieutenant Colonel Ransom's head, it had seemed unusually heavy, but maybe they were all that way. What did she know of Civil War uniforms? Her expertise was limited to the area of frag jackets and steel-toed combat boots.

Covered to his chin in his greatcoat, Rebecca noted Alexander's swarthy face appeared pale, his hazel eyes closed tightly against the flambeau's flame, but his breathing seemed regular as he dozed off the effects of the morphine she'd given him. Satisfied, Rebecca turned back to Cordelia.

"Do we have everything?"

"I believe so. The chaplain has already said a few words to Alexander. I have food, hot rocks at Alexander's feet to ward off the chill. We are ready.

Mount up, I will drive the wagon."

Good thing, too. I know less about driving that wagon than steering this horse, Rebecca thought to herself as the picket gave her a foot up into Alexander Ransom's saddle which was tattooed with the initials WAR—William Alexander Ransom.

Vedette danced sideways and Rebecca's reflexes took over. She dug her knees in, her shoulders straightening of their own accord, as she tugged back on the reins.

"Whoa, Vedette. Easy now," she cautioned intrepidly, her voice masking her alarm.

The horse settled affably to the tone of Rebecca's voice and the firmness of her hands. A loud puff of air, much like a human sigh, escaped her distended nostrils as she tossed her head, requesting adjustment of Rebecca's grip on her mouth. Rebecca responded, allowing the strips of leather to slide through her fingers several inches before tightening her grip again.

"Sorry, ma'am. I reckon I should'a warned you," the picket said frankly, "she's a mite skittish. Happens a stallion on line gave your mare a right smart nip on the rump this afternoon. I'd avoid touching the spot for a few days, iffen I was you. A might tender, I'd say."

"Right," Rebecca responded, wishing he'd said something a little sooner. Avoiding aggravating Vedette was high on her list of priorities. She couldn't turn off the ignition if the mare took it into her head to buck.

The chaplain assisted Cordelia into the wagon seat and handed her the reins. With a click of her tongue, they were off, Vedette pulling up the rear, the full moon lighting the way as the sounds of camp life faded and the methodical jingle of harness took its place.

Carefully avoiding the Federal lines, they skirted flat, plowed fields littered with the skeletons of damaged caissons. Dismounted cannons, blown apart by the ignition of residual gunpowder hurriedly and ineffectively swabbed from barrels, were strewn like the discarded paper carcasses of exploded firecrackers after a rowdy Fourth of July celebration.

Harsher to gaze upon were the bodies of both men and horses, profound abominations ripe for burial, grisly mannequins postured against the solemn backdrop of an undulating countryside.

The din of battle rang no more, but the horror was all too evident. Rebecca averted her eyes from the staggering loss of life—the unbelievable mass casualties. A sick feeling settled in the pit of her stomach.

How did they bury them all, without a backhoe, without dog tags to identify them? she wondered. Where? These warriors didn't have the option of being flown to a hospital unit, or failing recovery, home in nice, neat flag-draped coffins that glazed over the pain of a conflict fought overseas—out of sight, out of mind. Their war was being thrashed out on American soil—and they were dying, thousands at a time, for all the world to witness.

"Bad, isn't it?" Cordelia said, reading her mind.

"*Bad* doesn't even begin to describe war!"

"If it's any compensation, General Bragg will

see they're buried with full honor, right here on the field where they've fallen. He'll notify as many families as possible."

"It's not." Her mouth dry, it had suddenly dawned on Rebecca why there were national cemeteries in her time. They'd been a necessity, the direct result of the Civil War.

It was all so bewildering for a nurse whose primary directive was to save lives—never more so than today when she was out of her element, and could stand back and take an objective look. What she saw was depressingly clear.

You'd think people would have learned something from this, Rebecca reasoned, casting about for a more carefree pastime to occupy her mind than visualizing the row upon row of white crosses at Arlington.

Absently, Rebecca began to hum a popular ballad performed by Peter, Paul, and Mary—popular to "American Bandstand" anyway. The words came more slowly, as soft as a brush stroke across canvas.

After a few minutes of listening to "Blowin' in the Wind," Cordelia joined in to hum the background melody. Her smooth voice accentuated the haunting words, bringing home their meaning in a way Rebecca had never experienced before. She felt choked up, more by the timeless flavor of the song she herself had unconsciously chosen, than anything else.

"That was nice ... touchin'," Cordelia said when the song ended.

"I don't know what got into me," Rebecca said,

feeling suddenly ill at ease.

"You have a pleasant voice. And I insist you teach me the notes so that I may play it for Mother and Jubadessa. Alexander has a wonderful music room at Oak Mont."

"Oh, I can't read music," Rebecca was quick to remark, stopping herself before she added, "I just pick tunes up from radio and television shows aired in the States."

"Then I shall teach you, and we shall wrest the notes from the piano together," Cordelia said decisively.

Rebecca found herself surprised by Cordelia's accomplishments. Not only was she a competent nurse's aide when she chose to put her best foot forward, she was an accomplished musician. But the most marvelous thing was that she obviously knew the area through which they traveled like the back of her hand. She was such an effeminate contradiction.

Moved to question Cordelia's acute sense of direction, Rebecca was surprised by her answer.

"I admit I know this part of Tennessee fairly well, but not good enough to cross it in the dark without a little assistance. To be honest, I helped myself to Alexander's knapsack. He always carries a compass among other things," she added, patting her apron pocket. "You must thank him not me for the guidance when he awakens. We'll cross Stones River and a set of railroad tracks, then lumber on down along side the Nashville Turnpike. Mind now, step lightly round the toppled telegraph poles, or you'll turn your horse's leg for sure."

"What happened to them, the poles I mean?"

"I'm surprised you haven't run across it before. The Yanks have a nasty habit of fellin' our communication lines. They're also very good at tyin' railroad tracks into bow ties and issuin' blockcades. Keeps the countryside on its toes."

"I see." Strategy, Rebecca thought, settling in for the duration. Anyone in the service could understand the logic. Strategic maneuvers were the same no matter the century—a means to an end.

Several times in the ensuing hours, alerted by the rumble of heavy artillery and tramping feet, they pulled off the unpaved, rutted road to hide in a stand of trees while troops passed, avoiding Yankees and Confederates alike.

Rebecca was confused by this tactic.

"Why are we hiding from the Rebels, Cordelia? They're on . . ." she hesitated, "our side."

"I know that, but, don't you see? Many of our brave, desperate men have not received decent supplies in months. I just can't risk confiscation of the wagon, Alexander's weapons, our horses, and food. It seems cruel and unpatriotic, but . . ."

"I get the idea."

After that, they traveled on in silence for what seemed to be days instead of hours. For Rebecca, it was weird, and a little scary, traveling at night without benefit of headlights and the reassuring purr of an automobile engine to camouflage the forest sounds—the wind in the trees; the bark of a fox; the wail of a bobcat on the prowl; the rustling of an opossum as it ambled along the road, close enough to touch or so it seemed to a city girl.

By the time dawn arrived, its sharp rays cutting through the blanketing ground fog, Rebecca's rear end was tender and her back ached from swaying in the saddle for the better part of the night.

Rubbing her tired eyes with the back of her hand, she said, "Cordelia, we've got to stop. Alexander's had enough for the time being. *I've* had enough. It's time to take a break."

Cordelia sawed on the reins, the wagon grinding to a halt. "But we've barely covered ten miles, Becky! We can't stop now, we need to keep movin'."

"Ten miles! It feels like a hundred!"

"Nowhere near that far."

"Man, don't you ever sleep? I'm pooped!" Rebecca said decisively, stopping Vedette by the tailgate. Long hours filled with stress had taken their toll and her body, like Alexander's, demanded sleep to replenish itself.

"Man?"

"Forget it. I've had it. Call me a wimp, but I've got to get some rest." Dismounting and tying the mare to the back of the wagon, Rebecca surprised Cordelia by climbing in beside Alexander. Settling in, her hand brushed his exposed arm where he'd knocked off the great coat in his sleep.

"My God! He's like an ice cube," Rebecca gasped with concern.

"He's not—"

"No. He's alive, but we've got to keep him warmer than this or he won't be for long," Rebecca said with a frown of concentration. Rearranging the cape and blankets, Rebecca made a single cover, then crawled beneath it to share her body heat with her patient.

Her hand fluttering to her throat, Cordelia exclaimed, "Re—Becky. You shouldn't. It isn't seemly for a lady to...to...to be pressed against a man in such a fashion, especially when they aren't married to each other."

Rebecca cut her short. "That's the silliest thing I've ever heard, Cordelia! I'm a nurse, trying to keep her patient warm the only way she knows how—unless, of course, you'd like to stop and build a fire to reheat the rocks at his feet."

"We can't possibly do that right now. We'd attract attention for sure, so near the turnpike."

"Then give me some alternatives. You want to change places?" Rebecca asked, her fuse growing short. *As if traveling back in time wasn't enough, now I have to deal with some absurd moral code of conduct that would let an injured man die from exposure rather than allow a female nurse to rest beside him in the same wagon bed.*

"Good heavens, no!" Cordelia exclaimed, biting her lower lip. What would Alexander think if he woke up and found her, his own cousin, so intimate and all? It just didn't bear consideration. But then again, if he caught a chill from being out in the weather, what then?

Her conscience would kill her, that's what. She was having enough trouble living with herself as it was! Though raised mostly in the South, Cordelia was torn between her mother's family, and the deep-seated Yankee upbringing her father, a New York lawyer, had instilled in her. She could eat little and slept restlessly from the sheer worry of it all.

Why hadn't she listened to Jubadessa's advice and kept her nose clean! Cordelia asked herself. She wasn't good at choosing sides, was woefully inept at the art of deception.

Cordelia exhaled heavily. She just wasn't cut out to be an ear horn for her husband, James, via her volunteer work. She adeptly side-stepped the word "spy." It sounded so ... monstrous.

At the first opportunity, she'd find an excuse to ride to the Yankee headquarters in Nashville and reason with James, Cordelia decided. She hoped it didn't turn into a repeat of the last time she'd attempted to explain her position. He'd made a scene, ranting and posturing like a bull that had sat on a nest of fire ants. She despised it when he threatened her. Hated even worse, the times the golden-haired Adonis turned the tables and made love to her. Either way, he always managed to get what he wanted. She cared deeply for the South, but she was thoroughly bowled over by James Emory. It was like being caught between the devil and the deep blue sea.

At least she wouldn't be forced to betray the Confederate courier James's office was tracking. No feather for his cap this time. Her eavesdropping hadn't given her a clue to the officer's identity, though James insisted that he'd received recent information linking "The Gray Ghost" to the Stones River area. She'd been given only a sketchy description of the man. Thankfully, it had turned out to be like looking for a needle in a haystack.

I'm in over my head, trapped, Cordelia thought with resignation, *but for now there's nothin' to do but go on to Oak Mont as I planned.* "I'll drive on for a while. You...rest, keep Alexander warm, Becky," she said, clicking her tongue and sending the wagon into a jerky motion. "Get up there, old nag. We've got a l–o–n–g way to go, and a short time to get there."

I'm getting in over my head, Rebecca was thinking when Cordelia halted so abruptly, she almost rammed Vedette into the rear of the wagon.

"What now, more soldiers?" she asked wearily, beginning to turn her horse off the road. Would this thirty-five-mile trip never end?

Days on the trail, in and out of the back of the wagon trying to keep Alexander comfortable, his body pressed against hers, were beginning to pall. She longed for the modern, forty-minute-highway trip between the Murfreesboro and Nashville of her century—as much for her own sake as his.

Warming her patient had become a periodic ritual with Rebecca, but she'd never dreamed Alexander would begin to affect her so. She'd learned every masculine contour of his body as he'd tossed against her, memorized the curve of his brow, been pleased by the unexpected softness of his sable hair when it chanced to brush her cheek.

There was no doubt about it. She was physically attracted to Alexander Ransom despite herself.

And she hadn't realized how love-starved a woman's body could become! Though she'd never pictured herself as the alley-cat type, perhaps Cordelia's code of ethics had a firm foundation based on the natural order of things after all.

"No, wait. This way. It's not soldiers I'm thinkin' of. We have to cut off the pike here."

Rebecca looked dubious. "We've got to travel cross country?"

"Yes, but the trail is clearly marked."

To you maybe, Rebecca thought, shrugging. "You're the boss."

"There's an abandoned barn about a quarter of a mile or so ahead. Its hidden by a ring of trees, squattin' in a field run to waste. I stopped there on the way down with Mrs. Amehurst and the volunteers. I thought we could have a bite to eat and rest there for a few hours before we go on."

"Sounds good to me," Rebecca acknowledged thankfully, her uncertainty paling in comparison to the promise of a roof over her head. She was tired of camping in the open.

Cordelia led them unerringly down a woodland path to a weathered barn that smacked of a little piece of heaven as far as Rebecca was concerned. It was a sanctuary from the weather . . . safe. Cordelia pulled the wagon beneath the arched doorway, and Rebecca was close behind. Gathering up her skirts, Cordelia jumped down from the wagon and shut the double bay doors behind them, temporarily closing out the Tennessee landscape.

Rebecca dismounted awkwardly, her joints stiff as she stowed her gear in the wagon and led Vedette into one of the four stalls on either side of the central foyer to cool her down. She'd seen enough cowboy movies to know the importance of caring for the horse before the rider.

Flipping up a stirrup and unbuckling the saddle, Rebecca staggered under its weight, struggling to fling it over the stall's side railing in one clean motion. "And John Wayne makes it look so easy," Rebecca gasped, straightening the saddle so it wouldn't fall off its perch. Next, as if she enjoyed the attention of her rider, Vedette stood stock still, eyes closed, while Rebecca rubbed her down with the backside of the coarse horse blanket, careful of the healing bite on her rump.

The rubdown complete, Rebecca fumbled with the bridle, managing to get it over Vedette's ears and the bit out of her mouth without taking the contraption apart. Thus liberated, Vedette gave Rebecca a playful nudge toward the front of the stall, then turned her bobtailed behind on her mistress to partake of the water bucket wedged in the corner of the stall. Her thirst quenched, the mare settled down like a trooper to pick through the hay and grain scattered on the stall floor, undoubtedly leavings from another horse's meal.

Rebecca backed out of the stall and automatically hooked the grid-like leather stall guard behind the mare, proud of her handiwork. The picket had been right, Rebecca decided. Vedette was a fine figure of a horse. Not exactly a Mustang convertible, but she'd do in a pinch.

Cordelia, hastening toward the exit, stopped in mid-stride and turned toward Rebecca, a faint blush on her cheeks. "I'll be back in a lick and a promise. Nature calls," she said in a small voice, as if an explanation was needed.

Rebecca simply nodded.

Tossing her hat on the front seat, Rebecca climbed up on the wheel of the wagon to check on her patient's condition. Alexander still slept like a baby, though how he did it was a mystery to her. Her own insides were quivering like gelatin and she had another throbbing headache.

Damn, she wished she had an aspirin! Of all things to leave behind. *But aspirin seemed so trite, so readily available in my time*, Rebecca argued with herself. *How could I have known? No one in their right mind would think to pack a decent supply of aspirin, just in case they were suddenly whisked off to a time before it was invented!*

Rebecca reached out to touch Alexander's forehead. He stirred in his sleep, mumbling the word, "Cold."

Solicitous of his comfort, Rebecca tucked the greatcoat closer around him, adding her own cape and the waterproof gum blanket she'd found in his bedroll.

Reminded of the dreaded perils of pneumonia, so dangerous to the wounded during the first stages of recuperation, Rebecca climbed up into the wagon beside the lieutenant colonel. Careful not to disturb him, she crawled under the covers to once again offer her body heat as additional protection against the dewy air of the chilly January afternoon. Funny, how close a person could get to someone else in such a short time and with so few words.

Concern for her patient's well-being, and the rhythmic beat of his heart as she circled his chest with her arm and laid her head against his good shoulder, were the last things Rebecca remembered before she dozed off to sleep, wrapped in the straw-filled cocoon of the motionless wagon bed. She stirred from the uniqueness of a dreamless sleep as a callused hand gently caressed her hair, the fingers trailing a tentative path down the contour of her cheek, exploring the dimple in her chin.

Groggily and slowly awakening, Rebecca snuggled closer to the comfortable warmth of the muscular body stretched out next to hers. Her skin tingled as firm lips grazed her forehead, her eyelid, then moved lower to capture her mouth.

Her heart palpitating, Rebecca boldly responded to the lingering pressure of Alexander's insistent lips. The kiss seemed perfectly natural, appeasing the unaccustomed spark of raw desire his nearness provoked as her mouth opened to the penetration of his tongue. She drank of the nourishing kiss Alexander so expertly bestowed, fully knowing, by giving into the aching need gnawing at her hungry soul, she was going against her strongest conviction—not to become involved with a fellow serviceman.

"My God, you are so alive, so vibrant," she heard him whisper huskily, his ardor growing.

"Looks like I should have taken Cordelia's advice and slept *beneath* the wagon," Rebecca said dreamily.

"Wouldn't have been half as inspiring," Alexander breathed suggestively.

"No, I imagine not." Rebecca paused reflectively, then, "Hey! I bet you weren't cold at all awhile ago!"

"Yes I was. I've grown accustomed to your warmth, Rebecca."

"You know my name."

"I've been awake, on and off, heard some of the conversation between you and Cordelia enough to learn my nurse's name anyway."

"Why you little faker!"

"I've never been the kind of man to pass up a good thing when I see it and you're the best to come my way in a long while. Can you blame me for keeping quiet?" Alexander asked softly, and she was lost.

Rebecca reached out to Alexander as a drowning swimmer does to an extended hand. Entwining her fingers at the back of his neck beneath his hair, she pulled him invitingly against the softness of her body.

Alexander's hand trailed a path of fire down her arm, brushing her breast almost as if by accident. Immediately, Rebecca's nipples stiffened against the fleeting caress of his sensuous touch. She knew he could discern their hardened peaks beneath the fabric of her jacket by the glint of pleasure in his eyes. She felt gratified by his reaction, straining to mold her body more closely to his. And then it hit—an overwhelming sense of *déja vu*.

Their eyes locked for a brief, devastating moment, sapphire-blue clashing with hazel, as something treacherous flitted between them, touching Rebecca's heart. The sensation was like an old key turning the rusty tumblers of an ancient lock, or the last piece of a forgotten puzzle sliding into place. The relinking of lost souls, Rebecca thought, drawing back as if she'd been shocked.

"This is stupid!" Rebecca gasped.

"Why?" Alexander asked, stunned by the feeling that had overtaken him.

Rebecca wanted to say, "Because I'm not of your world. Because, in *my* time, you're already dead and buried, and in yours, *I* haven't been born yet. Because, I've got to find a way back. I don't belong here with you. That's why!"

Instead, her practical concern overrode her passion for an instant as she fought the rapturous fate threatening her more rational side.

"Because I'll hurt you," she fumbled. How could she possibly explain something to Alexander Ransom, she didn't fully understand herself? Rebecca thought. He'd chalk her up as a basket case for sure!

"You could never hurt me, Rebecca. I'm A–OK," Alexander breathed against her ear, defying the nagging pain of his wound to cradle this devastatingly sensual woman in his arms. She was no heavenly being as he had thought the night he was wounded, but a flesh-and-blood wonder.

Lighten up! Go with the flow, old girl, Rebecca's conscience argued, conspiring with her body. *How many times in your life have you been so moved by a man?* it whispered incessantly.

"You learn fast." Rebecca sighed in defeat, referring to Alexander's use of A—OK.

"Always, when there's a pretty woman involved," he responded with a disarming grin, and Rebecca realized Alexander was sufficiently recovered to do what she'd been tempted to all along.

"You owe me, you know?" she queried in a husky voice as she once again gave way to the passion he roused in her.

"I do?" He plucked a piece of hay from her hair, his knuckles brushing her cheek tenderly.

She captured his hand in hers. "Yeah. Good medical attention doesn't come cheap. But you'll be pleased to know, by careful evaluation, I've determined the cost doesn't exceed your capabilities."

"Really? Suppose I was moved to honor your demand for payment, what might that cost be?"

"Indulge my fantasy, Alexander Ransom, to have a genuine Confederate officer smoother me in kisses and I'll consider your tab paid in full," Rebecca said candidly, a provocative note evident in her voice.

Alexander searched Rebecca's face, and her breath caught in her throat as she awaited his answer. It seemed as if an eternity ticked by. Then in her stall Vedette nudged over her water bucket rummaging for food, and the clatter of tin against wood broke the spell.

With a groan of passion, Alexander turned slightly to face Rebecca more fully, his body brushing hers.

"You drive a hard bargain, madame," Alexander stated, though his moist lips gave lie to his words as he eagerly sought contact in repetition of their first kiss.

Rebecca sensed his passionate reaction to her unconventional request before her own registered in the sudden weakness in her limbs, the quickened breathing, and the exquisite tension building between her legs. The temperature in the barn seemed to escalate as she arched against him demandingly, cursing the clothes that separated their bodies as their kiss deepened.

When Alexander's hand slid down her thigh to lift her skirts, Rebecca's saner side cried out that she should stop him, but she couldn't bring herself to do it. Being in Alexander's arms felt too right, better than anything else she'd ever experienced with the other men she'd known.

Rebecca felt re-energized, the weariness that had stalked her for days vanishing as her libido spiraled. Somehow, she had been provided the means to feel, on a one-to-one basis, for the first time since war had come crashing into her life and she was going to snatch the tempest up, by heaven. No holds barred. She'd denied her own needs long enough. Now let the cards fall where they may.

Chapter Three

The silky texture of Rebecca's thigh beneath his fingertips brought Alexander to his senses. Though her sweetness was pure torment, he forced his hand to smooth her skirts back down to just below her knees with unbelievable tenderness. No lady deserved to be seduced under such unromantic circumstances—much less his cousin's friend, the woman who'd saved his life! Where had his mind been? He'd been so caught up in feeling, he couldn't seem to think straight.

"You were right. This is ... How did you put it?" Alexander fished for the word Rebecca had used. The last thing he'd expected while lying on the sawbone's bloodstained table was to awaken wrapped in the arms of a sumptuous female nurse.

He needed no added complications in his life right now.

"Stupid?" Rebecca guessed faintly, a moan of distress escaping her lips. What was Ransom doing? Didn't he realize he was driving her wild? she thought, her anticipation at a fever pitch.

"Exactly...stupid. For both of us." His mission took top priority over everything else, Alexander reminded himself.

A pained expression crossed Rebecca's face. Why had he stopped? Didn't he find her attractive enough? A mouthwash commercial flashed through her mind. Did she have bad breath? What?

Rebecca's wounded look tugged at Alexander's heart as it dawned on him she thought he was rejecting her. He hadn't intended to hurt her.

"You're quite remarkable. I thought you were an angel. I meant to practice a chaste kiss. I don't know what got into me, to take such liberties," Alexander expounded, conquering his emotions with an iron will.

How had the woman gotten under his skin so quickly? He hadn't realized a void existed in his life until Rebecca arrived on the scene. But tomorrow, or next week, or next month at the latest, he'd return to his company and where would that leave her? Like his brother's widow, running back to her family with three extra mouths to feed? Like Cordelia's mother, half-crazed with grief? Like himself? he thought bitterly. Any personal involvement during war time was cruel.

Alexander still held Rebecca against his broad chest, his lips close to hers, but he seemed to have drawn an impenetrable veil over his passion. She drew back slightly, puzzled by the unexpected turn of events.

Was it possible Cordelia's cousin was apologizing for his conduct? Rebecca frowned. She was an agnostic where men and apologies were concerned. On the brink of something wonderful, Rebecca plummeted back to earth unfulfilled.

Alexander's abrupt about-face was certainly a new one on her. Was it genuine? If so, it only served to make her ashamed of her immodest response to his advances and at the same time, she wanted to punch him out. This wasn't going to be as simple as she thought. The guy was a dyed-in-the-wool gentleman, and she'd been foolish enough to dive in the pool head first before she'd checked for water. What must he think of her wanton behavior?

"I'm not a member of the ethereal persuasion, Lieutenant Colonel Ransom," Rebecca responded practically, her smile fixed as she curtly disengaged herself from his embrace to straighten her skirts.

The barn, a cozy and serene haven, was disrupted by the crisp tone of Rebecca's voice. Unconsciously, she lowered it an octave, softening her words. "I'm just an ordinary woman, doing my job."

Alexander cocked an eyebrow at Rebecca. "A woman, yes, but hardly ordinary. Your kiss could resuscitate a dead man," he professed, wrestling for self-control over the demon that demanded he make this woman his, then and there in the hard

71

bed of the wagon. "Do you use the technique often?" he asked with deliberate calm, mastering the need she stirred in him by fanning her temper.

Rebecca was momentarily speechless. You'd think they were having a discussion on the pros and cons of CPR! Hadn't she just been writhing in this man's arms, absorbed with his body, his lips? How could he suddenly become so nonchalant about the whole thing? What....

Rebecca froze. She felt as if she'd been dashed in the face with a basin of ice water. *Now* she knew what he thought—that she was acting like a bitch in heat. *Remember where you are, Rebecca Ann!* Alexander was probably accustomed to more modest females, women like Cordelia, Rebecca surmised. She couldn't picture Cordelia requesting to be smoothered in kisses. Another *faux pas* on her part, a big one this time!

"No, not ordinarily. You were the exception," Rebecca said in agitation, hurling the words at him, burdening the still air with her blunt confession.

It was working. Rebecca was pulling away from him. Just a little more, and they would be on an even keel again. "You should probably be a little more cautious. Kissing with such abandon can lead some men to mistaken impressions," he reproached her gently.

That was all it took for her to fly off the handle. Rebecca's mouth dropped open. "Why, you pompous ass! You started it!" she snapped, her voice hardening with irritation as she collected the tattered remnants of her pride. Maybe he wasn't a gentleman after all. But just a jerk. "Who the heck died and left you king?"

"There are no kings in Tennessee, other than King Cotton," Alexander said speculatively, scrutinizing Rebecca more closely. Such an odd topic—kings.

A new thought occurred to Alexander. Maybe this nurse wasn't all she appeared to be. He sensed a threat in the strong-willed woman but whether it was personal or of national consequence was yet to be determined. In his line of work, it never hurt to be careful. Spies came in the most unlikely forms. Misplaced loyalties often spelled betrayal, even death, for an incautious courier.

Rebecca didn't like Alexander's riveted gaze, so like a glassy-eyed cat stalking its prey. What audacity!

"You don't have to stare a hole through me! All I meant was that I'm not your cousin, Cordelia, to be chastised for what you obviously consider my inappropriate actions. Why, I'd never even laid eyes on you before Stones River, so don't expect to bully me on this trip!"

"Just so."

She'd misjudged Alexander Ransom. He was neither a gentleman, nor a jerk. He was a nut! She hadn't thought to check for a head wound or brain damage from the fall off his horse. Maybe she should have.

"I'm going to let you in on something up front. You aren't my keeper, Lieutenant Colonel Ransom. No one is. I can stand on my own two feet, and I don't remember requesting pointers from you on how to do it."

It was Alexander's turn to be surprised. He wasn't accustomed to women speaking so boldly, especially to him. In his experience, the fairer sex liked to flirt, retreat, further entice, be coddled, romanced, then thoroughly kissed. Ultimately, they expected to be allowed to return to their shelves as perfect and serene as fine bone china thus salving their dignity against the baseness of life without climatic chinks in their bowls.

This auburn-haired saucebox was a law unto herself. A woman like her could really get a man's blood up—in more ways than one. She was volatile, exciting, unpredictable and more woman than he had parried with in a long while. He felt impelled to learn more about her.

"We are veritable strangers and yet, I think you would have yielded to me had I forced the issue," he said sagely, sparking her to further remonstration.

"Boy, I have to give it to you! You sure have an inflated sense of yourself."

"I could say the same for you. You have a certain ...arrogant defiance I find fascinating in a woman."

"And you, sir, are a...a..." What would Cordelia say?

"A blackguard? An overbold rakehell?" Alexander supplied.

"No! A cad, with a dirty face and badly in need of a shave."

"Touché."

74

Even as they exchanged jabs, Rebecca conceded, if only to herself, Alexander was right. He wouldn't have found need to force the issue. She was attracted to him, as if some pre-existent bond linked them. Ironically, she would gladly have returned to the security of his arms, if only he were to open them wide enough. But he did not.

Rebecca sighed. "This is idiotic. A nurse doesn't spar with a patient, even an aggravating one. Maybe I'm the one who should . . . apologize," Rebecca said, the word tasting like vinegar on her tongue. "It's simply that I'm not a reticent person by nature. I say what I think, do as I feel. I'm independent. If I want to take the initiative, I do. I'm neither lily-white, nor promiscuous. A noncomformist, so to speak. And I'm used to carrying a certain amount of authority, which sometimes causes me to appear slightly overbearing." After all, she was a lieutenant in the U.S. Army, Rebecca thought to herself, not deigning to explain her final comment.

"I'll accept your apology on one condition."

What in the hell was he trying to do now? Exasperate her, antagonize and offend her, throw her off guard? If so, his push-pull attitude was doing a great job on all four counts. Everything he had said hit too close for comfort, and distanced them.

Suddenly, Rebecca realized she'd hit the nail on the head. *That* was what he was doing—putting a healthy distance between them. Undoubtedly, their level of passion had been mutual, but it flaunted convention. She'd made *him* extremely uncomfortable, an officer who, under normal circumstances, kept his emotions tightly under control. He'd proved he could cope with the pain of injury, but could he handle the same amount of pleasure?

Was it possible he felt vulnerable, this Confederate man of steel? Ridiculous!

Alexander's shapely lips twitched at one corner and Rebecca could have sworn he was trying not to smile at her indignation compounded by her confusion.

"What's the condition?" Rebecca asked cautiously.

"That you first accept mine."

Rebecca nodded, almost afraid to speak least she say something to further incriminate herself.

Filling in the lull and abbreviating a most awkward moment for Rebecca, Alexander said, "I see you have forgotten your parasol more often than not."

Rebecca was dumbfounded by his off-the-wall comment. Noting her discomfort, he was being purposefully gallant in rerouting their conversation. She felt a burgeoning respect for Alexander Ransom.

"What? Oh, I see," she began, the meaning of his observation dawning on her, "the freckles. No, I don't carry a parasol, never have. Is that unacceptable?" There hadn't been one packed with the valise, and if there had been, she'd have tossed it with the corset.

"No, just interesting. Most women are rather vain. You see, they don't care for their skin to become darkened by the sun."

"Well, at least that's one thing you can't accuse

me of. Being vain," she said glibly, glancing down at her modest clothing.

Alexander followed her eyes. "You are delightfully pretty, but you hide your light under a bushel. A form of self-preservation, perhaps?"

Rebecca sensed that Alexander was a person normally controlled by logic. Maybe that's why he didn't understand her any more than he did the man in the moon. She was a distinct exception in this world of stringent standards that was crumbling around him as brother fought brother and old codes of conduct were transformed by the demands of war. Could it be she was looking at Alexander in the wrong light? She wasn't dealing with a modern-day stud, but a Southern cavalier, a man steeped in principle, fighting against the more earthly passions.

Their different worlds could only collide, hurting both of them in the process, Rebecca decided, and since the tragic loss of her brother, she'd resolved never to open herself to that type of pain again.

"I can live without your compliments and your insight, too, Lieutenant Colonel Ransom," Rebecca commented drily.

Alexander's expression hardened. "It's a pity you feel that way. It seems there can be little more between us, under the circumstances."

There was nothing like getting smacked in the face by one's *own* convictions. Keep things on a purely professional level, don't let anyone in, and you didn't have to deal with the criticism, or the pain of close association. That was the nursing profession's unwritten, intransgressible bylaw. She needed to keep it in mind while dealing with Alexander Ransom.

Thus released from the spell his touch had provoked, Rebecca backtracked. "Listen, let's begin again. Clear the air, shall we?" Rebecca paused, pulling herself into a sitting position beside Alexander and straightening her shoulders. "My full name is Lieuten—scratch that—Rebecca Ann Warren, a highly qualified nurse, if I do say so myself. And you, sir, are one outstandingly lucky patient." She extended her hand, and for a moment they were at odds again, he trying to kiss her knuckles, she attempting to shake his hand. Rebecca won the contest of wills. "I befriended your cousin back there at Stones River, and together, we intend to see you home."

"Please, continue," he requested, pleased by the change in their conversation.

"Cordelia thinks you are dying. You're not. But you do need to rest so that you won't suffer a relapse and I'm here to see to your recovery. As for earlier, my being in your arms was a mistake. I was half-asleep. Forgive my free-wheeling informality. I'll see that it doesn't happen again." Rebecca spoke to Alexander as if to a superior officer.

He answered her admission with a brief nod of salute, as he would with one of his men.

"Looks like we'll be thrown together a lot in the next few weeks as I've been invited to Oak Mont. I imagine, as you suggested, a platonic relationship would be feasible."

"Most appropriate."

"Yes. Well ..."

Alexander winced as Rebecca, suddenly the ironclad matron, leaned over to examine his shoulder bandaging. A frown of concentration marred his face and he gulped down a cross oath. The wound was as sore as a boil.

"Ouch! With friends like you, Rebecca Warren, who needs enemies?"

"Sorry, but this is for your own good. I think you're bleeding again," Rebecca said contritely, biting her lip in consternation. She hoped their foreplay hadn't opened up a gusher. Alexander had lost enough blood already.

"I'm going to get my bag," Rebecca informed him briskly, scrambling to the front of the wagon to retrieve her medical satchel. "Where is that Cordelia when you need her?" she muttered to herself, silently adding, *if she'd been around to chaperone, I wouldn't have thrown myself at her cousin*.

Alexander responded as if she'd addressed him directly. "Outside. She's built a cook fire, I think. Said she'd return when the food's ready."

So, he'd been awake, conversed with Cordelia while she'd remained dead to the world. He'd known all along they had a few minutes alone together, and he'd taken advantage of them to satisfy whatever curiosity he harbored about her.

Rebecca amended her verdict. Cordelia wasn't at fault. Alexander and she shared a mutual attraction, it was that simple.

Closing her mind to the previous episode, Rebecca doused her hands with alcohol, unwrapped Alexander's bandages, and sponged the area with an antiseptic swab. The wound was red and tinged with blood, but there was a minimum of swelling and little redness, with no sign of pus. Time to suture it shut, Rebecca decided.

"Your wound looks better than it feels, I assure you," Rebecca told him, preparing a local anesthetic. "You'll be back doing whatever it is you do in no time at all."

"I was a planter on our family estate. Now, I ride with Brigadier Major General Wheeler's cavalry and the Army of Tennessee," Alexander responded, eyeing the hypodermic as if he'd rather face a horde of Yankee soldiers than be pierced with the unusual apparatus. The last time he'd seen it used, the blind soldier wrapped in body bandages had summarily passed away.

"That needle...Is it absolutely..." Alexander began but Rebecca didn't give him time to continue the thought.

"Yes, it's necessary." Quick as a wink, Rebecca injected the painkiller beneath his skin.

Alexander felt a rush of heat that mellowed to a tingling sensation, finally spiraling to complete numbness in his shoulder. Satisfied the tissue-damaged area was sufficiently deadened, Rebecca threaded a curved needle with a strand of catgut and pulled the wound closed between a neat row of overhanded stitches.

The task complete, Rebecca repadded the wound and tightened the bandaging, discovering something she'd managed to miss before. A narrow scar ran along the side of Alexander's lower rib cage near the waistband of his pants, a puckered saber slash from a previous battle. "You've been in the thick of it before," she commented softly.

"Stones River wasn't the first engagement of the War Between the States, Mistress Warren," Alexander reminded her drily, catching his breath sharply as she knotted the gauze ends together over the bandage to hold it in place.

With his lucidity returning, Ransom was getting entirely too cocky for comfort! He'd openly gawked at the prepackaged, disposable syringe, the vials, and screw-cap bottles, the stainless steel needles—standard medical supplies she took for granted—that he hadn't appeared to take exception to before. Because of his inquisitiveness, Rebecca had thought it best to tie his bandages, rather than be cornered into a spiel about how she came by a roll of surgical tape that probably hadn't been invented yet. Now, she found it wasn't going to be so simple to dodge Alexander Ransom after all.

"Of course it wasn't. Fort Sumter in Charleston Harbor was. Everybody knows that!" Rebecca snapped back more forcefully than she intended.

What year *was* it? Rebecca had no concrete idea. *Concentrate.* The famous Gettysburg battle was in—what?—1863 maybe, she thought, attempting to figure the elusive dates. Therefore, Sherman's march through Georgia must have been around the summer of '64 she decided, visualizing the Atlanta Cyclorama in her mind. The situation didn't seem *that* desperate in the South yet. *It must be earlier. But how much earlier?* She asked herself.

"I didn't mean...It hadn't occurred to me..." she stuttered in growing frustration, unsuccessfully trying to cover her momentary disorientation. Alexander's mild frown stopped her dead in her tracks. "Damn! Never mind. This is crazy, all of it. I don't know what I'm doing here, what you're doing here, how I got here, none of it!" Rebecca exclaimed, exasperated with herself for making matters worse.

She was in the nineteenth century in body, but the twentieth in mind. No matter how smart she thought she was, she would never fit in. Even when she kept a tight rein on her actions, her mouth gave her away. She didn't have the faintest idea what the proper thing to say was without making a fool of herself, Rebecca thought with despair.

It was down right scary. They'd slap her in an asylum for sure if she didn't stay on her guard. Cordelia had reminded her as much for the second time only last night.

And what if, horror of horrors, she was trapped in time forever, never to see her own family again? The thought made Rebecca shudder.

Alexander discovered he felt a protectiveness toward Rebecca Warren. It rose to the surface, beckoning him to become her knight, albeit in slightly tarnished armor. He realized, for all her bravado, she was terrified by something, and he instinctively rallied to the roar of the beast riding her back.

"We all ask similar questions from time to time. War is an unpalatable feast for the wide majority of us. Few know how this country came to such ends," he said, and Rebecca could detect a momentary note of sadness. "The South is like an India-rubber ball, being pushed inside out. Yet we continue to struggle, each one frightened by his own worst nightmares," Alexander said gravely, a softness creeping into his voice as his hand, once again, found her cheek.

"And what is it that frightens you, Alexander Ransom?" Rebecca asked hesitantly.

"Nothing. You have to dream to have nightmares . . . and I no longer dream."

Rebecca's heart fluttered erratically. "You should have been a politician, the way you evade direct questions," she whispered, trying to lighten the conversation.

It worked. The tense atmosphere evaporated. "God forbid!" Alexander exploded with a short laugh. "I've not the silver-tongued facade necessary to an orator," he said, his hand relaxing at his side again.

"Amen," she said, her blue eyes twinkling with impish delight.

"Ah, so we agree on something," Alexander said with a disarmingly crooked grin that Rebecca couldn't resist. She responded with a half-smile of her own, her chin dimpling.

"The fresh dressing should do it for now, the bleeding has eased. You'll be as right as rain in no time."

"You seem to have an affinity for nursing. You are not the least bit squeamish, Rebecca Warren," Alexander said, his hazel eyes capturing hers. "You are no docile miss, but a woman of courage.

I think I'm fortunate that Cordelia befriended someone like you."

Well, I'll be, Rebecca thought. In spite of everything the male chauvinist had been taught about the genteel role a Southern woman played in society, he was condoning her uniqueness. Her uncertainty vanished, replaced by an unfamiliar shyness.

"Thanks for the compliment...I think. By the way," Rebecca gulped, "where *is* Cordelia? She's been gone an awfully long time, hasn't she?"

What was it about Alexander Ransom that had crept under her skin? She was actually shaking at the mere touch of his hand. It was queer, she'd had to travel clear across a century to bump into a man who affected her so.

About that time, the object of Rebecca's concern came bustling through the door. Using the tail of her apron as a pot holder, Cordelia toted a steaming kettle in one hand and a stack of wooden bowls in the other.

"There you are, both awake I see. Good. Luncheon, my dears, is served."

"Thank goodness. A body is likely to perish with you as cook. I feel as if I could eat a bear, fur and all." Alexander chuckled aloud, the serious air that had hovered about him and Rebecca evaporating with the aroma of chicken soup.

"Nothin' as substantial as bear today, I fear."

"Then, what I wouldn't give for one of Jubadessa's meals, with apple cobbler for dessert. But I suppose I dare not hope for such a spread, as you haven't graced a kitchen stool since you gave up short skirts." He grinned ruefully.

"Alexander, you never change! I can't *fly* to Oak Mont and Jubadessa, like a genie on a magic carpet, but I'll have you know I've done the next best thing. I've concocted a brilliant feast from next to nothin'. 'Tis true, the chicken came from a can, but I dipped water for the soup from the stream myself and gathered twigs for the fire and we have Jubadessa to thank for the corncakes from home."

"Who is Jubadessa?" Rebecca asked curiously.

"Our mulattress housekeeper, of course," Cordeila explained.

"Naturally," Rebecca remarked, and then fell silent again, contemplating slavery, the role of a plantation housekeeper in the Old South and what her duties might entail. She found the concept less than appealing.

"I can see you've been playing with fire by the soot on your cheek," Alexander interjected, but his thoughts were with Rebecca's pensiveness. He wished he could read minds. She was such an intriguing woman.

Rebecca wasn't sure the sassafrass tea held beneficial qualities, but she knew the chicken soup would put lost minerals back in Alexander's system, and her own stomach grumbled for a decent meal. Why, she'd eaten nothing save beef jerky and the rocklike soda crackers Cordelia called hard tack in over a century, Rebecca thought whimsically, smiling at the notion.

Cordelia misread the smile. "Are you and Alexander gangin' up against me, Becky?" she asked suspiciously, pouting prettily.

"Heavens no! I second Alexander's motion. You're groov...make that amazing, and I'm famished. The soup smells scrumptious!" Far more appetizing than the water buffalo and onion stew her friends in the MASH unit referred to as "the culinary delights of the rice paddy," she thought.

Cordelia's face shone with pleasure at their praise. It was obvious she idolized her cousin, though he seemed nonchalant about it. Rebecca had the distinct impression Cordelia was becoming quite fond of her, too, though she could find no reason for such immediate devotion.

Satisfied with Rebecca's response, Cordelia graciously dished up the chicken soup and passed out the bowls of chunked white meat floating in steamy broth.

"We must share the tea. I've only the cup from Alexander's canteen. I hope you don't mind, Rebecca."

"Not as long as its wet," Rebecca answered, thinking that drinking from Alexander's cup would be small fish in comparison to kissing him so thoroughly. How horrified Cordelia would be if she knew Rebecca'd been carrying on with her cousin while she was outside working. He must have been thinking something along the same lines, because he flashed her a knowing smile above Cordelia's head.

"It is wet and hot, too," Cordelia offered.

Alexander's smile broadened, and for the first time in her life, Rebecca blushed.

"G—good," Rebecca stammered, disconcerted.

"Can you manage your bowl alone, Alexander?" Cordelia asked politely.

"I believe so. Just the aroma of your soup makes me stronger," he said, rising on his elbow to sip from the bowl, done with teasing her for the time being.

"I must say, you do look improved today, almost like your old self," Cordelia commented, settling down on the tailgate of the wagon to consume her portion of the soup and corncakes.

"Don't encourage him, Cordelia," Rebecca stated, eyeing the molasses-sweetened corncake which reminded her of a cornmeal pancake. "You'll have him thinking he can rejoin his unit any time, and he can't. He needs bed rest to heal properly and the longer the better."

"Why, yes, of course, Becky. You know best," Cordelia said uneasily.

Outspoken, spirited, direct. He liked those qualities in a woman, Alexander thought with surprise. In Rebecca, traits that would otherwise seem domineering only mirrored the enthusiasm she felt toward others.

"I feel much more the thing, thank you ... both of you," Alexander stated, but they seemed oblivious to him for the moment.

"If it pleases, while we eat, might Alexander share news of the war with us, Rebecca?" Cordelia deferred. "At Oak Mont, we have only outdated newspapers to depend upon for information, and few enough of those. The war has so impaired postal deliveries that we'd be weeks behind without word of mouth."

Rebecca smiled benignly. Now *there* was something she could empathize with—disrupted postal service. "I do come off as a dragon lady sometimes, don't I, Cordelia?"

"You were only bein' honest, with Alexander's welfare foremost in your mind. Don't expect me to find fault with you for that," Cordelia said.

Both ladies finally looked at Alexander again. "If you hadn't noticed, you've been given permission to talk," Rebecca quipped, a wide grin spreading across her face.

Alexander shook his head. *Women!* "Most gracious, I assure you," he said.

Between swallows of savory chicken soup, Alexander slowly proceeded to caption the conflict. For Rebecca, it was almost like attending a history lecture. She listened without interruption, enthralled by the firsthand account of history in the making.

"I suppose Nashville got word of Lincoln's Emancipation Proclamation on the first?" Alexander remarked.

"The city was in an uproar when our volunteer group passed through for supplies on our way to Stones River," Cordelia responded.

"We received word on the field January second. The men were galled by Old Abe's nerve," he elaborated.

"I shouldn't wonder," Cordelia declared.

"There's speculation that the proclamation will turn English public opinion against the South."

"Never say so! I thought the self-imposed blockade on Southern cotton to England would force

England's hand to assist our country in its struggle," Cordelia said thoughtfully. "But perhaps you're right. All it's accomplished to date is to make current European fashion plates obsolete before American women can get their hands on them!"

Rebecca was surprised. She had never known the South had solicited aid from England during the Civil War.

"The ploy backfired, Cordelia. In my opinion, England doesn't look forward to involvement with the C.S.A. I think they'll look for other sources for their cotton mills. India perhaps."

Cordelia's face paled. "But that will hurt the Southern economy which is so precarious right now, will it not?"

"It puts the Confederate Treasury on tenterhooks, to say the least," Alexander agreed. "To counteract the side effects, a Louisiana gentleman of my acquaintance, John Slidell, has come up with a plan the government is leaning toward implementing."

"I remember Mister Slidell. We had him over once ... a soiree or some such. A gracious statesman, an eloquent dresser, as I recall," Cordelia interjected.

"That's the one. At present, Slidell holds the office of Minister to Paris. He represents the Confederate interests there."

Cordelia frowned in concentration. "I believe our neighbor and nurses' matron, Mrs. Amehurst, told me of his appointment. You know her, Madame Gossip. She keeps tabs on the up and coming in our circle."

"Anyway, to make a long story short, Slidell has masterminded a daring scheme to force-feed funds into the capitol treasury at Richmond," Alexander explained.

"How does he plan to accomplish such a feat?" Cordelia wondered aloud. If push came to shove, would this harmless little piece of information appease James in lieu of The Gray Ghost's name?

"You've always been more interested in books— Lord Byron, Shakespeare—than politics; you insisted they made no sense at all. Since when did you convert to a bluestocking, Cordelia?" Alexander answered with a question, his thoughts diverted to John Slidell's plan.

It was fairly common knowledge that a Parisian banker, Emile Erlanger, had agreed to underwrite the sale of Confederate bonds secured by cotton in several European countries. Slidell hoped to catch the eye of numerous speculators, and the proceeds from the sales would benefit Confederate coffers. The *real* beauty of the plan was less well publicized, Alexander mused to himself.

When purchased, the bonds couldn't be redeemed by the holders until the Southern blockade was lifted or until peace was declared, the only drawback being that if the Federals got wind of the stipulation, they could "bull" the market, thus dropping the value of the bonds. Only then could the ploy endanger the South's economy.

So far, things had gone off like a charm, though. Proceeds were already filtering through to the troops; the precious buttons on his coat proved that.

"That's a woman's preogative, Alexander!" Cordelia answered loftily, bringing his attention back to the present conversation. "B—besides, all the ladies talk of when they retire to the parlor these days is govern̄mental policy, the war effort. It's all the rage to be able to speak with some air of authority. Now proceed, if you please," Cordelia requested with exasperation.

Rebecca looked up sharply, catching Cordelia's gaze. She had the impression, call it intuition, Cordelia was hiding behind a woman's *supposed* ignorance for a reason. But for the life of her, she couldn't figure out why her friend was playing coy. Cordelia dropped her eyes first and a shiver ran up Rebecca's spine.

Alexander grinned at his cousin, visibly beginning to tire. "You've learned enough today to keep them buzzing for a while, Cordelia."

Had Alexander noticed something, too? Rebecca wondered, then shook herself. She was imagining things—and who could blame her? She'd been through plenty of disorienting situations in the last few days.

At that point, Rebecca called a halt to Cordelia's cross-examination, collecting the bowls from them as a means of unobtrusive intervention.

"Is there some place where I can wash these?" she offered, knowing what Cordelia's response would be. She was not disappointed.

"Yes. I'll help. Alexander, you relax while we tidy up. The stream's not ten yards from the barn.

91

We'll be back by the time you've finished your tea."

Once outside, Rebecca apprised Cordelia more fully of her cousin's condition.

"I hesitated to tell you before lunch, Cordelia, but Alexander's wound reopened during the night," Rebecca stated without preamble, his first name sounding funny on her lips.

"Oh, no! As I said, he seems so much better. I thought perhaps he would live after all."

"Not to worry. While you two were talking, I've been thinking of a way to circumvent the jolting ride. With your assistance, I think we can give Alexander a comfortable alternative to the wagon bed."

"Please, tell me what we can do."

"When I climbed up into the wagon earlier, I noticed there were hooks along the outside railing of the bed."

"Yes, it once had a fitted canvas tarp to keep the contents dry, but it is long gone."

"It doesn't matter. Vedette's stall has a leather grid door; it looks almost like a webbed hammock. If we used the hooks on the outside of the wagon to secure the grid in place of the canvas top, filled it with hay, don't you think it would act like a cradle?"

"Truly, I think it would! Whenever the wagon hits a rut, the guard would sway to accommodate the bump, cushionin' Alexander. That's a wonderful idea. You are so clever, Becky."

"It's less a matter of cleverness than necessity. Your cousin can't take much more trauma."

"Let's not tarry too long over this disagreeable chore. I'd like to get to Oak Mont and to a nice warm bath before dusk."

"Ditto," Rebecca agreed, thinking of the relative safety of the plantation as opposed to the open road.

"I declare, I believe the road dust has added five pounds to my draperies," Cordelia commented, drying the kettle and stowing it in a cotton sack. "I intend to soak and soak in a tub filled to the brim, until I am wrinkled right down to my toes, have Jubadessa lay out a fresh gown and attend to my coiffure," Cordelia chirped dreamily.

"That sounds sinfully wonderful."

Rebecca's words caused a lightning change in Cordelia's mood. Her face became somber and a faraway look clouded her otherwise bright eyes.

"Don't you see, dearest Jubadessa *must* help me scrub the blood stains from my hands, the moans from my ears, the horror of death from my eyes."

Cordelia looked to Rebecca as if for confirmation of the mulattress's ability to wash away her torment. Rebecca doubted any human being had the power to dissolve the traces of war that caked beneath a nurse's fingernails. Good thing Cordelia was only a candy striper.

Impatient with Rebecca's hesitancy, Cordelia continued, "Jubadessa can do that you know—absolve the cares of the day. She has a way about her that makes you feel as if everything will turn out all right," she insisted. "And I shall *never* go against her wishes and attend another battlefield with Mrs. Amehurst, no matter how much the woman begs," Cordelia vowed, much like a contrite child trying to bargain her way out of a spanking.

Rebecca was amazed at the change in Cordelia. She had calmed down volumes since the duress of Stones River. But Rebecca wasn't sure she liked the darker side of Cordelia's personality—so mournful.

A scarlet cardinal flitted to the ground in search of grubs near the muddy creek bank. Rebecca, discomforted, tossed it a leftover bite of corncake, watching with absorption as the merry-colored bird scrambled after the tidbit. She sensed something more to Cordelia's avowal than met the eye, but in a world already tilted at a precarious angle, Rebecca shied from delving too deeply into the implications. There was one indisputabe fact she would allow, however: Cordelia certainly had a poetic way with words.

By late afternoon, Rebecca was once again in the saddle, her posture erect, following Cordelia through rolling limestone land accentuated by meadows and forest copses. Alexander, despite his objection that there was no need to treat him like a babe in swaddling, rocked along quietly in his stall-guard hammock, a victim of Darvon-induced sleep.

Rebecca, unbeknownst to the lieutenant colonel, carried his frock coat folded across her saddlebow. She managed it gingerly, careful that it did not become too badly creased.

Chapter Four

"How much further?" Rebecca asked, standing in the stirrups to stretch, using them as she would have the foot pegs on a motorcycle.

"We've been on Ransom land for the past hour," Cordelia pointed out. "If you squint and look through the windbreak of evergreens to your right, you can just make out the house."

Rebecca turned in the direction Cordelia suggested.

It was as if someone finally flicked on a switch inside her head. Neon lights erupted, indelibly searing in Rebecca's brain the words: "You've actually transcended time!"

Although she'd toured innumerable historic homesites with her mother, the antique hound, nothing in memory compared with the real thing!

Oak Mont lived and breathed authenticity. Bathed in the rosy glow of twilight and spouting chimney smoke, the clapboard presented a sight for sore eyes.

Rebecca resumed her seat, mentally composing herself as they wound along the drive toward the whitewashed picket fence encompassing the isolated plantation's main yard. The phrase, "What if you gave a war and nobody came?" popped into her mind as she assessed the placid Southern estate.

Set on a pastoral plateau, the gracious *grand dame* spoke more of antebellum aristocracy, inherited wealth, and self-sufficiency than the privations of war. Dormant rose bushes, carefully pruned and maintained, hunkered in a circular rock garden in the center of the smooth front lawn, while bare dogwoods and spreading magnolia trees flanked either side of the veranda encircling the sturdy house.

An acre separated the main house from a stone springhouse standing spread-eagle over a gurgling stream that disappeared into the woodland belt. Adding to the landscape's picturesque quality, a hibernating apple orchard climbed the opposite hillside. Postured against the winter sky like brittle skeletons, the trees promised to be accommodating enough come fall. There'd be plenty of hot apple cobblers to appease Alexander Ransom's sweet tooth, Rebecca thought.

Along the front drive, an imposing carriage house with a bright red water pump and rough-hewn watering trough welcomed the weary travelers. Cordelia directed the wagon toward it.

Vedette, catching the enticing scent of water, tugged at her bit, excited by the prospect of a cool drink. Noting her impatience, Rebecca let the mare side-step the wagon and take the lead. She knew how Vedette felt. As ridiculous as it sounded, she too thrilled with anticipation.

Seeing Oak Mont for the first time was like catching a second wind after an uphill run or seeing the sun burst from behind a cloud on an otherwise dreary day. The world seemed more colorful, the air clearer and more promising than before.

"I think you were right, Cordelia. This is going to be like utopia compared to eighteen-hour shifts with more sick beds than you can count on your fingers and toes." She enjoyed the intensity of the O.R., but everyone needed a break now and then and the chance to unwind. What better place than a nineteenth-century plantation, her mother's fantasy come true?

Alexander, roused by the conversation, sat up in his makeshift hammock, thickening the air with words of caution. "Whoa, easy, Rebecca, Cordelia. We could be riding into a trap. I've no desire to end up in a Northern prison camp after coming this far," he said, warily judging the house's quiet facade.

Cordelia checked the hack, while Rebecca reined Vedette alongside the wagon.

"I know it seems I'm temptin' fate, bringin' you so close to Nashville, but the militia hardly ever bothers to come this far from town. Besides, the

Yanks in charge have issued restrainin' orders against civilian harassment. And with Mother like she is and all . . . Well, you know."

Before Alexander could comment, a friendly "hello" boomed from the front porch of the house. In a flurry of skirts, a woman bounded off the steps. Sailing out to meet the trio, she disturbed a pair of chickens scratching for earthworms at the edge of the rose garden. Squawking indignantly, they flapped from her path. She paused a moment to beg their pardon as if they were human, then hurried on only to stop abruptly and stare at Alexander from behind the protection of the fence.

As if resigned to a chronic problem, Cordelia jumped from the wagon and halfheartedly flicked her hand in greeting. "See what I mean?" she asked of no one in particular.

The middle-aged ash blonde, slim as a reed, but with a certain fading prettiness, teetered on tiptoes at the gate, swinging a croquet mallet in one hand and balancing a parasol in the other. She wore a taffeta bonnet, elbow-length silk gloves, a brocade ball gown with a wide hoop skirt, and a short cape with a cashmere shawl looped over one shoulder. Even Rebecca realized the outfit was unsuitable for yard games.

A rather imposing mulatto in a pokeberry red turban and homespun gown girded at the waist with a belt of keys followed sedately behind the blonde. In her early forties, the coffee-skinned woman was not only regal, but classically beautiful, with high cheekbones and the most bewitching almond-shaped brown eyes Rebecca had ever seen.

So enter the Mad Hatter and the Queen of Hearts, Rebecca thought without surprise.

"Jubadessa has set up the croquet game. Would you care to play a round, Alexander?" the Southern belle chortled inanely, as if her nephew being carted home in the back of a wagon was an everyday occurrence.

"Not today, Aunt Abigail. I'm slightly under the weather. Perhaps later in the week," Alexander answered gently, shifting his weight to face his father's sister.

"Oh my!" Abigail gasped, "I see now. You're wounded!" She leaned the mallet against the gate post and pulled a lace handkerchief from her bosom to dab at her lips.

"What nonsense, Alexander!" she chided, as her pendulum earrings danced in agitation. "I thought your job was to lead the attack . . . or is that cover the rear?" She blinked in confusion. "Personally, I would much prefer the rear. Anyway, West Point should have taught you to have a care! You're a brave boy with a right good will, but you aren't too smart. You and your rowdy brothers always seem to get into the worst scraps playin' cavalry," she admonished affectionately.

Abigail straightened, gazing down the lane as if expecting to see someone else dashing up to the house at any second. "Aren't Beau and Edward with you?"

A pained expression flashed in Alexander's hazel eyes, but he quickly masked it. Abigail had refused to accept his brothers' deaths. "No. I'm afraid they're not, dear."

"Oh, well, perhaps you can bring them along on your next visit." Her mind flitted back to his wounds. "Shall I fetch my volume of Francis Peyre Porcher's book on herbs and vegetation for healin' and medicinal use?"

"No need to dig out your textbook of pharmacology, Abigail."

"Then how about a hot water bottle?" she persisted.

"I think everything's under control," he stated, winking at Rebecca. His gesture was an obvious plea for her patience and understanding.

"As you wish, Alexander."

Alexander smiled kindly at his aunt's disjointed meandering, glancing at the woman who Rebecca deduced could only be Jubadessa, the housekeeper. The stately mulatto shook her head sadly.

"I'm sorry, *Monsieur*, Miss Cordelia. Mrs. Abigail forgets things, has trouble with names, confuses the past with the present. Some days are better than others."

"No need to explain, Jubadessa. I'm aware of the complexities that must be addressed when dealing with Abigail," Alexander stated.

"She had the blues this morning," Jubadessa continued, a trace of French flavoring her otherwise precise English. "She fancied a game of croquet while I made soap. I did not see any harm in it. She always loved sky larking when we were girls, would spend hours knocking the colored balls through the hoops. I thought the game a good way to keep her out of trouble."

"As I've told you before, I have every confidence in your judgment. I leave Abigail's care to your discretion. She stays with us as long as possible."

Rebecca's attention was drawn to the soap-making paraphernalia set up near the carriage house. An ash hopper, a triangular affair used to collect lye from wood ash, and a tray of pans filled with congealing soap were scattered on the ground while a dark-skinned youth stirred the grease-and-lye mixture bubbling in an iron caldron over the banked fire. Rebecca knew something of soap making. She'd seen it demonstrated while visiting a popular tourist attraction—historic Williamsburg, in Virginia. But it hadn't been nearly as intriguing as observing the genuine article.

While Rebecca surveyed the soap-making process, Abigail studied her.

"Who *is* that woman?" she burst out finally with the innocence of a child. "Have you brought another Jesse Scout to tea, daughter, or is this Alexander's new wife?" she demanded of Cordelia, pointing squarely at Rebecca.

"Honestly! Where *do* you get such ridiculous notions?" Cordelia squeaked in exasperation, reddening. "She's no Yankee spy, nor Alexander's wife either. Rebecca Warren is a nurse, here at my invitation. She'll help attend Alexander, while gleanin' a reprieve for herself," Cordelia spelled out defiantly, staring straight toward Jubadessa as if she expected the housekeeper to protest.

When she remained silent, Cordelia turned to Rebecca. "Allow me to introduce Abigail Ransom

101

Stoddard, my mother," she announced dramatically.

Why hadn't she noted the obvious family resemblance before now? Both had similar pale cornflower complexions, the same nose and mouth, a distant look in their eyes. "How do you do?" Rebecca said politely.

When Abigail failed to respond to Rebecca's salutation, Cordelia answered for her. "Not too well, I'm afraid, as you can plainly see."

Alexander repressed an oblique grin. Of them all, Cordelia dealt with her mother's sickness with the least finesse.

Cordelia, guessing his thoughts, glared at him. "Really, Alexander! I have as much forbearance as the next person," she claimed, stamping her foot. "It's just that I hate to see her this way."

"I know," Alexander soothed in a brotherly fashion. "We all do."

"We mustn't encourage her, you know. There are times, like today, when she's not responsible for her actions."

All this went over Abigail's head as she insisted in a monotone, "She can't be a nurse. Nurses are always of the male persuasion."

"Not this one, Mother," Cordelia answered automatically.

"I saw a female doctor once...most radical woman," Abigail chirped on as if Cordelia hadn't spoken. "She gave me an inoculation against smallpox after Alexander's wife died with the horrid affliction," she informed Rebecca, flip-flopping. "Would you like to see the scar?"

"No need," Rebecca replied faintly, humoring Abigail. Perhaps Cordelia's mother was suffering from an imbalance of some sort. She thought she recalled reading an innovative article in *The New England Journal Of Medicine* citing the lack of crucial chemical elements in the body in regard to metabolic disorders, much like decreased insulin production and diabetes. Could such a thing affect one's emotional state as well?

In which case, how much stock could she put in Abigail's statement concerning Alexander's wife? Was his aunt just rambling off the top of her head, or was he a widower? Funny, Rebecca hadn't considered the possibility of Alexander being married. Somehow, the notion bothered her.

Jubadessa cast Rebecca a measuring look, her lips compressed, her keen eyes sweeping from Rebecca's booted feet to slouch hat, ending with a piercing stab at her face. For a moment, Rebecca fully expected the imperious housekeeper to cry, "Off with her head!" Then, as if she'd made up her mind, and liked what she saw, her expression softened.

Rebecca had the fleeting impression Jubadessa was one of those women in constant search of someone she felt needed mothering. Rebecca reasoned judiciously she'd just been categorized for future reference should demand exceed supply.

"Mrs. Abigail, it was his intended who passed away. *Monsieur* Alexander has never been married," Jubadessa reminded her with inherent kindness, nodding in Rebecca's direction.

"Yes. I remember now," Abigail responded with a faint frown.

"Welcome to Oak Mont, Miss Warren," Jubadessa offered graciously, grabbing Vedette's bridle to hold the mare steady while Rebecca dismounted.

"Thank you," Rebecca said, extending her hand, for some reason measureably relieved Alexander was romantically unattached.

Instead of grasping Rebecca's hand in a handshake, as she'd anticipated, Jubadessa took the reins from Rebecca's fingers and tied Vedette to the hitching post at the front gate. "I'll ask Willy to see to the horses," she added, motioning to the boy who stirred the soap pot. He responded with a brief nod in Jubadessa's direction.

Jubadessa hesitated almost imperceptibly, then turned to speak directly with Alexander. "The barn burned a few days ago, *Monsieur*. We're using the carriage house as a substitute. We were able to save the cow and the mule team—Willy had turned them out in the high pasture—and enough corn and baled hay to see us through to spring."

"The boys in those pretty blue uniforms didn't torch our stable. Young scalawags did," Abigail interjected with wide-eyed wonder. "You should have seen the fire. Jubadessa ran the varmints off with Papa's old musket. It was glorious!"

"Honestly! She's worse today than usual!" Cordelia moaned.

"Your mama is right about the *outliers*, Miss Cordelia," Jubadessa confirmed quietly. While Alexander absorbed the bad news, Jubadessa finished the tally. "The thieves took the rest of the livestock and the horses the Yankees hadn't commandeered earlier, and raided the coop around back. The chickens that escaped, we've put in the front yard. It isn't as convenient to gather eggs, but they're a sight easier to keep an eye on."

"How about the watchdogs?" Alexander asked solemnly.

"Guinevere is in the house. They shot Sir Lancelot when he attacked them."

"Where were Max, Amos, the other servants and their families? You were in danger every second you faced those men alone!" Alexander almost shouted, angry that he'd been away, unable to defend his own land when he was needed the most.

"The Federals offered them jobs in Nashville for wages—building breastworks, as cooks and washerwomen. It has just been me, Willy, and Mrs. Abigail, since Christmas, *Monsieur*. I did what I had to do to protect *this* family."

A Jeffersonian, Alexander's father had taken the third president's theories a step further than the Declaration of Independence, absolving slavery at Oak Mont one person at a time long before Lincoln had the opportunity to turn the issue to the Union's advantage. But liberation was a powerful narcotic, and Alexander couldn't blame the Negroes for following its call. The gang of Rebel deserters was another matter.

Alexander's face hardened. "Damn this war for destroying so much of the good with the bad, for taking the men from their homes, for turning the more desperate into animals!" he spat between clenched teeth.

"Never to worry, dear. They pillage little as long as we stand our ground. That's one of the reasons Jubadessa and I remain, that and the roads are so crowded with traffic these days. I hate the dust you know. Makes me sneeze up a storm!" Abigail rattled on, relieving the tension with her comical dramatics.

"Oh, for goodness sake! I thought I told you to give Mother a tincture of laudanum each mornin' when she awoke, to keep her quiet. Her mind overflows like a teacup without medication," Cordelia cried, mortified by her mother's outlandish behavior in front of her guest.

"I saw no need—"

Cordelia didn't give Jubadessa time to finish her sentence. "What do you think, Becky? How would *you* deal with Mother?"

Before Rebecca could form a diplomatic reply, Abigail spoke up again, affronted by her daughter's forwardness. "Oh fiddlesticks, Cordelia!" Abigail spouted. "*I* think we should help Alexander out of the cold and into the house...plain as the nose on your face. There's a good boy, now. Give your old aunt your cheek, Alexander, and then in you go."

Alexander's face relaxed, and he did as he was bid, his aunt wrinkling her nose in distaste and brushing at the week's growth of beard on his face.

"I declare, I'd never have recognized you if not for your papa's serpentine ring. Hairy as a monkey's behind!"

"Aunt! You're a marvel!"

"Why, of course, Alexander. I've never pretended to be anything but. Now, on to more important matters. I've kept your room waitin'." She pressed her hands together in glee. "And there's smoked wild turkey, baked yams, apple sauce, apple pie, and apple dumplings for supper, all your favorites."

"I'm afraid we're running a little short these days, Mrs. Abigail. We used all the smoked meat and the remainder of last season's apples in November. We could cook a chicken in honor of *Monsieur's* return, but it would be a shame to give up the eggs. Now Willy, he caught a fine string of catfish this morning," Jubadessa said. "We *could* make a nice meal out of those, enough for everyone."

"Oh, yes. Dear me. I'm such a rattlebrain. I suppose we will have to use the fish before it spoils."

"That's right."

"Catfish and strawberry jam for supper then?"

"Yes."

Rebecca made a moue despite herself. She hoped they didn't cook the catfish *in* the jam. She could use a bite to eat, but she wasn't that desperate! Besides sounding unappetizing, she was allergic to strawberries. She broke out in an itchy red rash within minutes of eating the fruit. Her breathing became labored, her face puffy. It was awful.

This time, Alexander couldn't contain his mirth. He winced as, laughter rumbling in his chest, the bandages tightened over his wound.

Always the guardian angel, Rebecca rallied to her patient's side without realizing it was the look of revulsion on her face that had set him off. "Your mother is right, Cordelia. Your cousin is better off out of the weather, preferably in a soft bed near a warm fire," she added with an imperiousness that rivaled Jubadessa's.

With that, Rebecca hooked her hat over Vedette's saddle horn, gave Alexander her hand, and assisted him from the wagon. His strong grip sent tingles up her arm and she quickly drew her hand away. Gingerly, Rebecca handed him his knee-length frock coat, which he hefted over his uninjured shoulder.

The lieutenant colonel affected her tremendously when physical contact was necessary because of his condition. She had to be careful; she could still taste the moist warmth of his lips upon hers, feel the surge of desire he'd affected as his hands brushed her aching breasts. She yearned to feel him, hard and demanding, inside her.

Gosh! Such thoughts. What kind of nurse are you? She silently answered her own question. *The hungry kind. Too hungry for your own good. That's what.*

Using mind over matter, Rebecca forcefully pushed aside the immodest longing Alexander Ransom conjured. If she were honest with herself, Rebecca knew she could fall in love with a man like him far too easily, and in her topsy-turvy world there was no room for such a momentous blunder. She'd struck a bargain with Alexander Ransom and she intended to keep her half of it.

Taking a deep breath, Rebecca positioned her

shoulder under Alexander's good arm and her hand around his waist, taking the brunt of his weight. She hadn't realized he was so tall, six feet if he was an inch. She liked tall men—another strike against the handsome Confederate. She'd certainly have to watch her p's and q's.

"Incredible. After days in the saddle, your hair still smells of honeysuckle," Alexander whispered almost begrudgingly for Rebecca's ears alone. "Now, whenever the vines bloom in a thicket bordering some Godforsaken battlefield, I'll think of soft auburn hair and a kiss that could rival the mythical Aphrodite instead of Tennessee," he charged, as if his thoughts were criminal.

"Bull! You're stoned," Rebecca bluffed, trying to appear as if his words hadn't affected her in the least, but her heart skipped a beat at the notion that their desire ran neck and neck. For a fleeting second, she could have sworn Alexander's arm tightened around her in an affectionate hug.

Fear of involvement reared its ugly head. *Please, God, don't let emotion lean on me that hard again, as it did with my brother after his death,* Rebecca prayed. Like the South, Alexander's gallantry would have to serve as his mainstay, not her. He had already lost so much—would lose much more before the end of the war rolled into sight. She was ill-equipped to make it any easier. Besides, somehow she had to find her way back to her own time, to her own home.

"You mind your mama. I'll show Miss Rebecca to the house," Jubadessa stated, breaking into Rebecca's thoughts as, her carriage stiffly erect, she guided their steps up a gravel walkway toward the house.

"Isn't it about time for corn dodgers and tea?" Abigail asked vaguely, checking the timepiece pinned to her bodice as she retrieved her croquet mallet. "Tomorrow is Sunday, you know ... Church in town for sure."

"It's *Thursday*, Mother."

"Thursday? How odd. I could have sworn today was Saturday."

"I don't know how you put up with us, Alexander," Cordelia called, her words drifting up to them as they silently ascended the landing leading to the oaken front door.

Guileless, Abigail answered for them, "Because we're family and blood is thicker than water, Cordelia!"

"Whatever you say, Mother," Cordelia exclaimed, shaking her head.

Rebecca found herself agreeing with Abigail's observation. The woman might be a scatterbrain, but her spirit was intact.

"That's why Alexander would never let them put me away. He promised the last time I had a really awful spell at our flat in Nashville, after your daddy passed on, that I could stay at Oak Mont as long as I wished—with Jubadessa, of course."

Abigail's words grew fainter as Jubadessa pushed open the front door and they stepped inside. Now Rebecca knew what connection Cordelia had with asylums. Perhaps, unable to deal with her mother, she'd considered placing Abigail in an institution before Alexander intervened. The man was obviously a glutton for punishment, a cavalier of the highest caliber.

If she wasn't crazy before, Rebecca sure felt that way at the moment. Wading through the specifics of the Ransom family ties was confusing. At least Alexander felt good and solid beneath her touch, seemed reasonably sane, someone to hold on to as her own world spun just out of reach, gradually fading into the background of time as history established the upper hand.

Rebecca sucked a gulp of air, squeezed her eyes shut, and pinched her nose to submerge her head beneath the water. Her hair spreading like a fan, she rested on the bottom until her lungs reached the bursting point, then bobbed to the surface again.

Expelling her breath in a rush of satisfaction, Rebecca leaned back in the hand-filled brass tub. Her eyelids half closed and the water lapping against her chin, she relished the luxury of a hot bath. Bathing in the kitchen, warmed by a fire built in the belly of a cast-iron cookstove, was a far cry from the indoor plumbing she'd wished for earlier, but the result was the same—pure heaven.

The kitchen still smelled faintly of fried fish. But in retrospect, it wasn't an entirely unpleasant odor. Jubadessa had worked miracles with the un-impressive entree. The catfish had been done to a turn, crispy brown on the outside and succulent on the inside. The peas sauteed with onions were flavorful, the winter collards and cornbread seasoned with bacon drippings filling. The strawberry jam had been optional which Rebecca was happy to note.

"Now, if I only had a toothbrush and a tube of toothpaste, some mouthwash and a bottle of roll-on deodorant," she muttered, rubbing her teeth with the rough cloth and boxed tooth powder Jubadessa had provided. She grimaced at the flavor. "Mmm...lovely. Old shoe *à la grecque*. Mom always warned me not to take the little things in life for granted," Rebecca stated aloud, setting the dental powder aside.

The tan mastiff Jubadessa had spoken of earlier lay posted near the back door. Her massive head resting on her paws, she watched Rebecca's every move, her ears perked to better catch Rebecca's words.

"You sure don't look like a Guinevere to me, dog," Rebecca quipped, eyeing the powerful animal as she continued her bath. "Attila the Hun suits you better. Glad you're on my side."

The smooth-coated dog lifted her head. Cocking it to one side to consider Rebecca, she yawned, then settled down again as if she found no cause for alarm in the woman's mellow voice.

Lathering her hair, Rebecca mused that she had Cordelia to thank for everything: dinner, the brimming tub drawn up to a cheerful fire, fresh clothes, a place to stay. If not for her, Rebecca would have been left sitting alone on the banks of Stones River without a penny to her name or the least notion of how to proceed.

Her quarters, a cozy guest room with an adjacent dressing room and full-length pier glass, were located on the ground level sandwiched between the music room and kitchen. Rebecca mentally envisioned the rest of the house, beginning with the elliptical transom over the front door that supplied natural light to the main parlor. From there branched two rooms with ten-foot ceilings and hand-carved crown moldings, both accessible through sliding doors. A dining area, and a respectable library with a secretary, comfortable leather wing chairs, and wall-to-wall books and periodicals completed the circle.

Attached to the main house via a breezeway was the bake house, while upstairs were three cedar-paneled bedrooms, the largest of which belonged to Alexander. She'd been quietly informed that "the necessary house" was out back at the end of the garden path, past the smokehouse. Rebecca could only assume Cordelia had been speaking of the latrine, though she'd discovered a washbasin and chamber pot behind the screen in her room as well.

Decorated in heirloom oak furniture with petit-point pillows, Aubusson rugs, and an ample granite fireplace in every room save Jubadessa's off the kitchen, Oak Mont's interior was stately without being overpowering. But there were hints that, unlike the outside of the house, the inside had suffered from the war. Though dust-free and as neat as a pin, little things gave it away: a shadow on the wall in her bedroom where a painting had been removed, the hollowness of an empty china cabinet in the dining area, the void in the music room's plaster ceiling where a chandelier had once hung.

Rinsing her hair, Rebecca pondered the missing items, wondering if they'd been stolen, hidden, or sold piece by piece to supplement the family's income.

"Miss Rebecca, may I come in?" Jubadessa petitioned from the kitchen doorway, interrupting Rebecca's thoughts.

"Yes. Did you get it?" Rebecca asked.

"*Monsieur* Alexander let me bring it as soon as he had finished."

"Great!"

Jubadessa crossed the room, her hand hidden in the folds of her skirt. Parting the half-moon curtain that protected the tub from drafts, she paused at the head of the tub to deposit an ivory-handled straight razor on the soap ledge.

"You must be careful. It is very sharp," she warned, making no move to leave.

"I will."

"You aren't thinking of cutting your hair, are you?" Jubadessa asked with a disapproving frown when Rebecca flipped the wet strands over one shoulder, her dog tags clinking as she eagerly reached for the razor.

"No," Rebecca replied, flicking it open to test the cutting edge, "not exactly."

"Good. Ladies shouldn't cut their hair. You have nice hair, and it is short enough as 'tis. Perhaps tomorrow morning, you would allow me to help you dress it properly . . . with tucking combs?" Jubadessa hinted, her frown fading to a look of thoughtful speculation.

For a moment, Rebecca was startled. Did Jubadessa suspect something? She must stick out like a sore thumb. It hadn't occurred to her when she'd wrested the wavy mass into a braid that Victorian women wore their hair pinned up, like Cordelia's. But she'd never cared for topknots, hadn't considered the fashion etiquette of the day when she'd done her hair. Playing the chameleon under Jubadessa's astute curiosity wasn't going to be any easier than avoiding Alexander Ransom's sharp scrutiny.

"We'll see."

"Fine. For now, might I assist you with your bath?"

Rebecca lips curved upward in an unrestrained smile. The last person to help her bathe had been her mother. She'd been six at the time.

"I appreciate the offer, but I'm a big girl. If you wouldn't mind turning up the lamp a little before you go, I think I can finish up on my own."

Jubadessa twisted the knob on the oil lamp to raise the wick, then glided toward the door.

"Jubadessa, wait, please."

"Yes?" Jubadessa pivoted expectantly.

"Pardon me for prying, but, how long has Abigail had . . . spells? I mean, you never know. I'm a nurse; I might be able to help."

For a moment, Rebecca thought Jubadessa intended to play dumb. Then her stern facade relaxed slightly and she relented ever so slowly. "Close to a year now. The world can be a cruel place, Miss Rebecca, and some people are more fragile than others."

"And?" Rebecca prompted.

"Mrs. Abigail became one of the first war widows hereabouts. That should have elected sympathy from her peers, but it didn't," she said sadly. "You see, Carl Stoddard, Mrs. Abigail's husband, sided with the North. As the war grew more violent, *polite* society turned their backs on Mrs. Abigail. She's never been the same since, just sort of went off into her own little world."

"All because her husband fought for the Union?" Jubadessa seemed puzzled. "The Union?"

Rebecca quickly realized she'd have to watch her choice of words more closely. She sounded like a Northern sympathizer. "The Federals, I mean."

"No. More because she chose to marry a Yankee in the first place. Tennesseans are a hot-blooded lot when push comes to shove and they trust in only four things, Miss Rebecca: the land, the Holy Gospel as they see it, their weapons, and their hearts. They aren't afraid of a good fight. As sure as the sun rises, if they think they have been betrayed, they lash out. I feel for Mrs. Abigail, though luckily, the taint hasn't spilled over to Miss Cordelia, a child's sire being viewed as an unfortunate accident of birth."

"I assumed Cordelia's surname was Ransom."

"Until things cool down, it is just as well she play up her mother's maiden name, and down her Yankee heritage. Being kin to Carl Stoddard, though he is dead, is far from popular."

"It sounds as if you've been with the Ransoms quite a while."

"I was born in the French Quarter ... New Orleans," Jubadessa began hesitantly, "but I've been

116

with Mrs. Abigail, living at Oak Mont, since I was nine."

"As a slave?" Curiosity killed the cat, Rebecca thought.

"At first," Jubadessa said with tremendous dignity, "but no longer. I'm my own person."

"I know—the Emancipation Proclamation."

"No, miss! I was free long before Mister Lincoln's election. On Mrs. Abigail's fifth birthday, *Monsieur's* father gave her a pony. He delivered me my papers that same day. I was ten years old."

So, Alexander Ransom was an Equal Opportunity Employer. Interesting. "And you stayed, even after you reached womanhood?" Rebecca asked guilelessly.

"I've been luckier than most. Though some would disagree, Oak Mont is home to me. I have my position, my responsibilities, a roof over my head, food in my mouth, and clothes on my back. Where would I go?"

Rebecca fell silent. Torn between two worlds, where indeed? Rebecca wondered, her own thoughts mirroring Jubadessa's words.

"What of Alexander's father, Jubadessa? Where is he now?"

"Gone. Buried on the hillside, near the orchard. He was older, a grown man, when Mrs. Abigail was still a baby."

"And his mother?"

"Mrs. Ransom died birthing Beau, the youngest. *Monsieur* practically raised his brothers after that. He was not much more than a boy himself. Edward and Beau rest beside their mama. *Monsieur*

117

saw them home from Sharpsburg himself."

"Oh." *How terrible for him.*

Rebecca made a mental note to visit the family cemetery at the first opportunity. As gruesome as it sounded, the headstones could prove a godsend, supplying her with concrete dates without her requesting them outright.

As if she'd said too much, Jubadessa suddenly clamped her mouth shut. Following an uneasy pause, she said, "Well, if that is all, I'll go back up to Mrs. Abigail. She is too excited by *Monsieur*'s return to sleep."

"Do that," Rebecca said absently, her mind filled with Jubadessa's revelations. "Tell Cordelia I'll be up shortly to say good night, and thanks."

Detained by the dog looking for a friendly pat, Jubadessa's eyes grew wide as she watched Rebecca prop a slender leg on the side of the tub, soap it, then ply the razor in long, steady strokes from ankle to knee.

"Lay back down now, Guinevere," Jubadessa commanded, steering the mastiff back to the door by her collar. "Stay. *Monsieur* wants you on duty downstairs tonight."

Monsieur Alexander had been right! Jubadessa thought, backing through the doorway. Miss Cordelia's guest possessed a rare disposition, so full of questions, and with that *ugly* chain around her neck. Threaded with tinsel that jingled like wind chimes when Miss Rebecca moved, the noise set her teeth on edge.

Stopping by Rebecca's room to unpack her valise only reinforced Jubadessa's impression of Rebecca when she saw the clothes Rebecca had obviously rinsed out before taking her bath. The nurse had fashioned a makeshift clotheshorse from a ladder-back chair and positioned it near the hearth, arranging the clothes along the rungs to dry by the fire.

Attracted to the chair like iron filings to a magnet, Jubadessa examined the curious specimens. A flimsy piece of material she judged to be some sort of breast harness, and the legless drawers with elastic lace and a tag stamped with the words "Nylon and Cotton. Machine Wash Gentle. No Bleach. Tumble Dry."

Jubadessa fingered the curious material, as lightweight as silk, but with a sturdier texture to it, marveling at the methodical stitching and the rust-free hook and eye that adorned the harness. "Fancy that," she said aloud to herself, never having seen anything quite like these undergarments. "Where in the world did she find . . ." she began, then stopped short.

Of course! Hadn't Cordelia mentioned the nurse spent several years in England studying with Florence Nightingale. They had to be European, Jubadessa guessed. The coastal blockade had effectively cut the Southern women off from news of the latest European styles and England from their cotton supply for textiles early on in the war. Who could say what lurid changes had taken place to compensate for their loss since she'd last seen a current set of fashion plates?

Necessity was truly the mother of invention, Jubadessa decided.

Clucking over the sparseness of Rebecca's wardrobe, Jubadessa hung the dresses in the clothespress, placing the ornate brush on the bureau within easy reach. All in all, Jubadessa thought, flicking open the medical satchel, she'd never seen a lady travel so light, not even a descent wrapper or bed gown to her name. The one she'd discovered stuffed in the satchel was in dire need of a strong soaking and some elbow grease before it would be fit to wear again! she determined, holding it up to inspect the blood stains.

Well, in the meantime, it was incumbent on her to supply Miss Rebecca with night things. She certainly couldn't have a lady sleeping naked with *Monsieur* in the house, now could she? Jubadessa thought righteously, wading up the gown and tucking it under her arm to drop off in the laundry basket on her way upstairs.

And speaking of *Monsieur*, wait till she told him what the nurse was doing with his razor! Lord a mercy. Cordelia's friend bore watching almost as bad as Abigail.

Abandoning her usual aplomb, Jubadessa took the stairs two at a time. Within seconds, she stood before Alexander Ransom's bedroom door at the back of the house.

Jubadessa found Alexander standing by the window, staring out into the gloom blanketing the fallow fields. One hand was splayed on the ledge to steady himself. In the other, he clutched his uniform frock coat.

"Here now, *Monsieur!*" she cried, her voice overflowing with concern. "You can't be thinking of rejoining your unit so soon. Miss Warren's orders are that you stay abed for the next week, and that is where you should be, not by that drafty old window in nothing save your robe. You're not yourself. You're as weak as a new colt," Jubadessa fussed, taking the gray coat from his hand and draping it carelessly over the walnut valet before manhandling Alexander back into bed. "Even as a lad, you had no patience with illness, but you must heed your nurse."

"Where is the tyrant, Jubadessa?" he asked crossly, settling beneath the quilts.

"Mistress Warren? She is downstairs, shaving her legs," the housekeeper stated in a singsong voice, tucking him into bed as if he were still a child.

"Shaving her legs!" he sputtered. "Why the little hoyden." Alexander exploded in laughter, falling back on a pile of goose-feather pillows Jubadessa had stacked behind his back. It had been years since he'd found anything humorous. But that was before Rebecca Warren tripped into his life—an auburn-haired angel full of vim, with the tongue of a viper and the body of a temptress.

"Are you positive?" he asked, wiping the tears from his eyes.

"As the Lord is my witness, pretty as you please, she draped that, uh, limb alongside the tub, and scraped it smooth as a silk ball gown," Jubadessa elaborated, an inkling of a smile tugging at her own lips.

Alexander sobered abruptly, reaching for an am-

121

ber-filled tumbler on the night stand. "What next, I wonder?" He sighed, grimacing as he took a stiff shot of whiskey. But his thoughts turned to a more important matter. He had to get word to Major General Wheeler that he was alive, that the mission wasn't lost, only delayed! But how? He'd been wracking his brain for the last hour without discovering a solution.

One thing was for certain, though. Jubadessa was right. He shouldn't have tried standing alone so soon. His shoulder had begun to throb, the stitches drawing as the skin around them dried.

Oddly enough, with the dull ache rose visions of Rebecca, her soothing hands, her face, her confident smile, the way her breasts brushed his arm as she leaned to stitch the tattered edges of the bullet hole together. His loins tightened involuntarily, and he gathered the bulky covers at his lap, cursing the whim of fate that had brought them together at such an inopportune time.

Rebecca had driven him to distraction over the last few days. She was a woman after his own heart, but for her sake and his own safety, he could only risk possession of the enticing young lady in his dreams.

"I can't say what the future holds, *Monsieur*, but if we're not careful, what with the war, Miss Cordelia's shenanigans, and her new-found friend's presence, we could *all* wind up in poor Mrs. Abigail's shoes!"

Alexander polished off the whiskey in a gulp. "You might just be right, Jubadessa," he conceded, placing the empty glass on the night stand

122

and twisting to punch down ruthlessly the pillows behind his back. "By the way, I meant to tell you there's a storm brewing to the west. Ask Willy to see that the stock is bedded down securely."

"Right away. Now, close your eyes and get some rest," Jubadessa said sternly over her shoulder, snapping the drapes tightly together against the damp night air.

Alexander touched his brow in crisp salute. "Yes, ma'am."

Aye, he'd shut his eyes, Alexander thought, but he couldn't promise sleep. The weight of the world felt as if it was perched atop his injured shoulder. Between concern for his men left afield without a senior commander, the anxiety of an incomplete mission, Oak Mont's precarious position in occupied territory, and the seductive Rebecca Ann Warren haunting his thoughts, rest would be a long time coming!

Jubadessa tiptoed out into the wide hallway, closing Alexander's door quietly behind her.

As sure as she was born on a Monday, there was a storm coming, but it wasn't the one in the western sky that bothered her. The thunderclouds gathering over Oak Mont in the form of *Monsieur's* restricted activity did. The better he got, the more restless he would become, and it was only a matter of time before the bottom dropped out of his frayed temper.

The question was, which course would the rain take, and who would reap the downpour when it finally arrived?

"Jubadessa, thank goodness I found you!" Rebecca whispered with relief from the first-floor landing. "I wasn't sure which room was Cordelia's and the house seems so dark with only candlelight to guide the way."

Jubadessa turned to the sound of Rebecca's voice. A candle in her hand, her hair an unrestrained auburn nimbus about her face, barefoot and swathed in a blue matron's gown, she ascended the stairs.

Lordy, Lordy, Jubadessa thought, shaking her head. It had purely skipped her mind. She still had to round up proper night things for that poor young lady!

Chapter Five

The night rain began as a gentle drumming on the veranda roof outside Rebecca's bedroom window. It was not the watery tattoo, however, that interrupted her rest, but stealthy footsteps crossing the porch, punctuated by Guinevere's deep-throated growl.

Swimming up from sleep, for a moment Rebecca wasn't sure where she was. Then her memory came rushing back double time.

She heard the mastiff scratch at the threshold, then rise upright to plant her front paws against the kitchen door, sniffing at the jamb as the intruder bypassed the entrance and headed for Jubadessa's window farther along the porch. Rebecca waited for the bark that would undoubtedly rouse the rest of the household, but the alarm never sounded.

Confused by the watchdog's negligent response, Rebecca lay still in the single four-poster bed. Her ears keenly tuned, she listened to the code-like tap of fingernails against glass that rivaled the raindrops—three sharp, two dull, three sharp, two dull, three sharp.

Then, she detected movement in the kitchen, and heard Jubadessa's cultured voice shushing the dog. "Quiet, Guinevere. Stay."

The bolt was drawn, and the back door creaked open slowly. An instant later, with a rush of cool air and a feminine "Good gracious," the door swung wider to admit Jubadessa's rain-soaked caller.

A poker stirred the cookstove embers; dry kindling and a log were added with a rustle and a thump. Billows wheezed, whipping up the flame along with hushed voices, cloistered in urgent conversation. "People were packed into de city like sardines . . . *eruptive* fever. You've *got* to help," the unfamiliar baritone pleaded.

"Not so loud, you'll wake the others," Jubadessa cautioned in a low voice.

Mumbled words and disjointed phrases Rebecca couldn't quite catch followed, then Jubadessa's more solid reply. Her words were drenched in uncharacteristic anxiety. "Lord love us, Clayton! If it was in my power to help, I would, but there is shameless little I can do against the fever. And I've Mrs. Abigail to consider. She is as wild as the winter wind. Likely to set the house afire if I leave her tonight."

"For pity's sake, can't you ask Miss Cordelia to sit with Mrs. Abigail?" the man questioned in dismay. Then more strongly came words tinged with impatience, "What you stay here anyway for?"

"Clayton, Clayton. You will pull my heart in two for sure. You know Miss Cordelia is all thumbs where her mama is concerned, and I know her so well. I've spent most of my life beside that woman," Jubadessa answered.

Slow footsteps, emphasizing dashed hopes Rebecca thought, shuffled to the hearth. "If not you, den who, Jubadessa? You tell me dat! I been battling dis monster for weeks! Ain't done one lick of good for my family," he groaned. "You don't come down to de old mill house, do what you can, Dinah dies for sure, just like my wife and son. You want dat on your conscience? Me, I can't take no more!"

Total silence covered the gap in conversation for only a second before deep, muffled sobs filled the kitchen. *Why the man's crying*, Rebecca realized. *That does it*!

Galvanized into action, Rebecca swung her feet over the side of the feather mattress, her soles outraged at the coolness of the wooden floor. Hastily, she found her slippers, donning in one clean sweep the flannel robe Jubadessa had provided. Wishing Oak Mont boasted a thermostatic-controlled furnace like the one in her parents' home, Rebecca wrapped the cotton comforter around her for additional warmth before fumbling toward the doorway. The squarely built, dark-skinned man looked

127

up, his moist eyes filled with suspicion as Rebecca barged into the kitchen.

Dressed in her day clothes, her unbound hair, long and silky black, swinging freely, Jubadessa rounded on Rebecca. "This is no place for you, in the middle of the night, Miss Rebecca," she exclaimed, her face radiating surprise. Recovering herself instantly, she stepped in front of the big man as if to shield him from view.

"You can't hide him, Jubadessa, and there's no reason you should. I don't mean any harm. I only came to see if I might offer my assistance."

"Not this time, Miss Rebecca. Run along back to bed now."

Who did Jubadessa think she was dealing with? Mothering had its place. This wasn't it.

"What's going on, Jubadessa?" Rebecca asked, mustering her most authoritative tone. "This man seems extremely upset."

By Jubadessa's solemn expression, Rebecca realized the housekeeper would like nothing better than to swat her backside with a yardstick. Instead, she explained calmly, "Clayton was one of Oak Mont's folks, a field hand, and he's come back to have a word with me. His little girl sickened in Nashville. He brought her away from the city in hopes that it would curb her illness. The move didn't help . . ." Jubadessa's voice trailed off.

"But perhaps *I* can."

"Miss Rebecca, what are you saying?" Jubadessa snapped, her brown eyes flashing with gold flecks.

"That I'll go with your friend, examine the child."

"You will not! It is not practical. Dinah has the measles," Jubadessa stated flatly, as if Rebecca's suggestion was out of the question.

"I'm a registered nurse, Jubadessa," Rebecca reminded her. "I've dealt with viral infections before."

"What is wrong with you, with all this talk of ...viral...infections?" Jubadessa asked swiftly, her arms akimbo as she wrapped her tongue around the unfamiliar term. "Let us be realistic, Miss Rebecca. You don't strike me as a simpleton," she hissed in agitation. "You dare not go traipsing off into the dead of night! The Federals will arrest a Southern matron caught moonlighting as quickly as any Rebel officer."

She swiveled, glaring at Clayton, but speaking to Rebecca. "And how would you explain slinking around in the shadows playing peekaboo—a Confederate lady in possession of contraband fresh off the Federal breastworks in Nashville? Spies, or worse, that's how the soldiers would perceive the two of you. And what a pretty kettle of fish that would be!"

"Contraband? What contraband?" Rebecca asked, thoroughly confused.

"Clayton!" Jubadessa snapped.

"But he's a human being," Rebecca argued.

"A human being who is considered contraband of the war, at least as far as the Yankees are concerned."

"I'm still not sure I understand," Rebecca stated.

"Surely, you have heard about this before now?" Jubadessa insisted. When Rebecca shook her head, the housekeeper continued, "The Beast of New Orleans, Ben Butler, instigated the policy in the first place. A Yankee officer to the hilt, he suggested that because slaves were Rebel property, *enemy* property that is, by the unwritten code of war they could be confiscated."

"You told Alexander that the Federals offered Oak Mont's servants jobs in Nashville for wages. I just assumed they went of their own free will."

"They did, Clayton included. It makes no never mind to the Federals, though. They are always looking for an excuse to cause trouble."

"Jubadessa's right, Becky. Unless you have passes, the bluecoats would pick you up and send you off to prison up North quicker than you can wink." Cordelia yawned from the hallway door.

"Miss Cordelia! You go on back upstairs to bed. There is no need for you to get involved in this discussion," Jubadessa advised.

But the housekeeper's words went unheeded as Cordelia glided to the larder for a bottle of ammonia spirits. Mixing the small dosage in a dipper of water, she said, "I couldn't sleep if I tried. I've been tossin' and turnin' all evenin'." She swallowed the watered-down concoction. Massaging her temple, she set the brass kettle for tea, then plopped down in a cane chair pulled up to the cookstove.

"Your wisdom tooth is bothering you again,

isn't it? You pack it with cloves, it will ease the pain better than those nasty old spirits," Jubadessa said. "I keep telling you that molar needs to come out."

"It's not the tooth this time, Jubadessa, only a sick headache."

"Comes from nerves ... from running 'round the countryside, day and night, trying to nurse soldier boys, when you should be married to one of them and settled down by now. It is totally unladylike," Jubadessa said disapprovingly.

"I know you despair that I'll end my life an old maid, dependent upon Alexander's generosity for my daily bread, but now is not the time to harp on your disappointment in me, Dessa," Cordelia said firmly. "Besides, my 'runnin' 'round' saw Alexander home in one piece, didn't it?" she asked, drawing herself up to her full five-foot-four-inch height.

Jubadessa opened her mouth several times as if to speak, but said nothing, for Cordelia had a point.

Playing on their exchange, Rebecca interjected, "You had passes made up to bring your cousin home, didn't you, Cordelia? I could use those," she said, extending her hands toward the stove to toast her chilly fingers and to allow time for her idea to sink in.

"Yes," Cordelia commented after a moment's thought. "I suppose they'd do in a pinch, fool a patrol if we cut the date off the top and rewrote it further down. How are you at forgery?"

"When pressed into a corner, I've taken my turn

at signing school notes for my brother."

"Good enough."

Jubadessa threw up her hands, as a disgusted sigh escaped her lips. "Two peas in a pod talking. I might as well be invisible! Bound and determined to do as you please since joining the Ladies' Confederate Relief Society. You've been as hard to handle as a cat with its tail afire."

Much to Jubadessa's chagrin, twenty-eight-year-old Cordelia disdained proper female pursuits for more flagrant interests. The more harebrained the schemes she became embroiled in, the better it seemed to suit her. But for all her intractableness, Jubadessa hid a heart as malleable as butter, and Cordelia held the key. She had practically raised the girl for Carl and Abigail Stoddard, and because of that, Jubadessa knew that Cordelia had learned how to get her way from Jubadessa.

"Think of Dinah. You helped with her birth. Such a beautiful baby. You said so yourself. Remember?"

Clayton added his two-cents' worth. "I'd see de lady home by noon." His voice brightened with renewed hope as he realized Jubadessa was weakening.

"You're asking me to go against my better judgment. If *Monsieur* finds out about this escapade, he will skin us all alive! He's already commented to me in private on your presence at Murfreesboro," Jubadessa forewarned, weighing possible repercussions against her acquiescence.

Rebecca frowned. What did Alexander Ransom

hold over his family, to get such a rise out of imperious Jubadessa? No man should be so all-powerful, even if he had the dashing good looks of the devil himself.

"Lieutenant Colonel Ransom is confined to his bed. What he doesn't know won't hurt him, or us either," Rebecca said.

"Let's not quibble, Jubadessa. Allow her to go," Cordelia insisted sleepily as the ammonia took effect, easing her headache. "When all is said and done, Becky will do as she sees fit anyway," she predicted, vividly recalling the redneck incident at Stones River as well as Rebecca's insistence that she climb into the wagon bed and share her warmth with Alexander. "And Dinah is such a dear little thing. Alexander wouldn't care to see her ill if there was someone willin' and able to offer comfort," she added almost as an afterthought.

Jubadessa's face fell at the mention of a child suffering.

Her mind clicking, Cordelia realized that Rebecca's absence might benefit her as well as Clayton's daughter. With her house guest otherwise occupied, Cordelia could fake an abscessed tooth, seize Willy for the day as chaperone, and ride into Nashville on the pretext of seeing a dentist. From there, it would be simple to visit James secretly at Federal headquarters.

Wouldn't Jubadessa be appalled if she knew the truth? Cordelia thought. She hated lies, but she'd stumbled onto a windfall. She finally had a semi-legitimate excuse to go to Nashville. Jubadessa had suggested it, and Cordelia desperately needed to square things with James. This was the golden opportunity she'd been waiting for. All she needed to do was follow through on it, hypocrisy be hanged, Cordelia decided, pressing home her advantage.

"Rebecca is a wonderful nurse and avoidin' the Yanks comes second nature to her. Besides, Clayton would never allow anythin' to happen to someone from Oak Mont. You, of all people, know that, Jubadessa," Cordelia cajoled.

Jubadessa snorted with exasperation, her face tilted toward the ceiling as if beseeching divine guidance.

Monsieur would take the roof off if she consented to such a dangerous scheme. But Miss Cordelia was correct. If the nurse was willing and thought she could help, Dinah was worth the risk. Agonizing over her decision, in the end Jubadessa went along with Cordelia and Rebecca Warren, much to Clayton's relief.

The timber footbridge spanning the swelled stream was shaky, and water flowed over the plank floor like a shiny, polyurethane finish. Carrying an oversized wicker basket of supplies—Squibb and Sons quinine, dehydrated carrots, carbolic acid—and a blanket roll Jubadessa had contributed to the expedition wedged beneath his arm, Clayton reached out to steady Rebecca's step.

Rebecca accepted his hand, glad for the support. As luck would have it, when they'd left the house, Clayton's path had lead them past the family cemetery and by the early-morning light, Rebecca had made sure to read the dated script carved on Beau's and Edward's headstones. Rebecca's head still reverberated with her discovery. They had died in 1862, but the graves had still looked fresh!

Bundled in Cordelia's waterproof mackintosh and her own damp slouch hat, Rebecca shivered, sloshing through the water to gain the slippery bank. The day she'd arrived Cordelia had mentioned "September last" in conjunction with the Ransom brothers' deaths. Yesterday, Jubadessa had told Alexander that she, Willy, and Abigail had been alone at Oak Mont since Christmas. By Rebecca's calculations, it had to be early *1863*! Somehow she'd managed to land smack dab in the middle of the Civil War. Not at the beginning, as she had first thought when moral was high. Nor at the end, when the war was winding down and the worst was over. But in the middle, the most dreadful, uncertain, grueling part as far as she was concerned.

Just my luck! Rebecca thought. *Jump out of a hot frying pan, only to land in the fire.*

"Lookin' sorta pale. You doin' all right, miss?" Clayton asked, dropping her hand.

"Yes," Rebecca answered in monotone. *1863!*

"You cold? Probably shoulda worn somethin' warmer dan dat mackintosh."

The borrowed raincoat was too short to cover her outfit since she was a head taller than Cordelia. The difference allowed the hem of her skirt to get soaked, but at least it kept her upper body, and the medical bag tucked beneath, reasonably dry.

135

"I'm fine, Clayton...really." Suddenly a malodorous fragrance seasoning the air took her mind off the date. Wrinkling her nose, Rebecca asked, "Phew! What's that Godawful smell?"

"Skunk scent."

"Skunk?"

"Yes, 'um. Followin' a skunk trail now... quicker dan de road."

Quicker! Quicker than what? Rebecca wondered. Time seemed to creep along. They'd been walking along an overgrown labyrinth that wound through the forest so long, that she'd thought they were lost. But then Rebecca took heart for she sensed by Clayton's sure step that he knew his way.

It was amazing that Cordelia and Clayton had an uncanny sense of direction, Rebecca thought, the squish of her dank boots accompanying the songbirds' early-morning serenade as they turned to follow a winding creek bank. She could feel a blister rising on her left heel beneath her thin, cotton stockings. Oh, what she wouldn't give for a pair of tennis shoes!

"Sorry 'bout your boots, miss. Might uncomfortable, I 'magine," Clayton noted, his features carefully set in a blank expression as he lead the way, brushing back an overhanging branch before it had time to swipe Rebecca in the cheek.

"No problem. They'll dry." Her feet were of little consequence really, she'd experienced worse. And as they grew nearer the mill, it was the child who overshadowed Rebecca's thoughts, crowding out everything else, even the numbers 1863. Her growing concern was reflected in her next words.

"How high was your daughter's temperature when you last checked, Clayton?"

"Hot."

"That doesn't tell me a heck of a lot." Obviously mercury thermometers were a thing of the future.

"Real hot."

"All right, real hot," Rebecca responded. That could mean anywhere from 101 to 105 degrees she surmised, stopping to catch her breath and tug at her boot heel. Hiking had never been one of her specialities, though her father, the outdoorsman, had insisted she learn to read a compass and pitch an adequate tent right along with her brother.

"Have you been giving her plenty of fluids?" she asked, trying to collect as much pertinent information as possible before she arrived at the scene.

"What she'd take without a fight."

"Great!" Just what she needed, a dehydrated child in a world without Gatorade.

"Eating?"

"Some."

"Has she been going to the john regularly since she's been sick?"

The question obviously surprised Clayton, for his pace slowed. Glancing over his shoulder at Rebecca with a curious expression on his dark face he asked, "John?"

"Bathroom . . . latrine . . . outhouse . . . necessary."

"Oh. Yes,'um, suppose so."

"Good, very good. That's important with measles."

Relaxing slightly, Clayton resolutely offered a

tidbit more of information without Rebecca's prompting. "Got some congestion in her chest."

Not good, Rebecca thought. The most dreaded complications from measles were inflammation of the mucous membranes in the eyes, ears, and chest—mastoiditis, pneumonia, encephalitis.

"Is she coughing?"

"Yes, 'um."

"A–OK. That gets the fluid up. Anything else?" Rebecca urged in a gentle voice. The man was finally opening up to her.

"Runny nose."

"Like a cold."

"Yes, 'um. Same as my wife and son," he added dejectedly.

"I think that's all I need to know about Dinah for right now, Clayton," she said. "How much longer do you figure before we reach the mill?" Rebecca asked thoughtfully, trying to steer his mind away from his loss.

"Just ahead, 'round de bend where de bank widens out," he said, stopping to let her catch up.

"You don't waste words, do you, Clayton?" Rebecca asked with a smile, amazed by his stamina. He didn't even appear winded.

"No, 'um. Can't say as I do," he responded, with perfect seriousness.

The gristmill was built high off the ground on a solid rock foundation. Its overshot water wheel transferred power by leather pulleys and belts to the millstone within, Rebecca reasoned. The milldam looked washed out and Rebecca speculated that the owner probably abandoned the building to join the Army. It wasn't the quaint old mill, however, but the blankets spread like tarps, in the tree boughs near the front entrance with a small group of people camping beneath that captured Rebecca's attention.

"Why did I assume you and your daughter were alone, Clayton?" Rebecca asked sharply, cutting Clayton a sideways glance.

" 'Cause, I didn't say otherwise, miss?" he answered sheepishly.

"Probably so. Why did you feel the need to keep me in the dark and not tell me that other families were involved?"

"Figured you wouldn't come, if you knew."

"That wouldn't have stopped me, though had I known, I might have been able to bring more supplies," Rebecca explained, her momentary irritation evaporating.

"Yes, 'um. 'Pologize."

"Well, there's nothing for it now. Lead on."

To say that the group stared when Rebecca swept through camp bound for the mill would have been an understatement. Gaped was more the word. Audible whispers filtered skyward toward the blankets only to be muffled in their damp folds.

"They don't seemed to care for the fact I'm here."

"Surprised, that's all. Most white women . . . Well, you're taking a pretty big chance with measles."

"It's okay. I've had my shots."

Clayton stopped so abruptly Rebecca almost trod on his heels. "Shots, miss?"

"Never mind. Keep going. It isn't important. What I really need to know now is how many of the others have symptoms?" Rebecca asked, steering her way through the audience as well as through his question.

"I had 'em same time as my wife, but de spots passed. Lucky enough, no more so far."

"Thank goodness! Let's see if we can keep it that way, especially with the pregnant lady," Rebecca specified, nodding toward a young woman well into her ninth month, who was standing on the porch. "I don't want to see you near the mill house, not one foot on this porch, okay?" Rebecca directed to the wide-eyed woman in a no-nonsense voice, giving her a quick once over as she ascended the steps.

The woman shot off the porch like a doe hit with buckshot.

"I didn't mean to scare her, Clayton," Rebecca said, baffled by the woman's reaction. "I only want to isolate your daughter so she's less likely to infect the others. Since you've already contracted and survived the measles, your system has built up antibodies. You're the most likely candidate to assume the position of Dinah's designated provider after I leave. In that way, God willing, maybe we can contain this. Fourteen days or so should tell if we've succeeded."

Clayton nodded. Shoowee! The lady sure could talk up a storm.

"All right now, folks. You heard Miss Rebecca.

She's de nurse and she ought to know what she's talkin' 'bout. So go on about your business unless someone's feelin' poorly."

There was a shift to follow orders, but Rebecca's voice halted them. "One more thing, if you don't mind." Rebecca took a deep breath. "Jubadessa, whom I'll assume a good many of you know, has sent liquid soap, chloride of lime, and several bottles of carbolic acid from her larder. I can't emphasize enough the importance of cleanliness in a situation like this. Germs . . . microbes . . . can compound measles. All bedding that's been used by the sick, clothes, eating utensils, your hands *must* be disinfected against these microscopic bugs, particularly Dinah's things."

No one moved; they acted as if she was talking Vietnamese instead of English. How did she make these people understand the importance of such a mundane act? Rebecca wondered, suddenly at a loss for words. She turned to Clayton for help.

He read the plea for assistance in her clear blue eyes. "Everything washed," Clayton paraphrased, unloading the basket to distribute the supplies, taking a bottle of acid for himself.

"Exactly," Rebecca said with relief. "If you'll make a pot of the camomile tea Jubadessa included, I'll go in and examine Dinah," Rebecca said, picking up the blanket roll and disappearing into the mill house, a spring to her step. "And, Clayton, boil the water *real* well, then stir in an extra dose of honey to sweeten the cup," she added from the dark interior.

141

"Yes, 'um," Clayton answered, thinking Rebecca was a regular whirlwind.

Dinah was a tiny child, with round eyes, a button nose, and the most enchanting smile Rebecca had ever seen.

"You aren't Jubadessa," the little girl observed in a frail voice from her cornhusk pallet on the floor.

Rebecca smiled, relaxing for the first time since leaving Oak Mont. Incorporating her best Mary Poppins imitation, Rebecca conceded, "No, I'm not, little one, but maybe you can put up with me for a short while."

Setting down her bag and discarding the mackintosh, Rebecca kneeled to peer into the child's face, taking her small hand and cupping it in her own. She realized she was the happiest when she was working, doing what she was good at and was most comfortable with in this alien environment. She liked taking charge, making her own decisions, being useful.

The Koplik's spots, pinpoint-sized bluish-white specks on the inside of Dinah's lower lip, told Rebecca the child was two or three days away from the rash when she would have to be isolated. Taking out her thermometer, she got a good reading, checked Dinah's respiration then heartbeat with her stethoscope. With her vital signs out of the way, Rebecca covered the little girl with the blanket, then proceeded to crack open some windows for ventilation, careful of the light which could harm Dinah's sensitive eye tissue if left unprotected.

Stopping to rummage through her bag, Rebecca pulled out a pair of dime-store sunglasses. The sun was blinding in Vietnam, especially when one stepped out of a dark Quonset hut. It had become a habit with Rebecca to keep a pair of cheap sunglasses stashed in her medical bag, handy in an emergency.

Adjusting the glasses on Dinah's small nose, she commanded, "Wear those shades until you're all well."

"Yes, ma'am."

"I know you feel awful now, honey, but your dad's steeping something that's going to make your throat feel better and help you rest. And in a month's time, you won't even remember being sick," Rebecca said, once again kneeling by the child.

"Promise," Dinah asked, naturally accepting Rebecca as, crossing her eyes, she tried to see the glasses without taking them off.

Clayton's daughter was in good shape; she'd contracted a mild case of the measles. Rebecca felt reasonably sure Dinah would recover without a hitch. "As sure as my name's Lieutenant Rebecca Ann Warren," she responded, totally at home with the child. That was one of the things she liked best about kids, you could be yourself with them without appearing crazy.

"Until your dad comes with the tea, how about my showing you a game I used to play when I was a small?"

"Was that a very long time ago, when you were a little girl?" Dinah asked innocently, her fingers testing the plastic framed sunglasses.

"A v–e–r–y long time ago." Rebecca sighed.

Taking out a ball-point pen and a blank tablet, Rebecca drew Mickey and Minnie Mouse in a different pose on each consecutive page. By teaching Dinah to flip the pages through her fingers, Mickey danced a cartoon-style jig with Minnie.

Dinah was enthralled, not only with the glasses, and the comical characters, but with Rebecca. "How did you learn to do that?" she asked breathlessly.

"By watching a pro—Walt Disney. His company owns the patent on those guys."

"Does he draw a lot?"

"He did. All the time. Never seemed to run out of new characters," Rebecca replied, running through the story of Bambi before Clayton arrived with the soothing tea.

Unexpectedly, even though the drizzle had stopped and the day turned unseasonably warm, the creek had risen so high over the footbridge by the time Rebecca left the gristmill that she and Clayton had to go farther down stream to cross before cutting back toward Oak Mont. Consequently, it was late afternoon when Rebecca returned to the plantation.

Anxious to get back to his daughter, Clayton left Rebecca within sight of the house. "Now don't forget my instructions. Quinine and warm sponge baths every four hours for fever. *Don't* let her scratch when the rash appears even if you have to put mittens on her hands because it will cause scarring. Keep her on a light diet, carrot soup, with plenty of fluids. Clean the mill dust out of Dinah's room and don't hesitate to call if you need me," Rebecca said.

Clayton nodded, waved good-bye, then ducked back into the woods.

Rebecca smiled to herself, raising her hand in farewell. She'd thoroughly enjoyed the day. She hadn't realized she'd been squelching so much of her personality during the last week until she'd meet Dinah. It was like holding your breath when playing hide-and-seek so no one will find you out, she thought.

The mackintosh buttoned at her throat like a cape, Rebecca exhaled, her arms swinging freely at her sides as she limped toward the house thinking how good it felt to be herself, to be alive. It had been a pleasant change to work with someone who wasn't riddled with shrapnel and bullets.

Oak Mont's groom, as unlikely a welcoming committee as she'd ever had, met Rebecca at the picket fence surrounding the front lawn.

"Pardon, miss. We've not been properly introduced. My name's Willy McCorkle. I'm the groom. I've been watchin' for ya. Mister Alexander sent me to deliver a message. Said he'd like to see ya in the carriage house," Willy recited, doffing his billed cap, but keeping a good distance between himself and Rebecca.

Rebecca was mildly amused. Nearsighted without her driving glasses, stuck in the breast pocket of her fatigue jacket in the twentieth century, distances were deceiving sometimes. The person she'd assumed to be a dark-skinned boy making soap near the carriage house the day before was actually a jockey-sized Irishman with gray hair, and a construction worker's weathered skin.

"In the carriage house? Why, he should be in bed," Rebecca thought aloud, unlatching the gate. She couldn't *wait* to get her boots off!

"Jubadessa said the same thing, miss, but he's in a powerful temper, bound and determined to see ya down yonder before ya make yourself to home," the groom stated in his thick, Irish brogue, moving closer to block her path.

Rebecca frowned, slowly relatching the gate to face him head on. "Where's Jubadessa?" she asked suspiciously.

Willy blinked. "She's been regulated to her room for the time bein', miss, at least until this thing is sorted out."

"And Cordelia?"

"Same thing, only in her dame's room, Mrs. Abigail. As soon as Miss Cordelia and I returned from Nashville, and himself saw ya weren't with us ..."

This was making a little more sense now. "The feathers hit the fan," Rebecca finished for him. So, Cordelia had taken a ride into Nashville to try and cover her absence.

It was obvious by the groom's uneasy formality, Alexander had found out about her alternate trip to the gristmill, and was as angry as Jubadessa had warned he would be.

Rebecca cleared her throat. She squared her shoulders, wondering how disobedient women were punished during 1863.

"The carriage house, you say?" she asked, stalling for time.

"Yes, miss, right away," Willy pointed out, half in admiration, half in wonder. Usually, when Mister Alexander spoke, people jumped.

"Roger wilco," Rebecca quipped with a lively, if somewhat mocking salute, hanging her medical bag over a slat in the fence.

"As I said, it's Willy McCorkle, miss," the groom corrected, motioning for her to follow him.

Rebecca couldn't hide the smile that crept to her lips. He sounded just like her gruff old bootcamp staff sergeant.

"Yes, sir, Willy McCorkle, *sir*," she said under her breath, bending to tug her left boot off before, taking her satchel from the fence, her chin up, she marched along behind him.

Buggy whip in hand, Alexander stood in the arched doorway of the tack room neatly reworking the frayed leather around the flexible rod. Without the necessary manpower to maintain things, the longer he was away, the more Oak Mont fell into disrepair. He had to give them credit, though. Jubadessa and Willy had done an excellent job of keeping things going while he served Tennessee, but after all, there was only so much two people could do against the mountain of work piling up around them.

With the crop season fast approaching, things could only get worse. The corn would need as many as three replantings to ensure a good stand; the tobacco, started in seedbeds, would have to be transferred to the fields, pruned, topped, and the suckers removed. Both entailed hot, sweaty, back-breaking labor. The same went for any cotton or wheat they planted. Harvest consisted of eighteen-hour days when the plantation was up to par and it wasn't by a long shot.

But without Beau and Edward....

Alexander's thoughts veered from the graves on the hill. He'd love to be able to hire extra laborers, if they could be found with three-fourths of the South in uniform. Unfortunately, Willy would have to do the best he could alone. Alexander couldn't take the time to interview perspective employees, even if it resulted in his losing his shirt in the coming year. No one could know he was at Oak Mont. No one must find out. And, somehow, in the next few days, he had to devise a way to see General Wheeler, if only to let his commanding officer know he was still alive and that his preas-signed mission could and would be completed. Soon, he had to do that soon. But how could he without arousing suspicion in the district?

With supreme determination, Alexander turned his thoughts to something he could sink his teeth into immediately. Something he could act upon in his present recovering state.

"Where in the hell are Clayton and Rebecca? They should have returned long ago according to Jubadessa," he mused aloud.

Alexander gazed down the length of the carriage house. Once thoroughbreds had filled every available cubicle. With the death of his Morgan on the field at Stones River, however, Rebecca's sleek, dapple-gray mare was the only blue blood in sight.

The chocolate-brown mule team, stalled at the far end of the building, munched on the coarse hay he'd tossed in their manger. The Jersey dairy cow contentedly chewed her cud, rubbing her horns against a corner post of her stall every now and again to scratch an itch. Three unpretentious substitutes for his father's once-proud brood line, Alexander thought, glancing down at the valuable heirloom ring glinting on his right hand.

"I'm afraid the war's going to extract its toll in more ways than one, Father," he prophesied aloud.

Alexander set the whip aside to grab a handful of grain from the half-empty burlap sack leaning against the wall near his feet, extending it to Vedette. She snorted haughtily and drew back, rejecting the tidbit. With a switch of her fine tail, she presented her backside to him. Then as if reconsidering his offer, she wheeled, arching her elegant neck over the door to sniff at his hand. Alexander slowly unfurled his fingers, letting the grain rest temptingly in the center of his palm.

"Your disdain is admirable, pretty lady, but how long can you resist the temptation, I wonder?" Alexander coaxed in a soothing voice. She snorted, pretending disinterest. "So, it's to be a stand off then," Alexander said with a grin, remaining motionless, his hand extended invitingly.

It was a full three minutes before the mare deigned to acknowledge him, daintily lipping the sweet feed from Alexander's hand like a princess sipping champagne. Her eyes brightened at the flavor. She nuzzled his hand with her soft muzzle in appreciation when she finished, allowing him one quick pat between the ears before abruptly rounding on him again to gaze out the barred window on the far side of her stall.

"A lot like your mistress—spirited, fine-limbed and thoroughly captivating." Alexander chuckled aloud, his attention returning to the whip.

Willy ushered Rebecca through the carriage house doorway, but failed to accompany her in. It took a moment for her eyes to adjust to the light. Still, Rebecca spotted Alexander before he did her. She'd known her patient was handsome, but she'd never dreamed just how devastating a man the lieutenant colonel could be minus his dark beard and dirty hair, and dressed in civilian clothes.

A white linen shirt, carelessly unbottoned at the throat, displayed Alexander's powerful shoulders to advantage, while black pants tucked into worn leather riding boots offset his trim, muscular physique to perfection. Freshly washed sable hair hanging crisp and shiny at his collar, clean-shaven with a neatly trimmed moustache, he reminded Rebecca of some unattainable matinee idol. His overpowering masculinity took her breath away as an involuntary tingle of excitement fluttered in her stomach.

Who would believe plain little old me was actually kissed by such a hunk and held in his arms? Rebecca marveled, bemused by Alexander's blatant sex appeal. Wouldn't her friend, Janet, have a fit over him!

Reminiscing about the Quonset hut that doubled as a canteen for the MASH unit, where for a quarter Janet made a point of playing five easy listening tunes from the jukebox every Saturday night, Rebecca smiled fondly. A connoisseur where good-looking officers were concerned, the head nurse would give a week's pay to take a spin around the dance floor with this one, Rebecca conceded, making her way down the alleyway between the stalls toward Alexander—clump, pad; clump, pad; clump, pad.

Alexander glanced up at the sound of Rebecca's mismatched footsteps. She took one look at his troubled expression and her smugness vanished. It was obvious the man had a lot on his mind. Crow's feet radiated from the corner of his eyes as if light-hearted merriment came second nature to him, but grooves punctuating his full mouth reminded Rebecca of the hardships he must have endured over the last few years. She wondered fleetingly how high she was on the list of priorities, and if his somber reflection somehow pertained to her.

Her gaze dropping self-consciously, Rebecca halted mid-stride, noting the crisscrossed bandaging displayed beneath the thin material of Alexander's shirt rather than her own neatly angled design. Obviously, while she was away, someone had rewrapped the wound, with clean bandages Rebecca prayed, concern for his well-being overpowering her thoughts.

His eyes scanning Rebecca's outfit, Alexander's preoccupied expression changed. A harsh look replaced it as he zeroed in on her, advancing with a pantherine grace she'd been unaware he possessed while he lay flat on his back.

"I can tell by your swagger, you're feeling much better, but you shouldn't be up yet," Rebecca admonished softly, a bewildered frown marring her delicate features as a warning signal went off in her brain. Alexander Ransom was livid.

His hazel eyes twinkling with determination, Alexander disregarded Rebecca's concern, ordering without preamble, "Strip, Miss Warren!"

Rebecca was immediately defensive, the pleasant day spent attending Dinah disintegrating into dust. She mentally shrugged back into her hardshell coating, asking stupidly, "W–w–h–a–t?"

"You heard me. Strip." His words lashed her.

"You must be out of your mind," Rebecca stated coolly. Her action belied her calm words as she retreated a step, her eyes on the buggy whip he held.

"Hardly. Now will you disrobe or shall I help you?" Alexander asked sternly, caressing the handle of the whip with a strong, lean-fingered hand.

"Are you threatening me?" Rebecca asked, her voice resoundingly neutral as she fought for composure.

"Just stating a fact. One way or another, the gown, Miss Warren, goes," he parried, struck afresh by Rebecca's sense of control.

Wearing only one boot, her rich auburn hair wild from her trek through the forest, Rebecca still created an impressive picture, Alexander mused, repressing a smile in accordance with the gravity of the situation.

"Watch . . . my . . . lips—no way."

Rebecca could feel her pulse thrumming rapidly at the base of her throat, like a trapped bird beating its wings on the inside walls of a chimney, she thought as she awaited his response.

"Oh, yes. There's a way. But I don't think you'll find favor with it," he vowed ominously, so close now she could feel his warm breath fanning her cheek.

Shaken inside by the heat of his words, Rebecca's heart ran a gamut of emotion. She half-pirouetted, bound for the door.

Alexander cursed soundly as his face darkened. All humor aside, he couldn't allow her to infect Oak Mont with the measles if it could be avoided.

"I wouldn't if I were you," he stated grimly, grasping Rebecca's shoulder to turn her back toward him.

Their eyes clashed. Alexander's touch was firm but not hurtful, yet his familiarity angered Rebecca. This man was invading her space without an invitation!

Her narrowed eyes spitting sapphire fire, Rebecca dropped the water-marked boot she'd been clutching to her breast, managing to communicate her resentment without raising her voice.

"If you don't take your hand off me, Lieutenant Colonel Ransom, I'm going to demonstrate just how good a bring-you-to-your-knees Karate chop feels on top of a partially healed bullet wound. And make no mistake. I'm just the woman who can do it, too."

Chapter Six

Though a scowl remained on his face, Alexander's lips twitched. "Am I to understand that you're threatening me?"

Threatening you? I think you're the one threatening me. "Call it the way you see fit. I'm not afraid to defend myself when I have to," Rebecca affirmed.

"I take a dim view of threats."

"I bet you do."

Alexander's expression cleared somewhat as he relieved the tension in the carriage house by swearing, "You, madame, don't scare worth a damn!"

Rebecca tilted her chin pugnaciously. "Not if I can help it, although I have to admit the idea of being whipped isn't all that appealing."

Alexander glanced down at the whip, carelessly casting it aside and retrieving a beautifully crafted patchwork quilt folded on a nearby milking stool.

"Don't be a goose! You'd think a woman with your sensibilities would know better," he said, his mouth a tight line of exasperation. "Contrary to popular opinion, all Southerners don't believe a whipping is the answer to everything, even in cases of a guest's brazen discourtesy."

"I . . . Perhaps I was . . ." What had she done this time? She had the distinct impression she was somehow being accused of taking advantage of Oak Mont's hospitality.

Rebecca shook her head and took a deep breath. "Listen, Willy told me Cordelia and Jubadessa are on restriction for aiding and abetting me. You're doing them a disservice. They're not responsible; I didn't ask their permission. I would have found a way to go if they'd bound and gagged me. It's my duty to help people in need."

Rebecca felt the weight of his eyes upon her. "I don't require a sermon on duty. I understand the word far better than you think." He paused, then added, "I can see now why you are a spinster." There was a hint of challenge in his voice.

Rebecca's cheeks flamed. "Humph! You say that as if I was a piece of stale fruit, a withered, moldy old prune. The unpitted kind. I'm unmarried because I *choose* to be," she said, enunciating each word carefully, not quite understanding why she felt the need to defend herself.

Instead of blowing her away, Alexander threw back his head and laughed. The sound was husky, musical, almost seductive. It struck at Rebecca's heart and she shifted uncomfortably.

"Meek-mouthed and submissive, you're not. I find myself almost eager to see what you might say and do next." He sobered. "Your clothing, however, has still got to go."

"Is this some kind of a gag?"

Suddenly, Alexander's eyes were as hard and smooth as polished tiger's-eye. "If only it were. Your alacrity is admirable, dear lady. But there's something you forgot to take into account."

"What's that?"

"First of all, Cordelia informs me you carry no pistol."

"That's right. I don't care for guns."

"Traveling without one in times like these is folly." He paused for affect. "Secondly, except for myself, no one in my family has had the measles. In ministering to Dinah, you've exposed yourself to a locust that consumes young and old, black and white, rich and poor alike—entire households in one clean sweep. I've seen it happen before. As Aunt Abigail intimated earlier, and though it was smallpox, my fiancee's family was wiped out in just such a fashion."

"I'm ... sorry. I didn't know."

"Cordelia complains that I'm obsessed, that I'm taking this to the extreme. Be that as it may, I can't allow you to go inside the house until we've disposed of your contaminated garments."

Rebecca was finally beginning to get the gist of things. For once, she was at a loss for words.

"Willy has a fire built," he prompted.

"I see." There was no need to argue. Rebecca realized now that Alexander was firm in his resolve to carry out what he felt must be done to protect those at Oak Mont. Nothing she said would shake him.

Placing her medical bag on the floor, Rebecca slowly unfastened the taffeta-covered buttons on her woolen jacket. The lapels gaped to display the white, eyelet-trimmed camisole beneath. She shrugged from it without batting an eyelash, dropping it to the floor.

When she reached for the hook and eye on the hip of the green walking skirt, Alexander politely, yet abruptly, turned his back, the quilt clutched in his hands. She shimmied from the skirt, and the camisole quickly followed.

"Do you want everything?" she asked.

Alexander cleared his throat. "To play it safe, yes, except the boots. I'll soap those."

It was vain, and she knew it, but she couldn't help commenting as she disrobed, "I wish now, that I'd worn the . . . my blue matron's uniform. It seems such a shame. I'd developed a particular fondness for this outfit and I have so few pretty things with me."

Rebecca didn't add that due to the morning chill, she'd foregone her own underwear in lieu of the camisole, drawers, and a flannel petticoat and she had not worn her dog tags. Now, as she peeled the drawers from her body, she was glad.

"Brrr . . . The quilt, if you please," she said, reaching over Alexander's shoulder, her hand extended. His stance was as stiff as a board.

"I should have asked after her sooner. How is Clayton's Dinah?"

It seemed to Rebecca almost as if Alexander dreaded voicing the question for fear of her answer. She quickly allayed his concern.

"Terrific now that I've set things straight on the kind of care she's to receive."

"That's good," he said over his shoulder.

Only after she was fully swathed in the downy coverlet, did he turn. His head conspicuously bent to his work, he gathered the clothes with a pitchfork and handed them out to a leery Willy.

Almost as an afterthought, Rebecca said, "I guess, after this, you'll want me to clear out. I'll pack my bags."

Alexander swiveled. His eyes found hers. The gaze he levied was as broiling hot as the Vietnamese sun.

"Don't," he said, his voice low and gentle. He slowly lifted his hands, cupping her cheeks, his fingers trembling against her skin.

Trembling? Rebecca's eyes widened. It was as if, against his better judgment, he'd found himself forced to admit that he wasn't ready to lose her yet.

"But, I thought—"

His hands dropping to her shoulders, Alexander interrupted Rebecca. "Where would you go?"

She frowned. Where? The question was suddenly extremely intimidating. Scary.

"I'm not very good at playing twenty-one questions, but an established medical facility would be the proper place for me, I suppose."

158

"Richmond—Chimborazo Heights on the James River?" Alexander snorted. "You'll work yourself to death there. They have eight thousand beds."

"Eight t–h–o–u–u–u–sand?" Rebecca breathed. "I never imagined—"

"Or perhaps you could try Georgia and the fresh air pavillions? Unchaperoned, you should make a great splash. They hire five to one in favor of male nurses."

"Oh."

"Don't you have any family to take you in?"

Like you did Cordelia and Abigail. "I . . . No. There's far too much work . . . on the . . . um . . . battlefields . . . for me to go home just yet, I think." She wished she could go home. To Atlanta. Her Atlanta. She really did.

"Do you realize that a nurse's salary at those infirmaries is eleven dollars a month. With prices escalating, a decent hotel room can run that much a night."

"Why, that doesn't seem so terribly high. On the other hand, I'm afraid I'm not independently wealthy either. To be honest, I'm dead broke. Things could get rather sticky before I draw my first paycheck."

Alexander shook his head. "You are the most unconventional woman, far too spontaneous for a man's peace of mind." Without premable, his hands slipped to her waist. He drew her into the loose circle of his arms.

Rebecca stiffened.

"Don't worry. I'm not going to ravish you. I'm not recovered sufficiently to take on something that potentially horrendous."

There was no mistaking the teasing note in Alexander's voice. Rebecca was drawn to him despite herself. Even with his biting wit, changeable humor, and overinflated male ego, only a frigid woman could resist his compelling charm.

And Rebecca wasn't frigid.

"You certainly aren't. Now, if you'll let me collect my things from the house, I'll be on my way." She cut him a scathing look that failed miserably because her heart wasn't in it.

"I can't allow you to insult Cousin Cordelia. You're her guest. As your host, it is my responsibility to honor her invitation to you. You and I will simply have to tough it out until your stay comes to its natural conclusion."

Rebecca silently acknowledged they'd reached a stalemate.

"Will we now?" she asked quietly. She really had very little choice in the matter. Only Alexander didn't know that.

"Stay, Rebecca. What brand of person would toss a good Samaritan out on her ear?" His voice was too serious, the husky use of her name almost a caress.

"And what about my penchant for extracurricular activities?" Though her voice was even, Alexander's touch was doing strange things to her insides. Her heartrate accelerated until it was a steady drumbeat in her brain.

"I want you to consider Oak Mont your home away from home for as long as you wish. Therefore, we'll simply have to devise some less harmful way for you to occupy yourself."

Given the kindest reprimand she'd ever received from a fellow officer, plus the fact she'd nowhere else to go, what else could she do but comply? Still, she hesitated, troubled by the feeling that she was skating on thin ice where Alexander was concerned.

Instinct told her to shut him out but her heart wouldn't let her. She'd never had such a difficult time controlling her emotions. He'd appealed to her from the start, from the moment he tried to stand in her presence at Murfreesboro.

"Like what for instance?" she asked, stalling for time, trying to get her thoughts in order.

"You do sew."

With a mischievous sparkle in her eyes, Rebecca replied, "Yes, I sew rather well—wounds that is."

A wry smile curved Alexander's lips. "I have no doubt you're proficient in that area. My shoulder tells me that. I was speaking more along the lines of clothing."

"No, afraid not. I flunked Housekeeping 101."

Alexander cocked one eyebrow at her. "I assume that you mean your mother never taught you the proper use for needle and thread."

"You could put it that way."

"She passed away when you were young."

His words were a statement, as if he couldn't conceive of any other reason for her not knowing how to make clothes. Rebecca chuckled silently to herself. If Alexander only knew how much things had changed. That the women in her time voted, held down professional jobs along with their

wifely duties, shared equal status with the men ...
Well, almost equal, she amended to herself. They
were still working on that one. But they'd get there
eventually. Persistence was half the battle.

"Actually, my mother's very much alive. One of
the most chic women you've ever met, in fact. But
she wouldn't know a tape measure from a pincushion," Rebecca elaborated impulsively. Her
mother was a busy career woman with a thriving
antique shop. She bought old-fashioned things,
but she couldn't afford to *be* old-fashioned. Her
clothes and fashion accessories came from Belk's
ready-to-wear collection. "Does that shock you?"

Alexander's smile broadened. "In your case, no.
But perhaps lessons would be in order. Jubadessa
is a marvelous seamstress."

Rebecca extracted herself from his light embrace. To break the spell he seemed to hold over
her, she resorted to a comical little curtsy. "As you
command, me lord," she said, initiating an uneasy
truce between two duty-bound soldiers, both feeling their way into unfamiliar territory.

"I'm glad we've been able to sort that out."

"For now."

Rebecca drew herself up to her full height, her
shoulders back, her eyes aligned at a point on the
carriage house wall just above Alexander's shoulder.

"If that's all, I respectfully request permission
to be excused, Lieutenant Colonel, sir," she said,
thumping her heels, incorporating her best military air to counteract the inner turmoil she was
experiencing.

Alexander blinked. As if he couldn't believe his eyes. As if she'd done something exceptionally extraordinary.

"Yes. Of course. You must be getting cold. Jubadessa has hot water waiting for you at the house, and clean clothes once you've bathed."

Before Rebecca knew what he was about, Alexander had scooped her up in his arms. Put her in her place.

That was all it took to throw her emotions off kilter again.

"Alexander! What do you think you're doing? Your wound! You're going to tear it open...All that work," she groaned.

To make matters worse, her quilt slipped.

With only the thin linen of his shirt between them, the hard muscles of Alexander's chest pressed seductively against Rebecca's breasts. She hastily tugged the coverlet into place, but not before she realized he was doing everything in his power to pretend he hadn't seen, to remain the gentleman, not to embarrass her further.

Still, for a split second, she thought he might go as far as to kiss her.

Then his expression changed to one of iron self-control—a will power she envied. His jaw tightening, he rasped, "I'd have only myself to blame if you caught your death walking across the yard in your bare feet."

"Don't be ridiculous! I demand you put me down before you injure yourself."

"Cooperate, and I'll be just fine as far as the kitchen door."

"You're going to wish you hadn't done this to-morrow when your shoulder is so sore you can't move."

"If I don't do it, by God, I'll wish I had."

Did his words hold double meaning? "You're crazy!"

Alexander gritted his teeth. "And you're still struggling."

"But my bag! You won't let Willy burn my medical bag, will you?"

"No. I'll get it later and then I'll soap and oil it like your boots, and return the whole kit and caboodle to you, unharmed, when I'm finished. A–OK?"

"And if I refuse to be still? Refuse to be the cause of undue strain to your shoulder?"

"Willy's got the fire going."

"You wouldn't!"

"Don't force the issue, Rebecca. I don't intend to back down."

By the stubborn glint in his hazel eyes, Rebecca knew there was no use arguing with him any longer. He'd made up his mind. He'd carry her or fall flat on his face trying.

"Southern gentlemen," she muttered under her breath before clamping her mouth tightly shut for her patient's sake.

Though he never broke his stride once Rebecca settled down, Alexander sensed the hostile presence lurking in the tree line before he'd stepped two feet across the inner yard. He caught the flash of telltale Yankee blue out of the corner of his eye before he swerved toward the main house, presenting his broad back to the forest that bordered his land.

An icy shiver rushed through him as he speculated on whether he was about to receive a ball between the shoulder blades. He represented a walking target, but he dare not make a false move and expose Rebecca to a wayward shot.

Alexander swallowed, protecting Rebecca with his body, steeling himself for the worst. Against the searing pain of a bullet entering his flesh. Against the recoil of impact. Against another explosion in his semi-healed chest. Against another attack on his person, this one well laid and very possibly lethal.

Intent on making the porch before being cut down, Alexander was still amazed when his boots toed the back steps. He practically leapt onto the porch, standing Rebecca on her feet in one fluid motion.

"Alexander! Have you got a secret death wish or something?" Rebecca protested, gazing directly into his eyes. He saw concern reflected there, coupled with something else. Something elusive. Something she was obviously hell-bent on hiding.

"Is that what you think?"

It took her only a second to answer. "You get me so mixed up, I don't know what to think."

"The feeling's mutual, I assure you."

Opening the kitchen door, Alexander firmly propelled Rebecca inside the house by placing his hand strategically on the small of her back. While shielding her with his body, he wondered if the Yankee soldier who appeared content merely to watch the house had anything to do with Rebecca. His mind racing, he weighed the possibility that her determination to treat Dinah's measles had somehow been twofold—a mission of mercy as well as a chance to speak with a Yankee operative.

The thought sickened Alexander and he forced it aside. Nagging suspicions weren't concrete evidence, he reminded himself.

Before Rebecca could say more, Jubadessa materialized, sweeping Rebecca off his hands.

"Go on into the library, *Monsieur*. Read a nice book or something," the housekeeper said without preamble. "By the expression on her face, Miss Rebecca has had quite enough of you for now. You've done your duty right and tight. Now give her the necessary consideration to complete her toilet with some small measure of decorum."

Jubadessa had been a part of the family for as long as Alexander could remember and he was accustomed to her highhanded ways. Besides, he was only to happy to comply. He needed time to think.

Once in the library, he splashed a hefty dose of bourbon into a beverage glass. Rolling the cool glass across his temple, he sank into the leather chair behind his writing desk.

Alexander deduced that the man in the tree line was a harmless observer and a clumsy one at that. Still, he couldn't take a chance on being arrested before he met with Major General Wheeler again, "Fighting Joe" to his men. And yet, now that he'd tested his shoulder, he knew he'd need a few more days of rest before he would be sufficiently recovered to resume his duties at full capacity.

However, the cold hard fact remained that he had to do something. Move in some way. Drastic or otherwise. Mainly because the soldier's appearance suggested two important factors—that someone higher up in the Federal ranks was suspicious of Oak Mont, and that there was probably an infiltrator in his own ranks. At the moment, his nurse constituted a primary suspect. The notion stung deeply, but who else could it be? The Yankee didn't just happen along. Alexander was convinced of that, if nothing else.

He'd just have to outfox the fox watching the house.

A plan was already forming in his mind. The problem was to pull it off he needed an accomplice. A decoy. But who?

As if in answer, inspiration struck. Alexander swallowed the last of his whiskey in one gulp, smacking the glass down on the desk. There was one person he called friend who could and would assist him, and do it well. A retired jockey. A featherweight. A superb horseman. Knowledgeable of the area. Trustworthy. And a dyed-in-the-wool Confederate. All he need do was explain his daring plan to Willy McCorkle.

From the thick stand of Southern pines, the young Yankee private had watched with interest the uncommon theatrics taking place at Oak Mont. It had almost been as much fun as a circus. Clothes afire. Women being totted about as if they couldn't walk for themselves.

Following an early-morning visit to headquarters by Miss Cordelia Stoddard, Captain Emory had commissioned him to "lay low and keep an eye on the Ransom place. Nothing more, nothing less." The job had been as easy as pie. In no time at all, he'd discovered his captain's suspicions were right. Something *was* going on at the plantation. Exactly what, he wasn't sure, but he planned to impersonate a tree until he figured it out, no matter how long it took.

The sun would be setting soon, and his feet were beginning to numb with cold. He wished for nothing as much as a warm cup of soup, a mug of ale, a toasty hearth fire, his comfortable cot back at Nashville headquarters and a few minutes of uninterrupted slumber. But he had his orders and he'd carry them out.

The yard quieted and he sat down, his back against a tree, to wait. Before he knew it, the young private was dozing at his post.

The private was startled awake by a commotion in Oak Mont's inner yard. He wasn't sure how long he'd slept. Three or four hours. Maybe more judging by the moonlit darkness that surrounded him and the chill in his bones.

Stiffly, he stumbled to his feet, shaking himself, straining to see through the shadows. His eyes widened to saucer size as he focused on the apparition mounting a dancing gray horse. Before the rider was even in the saddle, the long-legged hunter pawed the air with its forelegs. As his caped greatcoat swirled eerily, the rider controlled the mount with ease, spurring it forward into the night.

"Fire and brimstone! Captain Emory will have my head on a silver platter," he exclaimed, scrambling toward his own horse hidden some twenty feet into the forest.

The private clamored into the saddle, urging the gelding in the direction the apparition had taken.

Alexander met the cloaked apparition in a predetermined spot two miles from Oak Mont.

"You lost him," he stated, grabbing Vedette's bridle to hold her still while Willy dismounted.

"Had to slow down so he could catch up with me. We played cat and mouse for a while. Then, when he was right on my tail, I pulled away as clean as a whistle. Fine fence jumper, that filly," Willy said, returning Alexander's greatcoat and slouch hat. Pulling his own billed cap from his back pocket, he fitted it firmly on his graying head.

"I expect her owner will be displeased when she learns I borrowed Vedette without asking."

"Oh, I don't know. The young miss strikes me as being a right reasonable sort. Besides, if she didn't draw and quarter us for what we did to her clothes today, I doubt she'll find fault with this. 'Tis all for the love of a good cause."

Alexander couldn't argue with that logic. He'd used it himself.

"Did you have any trouble doubling back here?"

"Doin' it in the dark was a wee bit tricky. My peepers aren't what they used to be. Proud to say I haven't lost my touch altogether, though. Ran the creek bed all the way back, just like ya suggested.''

"And the Yankee?''

"The last I saw of that poor, confused chap, he was headed for Nashville, lickety-split. Truth is, I think we started to spook him toward the end.''

"That's what I'd counted on," Alexander confirmed.

Willy grinned. "You're one man who knows you're business, all right.''

"I won't forget what you did, Willy," Alexander said solemnly. "I'd have had a devil of a time without you.''

"Come away with ya now. We both know The Gray Ghost has no trouble slippin' in and out of places when he has a mind to.''

Alexander smiled. "I can't speak for The Gray Ghost, but you won't find me complaining about a helping hand now and again.''

"Well, I was glad to do it. Kind of excitin' really. Now have a care, and we'll see ya ... Tomorrow, was it?''

"Late tomorrow, if I don't run abreast of unforeseen complications.''

"You'll not. I have a good feelin' about it.''

"Irish intuition?''

Willy's grin broadened and he winked. "By glory and sure it 'tis. I've a mind there's a bit of the Irish in all of us, even himself, The Gray Ghost.''

"You might be right," Alexander said, a twinkle in his eye as he mounted Vedette.

"Wheeler's camp is deeper south, less hazardous than usual. That's one advantage to the dead of winter. The antagonists go to their own corners of the ring for a while," Alexander commented.

"As it should be in any good fight," Willy responded.

"Sorry you have to walk back to Oak Mont."

" 'Tis nothin'," Willy assured him. "Luck to ya now."

Vedette, a natural born runner, pranced to be on her way, but Alexander stayed her with a firm pressure to the reins.

"Just in case something does happen, take care of the women, Willy, Rebecca included," he added despite himself, envisioning Rebecca as he'd last seen her wrapped in a quilt with nothing beneath but bare skin. Beautiful. Spunky. Enticing beyond compare. Maddening in more ways than one.

"Now you know you needn't have asked that," Willy said quickly. " 'Tis considered part of my job to see to the womenfolk when you're away. As long as Miss Rebecca's at Oak Mont . . . Well, I'll see to her, too."

Giving Vedette her head, Alexander saluted Willy, chiding himself for singling out Rebecca. She should have been the last thing on his mind, not the first. The safety of the campaign dispatches tucked in his breast pocket, letters from Jefferson Davis to each of his generals in the field outlining the Confederate States' spring objectives, held top priority, he told himself.

Yet for a good two hours into his ride, Rebecca remained firmly entrenched in Alexander's thoughts, no matter how hard he tried to put her in her proper place.

* * *

Rebecca lay in the narrow four-poster bed in the guest room at Oak Mont, wide awake and dry-eyed. Tense. Heavy-hearted. A little frightened. And definitely lost, she mentally added. The sensation topped even the trepidation she'd felt during her night flight from the U.S. to Vietnam when she began her tour of duty.

She'd seen Alexander slip past the smokehouse, down the garden path, and out into the forest beyond. She couldn't have missed him. She'd been availing herself of the necessary because she was still uncomfortable with the chamber pot.

Alexander hadn't guessed she was inside and she hadn't felt inclined to pop out and say, "Hi!" That would have been far too awkward, even for her. So, she'd remained silent until she was sure he had gone.

Rebecca rolled onto her side and punched her pillow, then hugged it tightly to her middle, wondering if sneaking away into the night without a by-your-leave was Alexander's customary way of saying good-bye.

The notion hurt. But then again, under the right circumstances, it might have been her way as well.

Rebecca closed her eyes, huddling beneath the bed covers, attempting to put the tall Confederate lieutenant colonel from her thoughts. He insisted on remaining there far into the wee hours of the night.

And at dawn, Rebecca's last coherent thought was a prayer that Alexander safely reunite with his unit.

* * *

Major General Joseph Wheeler, an astute gentleman with penetrating eyes and a neatly trimmed, full-faced beard that ordinarily served to hide his facial expressions, appeared startled for a moment. Recovering quickly, he relaxed back in his chair, resting his hand negligently on a desk overburdened with paperwork.

"Living up to your name, I see," he commented finally in a deep, resonant voice, critically gauging the man who stood before him.

"I try," Alexander replied, tossing his hat and greatcoat on a nearby cane chair.

"How did you get into my tent without being stopped by the guard stationed at the door?"

"I'm a ghost, remember? We have our standard tricks of the trade."

"And our bivouac location?" Wheeler asked.

"Educated guess. If you don't mind my saying so, you tend to like to be in the thick of things. The hotter, the better. I calculated on the fact you wouldn't be far from Nashville. The enemy supply lines between Memphis and Nashville would be far too hard for you to resist."

"I would that all my *ghosts* possessed your stealth and intuition," Wheeler remarked. "We've missed you, Lieutenant Colonel. Your kind adds spice to the game. You look haggard, though. Has hell finally caught up with you?"

"Several hours back, I think," Alexander responded in a voice fraught with weariness.

Wheeler stood, poured a steaming mug of black

coffee from the tin pot at his elbow, and extended it toward Alexander.

"Here. Take a moment to wash the dust from your throat before we proceed."

Alexander accepted the warm mug gratefully. The first swallow proved better than he'd expected, and he allowed himself a second one before commenting, "Um, real coffee. And damned fine, too. Some Northern general must be cursing your name to the high heavens tonight."

Wheeler allowed a slight smile to touch his lips. "Am I to blame if the Yankees haven't learned to sleep with one eye open yet?"

"The raids are going that well?" Alexander asked between sips.

"Better than well. Exceptional. No one has the pluck of our cavalrymen. Strike and strike fast, that's the ticket."

"I'll not deny that."

"Well, have a seat, Lieutenant Colonel, before you drop. I can tell by the gleam in your eye this is not a social visit."

"You're right, as usual," Alexander said, seating himself across the desk from his commanding officer. "I decided it was time to let someone know I was still with the living."

"We'd word that you were wounded at Stones River. Braxton Bragg sent me the message before he pulled the troops out of Murfreesboro. Said you were alive. That was all. You know Bragg, short and sweet. I assumed I'd hear from you sooner or later."

"Yes, sir." Alexander drained his coffee mug.

Wheeler generously refilled the cup.

"Well, let's get down to business. What have you got for me, Lieutenant Colonel?"

Alexander reached into his breast pocket, spreading out a stack of papers like a fan on top of Wheeler's already cluttered desk.

"I think it would be wise to send these out by separate couriers. I didn't have time to deliver them before being caught up in the battle at Stones River, and now the Federals are on to me—at least they think they are. I have a pesky gnat breathing down my neck, harmless, but there all the same."

"Why don't you just swat the bug and be done with him?"

"Because I think he's just one in a swarm."

"I see," Wheeler said, slowly flipping through the documents. "I'll arrange for these to go out separately as you suggest. In the meantime, what do you propose to do?"

"Play the stool pigeon. Perhaps if I do, we can clean up the ring of conspirators in Nashville once and for all."

"I assume you have something in mind."

"I'm working on it. You said the raids were going well. Does that mean my frock coat can be considered expendable?"

Wheeler frowned. His elbows propped on the desk, his forefingers steepled against his lips, he said, "I noticed you weren't wearing the coat. Thought perhaps you were incognito."

"Not this time. The coat is concealed in a safe place for the time being until I can make economical use of it."

"If you're thinking what I think you are, yes. Do with the frock coat as you see fit."

"I'll need some official-looking documents to replace the original ones sewn in the lining. Preferably dispatches you won't mind sacrificing for a chance at greater gain."

"Wise idea," Wheeler agreed, shuffling through his treasure of paperwork, selecting several likely candidates. Fishing out a sheet of tissue-thin blockade paper from the drawer, he scribbled a note, adding it to the stack of documents which he presented to Alexander.

"I imagine these will do nicely," he said.

Alexander scanned the handwritten pages, then responded by folding and pocketing the dispatches.

"By the way, I don't know how far out of touch you've been since your injury, but we've had some disturbing news recently," Wheeler began. "It concerns a set of dispatches your team of couriers was directly involved with before the holidays. The Erlanger bonds to be exact."

"I remember them well," Alexander interjected. "We had high hopes of those European-bound bonds stabilizing the government treasury."

"I'm unhappy to say that what the minister to Paris feared the most has happened. The Federals bulled the market. The bonds are next to worthless. John Slidell is livid. President Davis is seeking the crack in our security at this very moment. If you hear anything noteworthy along the grapevine, send the information directly to Richmond. The other couriers have already been notified to the same effect."

Wheeler had Alexander's full and undivided attention now.

"Where do they think the leak originated?" Alexander asked, carefully placing his empty coffee cup beside the pot on Wheeler's desk.

"That much is known. Nashville. Your home territory. Beyond that, your guess is as good as mine."

My God, Alexander thought, quickly searching his memory. Hadn't he and Rebecca discussed those bonds in the barn where they'd stayed for the afternoon during their journey from Stones River to Oak Mont? Actually, he and Cordelia had talked. Rebecca had listened, almost too attentively. No, attentive wasn't the right word, Alexander decided. Enthralled was more like it.

Alexander abruptly rose to his feet, suddenly impatient to be on his way. "Sorry to be so brief, Major General, but I must be getting back to Oak Mont."

"Is that where I can reach you?"

"On and off. But be careful. The Federals have someone watching the plantation," Alexander cautioned.

"Do you need a fresh mount? If so, you may have your pick of the stock."

"The dapple-gray I'm riding belongs to a lady I've just recently met. I'd best return it to her, if I want to stay on good terms."

Wheeler arched a dark brow at Alexander. "Need I remind you, Lieutenant Colonel, that war is not a time to cultivate relationships, especially for a courier."

"Not even if the lady in question might be a spy?" The instant the words were out, Alexander wished he could recall them. It had been pure folly to have said them in front of Wheeler in the first place.

Major General Wheeler straightened in his chair. "Sit back down, Lieutenant Colonel Ransom."

"Is that an order?"

"Don't get defensive. I realize that you aren't fully recovered, that you've taken quite a chance in coming here tonight. I'm merely requesting a few more moments of your time, Lieutenant Colonel, that we speak of this lady in more depth and you're intended course of action concerning the frock coat, as well. I sense there's more here than you've divulged, something Jeff Davis might be interested in hearing about personally. There's a possibility he *might* even have something to add to it. We do owe that much to our commander in chief. Don't you think?"

Alexander reseated himself, oddly reluctant to discuss Rebecca with anyone, even his superior officer. "You're right, of course," he conceded, though his eyes became hooded, his face an impenetrable mask that hid his inner emotions.

Major General Joseph Wheeler would discover only what Alexander wished him to know concerning Rebecca Warren—and he would learn it without Alexander naming names.

Chapter Seven

"I . . . Good heavens, Jubadessa. How in the world am I to choose from all these?"

Kneeling on a dust cover amid a vivid pool of cloth, Rebecca surveyed the contents of the sizable cedar-lined hope chest. Inky velvet swam with yards of linen, praline silk brocaded in violet flowers, saffron-printed calico, pewter taffeta, and gauzy mauve chiffon.

"Well, miss. I think the best thing would be to select the ones that we find need the least alteration."

Rebecca inhaled deeply. The gowns had been carefully folded, layered between with white rose petals, orange blossoms, and protective herbs. The warm spring fragrance was a welcome addition to the stale coolness of the musty attic.

"Alexander's mother owned the most beautiful gowns. It seems a shame to cut them up."

Jubadessa shook out a sedate broadcloth day dress. "Most things nowadays seem a crying shame. This isn't one of them. I only wish we'd thought of these clothes sooner. Mrs. Abigail and Miss Cordelia could have made use of them. Some flannel shirts and a new coat wouldn't hurt *Monsieur* either," she added, turning the day dress upside down and critically measuring the skirt's yardage. "And we will keep Mrs. Abigail busy turning the scraps into coverlets."

"Still, all things considered, it was nice of the lieutenant colonel to suggest I go through these."

Jubadessa eyed her almost as severely as the gown she'd been measuring. "His mama would have wished her things put to good use. Besides, that indigo nurse's uniform doesn't become you in the least."

She dropped the day dress to snatch up a back issue from a stack of *Demorest's Monthly Magazine*. Thumbing rapidly through the ladies' patterns, she said, "Now this ensemble, done up in the velvet and buttercream wool, with just a touch of silk puffing around the hem, would be perfect for you. I noticed a moth has been at the wool, but I think we can cut around the holes."

She thrust the drawing under Rebecca's nose for her inspection.

"Isn't that just a little bit too grand for me?" Rebecca questioned dubiously. What she really meant was that it looked terribly uncomfortable. She was accustomed to one of two things, the crisp line of a uniform, or the nonrestrictive hippie-style clothing of her own era—mini dresses, blue jeans and halters, loose flowing caftans with Nehru collars.

"Not at all. But I suppose I could redesign the pattern to more closely resemble the suit *Monsieur* bur–r–r—" Jubadessa quickly amended her statement. "The suit you lost, if you'd like."

Rebecca smiled. "Yes, I would. Thanks."

"You see," Jubadessa explained, her lower lip caught between her teeth as she concentrated on the pattern, "all we'd have to do is make the bodice more elongated, like a shirt front, and add a jacket. The skirt could..." Jubadessa stopped midsentence. Her words trailed off as she cocked her head to one side, listening.

"Did you hear that, miss?" she asked quietly.

"What? Guinevere barking?" Rebecca couldn't mistake the dawning alarm that registered on Jubadessa's smooth face.

"No. The jingle of harness."

"It's probably Cordelia and Abigail returning from church."

"It's more than a wagon. I hear saddle horses."

"How can you—"

Jubadessa didn't give Rebecca time to finish. Throwing the gowns aside, she scrambled to her feet and rushed to the window. Rubbing a clean spot in the pane with the corner of her apron, she peered into the yard below.

"Oh, Lordy, Lordy, Lordy!" Jubadessa said in rapid succession, spreading her hands against either side of the window frame as if for support.

"I warned Miss Cordelia not to take her mama to Sunday Services in Nashville. But nothing doing. They must go and try to be sociable, hear the visiting minister, the eminent Stephen Elliot, preach." She threw up her hands, turning to Rebecca.

Concerned by Jubadessa's uncharacteristic outburst, Rebecca rose to join her at the window. She gasped, as surprised by her own gut reaction as by the sight that met her eyes.

Red alert!

Gazing down at the Federal escort winding its way into the yard, dismounting, tethering a half-dozen saddle horses to the tenuous picket fence, she actually felt threatened! Her stomach lurched, and for a moment, Rebecca was totally confused. Then it dawned on her what was happening. Her body was beginning to acclimate itself to the past—and the future, her present, was slipping away slowly but surely.

"This is all becoming far too real," she whispered, her eyes glued to the young Adonis in the impeccable blue uniform conversing with Cordelia.

Jubadessa heard and responded. "Indeed it is. Those two have managed to bring the war right up to our doorstep—to *Monsieur*."

Rebecca instantly picked up on something that bothered her. Jubadessa spoke of Cordelia in conjunction *with* the Yankee.

"What do you mean, those two?" she asked.

Jubadessa brushed her question aside. "Just a slip of the tongue." Then she turned the tables on

Rebecca. "How are we going to hide *Monsieur*? He is in danger, dead to the world as he is."

Rebecca blinked, composing her chaotic thoughts. She realized the more deeply involved she got, the narrower her pathway home became but she couldn't seem to help herself. Jubadessa was right. Her patient, sound asleep in the room below, was a Confederate officer. And she'd taken it upon herself to add something soothing to his penicillin booster as she sensed he needed the rest. He'd seemed so worn out from his mysterious excursion.

Now, Rebecca mused, she'd have only herself to blame if he didn't hear the enemy and was put to sleep permanently.

"What do you think they want?" she pondered aloud. She'd been so relieved by Alexander's return, she'd failed to question him about what he'd been up to. He'd come back, and that was all that had mattered, all that she'd needed to know at the time. But that was then and this was now.

"They haven't stormed the house, and it doesn't appear they're going to. So I imagine it's safe to say they don't know about *Monsieur*, yet. Off the top of my head, I would guess that the officers plan to take dinner with us."

"Eat? But they're the enemy."

"It's not uncommon to sit down to table with Yankee officers, even at Oak Mont. The occupying army is well known for, shall we say, *inviting* themselves to dine."

"Which, in all likelihood, means that they'll be here all afternoon."

"Probably. And it's customary to do a house search before they sit down at the table. How will we hide *Monsieur*? We can't lift him without assistance."

Pivoting from the window, Rebecca instinctively took charge. "Go downstairs." She raised her fingertips to her temple, massaging away the dull ache that was attempting to hamper her thinking. "Detain them in the yard . . . ten minutes if possible."

"Ten minutes! How?"

"I don't know. You're resourceful, Jubadessa. I–m–p–r–o–v–i–s–e."

Jubadessa straightened, removing her apron and adjusting her head handkerchief. "I suppose it would be simple to lead Mrs. Abigail into suggesting a tour of the lawn. I doubt they would be so rude as to refuse a direct request from her. They rather hold her affliction in awe."

"Good idea," Rebecca interrupted. "Just give me as much time as you can without being obvious. If I can make it to the kitchen, the guest room, and back upstairs before they come inside, we might be home free."

"What are you going to do?"

Rebecca answered her question with a question. "I seem to remember Alexander's bed has curtains, am I right?" Rebecca fired, crossing her fingers.

"Yes, but *Monsieur* never pulls them to."

"He will today. Now listen. If it comes down to it and they ask who's in the master bedroom, tell them you have a sick guest staying with you."

"A what?"

"If pressed, tell them my name. Explain that I have the measles. Try to be straightforward. And make *sure* you plant the idea of contagion. Then, if they insist, knock first to warn me, then let them open the door to examine the room for themselves."

"But you don't have the measles."

Rebecca literally pushed Jubadessa toward the attic door. "Not now. But I will." She paused, a tense frown puckering her forehead, her hand on Jubadessa's arm to detain her momentarily. "You do have strawberry jam in the house?"

Perplexed, Jubadessa answered slowly, "Yes. Several jars. On the third shelf in the kitchen larder. It's Mrs. Abigail's favorite. But . . ."

Rebecca sighed, her face clearing. "Thank goodness for small favors. Now go. Hurry. Don't let them inside before I'm ready."

The women descended the stairs like rabbits with a pack of hounds hot on their trail. On the lower landing, they split, Jubadessa bound for the front door, Rebecca, skirts bunched in her hand, sprinting toward the kitchen. From the corner of her eye, Rebecca saw the mulattress strike her most regal pose, then glance over her shoulder as if for moral support. Rebecca stopped, shaped an *o* with her thumb and forefinger, and mouthed the words, "Everything will be A—OK," before scooting around the corner out of sight.

The larder was long, cool, and neat, with lighting from an unshuttered window at the far end of the room. "Why, it's almost like a miniature convenience store. All it lacks is a cash register and check-out counter," Rebecca marveled aloud as she hastily crossed the threshold.

Weaving her way between the staved tubs of meal, past the gaily painted pantry boxes stamped "pinto beans," "rice," and "hominy," she found the contents of the room fascinating. But this was not the time for a detailed study of early-American wooden ware, she reminded herself sternly. No matter how much of her mother she had in her.

Abruptly, Rebecca came upon what she sought, the "canned food section." Neatly labeled jars containing everything from homemade apple butter, pickled peaches, watermelon preserves, and bread-and-butter cukes, to vanilla brandy lined the sturdy shelves. But the jam eluded her, at least until she realized that Jubadessa had meant it was stored on the third shelf from the bottom, not the top. Half-hidden behind a lapped maple cheese box and a humungous tin of raisins.

Wrenching the sealed lid off one of the jars, Rebecca sniffed, pinched her nose, and tipped the container to her lips. The syrupy, seeded pulp filled her mouth, almost gagging her. She grimaced, crunched the seeds once, then swallowed.

"Yuck! I hate this stuff," she muttered, forcing down three-fourths of the contents before resealing the jar and placing it back on the shelf.

Rebecca shuddered, wiping her mouth with the back of her hand. "Ugh. Strawberries. Abigail can have 'em!"

Peeking from the larder first to make sure she

was still alone, Rebecca then streaked through the kitchen to her room, unbuttoning her gown and mussing her hair as she went. In two minutes flat, she'd changed from her nurse's uniform to the muslin crossbar nightgown Jubadessa had provided. She snatched up all her belongings, threw them into her valise, grabbed her medical bag, twirled once to scan the room, then raced through the kitchen back upstairs, as her heart pounded.

When she reached Alexander's door, Rebecca paused to catch her second wind, then burst into the master bedroom like a cyclone.

With single-minded determination, she flung open the wardrobe to stow her gear, then collected all signs of the room's true inhabitant along with the ledgers he had been working on before he dozed off. Shimmying under the bed, she stuffed them in a heap in the far corner against the wall. As an afterthought, she grabbed his revolver off the night stand.

Alexander didn't stir as Rebecca closed the drapes. But when she leapt upon the bed, and reached over her head to draw the curtains so that only one side of the bed remained exposed, he roused.

A look of amazement clouding his eyes, Alexander cleared his throat and stretched, attempting to focus on Rebecca's face. Eyeing the gun, he asked in a groggy, but solemn, voice, "Have you lost your mind? Or have I?"

"My gosh! Don't you ever know when to lie down and be quiet? Now *freeze*. Be *quiet*. That's an order," Rebecca hissed impatiently, juggling the gun from her right hand to her left. Straddling his hips, she planted a palm on his forehead and shoved him backward, brandishing the gun under his nose. Before he could protest the rough treatment, she rolled over him. Scrambling beneath the counterpane, Rebecca sank into the nestling comfort of the feather mattress, presenting her back to her astounded patient.

Rebecca couldn't help but notice the bed was toasty warm from Alexander's body heat. But the reflection was short-lived for she was jolted from her thoughts when he turned to press his hard body against her slender backside. He gracefully snaked his arm around her waist. Then drawing her tightly against him, he buried his face in her hair, one leg negligently resting across hers, pinning her down.

Inhaling appreciatively, Alexander commented, "I can't think of a more agreeable way to be awakened, but I thought we'd decided to keep things on a friendly basis. I'd say that this is stretching friendship to the limit, at least from my perspective. Most unsettling to think my freckle-faced angel can transform into a seductive swan at will."

Rebecca gulped. There was more to contend with than she'd counted on. Alexander was naked! Disturbingly vital. Every fiber in her being flamed, responding to him as naturally as a match to a striker plate.

Silence reigned as she struggled to control her reaction to his nearness when she had only a thin linen nightgown between herself and his physical arousal.

Finally she managed to marshal her chaotic thoughts. "Lieutenant Colonel, you don't understand what's going down. This isn't some kind of parlor game. I'm on a mission."

One brow flew up quizzically and the corner of Alexander's mobile mouth curved in a lazy half-smile. "Really," he mumbled, his hot breath tickling her ear, sending a rush of blood to her head. "A dangerous one, I think."

His voice, soft and vibrating, sent delicious tingles spiraling through Rebecca. Tingles that were incredibly difficult to ignore.

In a thready whisper, she managed to reply, "Y–y–yes. Dangerous. There are Federal soldiers in the yard. Guess who's coming to dinner?"

Alexander tensed, all pretext of play evaporating. He shook himself, sobering with amazing speed given the medication she'd administered. With an air of supreme self-assurance, he demanded, "Give me the gun. Though I wish otherwise, I suspect I'm going to need it."

As if she had forgotten she held it, she stared at the Colt Dragoon Revolver, then handed it to Alexander, watching as he tucked it beneath his pillow. His voice lowering accordingly, he asked, "How many are there?"

"Half a dozen."

"Are you sure?"

For a moment, Rebecca was rendered speechless by the masterful force radiating from Alexander. Here now, once again, was the indomitable officer. "I'm positive."

189

"I've got to try and get out of here. Through the window. Over the roof."

Rebecca hid her growing dismay for Alexander's safety behind her usual veneer of professionalism. "In your condition? You can't be serious! They'll arrest you before you get two feet."

"I'll have to take that chance. If they find me here, Oak Mont will suffer for it."

Lay a bigger guilt trip on him. "If they take you to prison, I'll have wasted a lot of valuable time patching you up, time that could have been better spent with other less fortunate soldiers."

She could tell she'd hit pay dirt when Alexander wavered, though it was obvious his pride was smarting.

"You expect me to play peek-a-boo from behind a woman's skirts. That's rich."

Rebecca raised a hand to her cheek and rubbed rather than scratched. "I expect you to do what any good soldier would. Lie low and live to fight another day when the odds aren't stacked against you."

"What makes you think this will work?"

"Chalk it up to experience in the fine art of tactical maneuvers. Believe me, I've thought this thing through. In another five minutes, they won't dare come close enough to the bed for you to be seen. So you're safer here than climbing across some roof in your birthday suit. Besides, they'll burn us to the ground for sure if they find out we've been covering for you."

This case of self-induced hives was going to be a doozy, worse than the time she'd eaten two slices of Shoney's signature strawberry pie, Rebecca added to herself. It had been so delicious—but the results! The itching and red welts, the puffy, watery eyes, had lasted for days. Horrified, her mother had bundled her up, jumped in the car, and whisked her off to the pediatrician only to discover Rebecca was highly allergic to strawberries.

Alexander pushed himself up on one elbow, gently removing her hand from her cheek. "God. No," he rasped, peering into her face. It was obvious by his expression that her face was already sufficiently Frankensteinish to strike fear into the heart of the boldest man.

Rebecca waited for the explosion of displeasure, for the accusation that her thoughtlessness *had* brought measles to Oak Mont. The harsh words never came. Instead, an unfathomable parade of emotions crossed his face, then were shuttered by a mask of concern. Rebecca labored under the curious conviction that Alexander really cared for her welfare. But whether as a host for a guest, or a man for a woman, she wasn't sure.

Slowly, Alexander skimmed the rising welts with the back of his hand. His touch was like a caress, almost an apology, though Rebecca could not think why. Then in a tone so tender that he might have been comforting a child, he said, "Don't be frightened, Rebecca. I won't leave you to see this through alone."

Before Rebecca could correct him, explain that she didn't really have the measles, they heard footsteps on the stairs.

"Please, Alexander. Trust me. Jubadessa has been laying the groundwork. There will be a knock on the door—a warning signal."

"Give me one good reason why I should trust you," he countered, wondering what kind of incredible charade Rebecca was playing. Wondering if she was the reason for the soldiers' arrival, if she had reported his return to the guard even after he'd managed to slip home undetected.

Rebecca was stunned. "Have I given you any reason not to trust me?" Rebecca asked, surprise evident in her hushed voice.

Alexander seemed rendered speechless.

Rebecca continued, "We don't have time for this, Alexander. If we had the time for anything, it would be an explanation concerning your moonlit jaunt. So stop giving me a hard time."

"You are the most...disconcerting..." Alexander never finished his sentence.

The rap on the master bedroom door came like clockwork, just as Rebecca had predicted. Well-trapped, Alexander pulled the pistol from beneath the pillow, then eased beneath the covers behind Rebecca. She tossed two pillows on top of him and forced herself to relax before calling out in her most feeble tone, "Come in."

The door creaked open and Jubadessa stepped inside followed by Cordelia and the Yankee Rebecca had glimpsed in the yard.

Holding his hat in his hand, he was exactly what Rebecca had thought. His uniform was impeccable, though it bordered on the garish with its showy epaulets and fancy braid. Golden-blond, trim and tanned, sporting a slightly clefted chin, the Yankee prep reminded Rebecca of a country club tennis teacher she'd once fended off. His pale blue eyes coolly scanned the bedroom, and his jaunty attitude told her he was determined to poke Jubadessa's story full of holes.

"Miss Rebecca. I hate to bother you, but the captain insisted he be presented."

The man stepped forward. "Captain James Emory, Federal Headquarters, Nashville, at your service."

"Captain. I'm afraid, as you can see, I'm not up to polite conversation. Perhaps another time," Rebecca said in a dramatically shallow voice.

Emory refused to be dismissed so easily. "I only wished to tell you personally that my men and I have noticed that supplies here are running low. We've chosen to share our day's ration of roast of beef with this fine house, if your woman doesn't mind preparing it. Perhaps you would like a cup of broth sent up when it is done."

He was crafty, but the Yankee captain didn't fool her one bit. Rebecca felt his intense perusal as he squinted to see her through the gloom that enshrouded her sick bed, and she had a strong suspicion Emory was good only from the teeth out.

Russian roulette it is then, she decided.

Playing the Southern belle to the hilt, Rebecca summoned the captain with a faint flutter of her hand. "Perhaps I can manage a bite or two. Come closer, that I might thank you for your kindness."

"Um, certainly." Obviously, her response wasn't the one he'd anticipated. Hesitantly, he called her

193

bluff, moving slowly to the center of the room.

"I was terribly sorry to hear that you'd contracted the..." He paused, a frown of concentration on his overly handsome face. "Funny, the illness escapes me."

"Measles, Captain Emory. Regrettably so. I declare, I feel as if I'm languishin' away. And I live in dread that my delicate skin will be damaged. I only hope that, should I survive this callous malady, my face won't be too dreadfully scarred."

She sat up in the bed and turned to face him point blank, coughing loudly for affect.

The captain stiffened, pulling a white handkerchief from his breast pocket and covering his mouth. Rebecca wasn't surprised when he warily backed to the door. By now, her eyes were swelled to narrow slits, and she had to clench her fists to keep from scratching the rash pimpling her body.

"A speedy recovery to you, Miss Warren. Perhaps we can talk further...next month...when you are feeling better," Captain Emory said in parting.

"If such a time comes. Measles are so...dreadfully deadly," Rebecca said as if their interview had exhausted her, all the while suppressing the grin that ordinarily accompanies success.

Emory blanched, vacating the room like a blue streak.

Why, I deserve a standing ovation, Rebecca thought. *Eat your heart out Bette Davis*.

Wringing her hands, yet remaining carefully in the hall, Cordelia interjected from the doorway, "I'm *so* sorry for sendin' you with Clayton. Really

I am. Forgive me, Becky. I should have known better than to use your absence as an excuse to go to Nashville." Abigail stood behind her daughter, as still and quiet as a startled doe.

Rebecca felt Alexander stiffen behind her.

"An excuse, Cordelia. Why would you need an excuse other than your tooth?" Rebecca asked, suddenly suspicious of her friend's motives. There was definitely something afoot at Oak Mont. A coil, as Cordelia would say. And it involved one or all of the Ransoms. The problem was, she wasn't sure which side was which anymore. Who was a Yankee, and who was a Confederate. Plainclothes people could be deceiving.

Jubadessa's voice broke the tension in the room. She shooed everyone back, saying, "Go on down with Captain Emory now, Miss Cordelia. And take your mama with you." Then more quietly behind her hand, "Keep an eye on him. He'll steal us blind, I fear."

Emory had already been downstairs several minutes, but Cordelia seemed extremely reluctant to follow him.

"Don't dawdle. Willy's in the kitchen to chaperone. What Miss Rebecca needs now is peace and quiet. I'll be down in a second to put on that rump roast," Jubadessa encouraged.

Cordelia finally complied. As soon as the unlikely pair was out of hearing distance, Jubadessa turned back toward Rebecca.

"Great day in the morning, child! You sure have done a job on yourself. Can I bring you anything else up with the broth?" she asked solicitously.

Rebecca smiled wryly, relegating Cordelia's behavior to the back burner of her mind—to simmer. "Since I know Benadryl is out of the question, a box of baking soda would be nice in place of the antihistamine," she said without thinking.

"Anti...antihis..." Jubadessa questioned, attempting to curl her French-accented tongue around the unfamiliar term. Finally, she threw up her hands. "Never mind, I'll see what I can do about the baking soda."

When the door closed, Alexander ventured somewhat dryly, "Now that we're alone again, would you mind explaining exactly what type of conspiracy you and Jubadessa have concocted?"

Rebecca was immediately defensive. "I hope you have a healthy sense of humor."

Alexander scowled. "I do. But you just put me through hell."

"Have I?" Rebecca asked with feigned innocence, but the slight edge to her voice gave her away.

"Most assuredly," Alexander growled.

"Well, it serves you right. You had me going there for a while, too, in the barn. Now you know firsthand how it feels to be caught at a disadvantage."

He cursed under his breath. "Tit for tat, is it?"

"What's good for the goose is good for the gander. That was my best set of clothes you torched."

"My father always warned me there is nothing like a woman's scorn. Now I know what he meant. You don't have the measles at all, do you? You're play-acting."

Rebecca's chin took on a decidedly mulish bent. "Wonderful deduction. And don't be so stiff-necked about it, Lieutenant Colonel. I just saved you from another early grave."

His expression grew stern, inscrutable. Then his face became carefully blank as he shot back, "At the expense of sounding ungrateful, did you have to scare me out of a year's growth in the process? I don't take kindly to being played the fool, Miss Warren."

"In a pinch, it seemed the best option. What's a year compared to a lifetime?"

"Well, be that as it may, we aren't out of the woods yet." He glanced meaningfully at the closed door.

Rebecca's face paled noticeably, and a bead of perspiration appeared on her upper lip. "You don't think they'll come back up here, do you? I don't think I can go through that again right now."

Troubled by the anxiety reflected in Rebecca's expressive eyes, Alexander's demeanor softened slightly. "I think you've effectively put an end to Captain Emory's search-and-seizure operation. I doubt he will request a repeat performance today." Reaching out to put a cool hand on Rebecca's forehead, Alexander turned to study her face in the dim light. Tipping her chin up, he frowned. "For the love of . . . These spots aren't drawn on! What *have* you done to yourself on my account?" he demanded.

"Don't read too much into this, Lieutenant Colonel," she answered pertly. "You're seeing a simple allergic reaction to strawberry jam. The prognosis is good. Nothing lethal, contagious, nor permanent." Then an astounded look crossed her face and her pertness wavered. Swallowing rapidly, she folded her arms across her stomach, adding miserably, "But if you would be so kind as to hand me the washbasin off your night stand, I'd appreciate it. I think ... I'm going ... to be sick."

Rebecca averted her eyes as Alexander jumped agilely over her, rising to his feet.

"What the heck did you do with the clothes that were on the foot of the bed?"

"Underneath. Hurry!"

Scrambling for his pants, Alexander wrestled them on. Then, grabbing the china washbasin, he held Rebecca's head while she threw up. Afterwards, he dipped a cloth in the tepid liquid of the matching water pitcher. Then he reached into the drawer of the washstand and withdrew a brown apothecary bottle. He emptied two drops of the liquid into a glass of water and then returned to Rebecca's side. Smoothing back her hair, he gently sponged off her face and lips.

Embarrassed, Rebecca took the cloth from him and finished the job herself, then taking the glass, rinsed her mouth. The peppermint taste made Rebecca think of Lifesavers and she was grateful for the soothing, clean tingling sensation.

Refreshed, she apologized weakly, "Sorry to be such a bother. But I've never experienced an upset stomach with the hives before. Nerves I imagine."

"There's always a first time for everything," Alexander responded matter of factly. "And after that, if the first was fairly decent and you're lucky, a second."

Before Rebecca could ask that he explain his statement, Alexander bent from the waist and planted a hard, unyielding kiss on her lips.

The casual strength, the hunger of the kiss surprised her, and for a moment Alexander's intimate touch almost drew Rebecca from her self-imposed shell. Long suppressed emotions skirmished with the carefully contrived numbness she'd learned to rely upon. But she couldn't have stopped him from kissing her, even if she'd wanted to.

Rebecca marveled that she no longer felt like Alice in Wonderland. In fact, she'd almost learned to trust the sensations Alexander aroused, because within the circle of his arms, she knew beyond a shadow of a doubt she wasn't hallucinating. Therefore, his kiss was both ecstasy and punishment.

Gazing into the depths of his ever-changing hazel eyes, stupefied, Rebecca spoke aloud her thoughts. "Punishment for my sins?" she asked in a shaky voice.

"Angels have no sins, nor swans either. So it would seem 'tis punishment for mine," Alexander murmured huskily, an odd smile on his lips as he withdrew from her.

Evidence was building daily against Rebecca that she was a Yankee spy and yet, things just didn't add up. There was a piece of the puzzle missing. Why would she save him, only to turn him over at a later date? Alexander wondered. Were the Federals afraid he'd stashed the campaign papers elsewhere, or were they waiting for him to exchange them so he would be caught red-handed with the evidence? What length would Rebecca go to in the attempt to further her cause? Lastly, why must this plague him so, when all he wanted to do was hold her close to his heart and never let her go?

"The world has gone mad, Rebecca, and I'm afraid it's trying to take me along with it," he said finally, almost as if to himself.

Rebecca's heart constricted. She searched Alexander's eyes, recognizing the momentary shadow of sadness that encroached on their clear green depths. She'd seen the same thing all too often when she glanced in the mirror. Mostly following a fifteen-hour stint in the O.R. when the surgical team lost more G.I.s than they saved. War was hell and always would be, no matter the time, place, or cause.

"I wouldn't worry about it too much. Right now, I think everybody in the South is pretty much in the same boat."

"I wonder," Alexander said thoughtfully. Astonished, Rebecca listened as he continued, confessing aloud something she'd been experiencing since the moment she'd met him.

"It seems there's something more that we share. I don't know what it is, but it exists. As surely as the moon and stars. Drawing. Pulling. Directing. As if it has some secret destination in mind."

"So you feel it, too." Rebecca had to bite her tongue not to blurt out her fantastic story, to relieve herself of the burden of her secret. That she was an involuntary time traveler.

"It's the most confounding thing. Neither of us wants it. God knows, I don't need the complications," he said honestly.

Rebecca could hear the shuffling steps of heavily booted soldiers as they gathered like a pack of hungry wolves in the kitchen below. The sound tangled with the excruciatingly sweet notes of a hastily prepared piano recital. "Amazing Grace," "Rock of Ages," "Nearer My God to Thee" drifted up the stairs to them. Music to soothe the savage beasts if she wasn't mistaken, Rebecca thought.

"You have your life. And I have mine." *And never the twain shall meet*, she added to herself. "I should be on my way as soon as the Yankees clear out."

Alexander's eyes darkened and in a low voice he said, "Stay." Again a single word. But it was enough, for Rebecca could still taste the sincerity of his kiss upon her lips.

An urge to fly from the room, from William Alexander Ransom's presence, assailed Rebecca. If only he knew that they were from two different worlds! That what they were feeling simply wouldn't fly.

Why had this happened? Rebecca agonized. She was usually so wise in dealing with her patients. Damn Alexander for getting under her skin. It was crazy. What did he want from her? Expect? He seemed so real. Too real. More genuine than any modern-day man she'd ever known. But how did a slightly tarnished flower child from the future cope with the original White Knight?

More upsetting still, what did she hope to gain

from Alexander? A road map home? Even a Nobel Prize—winning physicist couldn't hope to come up with that, not one whom she'd heard of anyway.

Did she want a quick toss in the sack? Much as she liked to play it cool, deep down inside she wasn't really that kind of girl. Security? Perhaps. Who wouldn't cling to something stable and strong if they were suddenly transported back in time with nothing more than a nightgown and a medical bag to keep them company? But security was only the tip of the iceberg.

Drawing a deep breath, Rebecca delved deeply within herself, acknowledging that she'd lost perspective on things. A fade in, fade out. It seemed the longer she remained with Alexander, the more his reality became hers. The fact was, despite her best resolve, she was falling in love with him.

There! As much as she hated to, she'd finally admitted it. If not to Alexander, at least to herself.

But it was absurd! Rational people didn't fall in love with individuals from the past. Did they? And if so, what could she expect when her bit part in the ongoing drama was played out? Would she simply vanish? Back to her MASH unit? Her own century? In which case, would her love for Alexander disappear, too? As if it had never existed? Or, as she feared, would it survive the trip across time to leave a hole in her heart the size of eternity?

So many unanswered questions. Too many. Her cranium ached, and with great difficulty Rebecca banished them one by one from her mind. At least temporarily.

Chapter Eight

Sprawled in a wing-back chair near the hearth, Guinevere lost in dog dreams at his feet, Alexander absently thumbed through a leather-bound volume from the library shelves. But his mind was not on Jonathan Swift's satirical tale of Gulliver's travels in the land of Lilliput. It was torn between the picket patrolling in the wintery shadow of the plantation's tree line and Rebecca Warren, in the kitchen, rolling out a pie crust for something she called a quiche.

Alexander slammed the book shut and rose to his feet, flexing his stiff shoulder. Startled by his abrupt movement, the dog opened her liquid brown eyes to stare at him.

"Sorry, Guinevere. But, by God, I wish it was dark so we could take a turn in the garden! I feel like a blasted prisoner in my own home."

The walks in the walled garden by night which Rebecca had suggested had helped relieve the tension, but the subdued activity was beginning to tell on him. He could actually feel himself regaining strength daily, and knew that he was finally almost fully recovered.

Alexander's expression hardened as he moved to stand to one side of the library window. Using the lace panel as a blind, he flicked back the drapes and studied the lone picket clad in basic blue. It had been a week since Emory and his men had foisted themselves on Oak Mont he mused, and though Rebecca's ruse had shaken the captain off his trail temporarily, things didn't look good. Emory's excuse for leaving the man behind had been that "he might be of assistance to the ladies during their time of need."

His square jaw clenched, Alexander snorted to himself, spinning away from the window. He'd never heard such humbug! He'd been warned of Captain Emory by Major General Wheeler during their interview. Emory professed to be a gentleman, but he was not. Plainly, the picket was a detective, ordered to watch the house because the captain suspected something. He didn't like the connotations. Clearly, Emory was receiving a steady diet of information, though Alexander had failed to catch Rebecca in the act of feeding it to him.

Either Rebecca was extremely crafty or totally innocent. One of which remained to be proved, Alexander reminded himself, going on to the next question that bothered him.

Why on earth was Emory treading so lightly where Oak Mont was concerned? In Nashville, he had a reputation for being a bull in a china shop when it came to the sanctity of private homes. Yes, the thought of measles had clearly frightened him, but Alexander sensed there was more to his caution than the threat of infection. But for now, all he could do was suffer and wait until the time was right to make his next move. The frock coat was planted. He could do no more.

Extracting a slender cigar from the carved box on his writing desk, he rolled it in his fingers, testing the weight, the compactness of the cylinder. The jewel in the ring on his hand caught his eye. A snake with its tail in its mouth. Symbol for eternal life. The Ransom family motto.

Even now, Alexander could envision his father, strolling proudly amid the rows of prime tobacco, down to the springhouse, then along the tree line, pointing out the numerous species of birds that inhabited *their* forests. As a boy, he'd scampered at his father's heels like an anxious pup in an attempt to match his strides, learning about his heritage, absorbing from his sire what it meant to be a man. Later, he'd tried to pass the knowledge on to his younger brothers in the same manner as their father had to him.

Alexander glanced at the daguerreotype that rested beside the cigar box. Almost hesitantly, he reached toward the silver-coated metallic plate, running his forefinger across the lifeless faces of Beau and Edward. Both had died as a man would have wanted, on the field of honor in a cause they supported. But it was small comfort, for now a Yankee picket walked Oak Mont's tree line in their stead. And to his chagrin, Alexander found himself wishing he'd been a less proficient tutor.

With a heavy sigh, he tipped the photograph on its face, bit the end off the rich, brown cigar, and viciously spat it out. Setting match to leaf, he inhaled deeply, allowing his thoughts to veer from the more unpleasant aspects of war to Rebecca.

What a brain teaser the woman was, even if he found in the final analysis that everything she'd said and done had been coldly calculated and that she was a spy. Rebecca was unique and nothing would alter that fact.

He'd never met a female who preferred to wear her hair cropped like Joan of Arc, though he had to admit the shoulder-length cut gave her auburn tresses a full-bodiedness that other women's lacked. The dimple in her chin was ordinary enough until she smiled. In combination with her full lips, incredibly even white teeth, and the freckles dusting her pert nose, it became an arresting feature.

Alexander liked tall women, and Rebecca was striking. But as much as her physical appearance, he enjoyed the economy of her movement, her bear-trap mind, her elegance of command, the way she looked you directly in the eye while speaking. Unconventional, nothing if not direct, she scorned social rule, falsity, public opinion, daring to behave as her conscience dictated. A fine example of that was the case of Rebecca's fitting.

"She was a horrid little spitfire, wasn't she, Guinevere?" Alexander said with a chuckle.

At the sound of her name, the dog lifted her head from her paws, looked at Alexander a long moment, then rose to join him behind the desk. He patted her head absently.

"I honestly think it would have been easier to have you stand in her place, girl." The mastiff licked his hand as if she too remembered the incident and agreed with her master.

The women of his household had closeted themselves in the parlor, leaving specific instructions that they were not to be disturbed until Rebecca had a descent outfit which would have thrilled most belles of Alexander's acquaintance.

Not Rebecca.

"You'd have thought she was going to an execution or that she had never been fitted for a wardrobe in her life," he muttered to the dog. But that was ridiculous.

She'd complained about "being mistaken for a human pincushion," of "the absolute necessity of simplicity, durability, and down-to-earth practicality." Things most females didn't care a fat fig about.

Alexander had to admit he was almost relieved when Jubadessa let Rebecca off the hook for the afternoon, deciding to pack up her sewing box and the excess material from his mother's gowns, along with Cordelia and Abigail, and to ride to the neighbor's house to attend the monthly sewing society.

Armed to the teeth with precious silk swatches

for flags and multihued quilting scraps, the Ransom women were sure to carry the day. Under the guise of recent illness, Rebecca had remained behind to keep an eye on the guard should he take it into his head to do some snooping.

Alexander sobered, snuffing out the slender cigar in the ashtray with a quick, stabbing motion. Raking his fingers through his dark hair, he turned to rest one arm on the mantel while staring into the hypnotic flames that lapped at the hardwood logs. For the first time since they'd met, he and Rebecca were alone together under the same roof. And all he could think of was sweeping her into his arms once again and resuming where they'd left off the day she'd eaten the strawberry jam ... for him.

The hours they'd shared while Emory's men consumed far too much of Oak Mont's depleted food supply had been priceless. He'd found, to his astonishment, that Rebecca was an astute poker player which had been her suggestion "to pass the time." And when that had paled, she'd managed chess shrewdly enough for a self-professed novice. He was especially pleased to find her well read. Witty, easily offended, yet quick to forgive an imagined slight, she was definitely entertaining.

But there were times, especially when she was excited, that he felt as if she were speaking a foreign tongue. Yet he rather enjoyed it all the same. Her unique vocabulary added zest to their conversations.

Still, by virtue of Emory's impromptu visit, the platonic tranquillity he and Rebecca had striven to maintain had been shattered. By silent yet mutual consent, they'd compensated for the breech in policy by keeping their distance. Emotions ran high. Consequently, a studied coolness had settled between them.

He wished the situation was reversed and therein lay the rub. He'd never wanted a woman as badly as he did Rebecca. The sight of her face, swollen with hives, and her upset stomach hadn't diminished his need one iota. In fact, it had been the strongest indication yet that he could easily overstep the boundaries decorum permitted. If the right situation presented itself, if he forgot that he was a gentleman, that he was duty bound, that she might be the enemy within....

"Damnation!" The devils in his head were about to gnaw through their chains, and he was hard pressed to stay them.

Selecting a wicked-looking tool from the matched set on the hearth, Alexander ran a hand along the length of the fire rod, as if testing a prospective sword for temperament and balance. Jabbing at the logs in the granite fireplace with the poker, he harmlessly vented a portion of his growing frustration on the burning hardwood.

"Of all the times to come into my life. Why now? Why not before the war, when love was an asset rather than a liability?" He grumbled then paused as if struck. Clamping his mouth shut, he found himself caught off guard by the noun his mind had so blithely supplied his tongue.

Love? God above!

His eyes narrowed, he rubbed his jaw with his

fingertips. He could use a shave. And, yes, love was the proper word to use in conjunction with his feelings for Rebecca.

With a decisive pop, the uppermost log he was jabbing at cleaved in half. Incandescent sparks swirled upward, waltzing in the puff of wood smoke created by the disintegrating wood. Like the passionate sparks dancing on the smoke of his crumbling resolve, Alexander thought to himself.

Ah, Rebecca. Where in God's name do we go from here? Perhaps it was time to remedy the distance between them. Perhaps he should go and talk to her. *Right now,* he mused.

Replacing the poker in its stand, Alexander strode toward the kitchen, purpose written all over his handsome, aristocratic countenance.

Rebecca stretched, massaging the small of her back with her hand. So where did she and Alexander go from here? The question was nagging. Persistent.

After spending several hours in close quarters with him, she'd found she not only loved the guy, she actually liked him as well. They'd talked books. Correction. *He'd* talked books. She'd talked movies—*Moby Dick* starring Gregory Peck, a new release of *Romeo and Juliet* with Olivia Hussey. *Ivanhoe. The Scarlet Letter,* which she'd seen *and* read.

They'd played several hands of poker; he'd been a good loser. Chess—he'd been a patient instructor. Kisser—he'd been, without a doubt, superb. Feather-light and firm all at the same time. Now, he seemed jumpy, uptight, on edge. Even angry since his mysterious ride, Rebecca thought, and she couldn't pinpoint the reason behind that either.

As for Cordelia. There was *another* problem. Rebecca sensed something elusive where the blonde was concerned. Cordelia was too free with the Yankee guard. She'd seen her chatting with him several times openly, to be sure. Still, it seemed in direct contrast to the way one would have expected her to behave.

"Oh, boy," she groaned. What kind of a place had she found herself in? What a mess. How was she ever going to sort all this out? She sure could use a Coke and an unopened box of Moon Pies. Pigging out always seemed to help her think things through. Besides, breakfast had been skimpy and cooking was hard work.

She'd considered making a thick, melt-in-your-mouth pizza. But barring tomato sauce, Jubadessa's larder didn't stock Italian, so she'd opted for quiche instead. It had seemed a great way to repay Jubadessa for the gown she wore, to have dinner ready when she returned from the sewing circle. Why, the housekeeper had spent days unraveling needlepoint samplers to recycle enough thread to alter a single gown. A meal was the least she could do. But then, who would have guessed collecting dairy products to put together a simple quiche would prove such an ordeal?

She'd had to fight the hen to collect the eggs. She'd never realized chickens had such sharp beaks. Thank heavens Willy had already milked the cow, storing the frothy stave-handled piggins in the springhouse along with a crock of freshly churned butter. The hen had been bad enough. She was certainly relieved she didn't have to take on the Guernsey, too.

She'd cracked the eggs then grated the cheese on a concave chopping tray with a pierced tin insert, along with the skin on three of her knuckles. She flattened the dough with a lignum-vitae rolling pin that seemed as heavy as a tree trunk. Rebecca knew it was made from the mahogany-like wood imported from the West Indies because her mother had once obtained an identical piece for the antique shop.

She missed the ease of mixing the custard with an electric blender, but in the end, Rebecca wound up with a reasonable-looking deep-dish quiche. And then she faced the *real* test of her ingenuity.

Rebecca had cut her eyeteeth on scavenger hunts. Any and everything that could be termed "old" found its way into her mother's shop in downtown Atlanta. Iceboxes. Furniture. Clothes. Jewelry. Even parlor cookstoves. Rebecca had seen them before. She'd even helped load them in the family pickup. But she'd never tried to fire one up. She hadn't counted on the stove being a test of her mechanical skills.

The contraption had no owner's manual. No control knobs. No timer. No electrical plug. The kettle of stewed raisins in the boiling hole on the top was doing fine. But she'd been baby-sitting the oven for over an hour in an attempt to regulate the heat with less than successful results.

212

"How does Jubadessa do it? Trial and error? Freakiest thing I've ever seen," she muttered aloud.

Rebecca eased open the heavy door, testing the pie with her fingertips while trying to keep the lace cuff of her new broadcloth day dress from dipping into the custard. The quiche was baking fairly well, except for the crust, which looked slightly overdone. *But you can't have everything,* Rebecca thought.

Then again, maybe the problem could be corrected. Maybe a wood stove was more like a back-yard grill. Perhaps you had to spread the embers for slower baking. With that idea in mind, Rebecca swung open the fire door located on the side of the stove to inspect the wood.

The cool air in the kitchen acted like a vacuum, sucking at the heat within the fire box. The fire surged, spitting red hot sparks toward Rebecca's knees, igniting her clothes—this time with her still in them. She could smell the cotton brown and ash, taste the acridness in the air as the holes widened even while she beat at them to smother the greedy, cloth-consuming flame.

A very natural fear rose in her, magnified by the vision of the crispy critters she'd nursed. Napalm victims mostly. Tragically burned.

"Fire!" Rebecca cried, but the word came out as a garbled croak.

Before Rebecca's brain could signal her hands to quit flailing, and her body to stop, drop, and roll, she heard the clang of the fire-box door being kicked shut. Then, strong arms enveloped her

213

shoulders, snatching her away from the stove.

Forcing her to the floor, Alexander executed the life-saving maneuver for Rebecca. His hard torso pressed against her softer breasts and thighs, he stifled the flames licking at her dress, cushioning their acrobatic tumble across the planked flooring with his muscular body.

When finally they came to rest, Rebecca found herself on the bottom of the tangled heap, Alexander on top, out of breath, balancing his weight on his hands to keep from crushing her.

"God Almighty! You gave me quite a start, woman. I vow, you're a hazard to your own health."

Her body trembled. Not from reaction to the accident, but to the man who hovered above her, to the concern in his voice. Eye to eye, Rebecca stared up into Alexander's hazel orbs. The kitchen was so quiet, the house so serene, not a footfall, not even the purr of a refrigerator to mar the sound of their mingled breathing. As if waiting for something momentous to happen.

Her soul, normally well guarded behind walls of self-control, rose from its long sleep, slipped past the shock of Alexander's nearness to dance in her eyes.

"You could have . . . thrown me a blanket. It . . . would have . . . done just as well . . . without half the effort," she faltered, attempting to recover, but Alexander had already met and seized the moment.

"You don't mean that," he said, his voice low and husky.

"I . . . Yes, I do. I could have—"

"Burned!" Alexander supplied roughly. "Do you think for a moment I would have stepped aside and allowed that to happen?"

"I only meant that I've been such a bother. The measles—and now this."

"You? A bother? That, dear lady, is an understatement. Now, stop chattering. The subject is closed." It was not a request, but a command, stated almost angrily.

"O—okay," Rebecca replied rather weakly, stunned by his outburst, using the time to strong arm her own rattled composure.

Satisfied, if not slightly surprised by her compliance, Alexander rose. In one swift motion, he scooped her up and headed for her bedroom, which ran directly off the kitchen. Tenderly, he deposited her in the middle of her four-poster bed. Then turned and marched back through the kitchen. She was alone only a moment before he returned with a pint of Old Crow Kentucky Bourbon, a tincture of cucumber, and a wad of lint.

"My quiche. It will burn."

"The pie is done. I took it from the oven," he assured her, twisting off the bottle cap and filling it with a stiff shot of the amberish-brown liquid. Passing it to Rebecca, he encouraged, "Drink. It will do you good."

Rebecca didn't have to be told twice. Tipping the cap to her lips, she drank, allowing the smooth, mellow alcohol to sear a warm path to the pit of her stomach.

"Has a nice kick," Rebecca commented.

"You never cease to amaze me. Now you're a connoisseur of fine whiskey."

Extremely potent, the bourbon was already beginning to relax her. "Not really. My dad isn't a drinker, but when he does drink, Old Crow is a favorite. I've sipped it before," Rebecca confessed, surprising herself. She'd thought of her family often, their reaction to her disappearance, her mother's shop, the loss of her brother, but it was the first time she'd actually mentioned any of them aloud.

"Your father must be a man of impeccable taste."

"Why, yes, I suppose he is."

Replacing the cap, Alexander set the bottle aside to tug off Rebecca's boots. With an air of unself-conscious assurance, he carefully inched her skirts up her calf. Then higher, slipping her lace garter from her thigh and rolling her stocking down around her ankle. And when she would have protested, he said with a reproving half-smile, "Don't you ever know when to lie still and be quiet?"

"No. Never," she answered faintly, charmed by his smile, relaxing when she realized he planned to push the damaged gown no further up than absolutely necessary.

"We're at a stalemate then," he said, sitting down beside her on the feather mattress.

"Has anyone ever told you that you're too bold for words?" Rebecca asked, thinking all the while how masterful he was. How he must have had the women waiting in line before the war, vying for the chance of a moment's attention.

"Saucy wench!" he muttered under his breath, but the words seemed more a caress than a put down.

Rebecca propped her upper body on her elbows, straining to examine her leg. "Move over and let me see how bad it is."

His hip pressed firmly against the shapely curve of her calf, Alexander ignored her demands, holding her leg immobilized in his powerful, yet gentle grip. "You're lucky. Your undergarments protected your leg for the most part. The kneecap's blistered, but I've seen worse," he said. "We'll have you fixed up in no time," he predicted, a determined note in his voice.

"Oh, honestly! I can handle this myself," Rebecca burst out, falling back onto the bed. "Who's the nurse around here, you or me?" she asked, trying to recall whether she had a tube of sulfur ointment in her medical bag.

"Quite an about-face, isn't it?" he responded, a hint of the smile still coloring his voice.

Rebecca regarded him darkly. "Humph! This is absurd. Totally absurd."

"Haven't you heard that turnabout is fair play?" he asked easily.

"Once or twice," she said dryly, her voice regaining strength with each passing second.

"I have to give it to you, though. Most woman would have swooned."

Did she detect a note of pride in his voice? Impossible!

"I'm not like other women. What you see is what you get."

"I'll consider myself forewarned," he said, redirecting his full attention to her injury, leaving Rebecca to wonder exactly what he meant.

The home remedy Alexander proceeded to swab on her knee did soothe the burning sensation. Or was it the wave of response she felt at the touch of his hand that washed away the pain? Oddly comforted, inside and out, by his ministrations, Rebecca wasn't sure. She knew only that if he kept massaging her knee with his sure, tender strokes, she was going to disgrace herself. Swoon, scream, or reach for him in a most "unladylike fashion," as Cordelia might say.

Rebecca's blood threatened to boil. "Enough already! My leg is fine."

Alexander's eyes met hers. He studied her for a long moment with eyes so arresting, so intense that the first stirrings of a warm blush blossomed on Rebecca's cheek. The tension in the room was palpable.

"No, it isn't. I'm not sure it will ever be enough," he said finally.

The annoyance she strove to maintain as a buffer between them faded.

"I don't know what you mean."

"Surely you can see fate has wrenched this from our hands, Rebecca," he said quietly.

Rebecca's thoughts scattered like four sheets to the wind as Alexander leaned over and drew her to him. An aching joy filled her when he didn't stop with the simple hug, but followed it with a kiss on her forehead. And then, a searing jolt to the lips.

"This is what you've wanted all along. What we've both wanted, though we stubbornly tried to fool ourselves into believing otherwise." His admission was agonized.

"No," Rebecca whispered against his lips, her tone carefully neutral. But the denial was a lie; it sounded hollow, out of place, with her blood speeding through her veins like a car in the Indy Five Hundred.

"Well, by heavens, it's what I've wanted, more than anything else in my life. It defies common sense," Alexander growled. "You enchant me with everything you do and are."

He was breaking every code of chivalry he had ever been trained to follow, but living daily in the shadow of death had given Alexander a great respect for life. And he saw the promise of life lighting Rebecca's angelic eyes. To him, spicy hot, vibrant, she seemed the very breath of it. The most essential part of it. Instinct asked that he release her. Necessity demanded that he not. He could no more have stopped himself from taking her than he could have stopped breathing without blacking out. Life was short, and he decided against all prior reasoning to throw caution aside and savor the moment.

Rebecca braced her hands against Alexander's chest. "We can't." It was all she could do to form the words.

"How can we not?" he rasped.

How could a man from the past sap her will

power? Break through her defenses? Incite such pleasure, such longing, when no other could? It seemed as if she'd waited forever for this particular man. And now that he was here, within touching range, conscience dictated she resist him with every fiber of her being. But it was impossible to do so.

"How indeed?" she asked softly, brushing his jaw line with her fingertips. "It would be so much better for everyone concerned if the things that you said weren't true."

It was all the capitulation on Rebecca's part that Alexander needed.

Once the decision was made, he undressed her with calm deliberation and she allowed it. No. She reveled in it. His warm touch. The delicate sucking sensation of his moist lips against her skin. He trailed tiny kisses across her shoulders as he unbuttoned her dress, across the swells of her breasts above her underwire bra. Her dog tags jingled.

"What's this?" he asked, holding the metal tags between his fingertips.

"Identification. All the...uh...Army nurses I know have them," Rebecca said. It was the truth. Where she came from they were part and parcel of the uniform.

Alexander lifted the chain over her head, placing the tags on the bedside table. "Good idea. But you don't need them right now. I know who you are."

"You do?" Rebecca asked breathlessly, reluctant to allow the future to intrude on the past—

which at the moment was all the present she ever wanted.

"Yes. You're the lady I'm about to make love to."

A tremor shook her body as he proceeded to divest her slowly of her garments, one article at a time.

"What? No stays?" he questioned softly as the gown was lifted over her head.

Rebecca bit her lips, shaking her head, almost afraid to look into his eyes. He had called her a lady, but ladies wore a corset.

"No camisole either?"

Again, she shook her head, wondering if she was doubly damned.

Her petticoats followed her day dress in a discarded pile on the floor. She waited breathlessly for his comment concerning the nylon panties. *What must he think of me?* What was the word? Harlot. Perhaps that would be his verdict.

"God in heaven!"

Rebecca squeezed her eyes shut, waiting for the worst, for him to draw away in revulsion.

"You're the most beautiful woman. Absolute perfection. It was insanity to have waited." He sighed as he found the catch to her bra, freeing her breasts from the soft, fiber-filled cups.

Their personal battle ended, his lips set about a painful awakening deep within Rebecca. A thawing. She released a puff of breath she hadn't realized she'd been holding.

Smoothing her hands across his back, down to his waist, Rebecca pulled the tails of his flannel shirt from his tight breeches, easing open the polished, ebony buttons, pushing the material from his broad shoulders to expose the dark, curly hair sprinkling his chest.

Alexander's bandaging was gone. The only sign of his wound was a neat row of ridges where she'd extracted the stitches—a permanent brand of her handiwork. Rebecca touched her fingers to the scar. He captured her hand, pressing a moist, intoxicating kiss into the hollow of her palm.

Shifting, he stood, stripping off his remaining clothes. Uninhibited, proud, he faced her, the pier glass to his back. Rebecca couldn't tear her eyes from him.

She'd been right. Trim, well-built, taller than most men, Alexander Ransom possessed star quality. He was a woman's sexual fantasy in the flesh, every magnificent inch of him. Unable to stop herself, Rebecca reached out to test the reality. He sucked in his breath.

"I can't believe I'm doing this."

"Believe," he rasped.

Rebecca made room for Alexander on the narrow bed as his mouth sought hers once more. Solicitous of her knee, he stretched out full length, gathered her to him and, rolling to his side, positioned her leg at an angle across his hard-muscled flank.

"Your skin is so soft, like silk," he murmured, cupping her breast, his head dipping, his tongue teasing the engorged nipple.

Like a windswept ferry bumping into its moorings, Rebecca arched against his lips, settling into Alexander's embrace. A liquid heat filled her, rushing into her head. There was no room for coherent thought, only for the strange, wondrous sensations engulfing her body.

He entered her swiftly with a half-starved urgency. They moved together with instinctive rhythm. Deep, deeper, deepest. Hot. Intense. Binding.

Two people, two worlds, two lifetimes merged into one seemingly inseparable entity. A miracle. Passion's precious timeless hour.

A healing so intense that it rocked her to the core shook Rebecca's soul. The tight bands around her heart burst as Alexander surged inside her. She eagerly met his onslaught, her brain shattering into a million tiny pinpoints of light. The relief was overwhelming, and for the first time in almost a year, tears welled in her eyes, overflowing, and trickled down into her hairline.

"Don't. Please, don't," Alexander said, smoothing her hair as he cradled her against his chest. "There's nothing to be ashamed of."

There was a flicker of something in his voice. Distress. Or could it be remorse? There was no doubt the principle of free love—love outside the bonds of marriage—was morally unacceptable in his time. Hell! She wasn't even sure she agreed with it herself.

Rebecca jumped ship and swam drunkenly to shore, clutching the cotton comforter to her breasts. "You, Lieutenant Colonel Ransom, are the most infuriating person I've ever met," she managed crisply, a glimmer of her usual spunk wading to the fore as she struggled to escape his arms.

"And you, Miss Warren, are the most changeable, bewitching creature I've ever had the honor of knowing. You wiggle in such an impressive manner, I'm loath to let you go."

The steel band of his grip tightened. The expression in Alexander's hazel eyes fractured to be replaced by the gleam of something recognizably physical—raw desire. Rebecca could feel the steady beat of his heart, his body heat, his warm breath against her tousled auburn hair. His arousal. She was *glad* he defied her, that he held her in place against his muscular form. There was nowhere else, in her time or his, that she would rather be than within the circle of his arms.

"Come." He tugged at the covers. "I have a terrible need for more of something only you can provide. The damage is done. What say we have another go-around. A slooooow one. For the sake of good measure," he added, a rakish smile with the potential to melt the heart of an Ice Queen punctuating his intent.

His mouth descended on hers. And though his words had appeared flippant, Alexander's lingering kiss said everything his words did not. Passionate, loving, giving, as drugging as morphine, the demonstration was Rebecca's undoing.

"I expect you will be returning to your military unit soon?"

He looked at her quizzically, tracing a forefinger

in a sensuous pattern back and forth along the sensitive flesh of her inner arm. "Regiment. Yes, soon."

"Then far be it from me to stand in the way of good measure."

Consciously or unconsciously, like it or not, for better or worse, heartbeat for heartbeat, she'd come home.

Chapter Nine

Abigail fidgeted in the doorway of the library, peeping at Rebecca from beneath the rolled brim of a plumed velvet cap.

Rebecca, lounging on a leather settee before the fire, glanced up expectantly from the papers in her lap. "What is it, Abigail?"

For some unknown reason, following the rockiness of their initial introduction, Alexander's aunt had taken a great liking to Rebecca. It was not unusual for Abigail to seek out her company and press a book of Byron's poetry into her hands, asking that it be read aloud. She was often invited to walk in the garden, or to play a round of croquet by the childlike woman.

Fingering the enamel brooch that pinned her paisley shawl together at the throat, Abigail tripped into the room, answering Rebecca's question with a question of her own. "Why are you readin' those dusty old newspapers? We use them to light the fire."

Rebecca had been pouring over the newspapers and periodicals, including a copy of *The Daily Rebel Banner*, a camp newsletter printed by Braxton Bragg's Army, and a packet of sheet music published by Blacknar and Werlein of New Orleans. Using them as a source to update herself, she'd hoped to get in touch with the era she found herself living in through the voice of its people, the mood of the nation, its politics.

From *The Charleston Mercury*, she'd learned that gold was weighing in as high as one hundred and thirty-eight. *The Charleston Daily Courier* covered a speech by Jefferson Davis. Victor Hugo was working on a romance entitled *93*. Queen Victoria had consecrated the mausoleum at Frogmore and then had the remains of her late husband, Prince Albert, removed to the tomb.

During her research attempt, Rebecca had also read a tribute to women and war, a notice to save rags for newspapers, and that some kind of war was going on in Mexico. Most interesting was that a band of smugglers had been arrested for spiriting cases of shoes across the Potomac—shoes bound for a needy and almost shoeless South. Which explained why Alexander hadn't burned her boots.

The Charleston Mercury spoke of intervention by England and Russia into the Civil War, with Switzerland, of all places, as mediator. There were estates listed for sale at public auction in the *Daily*

Dispatch from Richmond, Virginia. There were even casualty lists and battlefield accounts, substantiated with maps of the surrounding area where the combat took place—Murfreesboro included. She'd studied the Stones River map in detail.

Rebecca reasoned that if only she could discover her place in the scheme of things through reading the newspapers, the burden of her position might be lightened. She'd had some success, but Abigail wouldn't understand, even if she could explain. She didn't totally understand it herself.

Stacking the newspapers on the cushion beside her, she said, "I was just sorting through them. Thinking perhaps we could make a scrapbook from the more interesting articles. Would you like that?"

"You mean like a diary with sketches. Oh, yes. Let's do that, Rebecca. Such a pleasant way to pass the time of day."

"I tell you what. Why don't you look over these, see if you can find any articles you like, and I'll go ask Cordelia for a pair of scissors so we can start cutting them out."

Abigail's hand flew to her lips. "Oh, no! You mustn't ask Cordelia right now. She's terribly busy."

It was obvious something was bothering Abigail. "I don't think she'll mind the interruption," Rebecca responded as if soothing a youngster.

"Yes, she will," Abigail said adamantly.

Abigail's wide-eyed expression told Rebecca the older woman knew something she did not.

"Abigail, what's going on? Is there something you'd like to tell me about?"

"*Someone* should know, I'm sure."

"Then come here." Rebecca tossed the papers off the settee, clearing a spot for Abigail. Patting the cushion beside her, she said. "Sit down and tell me what's up. Maybe I can help."

"Do you think so?"

"I'll certainly try."

Abigail took the proffered seat, carefully arranging her voluminous white organdy skirts before launching into her story.

"Since that awful guard is no longer watchin' our house, and Alexander has locked himself in his room with his ledgers and legal papers, Cordelia has taken the opportunity to slip out and meet her beau."

It was true that the guard had been recalled to the garrison in Nashville, and that Alexander was absorbed with his paperwork. But the rest? Well, Rebecca couldn't credit it. Cordelia was too prim and proper to be involved in a clandestine affair. She was a virtual slave to propriety.

"You must be mistaken."

"No. I'm not," Abigail stated flatly. "He wears blue, like the guard. But he's not the guard. He's an officer, and he ate dinner with us one Sunday not too long ago. I took him for a stroll through my rose garden, though I must say I didn't care for his uppity attitude. I sensed he thinks flowers a waste of time. Thinks winter rose hips ugly, which they're not."

"Are you talking about Captain Emory, Abigail?

Surely not." Rebecca had to close her mouth with the tip of her finger.

"That's the young man. I saw them together."

Rebecca could hardly believe her ears. But Abigail seemed too coherent today, too sincere for Rebecca to disregard her tale totally.

"How often have you seen them, Abigail?"

"Oh, many times before you came. On our trips to Nashville, when Jubadessa wasn't with us. The day after you arrived, when Cordelia saw the dentist for her grippy wisdom tooth." Abigail began to count on her fingers. "Twice since the guard was posted...and...um...two, no three times since he left. Always when Alexander is otherwise occupied."

How dare the man! Who the heck did Emory think he was? Sticking his nose where it didn't belong?

"You're sure about this?"

"Of course." Abigail lowered her voice to a whisper, leaning so close to Rebecca's ear that she caught a whiff of fresh-baked bread on the older woman's breath. "The captain kissed her. On the mouth." She straightened, continuing in her normal voice. "I was outraged. They aren't even engaged."

While Abigail rambled on, Rebecca skimmed over the basic implications of Cordelia's involvement with Captain Emory. A Southern belle, and a devout Unionist. Bad karma.

"Does Jubadessa know about this?"

"Good gracious, no! Jubadessa is in the bake house up to her elbows in bread dough. But she would have already died of a cat fit if she did. Can you imagine the dreadful din? It gives me the trembles to think of it." Abigail rolled her eyes and shivered for emphasis, pressing her fingers to her temples. "What I wouldn't give for a glass of ratafia and a nice tray of sugar danties right about now."

"What's a ratafia, Abigail?"

"A most wonderful medicinal almond cordial. Cures a headache, just like that," she said, snapping her fingers. "But Jubadessa has locked it in the cupboard and I don't have a key."

Rebecca bit her tongue to keep from laughing aloud. There were times when Abigail's mind was as sharp as a whip, when she was as humorous as The Mad Hatter Rebecca had once likened her to.

"Maybe we'd better backtrack to our original topic—Cordelia."

"Oh my, yes. By all means. Well, you see, Cordelia made me promise not to tell anyone about the captain because he's a Yankee, like my own dearly departed husband was. Resembles the Stoddards, too," Abigail remarked speculatively, tapping her front tooth with her fingernail. "Anyway, the neighborhood simply won't tolerate such a repetition in behavior from another member of our immediate family. And havin' lived through it with me, Cordelia's horrified by the notion they might find out."

"How would you feel about it?"

Abigail batted her eyelashes as if she were surprised and slightly flattered that Rebecca had asked her opinion.

"Why, I wouldn't care to see my daughter ostracized from the sewin' circle as I was when the war began. Besides, polite society was down on us for so long that I have only just now managed to regain their good graces myself. Talk of this would surely put me on the fringes once again."

Public opinion was the last thing on Rebecca's mind. She was more concerned with Corelia, Oak Mont and Alexander's reaction when he discovered the liaison. He wouldn't take this affront lying down.

An instinctive protectiveness surged in Rebecca. She'd enjoy seeing Emory strung up by his thumbs! But not at Alexander's expense.

"You said that Captain Emory *kisses* Cordelia?"

"Rather exuberantly." Abigail wrung her hands. "Shockin' isn't it? But Cordelia is headstrong, just like her father was. Far beyond listenin' to her mother's 'ridiculous dribble' it would seem. So distressin'. I keep thinkin' I should turn this over to the head of our household. It's a man's job really, to put a stop to this...extravagant flirtation."

Rebecca balked. Alexander, an old-world gallant who had the absurd notion that women belonged on protected ivory pedestals, would go wild if he knew. No telling what he would be prompted to do in the name of family honor. This was really none of her business, and yet she'd grown to care deeply for the people of Oak Mont. Especially Alexander.

"No. That might not be such a good idea, considering the war and all. Perhaps I could talk to Cordelia for you."

"That might be a wise move. She has a high regard for you. Perhaps she would listen to reason."

"Do you know where they are right now?"

"Oh, yes. Most assuredly. She meets him in the family cemetery, by the apple orchard. I think if you hurry, you might catch them there." Abigail chewed her lower lip for a moment before adding, "But you won't tell her I sent you, will you? She would be so upset if she knew I betrayed a confidence."

"No. I've been wanting to go down to the mill and check on Dinah's progress anyway. Her measles should be almost completely cleared up by now. Since the path to the camp leads through the cemetery, I'll just *happen* across them on my way."

Abigail clapped her hands in delight. "Excellent idea. Thank you ever so much, Rebecca. You've lifted a great burdensome weight from my mind." Springing to her feet, she snatched up Cordelia's scarlet cloak from the wing-back chair near the fireplace. "Imagine that. Cordelia's forgotten her cape," she said, promptly draping it around Rebecca's shoulders. "No need to waste time collectin' yours. She won't mind if you borrow it. Now hurry along with you. That's a dear, sweet girl."

The moment Rebecca saw James Emory, standing in the cemetery alone, staring at the headstones of Edward and Beau Ransom, she wished she hadn't jumped the gun. Where was Cordelia?

"It's about time! Did you think I would allow

233

you to—" Emory snapped, freezing when he recognized Rebecca.

"Why, good afternoon, Captain. Fancy meeting you here," Rebecca said, an artificial smile pasted on her lips.

"Miss Warren. For a moment I thought you were ... Never mind. Exuse my manners," he said, recovering with the elasticity of Silly Putty, Rebecca thought. As if by rote, he immediately doffed his hat. "I hope I didn't startle you. I was just about to come down to the house and call upon you. To see how you've been feeling since the last time we met."

Now what? "You don't say?"

"Without a doubt," Emory responded.

"I'm flattered by your ... concern for my welfare."

The man was a pig! Not the least bit perturbed that he'd been caught trespassing on Ransom property. Of course, he probably didn't view it in that light.

"As you can see, I'm A–OK. As a matter of fact, I was just on my way to check up on one of my patients who's recovering from the measles, too." She wanted to ask him if he got his kicks from visiting private, family cemeteries, but she held her tongue.

"Really. And I thought the hamper of goodies you carried was for me." He reached for the wicker basket and Rebecca was instantly reminded of Little Red Riding Hood.

Their eyes clashed. "Not hardly," she said, reluctantly relinquishing the basket to his inspection.

"Borden's condensed milk. Fresh bread," he said. Plundering through the carefully packed items, Emory withdrew a cloth doll, dressed in red, white, and blue, which Jubadessa had sewn for Dinah.

"Sweet. And Union colors, too."

"Purely coincidental, I assure you," Rebecca said frostily.

Emory tucked the doll under his arm and carelessly broke off a sizable piece of bread. Rebecca silently fumed when he popped it into his mouth.

He chewed, swallowed, then broke off another bite. "Your woman is a good cook," he said between mouthfuls.

"She isn't *my* woman," Rebecca responded, thinking for two cents she'd gladly claw Emory's ice-blue eyes out and be done with it.

"That's right. The housekeeper is...was... Ransom's property. I stand corrected."

She could have argued Jubadessa was a freewoman before President Lincoln interceded, and highly respected by the Ransoms. But she decided not to waste her breath.

"That bread is for a small child, along with the doll. If you wouldn't mind putting them both back in the basket." She waited expectantly.

"Touchy today, aren't we?" he intoned sarcastically, breaking off a third piece of bread as if to remind Rebecca who held the power of occupation in their hands.

"A gentleman wouldn't find it necessary to eat

the entire loaf of bread just to prove a point," Rebecca parried in an even voice.

Emory jammed the items back beneath their terry towel, hooking the basket over her stiffly extended arm. Almost as an afterthought, he asked, "You don't like Yankees, do you, Miss Warren?"

Rebecca inhaled deeply, clutching her basket protectively against her hip. She'd never realized that being too handsome could make someone almost repulsive.

"Yankees don't bother me in the least. One of my best friends is from New York," Rebecca quipped, thinking of Janet, the head nurse in her MASH unit, for the first time in weeks. "But arrogant bastards? Well, now, that's another story all together."

He swallowed twice, and though a slight flush rose just above his collar line, the captain held his temper like a seasoned trooper. Rebecca would grant him that much. But no more.

"I have my buggy today." He pointed toward the shiny black, yellow-wheeled rig. "If you would allow me to drive you?" The invitation was too much like a command to suit Rebecca. Not knowing exactly where they'd wind up, she instinctively balked.

"No, thanks. I prefer to walk."

Rebecca was astonished when Emory grabbed her arm and yanked her against his body, nearly upsetting her basket. Too late, she realized she'd goaded him too far.

"Have a care. You *might* catch the measles

again," he said, his eyes mere slits as he gazed into her upturned face.

"You can't contract the measles twice," Rebecca responded, her jaw taut as she endeavored to tug her arm free.

He held her more tightly. "You intrigue me, Miss Warren. Cordelia said you spent a considerable time in Europe. Studied nursing in France."

The scenario was England and Florence Nightingale. Emory was attempting to trip her up.

Rebecca chose not to rise to the bait. Instead she countered, "Cordelia, Captain? I had no idea you and Miss Ransom were on such friendly terms."

"The lady has given me leave to call her by her first name."

The hidden shades of meaning were deadly.

"Aren't you afraid someone will see you here?" Rebecca asked, tilting her chin pugnaciously.

Emory regarded the plantation house as if the building itself were an adversary.

"No one of consequence."

His eyes swiveled back to her face. "Were you aware that you have kissable lips, Miss Warren? Practically irresistible, to my way of thinking," he said slowly, his cold eyes glinting with undisguised malice. His compliment was dredged in the granules of a threat. Rebecca almost recoiled, her gaze flying to the house, to Alexander's bedroom window.

The house was quiet. Too quiet. Almost as if its master was away from home. Had Alexander slipped out again without anyone seeing him this time? Undoubtedly, he had. Where to and for how long she wondered. On the tail end of that thought came another. Something was coming down! She could *feel* it. It zinged through every fiber of her being, setting her nerves on edge.

"When was the last time you were kissed, Becky?" Emory asked, breaking into Rebecca's chaotic thoughts. His smile was insincere, a travesty, reminiscent of a sneer. He leaned in close, as if he meant to back up his question with punitive action.

Rebecca's stomach fluttered as Alexander's precious countenance superimposed itself over Emory's. In stature, he was about the same size as Alexander. But that was where the similarities ended. Emory was so cocksure of himself that it made her sick. But this time he was out of his league. *She* was not Cordelia.

"Why did you call me Becky? I usually go by my full name."

"I must have heard someone use it before," Emory stated smoothly.

"Who? Cordelia perhaps?"

"Perhaps. Then again, perhaps not. It makes no never mind. Now, how about that kiss?"

Rebecca had an overpowering urge to punch his lights out as much for Cordelia as for herself. "I wouldn't try it if I were you, Captain," she warned, her eyes gleaming with sparkling blue fire. "*Becky* bites."

Straightening abruptly, Emory chuckled, a harsh, grating rasp that sent unpleasant shivers up Rebecca's spine. The man was dangerous.

"You are delightfully refreshing to say the least.

I had come to regard all Southern women as too delicate for words. Insipid flowers."

"I'd watch myself if I were you. Like the poinsettia, the most alluring plants can prove deathly poisonous."

"Is that so?"

How could Cordelia stand to be associated with such a jerk? "Don't fool yourself, Captain Emory. Mark my words. In the years to come, historians will prove these delicate women you so easily dismiss to be the backbone of the Confederacy."

"Can I take that to mean you support the C.S.A. over the Union?"

I'm a nurse. I don't take sides. "Take it any way you like."

"I had hopped we might be friends."

"Perhaps before I got your number."

He shot her an odd look. Dropping her arm, he adjusted his hat on his fair head. "Good day to you then, Miss Warren. It has been interesting. But I have more important fish to fry just now. Have a pleasant outing. And give my regards to *Miss* Cordelia."

She'd been summarily dismissed.

Rebecca seethed. The man knew she was on to him! She couldn't have stated it any more plainly. But he was crafty. He wasn't going to incriminate himself. It was almost as if he defied her to question him outright.

Rebecca decided her only recourse was to confront Cordelia instead. She would get to the bottom of this if it was the last thing she did.

* * *

From a distance, it appeared as if Emory had indeed kissed Rebecca. Standing in the shadows of the tree line where days earlier a Yankee picket had marched, Alexander trained his spyglass on Emory's back. His blood surged, threatening to boil in his veins. Rebecca, *his* Rebecca, *was* a Northern agent! Might even be the brains of the operation formulating in the area.

How could he have been so blind? He should have followed his original instinct. They knew so little about Rebecca. Her strange metal tags, even her tempting undergarments, could have been fashioned in the North. She hardly had a Southern accent. And all those peculiar words she used. Northern expressions—they had to be.

"Hell and damnation! How could I have been such an idiot?" he swore at himself. Major General Wheeler and he had discussed that Emory might have a female accomplice in his plot to sever the Confederate supply network that ran from sympathizers in Memphis clear to the Florida swampland. And Wheeler had agreed with Alexander that perhaps it was "his own obliging lady friend with the dapple-gray horse." How could he have forgotten so easily his own suspicions?

Emory must have grown anxious to risk meeting Rebecca so near the house, during daylight hours. Or perhaps, like him, he could no longer resist the temptation of her soft, pliant body, the lure of her generous lips. Bittersweet desire filled Alexander, while at the same time a sour bile rose in the back of his throat.

He wanted to howl his outrage, like a wounded

animal caught in a trap. The rage to dispose of Emory was overwhelming. He wished his spyglass a sword—no, a telescopic rifle to point at his enemy's head. He would call Emory's name, so that he could see his face when he killed him because he wasn't a back-shooter. Then he'd strike quickly with lethal precision.

His feelings for Rebecca were far less clear-cut. To watch her die would be to slice out his own heart. It was an odious proposition to contemplate, her death by hanging. The fate of a traitor.

But for now, his latest orders were simple, direct from President Jefferson Davis himself: No heroics.

Alexander had been charged to plant the frock coat and set the trap, then let the intrigue resolve itself while he cooled his heels. Whoever took the coat would implicate themselves. Emory and his cohort were to be eliminated in the C.S.A.'s own good time—beginning with Rebecca it seemed.

The mission was going along precisely as planned, and he was safe as long as the enemy thought he possessed the spring campaign documents, which they obviously did because he was still alive. Now all he had to do was to watch from afar and stay on his guard against further developments.

Alexander realized he must force himself to play along with Rebecca until he discovered what he and his compatriots were up against. It was his duty.

At great personal cost, Alexander determined to follow through with the mission assigned him.

Point; counterpoint.

The stairs leading to Cordelia's room seemed endless, largely because Rebecca wasn't looking forward to the forthcoming interrogation she'd planned. Balancing the modest meal tray on the palm of one hand, she tapped on Cordelia's bedroom door. She could hear someone stirring inside, but her knock was pointedly ignored.

"Cordelia. I know you're in there. Open the door. I want to talk to you a minute."

"Go away, Rebecca. I have a sick headache."

"I know. Jubadessa sent up a dose of salicylous acid for it, and I've brought you something to eat."

"I'm not hungry."

"I'm not leaving until you open up," Rebecca stated firmly.

"Really! Not a moment's peace in this house," Cordelia responded in exasperation through the door. "I told Jubadessa that I didn't want to be disturbed. You would think a servant would heed her mistress's requests. But, no, not here."

Rebecca could sense Cordelia leaning against the door.

"I saw Emory today," Rebecca said quietly.

The key twisted in the lock and Cordelia flung open the door, reaching for Rebecca's arm and pulling her inside. Once the door was secured, she asked in a hushed voice, "What did you say?"

The room was dark, filled with shadows cast by a single candle flickering in its cup. Rebecca placed the supper tray on the bureau before answering, "Captain Emory stopped me in the cemetery. I was on my way to do a recheck on Dinah's condition."

"How is Dinah doin'?" Cordelia asked woodenly.

"She's fine, thanks to your intervention. Clayton's decided to pack up and head for Memphis in the morning, hoping to find work there."

"That's nice." Cordelia slumped onto the bed, her head in her hands. "Did anyone else see James today?" she muttered through her splayed fingers.

"I think if they had, we'd know it," Rebecca said, thinking of Alexander.

"My mother has a long tongue," Cordelia said in resignation.

"I didn't say Abigail told me you were meeting the captain."

"You didn't have to."

"I know it's no excuse, but she's concerned about you, Cordelia. Who wouldn't be? I certainly am."

"I refused to meet him today, you know." There was an inner sadness evident in her voice.

"May I speak frankly?"

"Be my guest. You would anyway."

Rebecca smiled faintly. Cordelia knew her better than she'd thought.

"I don't mean to set myself up as judge and jury." Heaven knew, she was the last person qualified for something like that, Rebecca thought. "But you should have refused him period and you know it! Where is your brain? You're living in occupied territory. The man is your cousin's enemy. Your country is at war. More frightening still, what do you think would happen if Alexander stumbled onto this?"

243

Cordelia dropped her hands in her lap to stare Rebecca squarely in the face.

"Do you think I haven't gone over all that? If I had any say in the matter, do you actually believe I would willin'ly put Alexander's life in jeopardy?" she groaned. It was then Rebecca realized Cordelia had been crying heavily by the look of her ravaged face.

"Then what is this all about?"

"It's a coil...a never-endin' coil. That's what," she lamented, raking her finger through her blond tresses, sending her normally neat coiffure into rampant disarray.

"Calm down. Maybe if we talked this thing through—"

"Talk it through! You don't know what you're sayin'. The things I've discovered recently..." Cordelia threw herself face first across the bed, hugging a pillow to her breast. "...they're just too horrible to contemplate! And I can't trust anyone because Alexander's life is at stake. You and Jubadessa, my mother, you all think he's in his room, workin' diligently on his ledgers. Pooh! He's not! Go to the stable. To your horse's stall. You'll find her missin'."

"Cordelia, you're overwrought."

"I'm not. Alexander has gone to meet a Confederate courier. Only it's not a compatriot, as he believes, but a Union sympathizer with forged documents, a change in plans they say. And I'm the one who set him up. Oh, he'll return safely today. But it's only a matter of time. Tomorrow. Or the next day. Or perhaps the next, and it will

244

all be over. They're on to him. And I can't say or do anythin' to stop it! I tried, but James will brook no interference in his scheme."

"What are you saying?" Rebecca asked incredulously.

"That I've discovered that my dearest cousin, William Alexander Ransom, is the elusive Gray Ghost. An elite courier. Commissioned by the Confederacy to purchase black-market supplies via a *Union* quartermaster in Memphis. Famed for his darin'. A man who's been a thorn in the heel of the Union since the onset of the war," she finished with a flourish.

Rebecca gaped at Cordelia.

"Close your mouth, Rebecca. It's unseemly."

"Where did you hear such nonsense?"

"It's not nonsense. The other day, I slipped Alexander's frock coat from his room to repair the tear from his bullet wound as a surprise. Decent uniform cloth is so dear."

"Yes. I know. You've reminded me of it often enough."

"It was so heavy, you see, that I began to wonder what on earth the buttons were made from. So I uncovered one. It was filled with gold. And the hemline of his coat is sewn with dispatches and documents, written on blockade paper so thin that a full letter could be concealed in a hollowed pencil and stuck in the pocket in a pinch. Railroad schedules of mail trains carryin' Union gold shipments, maps, strategies." ·

Could what Cordelia said be true? Perhaps. She'd always thought the coat unusually heavy.

And the way Alexander refused to part with it had remained a curiosity.

"Why didn't the captain just raid the house and arrest Alexander?"

"Because he wants substantial evidence. Proof positive. Alexander has to be caught in the act. That's why he called off the picket. He realized as long as Oak Mont was watched, Alexander would never show his hand."

"What about his midnight ride several weeks ago?"

Cordelia covered her ears with her hands. "I don't know anythin' about that, and I don't want to! I know too much already."

Rebecca began to think aloud. "That's why the guard was posted. Emory knew Alexander was here all along."

"He only suspected," Cordelia insisted.

"And you confessed."

Cordelia dropped her hands to clutch up her skirts as she flung herself across the room in a dizzy dance of agitation. "I swear! I never did. But I might have. James is incredibly persuasive. If I had met him in the cemetery...alone...there's no tellin' what might have happened. That is why I did not," she confessed in a small voice.

"Good for you!"

"Don't be so quick with your praise, Becky. There's more. From all accounts, Alexander leaves to resume his duties within the week, and I don't know how to stop either of them. James is bound and determined to capture Alexander. He insists that for such a shrewd piece of handiwork, the war department in Washington will present him a general's stars. You see, James covets that position above all else. Even above the health of his unborn child."

"Unborn child! Cordelia?"

Tears gushing, Cordelia sobbed, "It's not as bad as you think."

"Explain!"

"I met James Emory at a soiree while visitin' my father's family up North several summers before talk of seccession began. He was the most dashin', debonair young swain I'd ever known. I'm two years older than he so I made up my mind to put him off. But he wouldn't take no for an answer. The man swept me off my feet."

"Miracles never cease."

"You don't like him, do you?"

About as much as rattlesnakes. She wondered how much *Cordelia* would like him if she knew that Emory had made advances toward Rebecca. "That's neither here nor there. Go on."

"James and I kept up a steady correspondence, even after I returned home to Nashville. Finally, six weeks before the first shots were fired at Fort Sumter, I consented to become his legally wedded wife . . . on paper. When he was stationed here after the war started, he asked me to honor the engagement. What else could I do? We were married quietly within the week," she said in a small voice.

"And you've been spying for him ever since," Rebecca prompted. It was all so clear. How had she failed to see it before now?

"Feedin' him harmless tidbits of information . . .

common knowledge after the battles, chitchat from the sewin' circle. Nothin' that would disrupt the supply lines, but enough to keep him happy." Cordelia sniffed, bowing her head and plucking an invisible speck of lint from the sleeve of her gown. "At least, I thought they were harmless, until I supplied him with information concernin' Mister Slidell."

"Slidell?"

"You remember. Alexander told us about him on the way home to Oak Mont. In the barn. Slidell's scheme was to underwrite the sale of Confederate bonds in Europe."

"I seem to remember something." *But I was too concerned with Alexander's condition at the time to really listen.*

"James was able to use the information to the Federals' advantage. And that only served to wet his appetite for more. No one but you knows the truth, Becky."

Rebecca collapsed on the foot of the flounced-canopy bed. "Let me get this straight. You're moonlighting as a spy for your husband, against your cousin, who is a gold courier for the South known as The Gray Ghost," Rebecca recapped, counting off the facts one by one on her fingers. "Now, your husband has concocted a plan to capture Alexander and cripple the supply lines."

"It's simple really. If a horse is lost in battle, the government is supposed to replace it. But mounts are runnin' short and many a veteran cavalryman is lost to the foot soldiers if a replacement can't be procured."

"And the South's strength is in its superior cavalry." Where had she read that?

"Exactly. Certain people in Memphis have been sellin' Kentucky horseflesh South. Good, strong mounts, Morgans mostly. Alexander has been directed to transfer the gold in his possession to a dealer in Memphis. When the money changes hands, James will have him, because only The Gray Ghost would know to request horses."

"Because the directive came from a Union agent incognito, planted by Captain Emory himself."

Cordelia sighed. "I feel like someone lost in a fog. Which way do I turn? Do I betray my husband to a cousin who has been like a brother to me, or Alexander to James? I love them both. Tell me. How can I make such a hateful decision and live with myself afterwards, Becky? You must help me devise a way to assure Alexander's safety without bringin' James's down," she pleaded.

Her mind racing, Rebecca pondered the particularly volatile situation. No matter Cordelia's choice, the repercussions would rip the Ransom family apart. Jubadessa, doing her best to mother the lot, would be crushed. Abigail might well go off the deep end. Alexander—who knew? There had to be a sensible way around this. *Think, Rebecca! Use some modern common horse sense here. Where there's a will, there's a way.*

Rebecca stood as if an incredible weight perched on her shoulders. Her hands behind her back, she paced the floor beside Cordelia's bed, her boots scuffing on the richly colored Aubusson carpet.

It seemed the only way to exonerate Alexander

was for him *not* to accept the horses from the supplier in Memphis, thereby blowing James Emory's plans sky high, she reasoned. But, of course, to stop him from delivering the gold payment would be to brand Cordelia an informant. Still, there were ways to turn things so topsy-turvy, twist them so intricately, that no one could be accused of anything. At least, not anything as serious as espionage, Rebecca decided.

Rebecca halted, straightened, dragging a dazed Cordelia to her feet. Her sapphire eyes shining brightly, she said, "If we play our cards right, perhaps it won't come down to a choice, hateful or otherwise. But I'll need your help, Cordelia. Preferably before Alexander returns home to stop me."

Perhaps this was the reason she had been sent into the past, to care for Alexander, save his life more than once . . . to protect those he loved from themselves, Rebecca mused. It made as much sense as anything else she'd come up with.

Chapter Ten

By daybreak, the wind had picked up, rattling the brittle brown cornstalks like Halloween skeletons arrayed in the fields. Only it wasn't October. It was January thirtieth, the Vietnamese New Year in country. The MASH unit would be breaking open extra cans of Army C-rations in mock salute to the holiday, playing the Supremes over and over and over on the jukebox in the canteen. Praying there were no new W.I.A's to disrupt the uneasy ceasefire.

Her year's service would be drawing to a final close. If she were there to sign her discharge papers.

Here, on the thirteenth of the month, Major General Joe Wheeler had struck at Harpeth Shoals, between Nashville and Clarksville. A red-letter day, he had captured or sunk four Yankee packets and a heavily armed gunboat, effectively suspending the flow of supplies up the Cumberland River to the Union soldiers.

The blow had been a shot in the arm for the Army of Tennessee. But for every action, there was a reaction. Now, the Yankees were plotting revenge. The capture of the Confederate States most renowned supply officer—Alexander Ransom. Code name—The Gray Ghost.

"What you thinkin', miss?" Clayton asked, drawing Rebecca's attention back to the situation at hand.

Dinah, saturated with every children's story Rebecca had ever known, slept in her arms. She hugged the child close, cushioning her birdlike body as the wagon bumped along the rutted road.

"Oh, I don't know. Lots of things. How the land has changed from the bluegrass meadows and hills of Nashville to bottomland and hardwood forests. How pretty the sky is at sunrise . . . forty shades of rose. How warm the weather for January." *How, in my time, we would be zipping along at fifty-five miles an hour, cruising on air shocks and asphalt-hugging radials. How Memphis would be a mere four interstate hours away from Nashville. How I'd be taking it all for granted.*

"Yes, 'um. We're really lucky, far as de weather's concerned."

"When will we reach Memphis."

"Makin' close to railroad time. Railroad time since de war, dat is. Reckon we'll be eatin' our breakfast at de city limits."

"That soon."

"Yes, 'um." Clayton turned intelligent brown eyes in her direction. "But I still don't understand why, Miss Rebecca."

Play dumb. "Why what?"

"Why you left a nice, cozy place like de plantation to travel to Memphis with me and Dinah? What have de plains got dat de heartland doesn't?"

"I told you. I was worried about Dinah traveling so far after her recent illness. Besides, I needed to purchase some things." At a tavern right off the turnpike on the outskirts of Memphis from a man with a full beard and a puckered scar above his left eye. She had Cordelia to thank for the specifics. "And since you were going to the city anyway, well, I thought we could kill two birds with one stone—your knowing the way and my having the wagon."

"Dat don't ring true. Nashville's closer to Oak Mont dan Memphis."

"Let it rest, Clayton. You don't want to know what I'm up to," Rebecca stated bluntly, putting all pretense aside. "Besides, in the long run, you're safer with me as a traveling companion. That soldier at the road block we passed through just before dawn was a bully."

"White trash to speak to a lady dat way."

"It wasn't anything I haven't heard before. I'm sorry he thought you were ...um ...my slave."

"Man was behind de times. When I asked, hadn't he heard of Mr. Lincoln's emancipation proclamation he turned four shades of red." Clayton laughed, squaring his big shoulders. "Felt real good to do dat."

"Yeah, well, I wish you'd keep a low profile. If you hadn't been carrying the freedom papers that Lieutenant Colonel Ransom's father gave you, I think they'd have trumped up some charges to arrest you. Just for the heck of it. And you've got Dinah to think about. You're all that stands between her and harsh reality."

Clayton cleared his throat, glancing at his daughter. "You're all wool and a yard wide, Miss Rebecca. I'll keep your advice in mind." Clicking his tongue to the hack, he said, "Still don't care to see you goin' back to Oak Mont alone, though. You've been kind to me and Dinah. Don't like to think of anythin' happenin' to you," he said gruffly.

"I appreciate that, Clayton, but we've been over this fence before. I'll be fine." Rebecca glanced at her bedroll.

With Cordelia's help, she'd commandeered everything she needed from Alexander's room. His compass and frock coat. Cordelia had loaned her the horse and wagon with her blessing and a hearty "Godspeed."

Rebecca couldn't help but feel uncomfortable for slipping away from the plantation like a thief in the night. But it couldn't be helped. Alexander would just have to hold Vedette as collateral until she returned. Besides, he'd started the trend of borrowing the horse without asking first, so he had no one to blame but himself.

"After you set us down, you think you can find your way back home on your own?"

Rebecca smiled, pointing over her shoulder in the direction they'd just come. "It's a straight shot. Nashville turnpike all the way. Dirt road. Bumpy as hel . . . lo," Rebecca said, quickly reconstructing the epithet she knew was considered unworthy of a lady. "I could do it with my eyes closed."

Clayton frowned. "How 'bout dis ornery horse? You got to hold the reins just right so de old cuss don't grab the bit in its teeth. Tear up your hands."

"I've got a pair of gloves in my satchel."

"What would Jubadessa have to say if she knew I let you go it alone?"

"She'd take both our heads off with a dull knife. But she doesn't know anything about this and won't find out if I have any sayso in the matter. She thinks I'm helping out at a local Army hospital for a few days. Now how much longer before we reach Memphis." She had an appointment, a very *important* appointment. She didn't dare be late.

"Like I said. 'Magine we'll be eatin' our breakfast at the city line."

Rebecca's eyes grew round. "Clayton. You won't believe this. I brought a canteen of water, but I forget to pack any food!"

"Yes, 'um. I noticed. Thought crossed my mind dat angels don't need to eat. Den I said to myself, nah, Clayton. Miss Rebecca's just got a heap on her mind. So I took care of it myself," he said with a grin, reaching beneath the wagon seat to extract a bulky pillowcase. He handed it to Rebecca.

"Wake dat child up and fix us all a piece of cornbread and cheese, Miss Rebecca. I smell de city up ahead."

* * *

The tavern was a rather crude affair with log cabin walls and a disreputable dirt floor. Two long tables with benches were stretched perpendicular to the open hearth where an iron kettle bubbled on a chain trammel over the flames.

Rebecca had no difficulty locating her contact, a man with a puckered scar dissecting one cheek. Wearing a blue uniform with food-stained lapels, the Yankee, the proprietor, and a young barmaid were the only people in the establishment.

Rebecca automatically swept up the hem of her cashmere traveling dress so that it wouldn't brush the floor as she stepped into the windowless, shoe-box-sized room.

"Excuse me," she said to her audience in general, "I'm looking for a horse trader, a Federal quartermaster by the name of Crumbum." Her voice was strong, authoritative, her words direct and to the point. Three pairs of eyes, three surprised gazes, impaled her. Obviously, she wasn't quite what they'd expected in a Confederate courier.

Good! Rebecca thought to herself.

Puffy-eyed and into his cups, the slovenly soldier said, "I might know where Crumbum can be found." His voice hardened as he patted the bench beside him. "I give you leave to take a seat, but first, what's the watchword, girlie? You never can be too careful."

For a moment, Rebecca was nonplused. Cordelia hadn't mentioned a password. And she had the strangest sensation that if she didn't dig one up

quickly, she might wind up in a back alley somewhere with her throat cut.

"*Gold*, Mister Crumbum. The watchword is
gold. And I prefer to stand," Rebecca stated
evenly, staring him in the eye without flinching,
though her stomach suddenly felt queasy.

The man actually laughed, winking at her as if
they were the best of friends, friends with a long
and sordid association.

"That is it, girlie! That's the word. For sure and
certain—gold," he said, taking a huge swig of ale
from the pint on the table, wiping his mouth with
his sleeve. "If you won't sit, can I offer you a
drink?" he continued. "On me, of course."

The proprietor and barmaid visibly relaxed,
going back to whatever they'd been doing before
Rebecca's arrival. Rebecca stepped deeper into the
smoky room.

Disgusted that a soldier could lose sight of his
honor in such a disgraceful fashion, Rebecca replied, "I never drink on duty." Too late, she realized her rebuke was less than subtle as the
quartermaster responded in kind.

"Stiff as a starched collar, aren't you?"

Rebecca frowned. "I didn't come here to trade
insults, Crumbum. I can walk out as easily as I
walked in. So either we get down to business right
now, or it's *adios*. Get my drift?" Rebecca shot the
quartermaster a look that said she'd do it, too.
Leave him high and dry without lining his pockets
as he'd expected.

Crumbum's eyes narrowed, reminding Rebecca
even more of golf balls than they had before. "Well,

now, they do say business before pleasure, so I suppose business it 'tis. What have you got for me, girlie?" he asked. The greedy twinkle in his blood-shot eye made Rebecca want to cut *his* throat—almost.

"Before I show you the merchandise, I need to clarify something. There's been a slight change in plans. I don't want the horses," Rebecca began, dropping her bomb with as much courage as she could muster, which for her was a considerable amount.

"What the hell!" the quartermaster bellowed, knocking over the bench as he jerked to his feet. The scar on his cheek flamed red in direct corre-lation with the engorged vein standing out on his temple. "Do you know how much trouble I went to just to see those Morgans out of Kentucky? Not to mention getting them to a farm on the outskirts of Memphis without every Tom, Dick, and Harry stopping me along the way? The governmental pa-perwork *alone* is worth any gold a mere slip like you could carry on her person!"

The proprietor and barmaid dropped any pre-tense of work and scurried off to the kitchen. Like frightened monkeys, they peered through the door-way toward the common area, afraid to miss any excitement. Afraid, too, to become personally in-volved, Rebecca supposed. Hear no evil, see no evil, speak no evil. But then, she couldn't blame them. Crumbum was an intimidating character.

Rebecca stubbornly stood her ground, thinking the middle-aged Crumbum a prime candidate for a heart attack if he didn't learn to control his temper. "I can imagine the trouble you went to," she said. "But the fact remains that I'm ill-equipped to see a herd of horses farther south alone. I'm not saying they won't be purchased later on. Just that they won't be purchased by me."

"So what the hell are you doing here, girlie? It's sure not for your health!"

The quartermaster was threatening her and Rebecca knew it. Stuffing her hand into the pocket of her cape, she fingered her Army-issue switchblade. She didn't intend to go down without a fight, to at least match his existing scar with a mark of her own if it came down to it.

"I'm still willing to part with the gold, but for medicine, Mister Crumbum. Morphine to be exact. Can you handle that?"

"Morphine, you say?" the quartermaster sputtered, his anger rapidly diminishing. "If that ain't a lark! I just received a shipment yesterday from our storehouse in Washington."

Rebecca could smell his fetid breath from where she stood. She stepped back a pace. "So we have a deal? Medicine instead of horses?"

"When will they come for the livestock?"

"I'm not sure...soon. They need fresh mounts as much as medicine," Rebecca assured the quartermaster.

"More so, to my way of thinking," Crumbum said sarcastically.

"Opinions are like..." Rebecca stopped herself just in the nick of time. She didn't intend to lower herself to Crumbum's level. "We all have our own opinion. Now back to the question of morphine."

"I'll have to go get it from the supply department."

"How long will that take?" How long did she have to wait in this creepy place for Prince Charming himself to return before she could be on her way? Rebecca silently wondered.

"An hour, no more."

"Then I guess you'd better get going. I don't have all day," Rebecca said.

"Me neither. But then I ain't the one who changed the plans," Crumbum grumbled, weaving his way to the front door. "Wait here, girlie—you *and* the gold." Then, "Give her something to eat and put it on my tab," he flung over his shoulder as he wrenched open the door.

"I can pay my own way, thank you very much," Rebecca responded, the tension draining from her limbs. *The Yankee is going to cooperate. Hallelujah!*

"Suit yourself," he growled, slamming the door shut behind him with a resounding thud.

More for something to do than anything else, Rebecca purchased a luncheon of boiled rice and toast for twenty-five cents out of the "pocket change" Cordelia had given her, and sat down to wait. Her back to the wall, she kept expecting a troop of Yankee soldiers to come scrambling out of the woodwork at any moment. But none materialized.

It wasn't long before the quartermaster returned with a gun-metal mesh bag of packaged morphine powder. Rebecca was amazed at the small quantity he offered for the price. Medicine, it seemed, was far dearer than horseflesh.

"Surely, you don't think I'm going to let you take advantage of me like that," Rebecca quipped, displaying an aura of confidence she didn't quite feel. "Either you're going to have to come across with more medicine than that, or we're going to have to renegotiate the price." Rebecca extracted the frock coat from her bag and spread it out on the table for him to examine. "You can have the collar and cuff buttons in exchange for the medicine, but that's all I'm prepared to offer."

The quartermaster looked as if he might strangle her, though his shaking fists were clenched firmly at his sides. "*Now* I know why those cunning Rebels sent a woman to deal with me. Knew she'd rattle me so, I'd practically give away my product to be rid of her!"

Rebecca decided Crumbum was sobering up, realized by his shaking fists that the d.t.'s were setting in with amazing speed. "Have another drink, Crumbum. To calm your nerves. Before you know it, we'll be done with this and I'll be on my way," she said as casually as possible.

"And none too soon!"

Rebecca mentally reiterated Crumbum's remark. "Have we got a deal?"

"I'll have the top two lapel buttons as well," Crumbum said petulantly.

"One and that's my final offer," Rebecca said, meaning it. She'd already accomplished what she'd set out to do—put a kink in Emory's plan to arrest Alexander. The medicine was an extra bonus—like buy one, get one free at the supermarket.

"You drive a hard bargain, girlie," Crumbum

snarled, yelling for the barmaid to bring him a mug of ale.

Rebecca smiled as the young woman scooted the mug of ale in front of the quartermaster and scurried back to the kitchen. "You aren't the first person to notice that, Mister Crumbum. Bargains are my specialty." Her mother had always said she was a real wheeler-dealer, had sent her to the antique auctions on more than one occasion because Rebecca always managed to come home with more for less.

Crumbum glared at her. "One it is then, but don't look to be in my good graces should you come this way again. 'Cause you won't be. If I wasn't hurting for the money, I'd send you packing quick as you could count one, two, three!"

And when the man would have ruined Alexander's frock coat by greedily attacking the covered buttons, Rebecca jerked it from his grasp, carefully removing them herself with her switchblade.

"Wait one red-hot second now." He put his hand on hers to stay her. "Where's the letters?" Crumbum asked when Rebecca finally rose to end their meeting. "There's supposed to be spring campaign dispatches, too, girlie. Maps. Strategies. Targets. Worth a pretty penny to me."

"Spring campaign documents?" Rebecca asked in a startled whisper, snatching her hand away. She didn't have them with her for they were hidden under her mattress in her room at Oak Mont. But Crumbum didn't have to know that. He also need not know that the papers she'd seen had nothing to do with the Confederacy's spring campaign maneuvers. Not even remotely.

Math had never been her strong suit, but Rebecca could add two and two. It took her only a moment to acknowledge she'd been set up. Not by Cordelia, but by Alexander. The force of his duplicity almost floored her.

Now she knew why the precious frock coat, a coat he'd never allowed out of his sight, had been left so easily accessible while he was away. Her taking the coat with its gold and the papers sewn into it and delivering them to the quartermaster branded her a spy. She'd been caught in a cruel game of intrigue, where every move made might be someone's last. Where everyone was suspect.

Alexander had outsmarted them all—Emory, Cordelia, even himself. Because she wasn't the spy. The pain that he should think she was became almost unbearable; it swelled her throat, making it a struggle to swallow around her suddenly thick tongue. *But you aren't guilty,* her heart cried. *He should know that.* But he didn't, and that hurt more than anything else.

Then anger rallied Rebecca's spirit. Alexander Ransom had put himself to an awful lot of trouble for nothing, and she couldn't wait to tell him to his face when she saw him again. At least she could prove she never gave the documents to the union soldier. On the tail end of her anger came another thought, however. If she told him everything she wanted to, she'd have to explain about Cordelia's entanglement with James Emory, her betrayal. And causing Alexander emotional grief was the last thing on earth she wanted to be responsible for. She cared too much for him.

Well, she'd just have to cross that bridge when she came to it. For now, she had Crumbum to deal with.

Drawing herself to her full five-foot-seven-inch height, Rebecca bluffed her way through, responding, "I don't do letters. I'm a nurse, not a postal carrier." Her fingers crossed behind her back, she waited for his response, counting heavily on his avarice.

"Well, now, I don't know about this. There are people waiting."

The moment of truth. "Tell them they were mistaken. That there wasn't any paperwork. No exchange for horses. That you don't know how it happened, but the courier obviously wasn't the man they sought."

The man's dull eyes narrowed. "You're interfering where you don't belong, I think. What's to stop me from doing you in and being done with it?"

Rebecca clutched her switchblade so tightly her knuckles turned white. "That's an awful lot of gold sitting in front of you. You do me in, and my . . . backers . . . will find out. You'll prove to them you can't be trusted. There won't be any money coming your way after that."

He licked his thick lips. "There's something to what you're saying."

The man might give her the heebie-jeebies, but he wasn't stupid. Rebecca pushed her advantage home. "Forget the horses. This is strictly a drug deal. Gold for medicine this time. Take it or leave it."

The quartermaster decided rather quickly a bird in the hand was worth two in the bush.

"Be on your way, girlie," he growled, jabbing his finger toward the door. "Cursed so-and-sos, sending a woman to do a man's job in the first place. The Confederacy's getting too smart for their own britches, I say! Going to turn on them one of these days," he muttered from behind the mug he'd raised to his lips.

Relieved, Rebecca recovered the precious frock coat, wrapping the morphine in it and stashing them both in her satchel. Backing to the door, she left the disgruntled quartermaster weighing his loot.

Under the circumstances, the entire exchange went as smooth as glass—as smooth as cut glass that is. And though her stomach was still tied in knots, Rebecca was rather proud of herself for pulling the whole thing off.

In no time at all, she was on the road again with medical supplies in lieu of horses. She was doing peachy-keen, until she was forced to cross swords with the bully at the road block once again.

While Rebecca attempted to reason with the young soldier, Alexander observed the argument from the cover of an overgrown thicket. He reminded himself that he was trailing a Union partisan, that he'd been royally duped, and that his precious frock coat had been stolen by Rebecca Warren—the enemy—just as he'd planned when he'd left it for her. That she was nothing more than a lightskirt and a traitor, and that she deserved whatever she got. That his job was to *watch* her movements. Not rescue her.

His brain demanded cooperation. His heart obliged . . . up to a point. Until the soldier caught the horse's bridle harness and demanded she climb down from the wagon. When she refused, he jerked the reins from her hands, and tied them across the horse's neck. Stomping back to the driver's seat, he placed his hands around Rebecca's trim waist and bodily removed her from her perch. For the first time since Alexander'd met her, she seemed suddenly delicate. Even fragile. Impossible to replace.

Alexander had entertained relationships since his fiancée's death. But they'd been of the informal persuasion. There was nothing casual in his relationship with Rebecca, however. She compelled him to do things, say things, *experience* things he'd never have thought possible a mere month before, as she was doing now without even trying.

He was angry at himself for being powerless against her unique charm, angry that she clouded his mind, that he couldn't trust her farther than he could throw her. Angrier still that no matter what havoc she wreaked, he continued to care for her.

Alexander fought himself, his attraction to Rebecca, his need to protect her—and lost.

Gray on gray, like a shadow against the sun, Vedette and Alexander cleared the thicket's hedge as one. The huge, dapple-gray mare's hooves beat a startling tattoo on the clay road as he wheeled her toward the road block.

Sliding his carbine from its saddle boot, he reined Vedette to a stop, aiming the muzzle at the blue-clad soldier's chest.

"I'd think twice before I put my hands on a lady again. You never know which ones will have a champion waiting in the wings," he cautioned sharply. Alexander found hiding behind sarcasm easier than dealing with his feelings, and so his voice held the cold-blooded ring of steel against steel.

The soldier threw up his hands and stepped away. His face paled to stark white. So did Rebecca's.

Alexander's double-breasted, caped greatcoat was flung back over one shoulder to expose his brass-buckled C.S.A. waist and shoulder belt, banded by a wide yellow sash beneath which bulged his Colt revolver. Swinging from a black leather sling at his hip was a curved saber, the signature of a cavalry officer. With his gray plush hat tugged down low over his glittering hazel eyes, and his knee-length boots sporting sharp-toothed riding spurs, he seemed more darkling than an avenging angel.

Practically swallowing his chaw of tobacco, the soldier recovered himself enough to spit. A thin strip of tobacco juice landed near the back wheel of the wagon.

"I'll be d—danged! Will you look at that! I swear on my mother's grave, we thought y—you were dead and buried."

"Being dead has its advantages."

The man went rigidly to attention. "Yes, sir. I suppose it does when you're workin' your way back and forth through enemy territory."

"I had no idea the regiment was within the immediate area," Alexander remarked speculatively.

The soldier cleared his throat. "It's not. They're winterin' deeper south, in Tullahoma."

"By God, man!" Alexander thundered. "Do you not know the penalty for desertion?"

"Beg pardon, sir. But I'm not a deserter. Rubin Atley lost his legs a while back. At Murfreesboro. I've permission, direct from Bragg himself, to see Rubin home."

The man hurriedly fished a crumpled note from his hip pocket and handed it to Alexander.

Alexander scanned the missive critically, then folded it neatly and returned it to the sergeant.

"Where are your horses?"

"Spooked durin' the night. Broke their tether line. Bobcat or somethin'. Rubin's about a quarter mile back in the woods. In a cold camp. Waitin'. I . . ." He swallowed several times. "That's how come I set up the road block."

Alexander raised a brow in question.

"You see, I let this woman pass once this mornin', but it's been poor pickin's on the pike since. Had second thoughts about lettin' her off the hook this time 'round. If I may say so, Lieutenant Colonel Ransom, I sure could use her farm wagon."

"You planned to leave the woman alone on the road?"

"No, sir! I would have seen her to the city limits before we hightailed it."

"Risky business, impersonating a Yankee, Sergeant," Alexander said, eyeing the blue uniform.

"Yes, sir. But Rubin's always been a good friend to me. From my home town. Saved my skin once or twice. I owe him. Besides, the blue-belly I took this off of didn't need it anymore."

With a sheepish smile, he turned to show the gaping hole in the back of the coat.

"Better keep your face to the opposition. They might guess you're up to something." Alexander holstered his rifle. "The wagon's yours, but I expect to hear you've returned to the unit come week's end."

"Yes, sir. Thank you, sir." The soldier saluted.

"Now, if you'll excuse us. The lady and I have some pressing business matters to discuss. I appreciate your detaining her for me, but I'll take her off your hands now, Sergeant." Alexander turned to Rebecca, extending his hand.

"Would you do me the honor, ma'am?" he drawled.

Rebecca dropped her gaze from Alexander's face. She didn't want him to see her pain. In doing so, they would be sharing something, and at the moment, she didn't want to share the briefest portion of her inner soul with him. Not until she'd recovered from the shock of seeing him materialize right before her eyes. When she needed to lean on him the most, and couldn't allow herself to.

Finally, Rebecca found her voice, coaxing her eyes to meet Alexander's head on. "I'm not a *com-*

plete fool, Lieutenant Colonel Ransom. You've
been trailing me! That's where you went the night
I saw you leaving Oak Mont through the garden.
Not to rejoin your unit as I thought, but to plot
this thing out with your cohorts. This was a set
up from the word go and you know it, but you've
got me pegged wrong."

"Have I now?" Alexander asked dryly. Their
gazes clashed, his entrapping hers.

"Yes. I'm not who you think I am. I didn't take
the coat for myself or for the Yankees either. And
those phony documents are still at Oak Mont. I'm
not guilty," Rebecca stated, tensely awaiting his
response.

"You took the coat with or without the papers.
But it's not for me to judge. You've gone far beyond
that," Alexander said with solemn assurance.

"You don't believe me!" Rebecca gasped indignantly. "After all we ..." She fumbled for words
that would not come. "I honestly can't *believe* that
you think I would do such a thing," she finally
sputtered, lightning in her sapphire eyes and thunder in her soul.

Alexander scowled, his eyes the color of tem-
pered steel. "You may come peaceably, Miss Warren, or tied over the mare's rump like a sack of
potatoes. It makes no never mind to me. But come
you will. You've no option whatsoever."

The storm raging within her dissipated. If she'd
ever wondered what it felt like to be arrested, now
she knew. Deflated by Alexander's cold anger, Rebecca collected her bedroll, shouldered her medical satchel, and allowed him to lift her in front

of him. His touch sent her senses reeling, scattered her thoughts, made her knees weak, and her mouth go dry. It wasn't fair! she thought, the things Alexander did to her when he was so obviously cool, calm, and collected.

With a nudge to the ribs and a shifting of the reins, Alexander sent Vedette into a canter. Rebecca hooked four fingers beneath the saddle pommel.

When they reached the thicket, he growled, "Might want to hold on a little tighter. Wouldn't want you to break your pretty neck."

"Where are we going?" she finally managed to whisper past the growing lump in her throat.

"Hell most probably," he replied in a scathing tone.

Her heart lurched. Rebecca clung to the pommel for dear life, wrapping her free hand in the mare's black mane as they thundered over the thorny hedge and merged into the cool clutches of the shadowy forest.

Chapter Eleven

Dusk was falling, and a full moon rose in the twilight by the time Alexander reined the mare back onto anything remotely resembling a road. It wasn't long before Rebecca spied a small frame structure looming ahead in the curve of the narrow lane.

"We'll stop there for the night. No need to push Vedette beyond her limits," Alexander informed her curtly. Distant, impersonal, they were his first words all evening.

Rebecca could have cried with relief. Propped on blocks off the ground, the building might have been a palace for the rush of delight she experienced. Not only was she happy for poor Vedette, who was bearing double weight, but for herself as well. Because her rear was as sore as a boil, rest was a stone's throw away, and Alexander had finally broken the ice.

Alexander dismounted, leading Vedette into a lean-to attached to the side of the building. He tethered the mare, then as if by reflex, raised his arms to assist Rebecca's descent. She hesitated, feeling an urgent need to somehow clear the air, to redeem herself.

"I hate that I cost you the use of the wagon," she began.

Alexander laughed shortly. "You've cost me a lot more than the wagon."

What could she say to that?

Rebecca lowered her eyes in chagrin. Her arms wrapped around her bedroll, she slid from the mare's withers. Simultanesouly, Vedette shifted her weight from one side to the other, unbalancing Rebecca, sending her headlong into Alexander's embrace, hard against his chest. There was a soft "umph" as he wrapped his arms around her to break her fall.

She could feel the swell of him against her hips, watched desire darken his hazel eyes as a familiar ache seeped through her body, her heart, and mind. How was it possible to feel such safety in the arms of one's jailor? Rebecca wondered.

Alexander inhaled deeply, closing his eyes as if their contact was physically painful to him. He quickly thrust her from him, even before she was ready to be released.

Turning to rummage in his saddlebags, he dug out a lard candle and flint. Shoving them at her, he said, "Go on inside. I'll be in after I bed down the mare."

Rebecca took the candle, nodded numbly, feeling curiously bereft without his arms about her.

"And don't attempt to escape. There's only one way in and one out. You wouldn't get twenty feet."

Rebecca knew his stiff words were meant to form a boundary, to draw a line between them and they worked.

"Where would I go?" She was a time traveler. The only home she knew was Oak Mont, the only family the Ransoms. "You've got me so turned around, I don't know which end is up," she remarked defensively.

"A compass could remedy that." The steely evenness was back in his voice.

By Rebecca's interpretation, Alexander appeared to be calling her a thief.

"I only borrowed it, just as you did Vedette," she alleged. Her throat tightened as she wiggled her fingers into the center of her bedroll and extracted his compass. She pushed it into the palm of his hand. It had been a sickening day of suspense, one that wouldn't end with the darkness, Rebecca suspected.

"There," she said swiftly, holding her eyes level with his. "Now you don't have to worry about a prison break. Geography never was my bag. North, south, east, or west. It's all the same to me. *Especially* without a compass."

Dropping the compass in his breast pocket, Alexander once again turned toward Vedette. His back to Rebecca, he threw the iron stirrup across the seat and uncinched his saddle girth.

"You should have thought about the consequences before you decided to stick your oar in
another man's boat," he advised without turning
around.

*I was thinking of the consequences. Otherwise, I
wouldn't have done it.* "That's rich. Elegantly
stated. But you're the last person I'd expect to
convict me without benefit of a trial," she quipped,
though tears threatened. Tears of pleasure; tears
of pain. Liquid feelings. Alexander did that to her.

"I'm responsible for seeing you apprehended
and brought to justice. The Confederate government will do the rest."

"What exactly does that mean?" She was beginning to feel the slightest tinge of apprehension.

"Libby and Son's Warehouse at Richmond. If
you're lucky."

"*Libby Prison*? Why, that place was a . . . is a
pesthouse. You've got to be joking!"

"Dammit, Rebecca!" Alexander exploded,
wheeling to face her once again. "Why would I do
that? Don't you realize what you've done! Treason
carries as high a price as desertion. I would throt-
tle you myself if it would help, but it won't. It's
out of my hands. Only word from President Jefferson Davis can save you now."

That's what you get for trying to help someone,
she thought bitterly.

"Well then, call . . . write . . . no . . . wire Jeff
Davis. Tell him a nurse went completely bonkers
and absconded with your gold to buy medicine
while you had your head turned." Rebecca reached

into her satchel and tossed the bluish-black mesh sack of morphine powders at his feet. "Explain she's given over the loot to the proper authorities for distribution south. And the papers are tucked under my mattress at Oak Mont, useless ones as I said, but safe all the same." *That should clear me, because, for all intents and purposes, I don't exist anyway—at least, not on any of their records,* Rebecca thought.

"What about the coat?" Alexander asked evenly.

Rebecca stared down at her leather satchel. A gray sleeve trimmed in yellow braid fell over the lip, like a body trying to crawl out of a sack. A witness to a crime.

Yanking the frock coat out, she tossed it at Alexander. "There! Are you satisfied?" she asked in a huff.

Alexander examined the coat. His next two questions almost blew Rebecca's mind.

"Were you planning to keep these for yourself?" he demanded, holding the coat by one button.

Rebecca laughed, but her tone of voice held no mirth. "No. I just drive a hell of a hard bargain."

"Now is not the time to be flippant with me, Rebecca. Why did you take the coat, and leave behind the papers that were inside the lining?"

"Is this an inquest or something? If so, I'd like to have my lawyer present."

"Just answer my question, Rebecca. Make it easier on the both of us."

"A–OK, Lieutenant Colonel. I took the coat without the papers because I'm not a spy. Or would you prefer I make up something more suitable to the picture of me you've drawn for yourself."

"I can see you're not in a cooperative mood, Rebecca."

"Under the circumstances, I can't think of a single soul I know who would be. This is serious stuff you're trying to lay on me. If you'd just wire Richmond, they'd tell you—"

"I've already done that," Alexander interrupted. "But until they've had time to investigate you, until I receive word one way or the other, you're still a prisoner of war," he said, stowing away the medicine and the coat in his saddle bag.

"A POW? Now I've heard everything!" Rebecca said, though she couldn't help admiring him for doing what he felt was right.

Batting back her emotions behind thick, auburn lashes, Rebecca twirled smartly. "If you'll excuse me, I've had enough of this for the time being. It's been a terribly long day and I'd like to freshen up."

"One more moment, Rebecca." Alexander's solemn voice gave her pause. "Why did you do it? If you're not involved with the enemy, why implicate yourself after shielding me from Emory the day you pretended to have the measles? Explain it if you can."

Rebecca turned ever so slightly, casting a long look in Alexander's direction. "That's the whole problem, Alexander. I can't explain it," she said with a catch in her voice.

It would be so easy to spill the whole sordid story, Rebecca reasoned. Like turning state's evidence. But she simply couldn't face the hurt in

Alexander's expressive eyes when he learned he'd been betrayed by someone in his immediate family. It wasn't her place to explain, even if she had the stomach for the job. She'd just have to wait and hope that Confederate President Davis would exonerate her name. And that Cordelia would take her cue from this mess, and clean up her act! Flipping her cashmere skirts over one arm, she regally ascended the front porch steps, and, after several fumbled attempts, lit the candle. Cupping her hand to protect the feeble flame, she shouldered the knobless door open.

Again, Alexander's voice stayed her. "Can't—or won't, Rebecca?" he growled.

"Can't. Won't. Same difference," she answered. *God, how I wish I could spill it all to you. I'd feel so much better. So much safer. So much happier.*

"You'd think someone in your position would try to be a little more obliging," Alexander said, anger and frustration marring his handsome features, deepening his hazel eyes to the gray-green of a storm-tossed sea.

"I guess I'm not quite right in the head," Rebecca replied with a practiced shrug, opening the door to disappear inside. The door swung shut behind her with a resounding thud.

White-lipped, Alexander cursed. Seething with contradictory emotions, he tossed his saddle as hard as he could against the lean-to's back wall.

The vibrations of the saddle hitting the wall followed Rebecca inside the building. Her shoulders sagging, she leaned against the door for support. To deny Alexander the truth, to direct his anger against herself, was to cut out her own heart.

But as Cordelia's friend and because she loved Alexander, she felt she had no other choice.

To Rebecca's surprise, the Spartan building turned out to be an abandoned schoolhouse. Crude student benches, three deep, comprised two crooked rows on either side of the room.

"Imagine that. A schoolhouse, in the middle of nowhere."

The blackboard at the front of the room drew Rebecca's attention like a magnet. She lifted her candle to better read the faded chalk inscription.

A line down the center separated the board into two halves. On one was a homework assignment from *Webster's Elementary Spelling Book*. On the other, "I will not disrupt the class," listed fifty times in a childish scrawl. Rebecca noted the hickory rod propped against the free-standing chalk board.

"Some things never are as they seem. Others never change," Rebecca said, picking up a stick of chalk and defiantly writing "JABBERWOCKY" in block letters across the center of the black slate. Plunking the chalk back in its tray, Rebecca removed her slouch hat to discard the loose net Cordelia had insisted she wear. Her auburn hair cascaded freely against her shoulders as she slumped down on a dusty bench.

It wasn't long before Alexander joined her, his arms loaded with wood. He built a fire in the hearth, boiled coffee along with huge mug of beans, and rubbed a pinch of salt into and spitted a freshly dressed squirrel. He heated a wedge of Jubadessa's loaf bread then warmed some water, motioning for her to wash her face and hands. Mundane, but necessary tasks.

They shared supper in bleak silence, in opposite corners, on separate benches. Rebecca thought how strange it was, when they'd shared so much only recently.

She caught herself watching him when he wasn't looking. He ate heartily, yet with the same leisurely appreciation with which he made love, Rebecca thought.

Dinner finished, he banked the fire, cleaned up the dishes, and unrolled their bedding at least five feet apart. He positioned himself between her and the door.

"Better get some sleep. We leave for Oak Mont at daylight," he said gruffly before crawling beneath his blankets, his face toward the entrance.

Within minutes, he was snoring softly.

The candle sputtered, went out. Only the feeble firelight illuminated the still room, casting grotesque shadows across the stark walls.

An owl hooted outside. Wings flapped. There was a quick skirmish on the porch. A rodent's eerie, high-pitched squeal cleaved the night, followed by the scratch of claws digging in for a running start. The heavy whoosh of wings. Then silence reigned once again, save the crackle of the fire and Alexander's steady breathing. The ruckus hadn't fazed him at all.

Shuddering, Rebecca imagined the owl flying off

into the night sky, its helpless victim dangling in its talons.

She wasted no time scurrying into her own bedroll, tugging the covers to her chin. Attempting to block the day's sordid events from her mind, Rebecca tossed and turned on the hard plank floor until she finally dozed into a fitful slumber.

But the nightmare began almost immediately. The plot line was the same. Rebecca recognized it immediately, though she hadn't dreamed it in eons—not since she was a child. Usually after munching down a midnight snack while watching a Count Dracula movie on TV. Only this time, the stalking vampire was after something far dearer than blood. And she wasn't sure how to stop him, wasn't entirely sure what he wanted from her, or how she fit into the scheme of things.

This time, the vampire wasn't Bela Lugosi, who had ceased to frighten her years before. When it reared its sleek head, its lips drawn into a sneer to display gleaming white fangs, it was James Emory's pancake face she saw. And she knew whatever diabolical thing he planned would be more horrible than anything she might see on television.

A shiver ran through Rebecca as a film of cold sweat beaded her body. He reached for her and started to shake her. "Emory," she gasped in her dream, and fought him for all she was worth.

"Rebecca. For the love of...I'm not Emory! Stop fighting me," Alexander growled. "I'm not going to hurt you. You're dreaming."

Rebecca snapped awake. It was predawn, and

Alexander was on his knees at her side.

"Emory?" she repeated blankly.

"You cried out his name in your sleep. Sweet heaven, Rebeeca! For the sake of my sanity, tell me what power that man holds over you. Is he your lover?" Alexander demanded harshly, glaring down at her, unmistakable jealousy radiating from his eyes. Its beam singed her with its intensity.

His voice lowered an octave. "Better still, explain what power you hold over me," he said, crushing her against his hard body. She huddled in his warm embrace.

He wanted answers, Rebecca thought dazedly as her arms crept around his waist. And he deserved them. Okay, she resolved. She'd tell him the truth. Not about Cordelia, but about herself.

"Alexander, earlier, you asked me to explain all this to you," she began tentatively. "There are ... others involved. People I wouldn't want to see hurt by the backlash."

Alexander released her, rocking back on his haunches. "Go on," he prompted gravely.

"When I tell you this, you're going to think I'm psychotic."

A trace of his lazy half-smile appeared. "And I don't already?"

"*Touché*." Rebecca took a deep breath and exhaled slowly as she sat up in her bedroll. *Where to begin?* she wondered.

"What would you say if I told you that I don't belong here?"

"Neither of us belong in this situation. In a dilapidated, one-room schoolhouse. Together. Over night."

"I don't mean here. I mean *here*. In this century. In your time frame." There. It was out. Her deepest, darkest, most dreadful secret.

Alexander's eyes narrowed perceptively. "I'd say you're worse than Abigail," he said softly.

"You're probably right. But, be that as it may, it's the truth."

Alexander sprang to his feet. "Preposterous," he said with a mirthless puff of laughter. He yanked Rebecca to her feet as well.

Nose to nose, his eyes flashing gold-flecked daggers, he expounded, "You test me to the limits. I think you'd say or do *anything*, beard the devil himself, if you imagined it might lessen the severity of the situation. I misjudged you. You *are* adept at lying."

His words pierced her soul.

"I swear, I'm not lying," she denied in a hushed voice.

"You think me a fool?" he demanded angrily through gritted teeth, his forefinger beneath her chin, forcing her head back.

"No," she choked.

"You must, to expect me to believe such a fairy tale. What make-believe will you conjure up next? Perhaps, like the owl on the porch last night, that you can fly?"

Rebecca broke away, straightening her skirts, meeting the challenge in his eyes. "If you must know, yes. With the right equipment, I *can* fly."

Alexander blinked, so astounded that for a moment he couldn't speak. Finally, he scoffed, "Is that how you got here? Hitched a ride on a comet!"

"I'm not sure how I traversed the t—time barrier," Rebecca stuttered. "I've asked myself that same question a million times over the last month."

Alexander said nothing. But Rebecca could feel his reproof.

"Listen. Maybe our dimensions are back to back. Maybe I've stumbled onto the black hole all the research physicists are yacking about. The dates when all this started coincide. Sort of. January 2, 1863. January 2, 1968."

The more she related to Alexander about her theory, the more excited she became.

"My brother was killed in Vietnam by a sniper's bullet. I've always wished I could have been there to save him. I was here for you. My initials are RAW. Yours are WAR. I'm a nurse, a good one. You needed a nurse, a good one. Maybe you weren't supposed to die. Which you surely would have done had I not been here with a vial of penicillin."

"Penicillin."

"It's an antibiotic, discovered in 1929. It's produced by molds. A wonder drug by any standards. Used for treating infection."

Alexander studied her for what seemed an eternity. "I fear, like my aunt, this war has been too much for you, Rebecca."

"It has not!" Rebecca exploded defensively. "I'll have you know, I've barely gotten my feet wet in *this* war. I could tell you things that would curl your toes, Lieutenant Colonel. If you think medicine has come a long way, you should see military warfare," she added.

"This gets crazier by the moment."

"I may not know how I got here, but I know my name, rank, serial number, and date of birth. Who I am, and where I come from. And it's not here," she insisted.

Alexander ran a hand through his hair. "Who in their right mind would believe time travel possible?" he retorted.

"Me! I'm living proof."

"Ha!"

"I'll tell you something else. I love egg rolls, bottled soda, and baklava. My two favorite movies are *The Graduate* and *Dr. Zhivago*. Bob Dylan and the Beatles are all the rage. They're trying to put a man on the moon and *Gone With The Wind* was as close as I ever expected to be to the Civil War!" She was practically screeching.

"Calm down," Alexander advised, concern creeping into his voice.

In rare form, desperate that he believe her, Rebecca ignored him. "The world has discovered DNA and the Mekong River Delta. A mustang is a car. There's only one President in America. And his name doesn't end with either Jefferson *or* Lincoln!"

"You're overwrought. Control yourself, Rebecca."

How could she control herself when she was near him. "I won't! I'm trying to tell you I'm—"

"I don't understand one-tenth of what you're

saying," Alexander interjected.

Rebecca nodded sagely. "I didn't expect you to. That's the point," she said, her mouth grim, her eyes troubled.

Alexander reached for her, turning her, holding her back tightly to his chest. One arm encircling her waist, he brushed her cheek with his knuckles.

"Shh. Hush now, love," he whispered in her ear. His last word sounded as if it had been dragged from him against his will.

Rebecca struggled for a moment, but he held her firmly in place.

"I'm not crazy," she almost sobbed. "Can't you understand? Your life consists of weeding fields, riding horses, boiling lye, tracking deer. Quilting bees, picking wild blackberries, and tavern luncheons that only cost twenty-five cents are everyday occurrences. My world is light years away from that sort of simplicity. Good grief! When you take into account the sales tax, a quarter barely buys a pack of gum where I come from."

"And I suppose you expect me to believe James Emory is from the...What? The future, too?" Alexander remarked dryly, though he refused to relinquish her.

"Don't patronize me! In my world, I wouldn't give that man the time of day," Rebecca exclaimed indignantly.

"But here, you would." His hands tightened, biting into her waist. "Why didn't you tell Emory I was in the house in the first place? It would have saved us both a lot of grief!"

"What are you talking about?" Rebecca asked in confusion.

"I saw you with him in the orchard, Rebecca. I wouldn't have been surprised to see him press you across one of my brother's headstones and have his way with you," he accused.

With a surge of adrenaline, Rebecca wrenched free, swung around, took careful aim, and slapped the fire out of Alexander Ransom. The thwack of flesh against flesh reverberated in the room.

No more startled than she by her reaction, Alexander massaged the handprint marring his cheek.

"I...I won't apologize for that. You deserved it," Rebecca said defiantly, taking a giant step backward.

"I don't expect you to, spitfire," he replied, taking two steps forward, his lips capturing hers in a punishing kiss.

Rebecca was appalled by the anger transmitted in the kiss. She was also aroused by Alexander's barely suppressed passion, to know that she could affect him so.

Flabbergasted by the havoc he was wreaking on her senses, she argued against his lips. "Alexander. I wasn't lying. I keep telling you! I'm not a spy. I'm a time traveler. *Listen* to what I'm saying, would you? Think of my machine-shop dog tags. My medical satchel and stainless steel instruments. When's the last time you saw such a neat bag of tricks? And doesn't the medical knowledge that goes with them count for anything? I stick out in your world like a sore thumb. I...I can drive a jeep far better than I sit a horse and I bet you don't even know what a jeep is," she said, grasping at straws.

Alexander drew back. "Rebecca, this is ludicrous."

Like a flash of lightning, inspiration zigzagged through her brain. "Then what about my skimpy, synthetic, nylon underwear? Bra and panties is the generic term."

At the mention of her sexy undergarments, Alexander's anger diminished. She was right. He'd never seen anything like them. His certainty wavered.

"I must admit. Your undergarments are decidedly fetching, but they could be some kind of new invention from the North. And even if I did believe you, and I'm not saying that I do, I couldn't let you go until word arrived from Richmond to validate your innocence," he responded, torn between loyalty to his home state of Tennessee and Rebecca.

"I see." And she did. Rebecca understood his line of logic. Empathized. Accepted his decision. After all, she was an Army officer herself. Still, somewhere in the back of her mind, she knew he was going to throw caution to the wind and kiss her as he had once before in the kitchen at Oak Mont.

And he did.

Instead of continuing to fight him, Rebecca yielded to the pressing desire seeping into her as what had begun as brutal punishment, became an intimate caress. Soft passion. Their kiss held a tangible sense of rightness despite everyone and everything that stood in their way.

"This won't settle anything," Rebecca breathed, reveling in his nearness and musing that because of it, she felt less lost, less vulnerable to outside forces.

"I know," Alexander acknowledged hoarsely. "But you are the most exasperating, uninhibited, thoroughly bewitching creature I've ever met."

"I might stab you in the back while you aren't looking. Remember I'm the hoodlum who ran off with your coat," she warned, her tone husky, unconsciously sexy.

Alexander had stopped asking the meaning of certain words Rebecca used like "hoodlum." What did it matter, when she was driving him wild, blinding him to anything other than her immediate nearness? Her potential accessibility? "I'll just have to take my chances. I want you so badly I can taste it. Want to taste you. All of you."

"This is emotional suicide," she moaned, thinking what potentially violent emotions love and hate could be. She wondered how she would ever adequately satisfy her need for this man.

"Fear of allowing this moment to pass outweighs the risk. Besides, I find I'm no longer so sure about my previous convictions," he answered with a groan of desire, nibbling hungrily at her ear lobe. His lips reminded her of the delicate brush of a butterfly's wings as he tenderly worked his way across her heated cheek covering her mouth with his, claiming it for his own.

His questing hands skimmed down her body to the warm curve of her back, grasping her buttocks, tucking her more firmly against his groin as their kisses grew more ardent, less gentle.

Their tongues searched, teased, plunged, plundered. Anticipation was an ache welling in Rebecca's chest as Alexander slipped his fingers down the bodice of her cashmere traveling dress, flicking open the pearl buttons to expose her lacy bra. Then the fine mauve wool gaped open to her waist like the petals of a flower.

Her lips swollen and trembling with pent-up passion, Rebecca tore her mouth from his. "What are you doing?"

His movements grew more possessive still as he drew her to her knees on the bedroll.

"What does it *feel* like I'm doing?" he asked thickly as he hastily shed his shirt.

The teasing note was back in Alexander's voice, the humorous side of him that Rebecca so enjoyed.

Her eyes dropped below his belt then swerved to a neutral point on the wall.

"Exactly what I want you to." She sighed, laying her heart at his feet.

"In this there is no doubt we are well-matched, angel mine," Alexander said, retrieving her heart, and reaching to pull her atop his hard body.

Warm skin grazed warm skin as Rebecca's bra pushed her breasts upward against the soft dark hair sprinkling Alexander's chest. Her skirts rode up to her thighs. He impatiently gathered them higher, as if to completely disrobe her would be to waste precious moments that might never be recaptured.

Fumbling with the buttons on his pants, Rebecca silently agreed and grew frustrated with the tight button holes.

"Here. Allow me," he rasped, loosening the fly for her. A deep groan and a soft rush of air escaped his lips as Rebecca's hand slipped inside.

Rebecca opened to Alexander as if it were the most natural thing in the world. Her body throbbed, flexed, meshed, fused with Alexander's. Swiftly, she carried him to the brink of fulfillment. His breath ragged, he reciprocated the gift with a final driving stroke that sent them both tumbling into a realm where sensation was the ultimate guiding star.

Their coming together was inevitable, seemed preordained, as Rebecca was beginning to believe it had been from the start.

Afterwards, satiated, they slept soundly in each other's arms, defying, if only for a brief, fleeting hour, the ever-present ticking of Father Time's merciless clock.

When she had been a small child and had fallen down, her mother had dusted her off and said, "You'll survive." Now, as Rebecca readied herself for the last leg of their journey to Oak Mont, she had her doubts. Just how far could someone fall and still survive? As far as she had? Rebecca wondered. It was doubtful. Father Time had pulled a real lulu on her this go-around. This was worse than falling down as a child, than living through her first teenage crush, than wrecking the family car. Worse than passing from puberty to womanhood. Worse, if it were possible, than Vietnam.

Unlike the other ups and downs in her life, this time it was difficult to make heads or tails of anything. Anything except Alexander's abrupt change in attitude between dusk, dawn, and now. Since waking, he had withdrawn from her, placing an impersonal distance between them. She could only guess that he was closing ranks on her so he could come to grips with the fantastic story she'd recounted, and deal with his suspicions against her and the basic need they seemed to share. Perhaps even to protect himself. Most probably from her, Rebecca mused. She could deal with that. What she couldn't figure out was what cosmic source had predetermined the present set of events? What curvaceous path had she and Alexander followed? To what incredible conclusion? And most importantly, why?

Fully buttoned into her cashmere traveling dress, Rebecca paced the floor as she waited for Alexander to finish saddling Vedette. She pondered the pros and cons of their relationship until a vaguely familiar voice on the other side of the schoolroom wall arrested her attention. Rebecca stopped in mid-stride.

Who in the world was Alexander talking to?

On tiptoes and quiet as the proverbial mouse, Rebecca crossed the room to press her ear against the wall adjoining the lean-to, listening to the conversation taking place outside.

Muffled, yet audible, the voice ordered, "I suggest you ease that revolver out of its holster and toss it this way. That's right. Good move."

Rebecca could only imagine Alexander was

doing as he'd been told—dropping his Colt revolver. Her suspicions were confirmed when Crumbum continued.

"Nice gun, even balance. Expensive piece I reckon." There was a pause, then, "The woman you're with, she led me a merry chase, and I can't see letting you stand in the way now that I've caught up with her. She's a looker, that one. I'll give her that much. Smart, too. Smooth as fresh cream. Took me awhile after she left the tavern to figure out she'd cheated me."

"I have no idea what you're talking about," Alexander stated evasively.

Rebecca's heart constricted. She knew she was hearing a new facet of Alexander's character—a deadly one. His tone of voice was low and quiet to be sure. Still, it reminded her of a panther's guttural warning snarl just before it attacked. She shuddered. Should she stay put or intercede? Which would Alexander appreciate more?

"Don't play games with me. I know the woman's here somewhere...uh...Lieutenant Colonel, is it?" Crumbum asked.

"This is getting interesting. And how did you deduce that I was a lieutenant colonel?" Alexander questioned even more quietly, his voice infinitely more menacing to Rebecca's way of thinking.

"Come on now! We both know that coat belongs to you. The cut, the size, the gentleman's quality. Figured out it was a lieutenant colonel's frock coat right off the bat by the number of buttons."

"How astute." Alexander offered.

"I can count, can't I?"

Alexander snickered. "The question is, how high?"

"She's good at that, too. Rattling people. But it won't work this time," Crumbum professed. "I've made up my mind to that."

"Have you now." Alexander's statement was dry, slightly sarcastic.

"I'm curious. What are you to her anyway? Her lover?" Crumbum asked, taking a stab at a little rattling of his own.

Keenly attuned to Alexander, Rebecca sensed his carefully controlled indignation as he responded, "That's really none of your concern, now is it?"

Crumbum's voice became excited. "Whoa now! Don't drop those hands. Keep 'em up where I can see them. Higher. That's right. Guess you two slippery eels thought I'd lose you for sure when she switched from the wagon to your horse awhile back. It was a might tricky, but I'm smarter than that."

"I bet you are, like a bloodhound on a scent," Alexander taunted harshly. Rebecca imagined how much he itched to take Crumbum physically down a notch or two. She did herself.

"You see, I got to thinking about that gold. The deal was . . ." Crumbum began. "Well, you don't need to know all the details. Fact is, she cheated me. I know that as sure as I live and breathe. I'm thinking right now that you were in on it, too."

"Dangerous business for some people—thinking," Alexander said grimly.

There was another pause. Longer this time.

Crumbum swore. "That's what I hate about Southerners. Too hoity-toity for my liking."

"The same could be said for some Northerners I've met."

Rebecca could visualize the glint in Alexander's hazel eyes, and she knew Crumbum's temper was beginning to fray when he said, "Making fun of me, huh? Think you're sharp, don't you, Mister Confederate Officer? Think I don't understand your jabs. Well, you'll be laughing out of the other side of your face when I put a bullet in your gullet. Rebels in occupied territory ought to be more careful. Too absorbed with the young lady to notice me sneaking up on you, I'll warrant."

Alexander spoke up, his words measured and distinctive. "You, sir, are contemptible." There was no mistaking the steel-cutting edge in his voice. It slashed the air in dire warning.

There was no doubt in Rebecca's mind Alexander was about to do something that would put him in grave danger of being shot on the spot. Impulsively, she whirled, dashing out through the schoolhouse door toward the lean-to, her foremost thought to distract Crumbum, to somehow protect Alexander from *her* mistake. She mentally chastised herself for not handing Crumbum the entire coat in the first place, and being done with the odious quartermaster.

Halfway down the steps, Rebecca yelled, "Crumbum, you louse! Where do you get off calling me a cheater? We had a deal. Fair and square! If anyone reneged, it's you."

Crumbum pivoted a fraction, the gun still precariously trained on Alexander's throat. "Ah, the lady in question makes her grand entrance. *Had* is the key word. I've since experienced second thoughts concerning our recent transaction."

"You have? That's just too bad," Rebecca said curtly.

"We'll see about that," Crumbum said with a sneer.

"I wouldn't turn those buttons over to you if my life depended on it. No way. Not now. Not ever. Forget it! You've come all this way for nothing. A pure waste of time. Got it?"

As if on cue, Crumbum's scar reddened, his temper soaring as he twisted to face Rebecca.

"You are a stubborn chit, girlie. Let's just see how stubborn you are when I—"

Crumbum never finished his sentence. Alexander struck with lethal precision, wrestling both guns from the stunned quartermaster, knocking the stockier man senseless with the heavy butt of his retrieved Colt revolver.

The Yankee quartermaster sagged, collapsing like a punctured air balloon.

Alexander and Rebecca stood on either side of Crumbum's prostrate form, staring at one another. Finally, Rebecca said, "I thought that was just a trumped-up movie stunt, knocking a man over the head with a pistol."

Alexander scowled. "I don't know much about moving stunts, but you of all people should know that if you hit someone hard enough, and in the right spot, they're going to go down," he said, reholstering his gun and placing Crumbum's in his waist belt. "You should also know that your friend is going to have a walloping headache when he regains consciousness."

Rebecca frowned down at Crumbum, haphazardly sprawled at her feet. Bending at the knees, she checked his pulse. It was perfectly normal, as was his breathing. "Nothing he hasn't contended with before. The man chugalugs alcohol like a fish does water. I'm sure hangovers are a way of life with him." Rebecca straightened to face Alexander eye to eye, cloaking her growing frustration in dignity. "And he isn't my friend."

"Be that as it may. I allowed him to live, not because he knows you, but because he's a crafty supply contact for the Confederacy."

Rebecca's sapphire eyes snapped fire at Alexander. "You simply refuse to believe that I—"

Alexander interrupted her, waving her away. "We don't have time to rehash that now. I suggest you collect your things so we can make tracks before he comes around."

With a curt nod, Rebecca closed her mouth. Reentering the schoolhouse, she quickly gathered her cloak and slouch hat before returning to Alexander's side, only to discover him already mounted.

Vedette snorted and side-stepped as Alexander lifted Rebecca into the saddle behind him. He gently soothed the horse with soft words and a firm hand. Just as he might have a rebellious child, Rebecca thought.

"I don't think she likes riding double," Rebecca commented, more to break the uneasy silence between them than as a protest against Alexander's handling of Vedette.

"She's strong. Lots of pluck. She can carry the weight. Besides, she doesn't have much choice, unless you'd care to walk back to Oak Mont," Alexander said tightly.

"No. I think I'd rather ride, thank you," Rebecca said truthfully, biting her lip to keep it from trembling.

As he nudged the dapple-gray toward the plantation, Alexander offhandedly said, "You realize I'm falling in love with you, Rebecca." The unexpected confession was almost an accusation. An accusation that sufficiently distanced them as nothing else had.

"I never asked for this," Rebecca responded in a soft voice, wrapping her arms around Alexander's waist, when what she really wanted to say was, "I'm in love with you, too." But she knew in her heart he wasn't ready to hear that his love for her was reciprocated. The closeness they'd shared, the emotional sensation, the sensual passion of the night before, had been shelved in lieu of a studied indifference. A distance that was far easier to deal with under the present stressful circumstances.

Still, Rebecca felt a gnawing sense of hunger deep within her, an emptiness that had little to do with the lack of breakfast. She knew she rode behind Alexander so he wouldn't have to look into her face and see her eyes and what might be reflected there.

With a sigh of resignation, Rebecca pressed her cheek against Alexander's broad back. She could

hear the strong beat of his heart, and she longed
for him to turn to her and smile his mischievous
smile or his seductive one. His sad one. Or even
his angry one. If only he would look at her.

But he didn't.

Rebecca found herself wondering, why when
you loved someone, it had to hurt so? Her skin felt
stretched tight from holding in the pain of her love.
Overly sensitive. Uncomfortable. As if she really
didn't belong in it. As if her skin might split apart
at any moment.

Finally, forcing herself to close her eyes, Rebecca let the rhythmic beat of Alexander's heart,
plus a liberal measure of her own iron resolve, lull
her soul toward an uneasy peace.

Alexander felt Rebecca relax against him, reveled in her clinging, vibrant presence at his back.
When she'd stepped outside the schoolhouse to
call the Yankee quartermaster out, he'd died a
thousand deaths, thinking she might come to
harm. In the same breath, he'd also cursed her.
Himself as well.

Before he'd met Rebecca, he'd been certain that
nothing could come between himself and his powerful sense of duty. That's why he'd become a courier for Major General Wheeler in the first place!
He'd seen far weaker men succumb to the charms
of a comely face and a pliant body, but he'd never
imagined that one day he would.

And yet, it was much more than Rebecca's physical beauty that drew him, Alexander conceded.

She'd stolen his frock coat from his room with

all the aplomb of a seasoned warrior. He admired her for that.

She'd *had* to realize she was going to get into a world of trouble, and yet, she'd bought medicine with the buttons instead of horses. She'd surprised and intrigued him.

At great risk to life and limb, she'd placed herself between him and the Yankee quartermaster and then she'd turned right around and shown a true nurse's capacity for compassion by examining the unconscious man—a confusing feat that only served to make her even dearer to him.

Rebecca was so erroneous in her actions, and yet, with every ill-advised move she made, he loved her all the more.

Insanity, Alexander thought. Sweet, exquisite, pain-filled insanity. An insanity that wouldn't be remedied until he knew for sure, in his own mind and heart, who and what Rebecca Ann Warren really and truly was.

Chapter Twelve

The next week was torture for Rebecca; the waiting unbearable. She had never ventured into the windowless tack room of Oak Mont's carriage house. Now, it was her prison. And every chink in the wall, every plank, every wood grain swirl, that like clouds formed any sort of picture, had become old friends. Even the bold little field mouse, who shared the warmth of her brazier and was tempted by the crumbs from her table, was considered a companion, for no other was allowed admittance into the tack room for any unjustifiable length of time.

Of course, the family could talk to her through the door, but it had grown wintery again. A powdery snow covered the ground. And who could blame them for preferring the house to the chill of the carriage house? Oh, Abigail tripped out to keep her company once in a while until her toes became numb with cold and she was forced inside once again. And Cordelia had slipped her a guilt-ridden, tear-stained note of apology, which she'd promptly destroyed after reading it. Apologies confirmed guilt in any language, in any time frame.

Jubadessa shouldered the essentials—meals, bathing water, fresh clothes. Willy supplied coal for the brazier, always careful that the padlock on the door was in place when he finished. But she'd not seen or heard from Alexander since they'd returned to Oak Mont.

Alexander.

She had known making love would not affect a cure-all for them. If anything, it had made matters worse. Perhaps that was why he hadn't been down to visit her. Because even if he had found the false papers he had nothing more to say until word arrived from Richmond. Or because it was too painful to see someone you cared for incarcerated. She hoped it was the latter. Because she cared for his state of mind and she was hurting, too. With him. For him.

"How long can it take?" Rebecca questioned aloud. "It's been days since he sent the telegram!" *Days that seem like years*.

Rebecca picked up one of the books stacked neatly on the table beside the oil lamp. She thumbed through it then set it aside in exasperation. The framed sampler went the same route. Busy work held no appeal for her. Besides, she'd never get the hang of chain stitches, button-hole filling, and whipped webs. She felt a vague sense of relief that embroidery was outside her realm of expertise.

Hiking up her skirts and tucking them in her belt, Rebecca decided to do a series of jumping jacks, some windmills, a few deep knee bends, along with several minutes of running in place to temper her restlessness. She put her hands over her head, stretched, bent double, touched her toes. Bobbed. Sagged like a rag doll and shook her head to loosen up and help kick off her routine. The exercise felt good, eased some of the tension, drained away the weariness that weakened her body.

Afterwards, she lay down on the canvas cot, settling into the ticking mattress filled with pine straw that padded it. Closing her eyes, she threw in a heavy dose of meditation exercises to salve her spirit and temporarily relieve the burdensome thoughts marching through her brain like a troop of termites.

Rebecca concentrated instead on home. The home that existed in her own time. Of her parents, working in the yard on a summer day, mowing grass, making lemonade with a juicer. Of cars with speedometers and gas tanks. Of supermarkets and fast-food restaurants. Of movie theaters. Washing machines and electric stoves.

Of toothpaste. Mascara. Passion Pink nail polish. Bob Dylan records. Concerts. Spin the bottle. Even of war as she knew it.

Life had never before seemed so simple.

* * *

"Rebecca. Rebecca."

There was a scratch at the door. A familiar voice intruding into her subconscious. "I've got the k–e–e–eys."

Rebecca sat up. "Cordelia? Is that you?"

"Yes." A key scraped in the lock. The door flew open and in stepped Cordelia Ransom with a knapsack in her hands.

Without preamble, she thrust it at Rebecca. "Get up. You've got to get away from here!"

"Where did you get the key?"

"I stole the spare from Jubadessa's room. Now hurry! James will be here any minute."

At the mention of Captain Emory, Rebecca swung her feet over the side of the cot and stood up.

"What's going on? Alexander hasn't—"

"Not Alexander. *James*. He's put two and two together and come up with a plausible four."

"What are you talking about?"

"I've only just arrived from Nashville. From James. You see, I refused to siphon him any more information. That only served to fuel his temper. He's absolutely furious that his plan to apprehend The Gray Ghost in Memphis failed. And he's figured out what we did."

"How did you get into Nashville without the wagon?"

"James sent a buggy for me. He's threatened to extradite you to his headquarters in Nashville for extensive questionin' if I don't come across with proof positive of Alexander's involvement." She visibly shook in her agitation. "He simply wouldn't listen to anythin' I had to say. Now for heaven's sake. Run! Get out while you can!" she wailed. "James isn't ten minutes behind me. He'll .be all over us like hot wax in no time at all."

"Where is Alexander? I can't imagine him allowing you to go to Nashville at Emory's request."

"Lord, I don't know for sure!" Cordelia twisted her hands together. "He's been livin' up to his title of Gray Ghost. In and out so often since you two returned I haven't been able to keep track. Doesn't know I've been to town," she said, her sentences cursory and stilted. "And you've no time to worry over that anyway. You're the one in trouble this time and I feel so . . . horribly responsible for it all."

"I can't leave without speaking to Alexander."

"You must!" Cordelia said, breaking into great, wracking sobs that convulsed her tiny body.

"Stop that, Cordelia. Think of the baby, your blood pressure. Upsetting yourself like this can't be good for the child. Besides, you aren't responsible for my, or Alexander's, or even your husband's actions. You're a victim, stuck between a rock and a hard place. Like so many others," Rebecca soothed, steering Cordelia down on the cot, patting her shoulder, comforting her as only a best friend could. At the same time, she tried to decide if she should indeed run. Should she take the horse? That didn't seem fair considering she'd lost them the wagon. And if she did, with or without the horse, where would she go?

Before she figured it out, time pulled a fast one, and ran out on her.

* * *

Jubadessa was not stupid.

Though she hadn't needed them in so long she'd almost forgotten they existed, she realized the duplicate tack-room keys were missing the instant she reached for her cloak. They ordinarily hung behind the cloak on the same peg and gave a telltale clink when disturbed.

She also correctly deduced the one who had helped herself—Cordelia.

The young miss had been acting peculiar for weeks. Sickly. Jumpy. What she was up to, Jubadessa wasn't sure. But she sure was going to find out. She hated seeing Rebecca locked up. But the only alternative was to disobey *Monsieur*'s wishes and set the nurse free. And she didn't plan to do that. Nor allow Cordelia to do so either. *Monsieur* had his reasons, though they were difficult to comprehend at times. They'd both best content themselves with the fact that if it wasn't important, *Monsieur* wouldn't order such a thing.

Flipping her cloak around her shoulders, Jubadessa snatched up Rebecca's dinner plate and headed for the carriage house. She should take Mrs. Abigail with her, she thought fleetingly. But she was having a bad day, and it seemed unkind to rouse her from her nap when Jubadessa planned to be away from the house only a moment. Perhaps, if she allowed her the sleep, Abigail would awake refreshed. More her old self.

Juggling the tray to close the side door, Jubadessa stepped onto the wrap-around porch to find Rebecca, Cordelia, and James Emory standing in the snow-covered carriage house yard. What she saw appalled her—so much so that she almost dropped the plate of food.

It was obvious that the captain and Cordelia were arguing.

"I'll be damned if I won't arrest her, despite you. You know how important this is to me!" he spat.

"Please, James. No. There must be some other way to earn your stars," she entreated.

"Cordelia, you must understand. This is a means to secure our livelihood," he preached.

But the drama didn't end there. Not with a simple verbal disagreement. When the argument became physical, when the captain pinched Cordelia's arm, Rebecca pounced at him, her nails drawn, going for his throat like an angry she-cat protecting a cub.

In the struggle that ensued, Emory raised his arm as if to defend himself from attack. Cordelia was inadvertently caught under the chin by his balled fist. She toppled to the ground in a dead faint. Astonished, both Rebecca and Emory dropped to their knees, grappling to assist Cordelia.

Jubadessa's *café-au-lait* skin turned pale. Incensed, terrified for their safety, Jubadessa's first instinct was to fly to the womens' aid. Then common sense prevailed. She was a Negro woman against a white man. A Northerner. She had no rights where he was concerned, no more than Miss Cordelia or Rebecca Warren. She had no weapon handy to back up her innate courage. Not a leg to stand on.

No. Jubadessa was not stupid.

Melting back into the shadows of the porch, she eased open the side entrance, set the plate on the counter, and sped through the bowels of the plantation house. Wrenching open the back door, she dashed down the garden path, bent on alerting *Monsieur* to Emory's presence. *Monsieur* was in the lower quarter with Willy, discussing the spring planting season. *Monsieur* was the one person in all of Christendom who could, by divine birthright, protect the women of Oak Mont against a Yankee invasion.

He appeared like the name he was so well known for. A gray ghost. A gray ghost with a turbaned mulattress, and a wiry little Irishman guarding his backside.

Emory didn't even have time to draw his weapon, to rise to his feet, before Alexander was upon him. His hazel eyes blazed a feral golden-green as he clicked back the hammer on his Colt revolver and placed it against James Emory's temple.

"I suppose a man of your caliber would deem this satisfactory behavior. I, on the other hand, do not," Alexander snarled, making a slow, almost insolent appraisal of Emory. "Prepare to meet your Maker."

It was amazing, Rebecca thought, as she gazed up at him, towering over them. She'd always assumed she'd seen Alexander's angry side.

She'd seen him testy, perturbed, out of sorts, but

not angry. She knew that now. His anger was lethal. A palpable thing.

Cordelia stirred and opened her delicate, china-blue eyes. She clutched convulsively at Rebecca's hand.

"Alexander," she pleaded in a wispy voice. "Please don't shoot him. He didn't *mean* to hit me; I *know* he didn't. He's . . . he's . . . The captain . . . is my husband. I'm carrying . . . his baby," she confided at last.

Rebecca almost passed out. Every atom in her body tensed as she awaited Alexander's reaction. Perhaps he would simply shoot them all and be done with it.

"That complicates matters, doesn't it?" he said finally, lowering the gun a few inches, but holding it still poised in the direction of Emory's head.

Jubadessa danced around Alexander, brushing Emory aside. "Miss Rebecca. Here. Help me get this child to her feet," she said.

James Emory rose then stepped back away from the women.

Rebecca clasped Cordelia under the elbow while Jubadessa did likewise. Together, they hoisted the frail woman to her feet.

Cordelia's bruised chin was already beginning to turn purple. Jubadessa clucked her tongue, glaring at the captain. "How could you!" she exclaimed with considerable bravado, Rebecca thought.

His face like stone, James ignored Jubadessa's heartfelt reproach, his wife's sad eyes, Rebecca's silent condemnation.

"How do you intend to settle this, Ransom?"

"That depends on how many men you have waiting for you over the hill."

"None. I came on my own today. To ... er ... speak with my wife."

"And perhaps arrest Rebecca Warren in the process?" Alexander asked with barely concealed malice.

Emory's cold gaze slashed across Jubadessa's face then back to Alexander. "It would seem the cat is out of the bag."

"My housekeeper had nothing to do with it. As a matter of fact, I've been expecting you. The grapevine has not only a mouth but ears as well, Emory.

"Willy," Alexander directed. "Gather up my father's dueling pistols. Ball and powder. Meet Captain Emory and myself in the meadow behind the house when you've done that. We'll have need of a witness."

A duel? How ridiculous! Rebecca thought. She started to protest but Cordelia usurped her.

"Alexander!"

"Go in the house, Cordelia." He turned to Jubadessa. "Take her inside, Dessa. Keep her there until Willy returns with word on the outcome."

He faced Emory with his challenge. "Afterward, whatever happens, I want your word of honor, such as it is, that Miss Warren will not be troubled again with questions concerning The Gray Ghost."

"That would be hard to do, if I were dead. And if you die, well, The Gray Ghost episode will be ended. Won't it? And I suppose, in that case, I *could*

310

write Miss Warren's untimely intervention outside Memphis off as, shall we say, purely accidental. If the mood struck me."

"You imagine you have it all figured out, don't you, Emory?" Alexander growled. "There's only one minor detail you've overlooked. Those who subscribe to the Confederacy are smarter than you give them credit for being. Perhaps there are several Gray Ghosts. Dozens, in fact. A whole intricate brotherhood of couriers fanatically loyal to one another. Perhaps, if one is struck down, two more will rise up in his place to avenge him. And if those two fall, four. And each and every one will have orders to protect Miss Warren throughout the war, no matter the cost."

"Damn," Emory seethed.

Cordelia shook herself free of Jubadessa, interrupting the men. "I won't go into the house," she cried hysterically. "You can't make me, Alexander. He's my husband. I'm going down to the meadow, too."

Rebecca couldn't believe her ears. Cordelia wasn't protesting the duel, but the fact she might not be allowed to attend.

"This is *way* too far out! Duels were outlawed long before the Civil War. Weren't they?" Rebecca cited. It was archaic, barbaric, incomprehensible behavior for a contemporary woman's approval, Rebecca wanted to scream. After all she'd been through, would Alexander live to be killed in a stupid duel at the hands of his cousin's husband?

For the first time, Alexander turned his hazel eyes toward Rebecca. They lingered on her lips a moment then leveled off at her eyes. Sapphire and hazel. Blue heat and molten gold.

"All this turmoil isn't good for Cordelia in her condition," Rebecca said woodenly, mainly in an effort to stall the proceedings.

"That's right," Cordelia interposed, twisting Rebecca's words. "You see. I must be allowed to attend the duel. It would upset me too much otherwise."

Jubadessa spoke. "Perhaps it is her place, *Monsieur*. I'll accompany her to see that she's no problem."

Alexander nodded. "As you see fit. I leave the matter to your discretion."

His attention returned to Rebecca and she almost dissolved under his intense perusal.

"There should be a surgeon in attendance. I'd like you to take his place, Rebecca," he requested solemnly.

Rebecca realized the duel was a foregone conclusion. She could see it in Alexander's stance, hear it in his voice, feel it in the inflexible gaze he turned on her. Jubadessa agreed with him. Cordelia. Emory. Even Willy, quietly standing in the background, scuffing at the snow with the toe of his brogans.

It was a question of honor and as inevitable as their love. And though she didn't understand their reasoning, there was nothing she could do or say that would change anything because Alexander was honest, forthright, a gallant. But more important, he was a gentleman. Her only option was to be available, to once again lend her superior medical knowledge in the event he should fall.

God have mercy. Not that. I don't know what. But not that!

"Yes. I'll come. Let me get my bag." Rebecca was shaking so much inside, her legs felt like taut rubber bands. But her voice was strong, calm. Her actions sure.

Alexander nodded. "Of course. Willy will wait for you and escort you to the meadow."

Chapter Thirteen

Willy flipped the coin between the two combatants. It spun in the air, reminding Rebecca of the coin toss preceeding the Super Bowl football game.

Emory called heads. The piece of silver landed at his feet. Heads.

The golden-haired Adonis had earned the right of initial choice from the velvet-lined weapon case which held a pair of flintlock pistols with embossed dark wood, eighteen-inch extended barrels, and intricate gold grips.

Rebecca thought how expensive such a set of eighteenth-century mint condition aristocrat dueling pistols would be at her mother's antique shop. How pleased she would be to acquire such a rare item. How, as Alexander had been quick to point out, no one in their right mind would believe she was a time traveler, attending her first duel.

Emory inspected the gun, aligning it with his eye to check the sights. Turning, he pretended to target a turtle dove in a tall oak tree. Obviously, he wasn't satisfied, for he frowned, rejecting the pistol, reaching for the matching weapon.

Rebecca wished she had an electric cattle prod to hurry him along. She desperately wanted this ordeal over.

He went through much the same procedure as before, finally selecting the weapon he held.

Alexander lifted the remaining pistol from the case, and handed it to Willy who gave it a quick once over.

"Do you know the rules? Or should Willy go over the duello with you?" Alexander asked, accepting his gun from the Irishman.

"No need to put yourself out, Ransom. With a little luck, I think I can muddle through," Emory blustered, and Rebecca experienced the weirdest sensation that something wasn't quite right. But she couldn't put her finger on it.

Willy closed the case and placed it on a nearby tree stump. Bareheaded, the men merged into a huddle, then broke apart. Alexander and James Emory stood stiffly back to back as if they couldn't bear to touch one another, their pistols angled toward the laden sky, Willy acting as referee.

Snowflakes began to spiral toward the earth, topping the already virginal white ground as Willy counted off the paces. "One, two, three, four . . ." he droned in his lilting Irish brogue.

Rebecca had seen the same thing staged so many

times on film that she felt as if she could recount the story line by heart. Ten paces and the men would turn and fire. Ten paces and one, perhaps both, would fall.

Each number was like a slap in the face to Rebecca.

Shivery-cold with goose bumps on her skin, and chilled to the bone, Rebecca felt the frozen snow crystals melt as they landed on her burning cheeks. Odd that she should be so cold on the inside, yet so hot on the outside, Rebecca thought as she prepared to rush out onto the field. She'd learned the hard way that mere seconds could mean the difference between life and death.

An eerie stillness pervaded, as if an acoustical shadow had descended on the meadow. There was no motion. No sound, save the men's crunching footsteps as they paced out their lives. And then, midway through the count, Alexander's pistol misfired into the air, emitting a puff of smoke that curled above his head like a vaporous halo.

He turned slowly on his heel, staring at Emory across the clearing.

Rebecca knew what had happened and yet couldn't fathom it. Somehow, Emory had tampered with the first weapon.

A wicked grin curling his lips, as if he'd been waiting for just such a signal, Emory turned. "It seems your Irishman there wasn't such a good choice for a second. He obviously knows nothing about a gun."

He squinted, aimed, holding his pistol arm at the elbow to steady his bead.

"My only mistake was underestimating the audacity of my opponent," Alexander said, his tone cool and unruffled.

Rebecca suddenly felt ill. Was Alexander going to just stand there and let Emory shoot him down in cold blood?

She cast a glance at Jubadessa and Cordelia, positioned near the meadow's outer fringes out of harm's way. Their eyes as big as saucers, they seemed rooted in place. Rebecca didn't have that problem.

But before she could take the first step toward him, Emory squeezed the trigger, oh so carefully. The pistol barked.

Concurrently, a keen, crooning voice united with the dull pistol shot and somehow managed to usurp it.

"Carl. My dearest, Carl. I *knew* you'd come back one day. In your fine blue uniform, I see. I told them all you wouldn't leave me to fend for myself, but they laughed in their sleeves. How wrong they all were."

Fate couldn't intercede to stop the leaden slug spiraling toward Alexander, but a softly padded, substitute body running interference could.

Rebecca spied a flash of ash-blond curls, a splash of taffeta and brocade, as Abigail, her arms open wide, raced in high gear toward Emory and between the two men who faced each other.

The unwary woman caught the projectile destined for Alexander's heart. There was a hollow "whumpf." Then Abigal crumpled in a dainty heap on the ground.

It happened so quickly, for a moment Rebecca wasn't sure where the ball had landed. All she knew was that, miraculously, Alexander was still on his feet.

Then her glance strayed to Abigail, and she saw red. A red more brilliant than an intersection stop sign. More vivid than any hybrid tea rose Rebecca had ever seen. A puddle of red, growing more impressive by the moment as it seeped from the hole in Abigail's chest. Spreading. Staining the soft blanket of white on which she lay.

Blood-red.

For a deafening second, no one spoke. Then Cordelia gasped, wailing at the top of her lungs, "Mama!"

Appalled, Rebecca was running before she knew her legs were moving. Reaching Abigail's side, she frantically tested the pale wrist for a pulse. The beat was so faint as to be almost indiscernible.

"Carl, I love you," Abigail babbled almost incoherently. "Carl. I don't care what my friends say. You're my husband and I love you." Crimson spittle bubbled on her lips.

"Don't try to talk. Save your breath, Abbie," Rebecca commanded.

Ripping open her medical satchel, Rebecca seized a pressure pad, packing the ugly wound. Gobs of sterile gauze followed and when she ran out of that, strips torn from her flannel petticoats. But Rebecca was losing Abigail, and she knew it.

She continued to try and staunch the blood until Abigail quit breathing on her own. Fishing for her stethoscope, Rebecca listened for a heartbeat.

She found none.

With the precision of a fine-tuned Swiss watch, Rebecca valiantly switched to CPR as a last resort.

It was no use. The wound was too severe, even for a hospital emergency room armed to the teeth with modern X-ray equipment, oxygen, bottled plasma to diminish the shock. It was a hopeless proposition for a young, registered nurse kneeling in the snow, with only a medical satchel to assist her.

Rebecca straightened, closing Abigail's eyes. "I've lost her," she whispered softly, as unemotionally as possible. It was much harder to stay cool when you were personally involved. That's why she'd always avoided it like the plague. Played it smart—until now.

Jubadessa put her hand on Rebecca's shoulder.

Rebecca looked up. It seemed she'd had an audience ringed around her, supporting her, allowing her to do her job.

"I've never seen the like. You did everything in the world you could for poor Mrs. Abigail. I'll take care of her from here," Jubadessa offered in a shaky voice, sinking to the ground, placing her cloak around Abigail, cradling the frail woman's body in her arms.

Tears gathered in Rebecca's eyes as Alexander held Cordelia back. "She's gone, Cordelia. There's nothing you can do now," he said quietly.

Cordelia wrestled free and sailed headlong into James Emory's arms.

"James, oh, James, what have we done?" she whimpered.

Even Emory, honorless scoundrel that he was, couldn't believe he'd killed his own mother-in-law. But the evidence was indisputable.

"I'm ruined," he said incredulously.

Dropping the dueling pistol in the snow, Captain James Emory gulped down his astonishment, and did what was probably the first decent thing in his adult life. He gathered his wife in his arms and rocked her as she sobbed against his chest.

James took the brunt of Cordelia's pain as was his due. It was the closest he would ever come to attaining the coveted title of "gentleman."

"Emory," Alexander said with calm authority. "I think it would be best if you and Cordelia returned to the house and gathered her things."

"W—w—what?" Cordelia stammered in a watery voice, twirling to face Alexander.

"Your place is with your husband, Cordelia. I don't know why you didn't see that in the first place."

Cordelia dashed the tears from her eyes, staring at Alexander for a moment as if she'd really seen a gray ghost, as if trying to grasp the full meaning of what the ghost had said. Then she slowly reached for her husband's hand.

"Y—y—yes. Of course. You're absolutely correct, Alexander. A wife's place is with her husband. I've said so all along," Cordelia affirmed dazedly.

Alexander glanced down at his aunt's body. The pain Rebecca had feared was in his eyes. He recovered quickly, masking it, turning a harsh eye on James Emory.

"I don't think this is the time or place to resolve

our differences. Perhaps a future battlefield, at some more appropriate time. I'll see that Abigail receives a proper burial."

The man gulped, nodded dumbly almost as if he were afraid to believe his good fortune.

"I'm only doing this for Cordelia's sake," Alexander clarified. "It's obvious she loves you, prefers you to her blood relations, though there's no accounting for taste. Plus, by her own admission, she carries your child. I doubt she would survive the hullabaloo this disagreeable affair would create. Not to mention the stigma that would follow the child its entire life."

"What of the authorities? Do you intend to report this to them?"

"Report you to which ones, Emory? To the Confederates, who would hang you on the spot on sheer principle? Or to the Yankees, who deplore 'the South's uncivilized tendency to solve arguments by armed contest'?" he quoted. "It's just as likely they would hang you as well, as an example to others."

"You simply couldn't do such a dreadful thing," Cordelia demurred. "Please, Alexander. Say you won't even think of it."

Alexander sighed. Cordelia was a spy. A traitor to the cause. And due to that, the Confederates would destroy her along with Emory, and ask questions later. Of that, he was certain.

The Yankees? He hated to see any Southern woman at their beck and call. Cousin or otherwise.

For love of family, blood ties, he must let Cordelia go, Alexander decided. His deep passion for his country, however, made it a grueling proposition. One that would ride him hard in the wee hours of the night when he rested by a Confederate campfire, expecting any moment to be ambushed.

"As you can see, either course would be detrimental to Cordelia," Alexander stated. "The war has had many casualties, Captain Emory," he continued wearily. "It's sad to say that not all of them are soldiers. Abigail's death was an unfortunate accident. Everyone present knows that."

"I see."

"Do you? Do you really? I seriously doubt it."

"Well ..." Emory faltered, tucking Cordelia under his arm, making as if to cut and run before any more misfortune befell him.

"A moment, Emory."

James rounded on Alexander, his golden brow raised in question.

"If I were you, I'd treat Cordelia with kid gloves, as if she were spun gold. I'd tiptoe around her wishes as if you were walking on eggshells. Because you are. Otherwise, it might get around that you shot and killed your mother-in-law. The society you seek so diligently would blacklist you."

Emory blanched.

Alexander had driven his point home.

"It would most assuredly nip your military career in the bud, kill any hopes you might harbor for financial success. Yes. I think if word leaked out that you were anything other than an exemplary husband, information concerning this fiasco *would* most assuredly find its way to the appropriate channels," Alexander pledged dispassionately. "Need I embellish further?"

Emory cleared his throat. "I'm well aware that discretion is the best policy."

"I'm glad we see one thing eye to eye."

Gaping, Rebecca watched James Emory guide his wife toward the garden path that lead to the rear of the plantation house. To her chagrin, despite all her best efforts, the Ransom family had been destroyed after all.

Perplexed and totally disconcerted, Rebecca eased to her feet.

Nothing, up to now, seemed more senseless than Abigail's death and Cordelia's exile. It was all so cut and dried.

Besides, Cordelia had never even gotten around to teaching her to play the piano, Rebecca thought.

And Alexander need only await word from Richmond to release her.

Yet, Alexander didn't release her.

Not the day after Cordelia left Oak Mont with James Emory. Nor the day after word arrived from Richmond exonerating a woman named Rebecca Ann Warren of guilt in association with the Nashville spy ring. Nor the day Alexander told her he believed her fantastic story, that she was a time traveler from the future, and that he was mad about her anyway.

Nor the day after that. Nor the day after that. Nor the day after that.

Instead, Alexander and Rebecca became willing prisoners to their enduring love for each other.

Chapter Fourteen

To Rebecca, gazing out the open door of the carriage house, the world seemed oddly monochromatic. Like old photos, she thought, neither black nor white, but gray, as gray as the frock coat, with its newly replaced buttons, that stretched so superbly across Alexander's broad shoulders as he saddled Vedette.

Leaning with her hands tucked behind her, her back against the doorjamb, she could see the blossoming apple orchard where Abigail rested; the gracious house that generations of Ransoms had called home; the crowns of the bud-tipped dogwood trees that flanked the veranda; and the leafy roses through the slated picket fence. She could see the mountain bluebells on the hillside, could smell the fragrance of wild honeysuckle permeating the air, could feel the delicate brush of a spotted ladybug's wings as it landed on her cheek, then just as quickly changed its mind and flew on about its business.

A dove cooed, a peaceful sound—almost too much so. How long could Oak Mont retain its serenity, what with the war so close, its outcome so terribly final? she wondered morosely.

Rebecca caught her lower lip between her teeth, a frown puckering her brow. *Spring's here. You're in love and that love is reciprocated. You have a new family of sorts. Willy, Jubadessa, Alexander. Most definitely Alexander. You should feel happy.* But she couldn't. There was an aura of foreboding in the air and she couldn't seem to shake it.

"Rebecca?"

She slowly turned into the carriage house, her skirts swishing around her ankles. She wore no hoop, had refused a corset in lieu of petticoats and her own undergarments, but Jubadessa had ceased to chide her over her "eccentricities." Now, she was accepted for who and what she was. She belonged. No longer did she feel like Alice, trapped in a bewildering Wonderland.

"Come here," Alexander commanded sternly, his arms spread wide to receive her.

Rebecca hurriedly crossed the distance separating them, gliding into his arms and pressing her cheek against his heart. He caught her in his firm embrace, kissing the top of her head, holding her as if he might never let her go. He smelled of homemade soap, bay rum, and leather, spicy and tantalizing, a scent of which she was positive she would never tire.

They were silent for a moment, then he murmured, "You're unusually quiet. What did you see outside?"

"Nothing. Please, don't go. Not just yet," Rebecca whispered on a pleading note, her eyes involuntarily filling with unshed tears.

"Here now," Alexander cajoled softly, tipping her chin so that he could read the expression on her face. "What's this? Women simply don't cry in public, not at the depot, not on the battlefield, and *never* in front of a gentleman. Where's my fiery saucebox, the lady who crossed Federal lines under fire without flinching, who saved my worthless hide more than once, the temptress who warms my bed with such gusto?"

"If you're trying to make me angry, it won't work today. And your hide isn't worthless." Rebecca sniffed, stretching her eyes like a Chinaman's and blinking several times to keep the tears from overflowing. Stepping away from him, she squared her shoulders, reminding herself that she was tough, that she was an Army nurse, that she knew a soldier's duty as well as Alexander did. And that she loathed simpering females who cried at the least provocation.

"Major General Wheeler has sent orders that I'm to return to my command. Tennessee needs all her able-bodied sons. Besides, it's unfair that my men are without me. Their welfare is my responsibility, Rebecca. I have to support them, no matter the cost."

"I'll go with you." Her sapphire-blue eyes sparkled from her tears.

"Impossible." His statement was not unkind, only irrefutable.

"I know." Rebecca swallowed hard. She was afraid for Alexander and couldn't bring herself to explain that the cost he spoke of would be so dear, that a fourth of the soldiers probably wouldn't survive to witness the war's end. With that thought came another, that when all was said and done, *she* might be one of the unfortunate women waiting in vain for her loved one's return. There were no automatic guarantees in this life, or in any other for that matter, even though she'd resolved to remain at Oak Mont.

Rebecca shivered, unable to control the words that tumbled from her lips nor hide the anxiety in her voice. "Come back to me, Alexander. I'd be lost without you."

"Nonsense," Alexander corrected, his lips lifting into a beguiling grin. "If my command could maintain half your pluck and high spirit, we'd be home free."

"How I wish that were true," she responded with a heavy sigh.

Alexander drew her securely back into his arms. "You know something you're not telling me. But I won't push you. Some things are better left alone."

"Yes," Rebecca agreed.

"There's something I've been meaning to ask you. A favor," he began, rerouting the conversation as he kissed her mouth lightly.

Rebecca licked her lower lip with the tip of her tongue, tasting him, cataloguing the flavor away for the lonely days ahead. "Anything."

"Jubadessa is a fine woman. She will be a comfort to you in my absence, a good companion."

"She's been that already."

"To all of us. If not for her cry of alarm, James Emory would have caused more harm than he did."

"Do you think he'll be back?"

"He isn't stupid. Emory knows if he harasses Oak Mont further, I'll see that he's blacklisted from here to kingdom come. I only allowed him his life for Cordelia's sake."

"I hate it for her. Banishment must be awful, but then again, she has a baby on the way to take her mind off more unpleasant things."

Alexander chose not to comment. Instead he said, "Jubadessa may not show it, but quietly and in her own way she still mourns the loss of Cordelia and Abigail. Now, the roles have reversed and she's the one who needs mothering. Keep an eye on her for me."

"I will."

"And help Willy hold down the fort."

"I'm game. As long as he shows me what to do," Rebecca quipped, attempting a lightheartedness she didn't feel.

Alexander brushed a wavy tendril of auburn hair from her cheek, gently tucking it behind her ear. Running one long finger lower, he traced the delicate column of her neck, traveling diagonally to graze her collarbone beneath the fabric of her day dress. His touch was wooing.

Presently, Alexander withdrew his hand only to plant a hot, moist kiss on the throbbing pulse at the base of Rebecca's throat. Her blood surged so passionately that she could almost feel its movement.

"There's something else," he said huskily, flicking apart the first three hooks on her bodice to expose the deep vee of her breasts swelling above her bra.

Rebecca arched one eyebrow in silent question, waiting in anticipation. She'd expected him to say, "Make love to me," as he'd often done in the past two weeks since James Emory had attempted to arrest her.

"I love you, Rebecca. I want you. Marry me this evening before I go."

Rebecca felt as if everything inside her was melting under the heat of his proposal, her heart, and mind, and bones draining in a molten path out through her toes, leaving her body a hollow shell. Her fondest desire was within her immediate grasp—again. He'd proposed so many times since Cordelia left, she'd lost count.

Watching Alexander as if at any moment he might vanish into thin air, Rebecca opened her mouth several times to speak, unable to find the words. Finally, shaking her head to clear it, she whispered in a strained voice, "I can't. You know that."

The aching emotion in his eyes was hidden by the lowering of his lids as he asked gravely, "Why?"

It was a simple question, with an extremely complex answer. Rebecca reached for his hand, making a show of studying the serpentine ring on his finger, smoothing her thumb over its cool garnet orbs. The heirloom stood for tradition and honor, plus a code of ethics and a way of life she was only just beginning to comprehend.

"Because I'm not a chameleon. I'll never be able to commit myself to being a proper young lady. I'm a nonconformist. You'd be stuck with a wife who's subject to ... to ..." She glanced toward heaven as if searching for an example, then continued, "... dashing off without a moment's notice to nurse a family with measles or diphtheria. I have no diplomacy. I'll blurt out what I think at the most inappropriate times. Polite society will be appalled, if it even understands what I'm talking about. Most people will probably have a good laugh at your expense because you've freely chosen to tie yourself to a woman who speaks such unusual English."

"Laughter is good for the soul," Alexander said, the stubborn tilt of his jaw assuring Rebecca that convincing him to accept her refusal wouldn't be easy. She relentlessly forged ahead.

"I *despise* restrictive underwear and I won't wear it ..."

"Not even in public?" he teased gently.

"Well ... maybe in public, but that's not the point. Don't you understand? *Look* at me. I'd rather wear pants and a T-shirt than skirts. My hair's a mess." She lifted a wayward lock that had escaped the bun at her nape then dropped it. "I'm hopeless without hair spray ... Can't get the pins to stay in to save my life."

Rebecca was desperate, crying now despite herself, the salty tears scalding her cheeks. She hadn't allowed her emotions to get the better of her since her brother had been killed near the DMZ. Alexander had that affect on her. He made her feel. The tears hurt. They were also a release, a rehumanization because his love drew her out of herself.

Alexander's face was suddenly solemn. He dried her tears with the back of his hand. Then with infinite reverence, he reached up and began to extract the hairpins from her coiffure, tossing them to the straw-strewn floor. When he was finished, her hair hung in carefree abandon on her shoulders.

"I don't care about those things. If it was within my power to alter you one wit, I'd decline the option. When I think of all the mamas who paraded their 'proper' young daughters before me, spineless wonders for the most part, I shudder. They were all so boringly pale in comparison to you. Once seen, you could never be forgotten, Rebecca," he said, eyeing her steadily. "You've left your imprint on my soul, and like this war, there's no turning back. If we're going to do this, and we are, then let's do it right. I couldn't stand the notion of another man sweeping you off your feet while I'm away."

Rebecca could have kicked herself. She'd managed to do what she'd always avoided before—gotten personally involved, deeply and irrevocably. "What if something happens? Not to you, but to me? I don't know exactly how I got here. What if . . ." The idea was almost too horrible to contemplate, but she forced herself to voice her fear. "What if I'm no longer here when you return?"

She was speaking of time somehow sucking her back into her own century, and Alexander knew it.

"That's been the *real* reason you wouldn't marry me. The problem all along. Hasn't it?" Alexander asked.

"Yes," Rebecca replied in a hoarse whisper that sounded almost like a sob.

"You have my word on it. When the war's over, I'll return to Oak Mont. If you aren't here, I swear I'll find you."

"How?"

"Put a candle in your window, darlin'. That's all I need," he said hoarsely.

The endearment almost broke her heart. "Candles are so feeble in a storm. I would hate to depend on one to light your way."

"Then let it burn where it's protected—in your heart. I can't fail with a flame that bright to guide me."

A smile curved Rebecca's lips. A funny thing had happened; now she knew where all the color in the world had gone. All of it, every single drop, was in Alexander's eyes. They were so vibrant, so intense, that she was overwhelmed by the promise she saw reflected there. Like the bold green traffic light at a crowded intersection, they said, "It's finally your turn. Go for it, Rebecca!"

Rebecca was married at dusk in Oak Mont's main parlor, bedecked in Alexander's own mother's wedding gown. The dress was a grand affair, yards and yards of sheer silk overlaid with delicate Venetian lace adorned in luminous seed pearls. Willy and Jubadessa were their only witnesses, with the minister who was a close neighbor and family friend performing the ceremony.

"I, Rebecca Ann Warren, take you, William Alexander Ransom, to be my beloved husband," she intoned.

"I, William Alexander Ransom, take you, Rebecca Ann Warren, to be my wedded wife, cherished above all others faithfully," he said in turn.

Alexander's solemn words echoed softly in Rebecca's ears, stroking her senses like a caress. Then, the minister asked for the ring. Without hesitation, Alexander slipped the serpentine off his hand and slid it on Rebecca's finger. It was far too large, and she balled her fist to keep it from falling off. Then he kissed her to seal the commitment. The kiss was warm, deep, and lingering, as if he could never get enough. The feeling was mutual and she savored the intimacy.

They toasted their marriage by sharing the last bottle of fine old Madeira with their guests, then Alexander mounted Vedette and rode off into the night. For a solitary Confederate, travel was wiser under cover of darkness.

Rebecca stood on the veranda and listened to the pounding of Vedette's hooves until she could no longer hear the bittersweet sound. Eventually, she followed Jubadessa into the house.

"Here, let me help you off with that gown. It is so beautiful on you," Jubadessa offered gently, lighting an oil lamp to escort Rebecca up the stairs to her room—Oak Mont's master bedchamber.

"No need," Rebecca mused aloud, suddenly incredibly weary now that Alexander was gone. "I can do it."

"But, *Madame . . .*"

"*Madame?*" Rebecca said thoughtfully, a small chuckle escaping her lips. "Never *Madame*. I won't tolerate formality between us. Rebecca will do. From here on out, you've got to try and remember that." She smiled.

Jubadessa looked at her strangely as she took the lamp and turned toward the oaken staircase.

"Rebecca," she said, testing the word as she followed Rebecca up the first step. Her version possessed a romantic French inflection that pleased Rebecca.

Her heel tangling in the hem of her gown, Rebecca stumbled. Jubadessa caught her elbow, steadying her. "Are you okay?" she asked with concern.

Rebecca paused to unhook the shoe, her smile broadening. She *had* rubbed off on them for better or for worse.

"A–OK. I just need to be alone for a little while, that's all."

"If you want anything, ring the house bell. I will be right up."

"Thanks, but I won't be needing anything else tonight."

On impulse, she surprised Jubadessa by giving her a peck on the cheek, then left her standing as if frozen in place at the bottom of the staircase.

Once in her room, Rebecca swept back the brocade drapes and opened the window wide. The silvery moonlight poured in, the cricket's music rivaling that of the tree frogs.

Jubadessa had neatly laid out her nightgown on the massive poster bed. It proved to be the antique cotton gown her parents had given her. She hadn't worn it since the day she'd arrived. Picking up the skirt, she rubbed the material between her thumb and forefinger, wondering how clever Jubadessa had gotten out the blood stains. It was as pure and white as the day she had unwrapped it in Vietnam.

Placing her wedding ring on the night stand, Rebecca made a mental note to ask the housekeeper for a spool of twine to wrap the ring so she could wear it without fear of losing it. Carefully, she unhooked the silk gown and stepped from it, spreading it over Alexander's walnut valet.

Stripping out of the starched petticoats and horsehair crinoline that had been absolutely necessary to accommodate the fitted hourglass-shaped finery, she donned the nightgown. It cascaded against her lower body, conforming to the slender curves of her figure to fall in a whisper about her ankles.

With a start, Rebecca recollected the card her parents had enclosed in her Christmas package. She sank down on to the bed. What had she done with it? It seemed that only this morning she'd held it in her hands. Like neon lights exploding in her brain, she remembered.

Rebecca scrambled to her feet, dashing to the wardrobe where Jubadessa had stored her leather medical bag. In desperate need of the comfort her parents' words might offer, she dropped to her knees and rummaged in the free-standing closet. With an exclamation of success, she slid the bag out onto the floor, tore it open, and un-zipped the side pouch. If only her parents could know how happy she was, how confident and secure she was in her husband's love. How pleased they would be.

The instant her fingers touched the precious card, Rebecca knew she'd made a fatal mistake. *Wham!* It seemed as if she'd been hit in the head with a two-by-four. An electric charge surged through her fingertips, painfully penetrating her heart. The room dimmed as if the lamp had blown out, though glancing at it in horror she realized it hadn't. There was a whistling in her ears. Her body burned. Her mouth watered. She felt nauseous and began to perspire profusely, compensating for the internal rise in her body temperature. *Oh, God! What's going on?*

The momentum of the moment propelled her as she crawled to the window, dragging her bag be-hind her. Reluctantly, as if she had no control over the matter, she slanted the stark-white card embossed with angels toward the streaming moon-light and took a deep breath. The night air seared her lungs with its coolness.

With a dread that made her teeth chatter, she squinted, reading aloud the ball-point penned words her mother had written. "We love and miss you, Rebecca. Come home to us safely. Mom and Dad." The whistling increased as did the nausea.

Don't panic! "Jubadessa," Rebecca called in a faint, stricken voice, wondering if she could make it to the chamber pot before she threw up. "Juba—" Her throat tightened and her words were choked off.

More threatened than she'd ever felt when the MASH unit was shelled, she raised her face to the night sky, grappling for the windowsill to pull her-self to her feet. "Must...reach...the...house bell," she stammered to herself. But she couldn't seem to lift her body. Time had finally caught up with her.

She felt herself slowly fading, not at all like the abruptness she'd experienced with the first trip across the time warp. "No–o–o–o–o–o!" she cried in strangled amazement, staring at her hands. They were mere shadows through which she could see the Aubusson rug. She supposed it was because she was so unwilling to cooperate that she was being sapped back, one cell at a time.

With grim resolve, Rebecca tried to fight the force, quickly realizing the struggle was lost before it had gotten off the ground. Time was too pow-erful. Like a coat of honey, the cloying sense of foreboding that had dogged her throughout the day enveloped her. "Alexander, I tried," she said on a stifled sob. "I'll love you...always."

Rebecca's words were borne off into the darkness by the gentle spring breeze. Then complete and total blackness descended, robbing her of further thought.

Epilogue

Rebecca smelled alcohol. Cold, strong, and pungent. It was stinging her eye. She reached up to fan the fumes away only to find a wad of saturated gauze pressed firmly to her throbbing temple.

"Stop struggling for a minute, Rebecca. Let me get this dressing on." The gauze was replaced with the tight bulk of a wrap-around bandage. "Now, sit up, carefully. Stand. That's it. Lean on me."

"Janet?" Rebecca ground out, disoriented, grit crunching between her teeth as she spoke.

"Yeah."

"What the hell's going on?"

"Empty can from the trash dump hit you in the

head. Knocked you out like a light. How many times have I told you to wear that damned helmet on your *head*, instead of slinging it over the crook of your arm like a freakin' pocketbook?"

"A million."

Vedette's pounding hooves echoed in the distance, receded, then disappeared. In their place, Rebecca could hear the modern whir of chopper blades, momentum decreasing as they stilled to a quiet hum. She'd been dreaming ... Alexander, the plantation, all a dream. Tears filled her eyes, spilling down her cheeks as she slumped against Janet for support.

"Don't cry, hon. It's not that bad." Janet adjusted Rebecca's stethoscope more securely around her neck. "You'll be okay. Your head's going to need a few stitches. Later, though. Wounded first."

"Of course," Rebecca agreed, her head aching so badly she could hardly think straight. "The Civil War ambulance ... chopper, I mean."

"On second thought, maybe you'd better go on over to surgery, let the major have a look at you," Janet stated in concern.

"No, I'll be all right ... the men. I'm just a little woozy." Sluggishly, Rebecca placed one foot in front of the other, heading for the grounded medevac unit. Janet pranced beside her.

"If you say so," she said with a shrug, letting go of Rebecca's arm as her friend's steps steadied, turning her own attention to the helicopter.

The corpsmen were rapidly handing men out to the other medical personnel gathered around the

Huey. Four, five, six stretchers passed within reach, but Rebecca couldn't seem to focus on them. A young crew chief, wearing a tourniquet on one arm and a grin from ear to ear, trailed them. Janet directed him past Rebecca toward the surgical unit.

"We did it! We got her down safely, Lieutenant Colonel, just like you said we would," Rebecca heard him shout over his shoulder, his words blowing back into the chopper's open bay door to the remaining passenger inside.

Rebecca had just reached the door when the corpsmen wheeled the pilot out on a gurney. His chicken plate had already been removed, the bullet-proof flight vest having had little effect against the bullet that had entered at an angle via his upper arm, tumbled, then strangely enough exited his shoulder.

Rebecca squeezed her eyes shut and concentrated hard, forcing everything except the moment at hand and her patient's welfare from her mind. Finally, her nurse's training rallied, carrying with it a mechanical professionalism that coated her emotions without hampering her efficiency. When she opened her eyes, her mind was as clear as a bell and she was once again in control of the situation.

Rebecca placed her leather medical bag on the gurney and methodically went to work.

The pilot's flight suit was torn, his shirt gaping, his dog tags bloody, but Rebecca could see his breathing was steady. She established a pulse through the carotid artery in his neck, then fished her scissors from her bag to cut off his shirt. With lightning speed, the officer grabbed her hand in a crushing grip. Numbly, she dropped the scissors.

Pulling Rebecca closer, he drew her hip firmly against the gurney. Then, raising her hand gently to his parched lips, he turned it over and brushed the palm with a feather-light kiss.

"Rebecca." Her name was a deep sigh, uttered as if it were the long lost answer to an often-repeated prayer.

Rebecca's heart almost stopped. Her gaze flew to his hand, to the ring he wore—a snake, with domed garnet orbs that winked at her. Her eyes widening, she anxiously scanned the helicopter pilot's beloved face, and a thrill of pure ecstasy assailed her soul.

"Alex . . ." Rebecca whispered incredulously, a thick sob catching in her throat as she returned the pressure of his hand. Then more strongly, "Alexander. My God! How?"

"I followed your light."

It was then that Lieutenant Colonel William Alexander Ransom tugged her down and kissed her trembling lips, a proclamation for all the world to see. The kiss was warm, deep, and lingering, so filled with his love for her that she could barely contain her joy.

"I promised I'd find you after the war, darlin'. A Southern gentleman never goes back on his word. You should know that by now," he professed when his lips finally released hers, his endearingly crooked grin surfacing through a grimace of pain as he attempted to sit up on the gurney.

She pushed him back down, softly admonishing, "Please. Lie still for now, my love."

Rebecca reluctantly extracted her hand from Alexander's to examine his chest wound. It was clean through and through, and not too bad. The modern day on-the-spot medical attention and the MASH surgeon's expertise would fix him up in no time. Hardly as tricky as before, she decided with intense relief.

"I can't believe . . . I thought I had imagined it all," Rebecca rasped, tenderly smoothing back the sable curls from Alexander's brow as she held a pressure pad against his shoulder to control the bleeding and to minimize shock.

"No. It was real enough, as real as you and I are now," Alexander stated solemnly, covering the back of her hand which held the pad with his larger one, squeezing reassuringly.

Rebecca nodded. Who was she to doubt the power of love, question the mysteries of the universe . . . eternity? All that mattered was that, by some miracle, she was once again at Alexander's side.

"You're not going to die on me, soldier." It was not a question, but a command, voiced as Rebecca raced beside the gurney toward triage.

"Not a snowball's chance in hell," Alexander vowed. " 'Fraid you're going be stuck with me a long, long time, ma'am—several lifetimes in fact."

"Promise?"

"With all my heart."

SPECIAL SNEAK PREVIEW!

TIMESPUN TREASURE
by Thomasina Ring
Author of *Timespun Rapture*

When a storm transports Meredith Davis back to Colonial Virgina, she can't believe her eyes—especially when a dashing stranger vows he must take her for his wife. But all too soon, Meredith discovers that her delicious fantasy might really be a nightmare. For dark secrets threaten to destroy her newfound bliss with Benjamin Foxworth. And even if she can solve the mysteries behind the curse that plagues Foxworth's plantation, Meredith fears that at any moment she might awaken and lose the dream for all time.

**ON SALE IN FALL, 1992
AT NEWSSTANDS AND BOOKSTORES
EVERYWHERE**

Chapter One

The afternoon got off to a rotten start.

Patrick Henry arrived with a bad case of laryngitis, George Washington's fly was missing two buttons and Thomas Jefferson's wig had sprung a curl.

Clucking like a mother hen, Meredith Davis searched through her oversized leather shoulder bag and within seconds had everything under control.

For Mr. Henry, Meredith found a package of herbal cough drops. "Suck two of these slowly and another two shortly before the big speech—they should do the trick," she assured him.

Mr. Washington received a couple of safety pins and an admonition. "Please, for God's sake, pin them on the *inside* so they don't show."

A strategic placement of a small clip and a whiff of hair spray took care of Mr. Jefferson.

They were beholden, they told Meredith.

With a warm grin, she dipped a mock curtsy and left the men standing amid the gravestones behind the small church. She couldn't help but chuckle as she hurried around to the front. Lord, even the Founding Fathers were depending on her now. The irony struck her. Back there stood the so-called "Voice, Sword and Pen" of this country's noble struggle for independence, and without her assistance they surely would've made a sorry spectacle of themselves today.

Rounding the corner, she saw Kelly McGee already stationed in St. John's open doorway. Meredith glanced at her watch and frowned. She was five minutes late, thanks to the delay out back. Even as she quickened her steps she remembered to unfasten the black-strapped watch and stuff it into her bag—it would have added a jarring note to her colonial garb.

Scurrying through the door, she offered Kelly a shrug of apology, tossed her purse over into the corner of the vestibule, grabbed a handful of programs and joined her fellow docent out by the entrance.

The bright, sunny day was unusually warm for late March, and early arrivals for the afternoon's performance chose to linger outside, many of them wandering around the old graves in the historical churchyard.

"Like your new costume," Kelly complimented her in a properly subdued voice while they waited.

"Fits you better than that brown thing you wore last year, and the lower neckline is becoming as all get-out."

"Even managed some tantalizing poofiness, I hope you noticed," Meredith whispered with a wicked smile. "Found an underwire push-up bra at Victoria's Secret that works miracles."

Kelly lifted an eyebrow. "Am I hearing right? *You*? Ms. No-Nonsense, Professional-Image Davis into tantalizing and shopping at bimbo heaven, of all places! Did you get a personality transplant during the winter?"

Meredith's cheeks warmed though she'd expected Kelly's teasing. Good grief, she'd long ago proved her levelheadedness and professional competence. Now, at 29, she figured an attempt at a bit of feminine allure would hardly create the impression she was an airhead.

"The personality remains the same, Ms. McGee," she retorted. "It's just that I've decided to stop hiding my drop-dead beauty from the impoverished world."

Kelly tilted her head and gave her an appraising look. "Hmmm. A dynamite new blunt cut, obviously a first-class salon job. Green contacts—startling green, like a cat in heat, I'd say. A touch of matching shadow, a hint of mascara, a light brush of blush, lip color." She giggled. "Not drop-dead, Meredith, but you show some promise. Estee Lauder or Clinique?"

"Lancôme. And, if you can believe it, I splurged on a set of violet contacts, too, for a change of pace."

"You needed one, girl, and it's about time." Her hazel eyes sparked a saucy twinkle. "And way past time you started looking for a man."

Meredith bristled. "I'm doing this for me, Kelly, not for a man. I've found I like being a touch more attractive, and it's something I feel secure enough now to come to grips with—a big something I've had to work out for myself. Besides, the last thing I'm interested in at the moment is a man. *Any* man. When Sam and I broke up last year, I swore off involvements." She wrinkled up her nose. "Shoot, they're all wimps these days—half-baked wimps, the lot of them."

"But your eyes, love," Kelly said with a wry grin before turning to face a group of people heading their way. "Definitely like a she-cat in heat," she tossed over her shoulder in a low voice.

Blast her, Meredith grumbled, though she had to admit perceptive Kelly had punched a sensitive button. It had been a year since Dr. Sam Whitson had crawled out of their stormy relationship to marry that simpering, docile nurse. But Meredith hadn't missed him a minute, if truth be told. Like the pitifully few other men she'd ever let get close to her, Sam had protested her strong will and independent ways, but whimpered like a lost puppy if, God forbid, he had to exert some gumption on his own.

She was a hard woman to please, she guessed. What she wanted in a man simply wasn't out there to be had—someone who would love her for her strength because it dovetailed with his strength. Someone she could respect, for Pete's sake.

She shrugged. Since such a paragon didn't exist, she'd decided she could get along just fine without a man.

True, her hormones had been rebelling a tad lately; but, like the rest of her well-ordered life, she had those primitive urges under complete control.

She lifted her chin a resolute notch higher. Despite her new vivid-green contact lenses, she was *not* a she-cat in heat. So there, Kelly McGee!

Meredith greeted a trio of elderly ladies with a pleasant smile and led them inside to a pew near the front. "Please leave this seat at the end here vacant," she said in a conspiratorial whisper, knowing the gray-haired women would be thrilled beyond measure when the actor playing George Washington, resplendent in his bright red coat, would enter soon and take his seat there beside them.

She hoped like the dickens his fly was suitably closed.

After the audience had been seated, filling the tiny white wooden church, the annual anniversary reenactment of the proceedings of the March 23, 1775, Second Virginia Convention got under way. Kelly had stayed inside for the performance, saying she'd never tire of hearing those wonderful words.

Meredith felt the same way. Today, however, the church was sweltering, and she hated crowds. She'd opted to stand out in the vestibule, near the open door where she could benefit from the fresh breeze that had kicked up. Besides, she could hear well enough, and she practically had the thing memorized.

Like Kelly, she got tingles in her spine every time Patrick Henry stood to deliver his immortal "Liberty or Death" speech, though she'd heard it in dozens of similar reenactments by dozens of Patrick Henrys—none of them bearing the slightest resemblance to portraits of the gaunt red-headed Virginian, but all of them gifted with proper verve and silver tongues.

Being a Richmond native, Meredith loved history, especially Virginia history, so she'd happily taken on this part-time job as a docent for the Patrick Henry Association.

Lord knew, it wasn't the little bit of money she was paid that attracted her. Her small physical therapy private practice was doing exceedingly well. Referrals from orthopedists and other physicians had grown to the point that she'd have to expand soon and increase her staff.

She truly enjoyed ushering at these St. John's reenactments, and the activity took little time away from her busy schedule. Other than this anniversary performance every March, the events were held only on Sunday afternoons during the three summer months.

A grumble of thunder disturbed her thoughts, and she stuck her head out the door to study the sky. Uh-oh. Angry clouds had gathered in the northwest and were fast approaching.

"The question before the house is one of awful moment to this country. For my own part, I consider it as nothing less than a question of freedom or slavery." Mister Henry had started his speech. Her cough drops had worked, thank heaven. His voice was as clear and resounding as the Liberty Bell. She prayed the storm would hold off till he finished.

But it didn't look promising. A strong wind buffeted the trees lining the church's narrow brick walkway. Maple seeds and dried magnolia leaves skittered across the weathered gravestones.

"I have but one lamp by which my feet are guided; and that is the lamp of experience. I know of no way of judging the future but by the past."

Grimacing as a speck of dirt blew into her left eye, lodging beneath the contact lens, Meredith quickly grabbed for her shoulder bag and dug for the bottle of saline solution. She squirted a few drops into her eye and blinked away the irritation. A sharp spear of lightning flashed through the vestibule, triggering an added blink.

"Sir, we have done everything that could be done to avert the storm which is now coming on."

As if on cue, a loud clap of thunder provided a dramatic response. She tightened her lips. "Hold back," she muttered her plea to the turbulent sky.

The actor's voice rose for the soul-stirring climax. "Gentlemen may cry, 'peace, peace'—but there is no peace. The war is actually begun. The next gale that sweeps from the North will bring to our ears the clash of resounding arms!"

She leaned against the paneled wainscoting and closed her eyes. He was nearly through. For a moment, the wind quieted, the thunder stilled. The voice back in the crowded church lowered; the audience was hushed, waiting. The small building itself, like the storm above, seemed to be holding its breath. "Why stand we here idle? What is it that gentlemen wish? What would they have? Is life so dear, or peace so sweet, as to be purchased at the price of chains and slavery?"

And then, that glorious primal shout: "Forbid it, Almighty God!" Meredith loved the poignant pause, knew the actor's arms were stretched high. "I know not what course others may take; but as for me, give me liberty or give me!"

A blinding stab of lightning pierced her closed eyelids, a blast of thunder tore through her ears. Jolted, Meredith stiffened against the wall. But the wall wasn't there! She fell backward, through dark nothingness, landing on her rump with a teeth-shattering jar.

Stunned, still clutching her bag, she sat in the darkness, unwilling to open her eyes. Dear God, had a tornado struck? Was everyone all right? Was she all right? Nothing hurt; she could move her arms and legs, wiggle her fingers and toes.

She opened her eyes and gasped. Wherever she was, Meredith Davis was no longer in the vestibule of St. John's Church.

She took a quick, deep breath, trying to ward off the icy panic that gripped her. *Where am I? Good God, what's happened?*

Ordering herself to stay calm, though her thumping heartbeat refused to obey, she did what she could to assess her situation. She was seated on weed-covered ground, beside a small white clapboard building. On a dreary hillside. Alone. The day was heavily clouded; the wind, brisk and cold, like winter. But the scattering of trees on the steep hill bore the tenuous green sprouts of spring.

Her astounded brain raced, searching for a logical explanation. Had the storm swept away Richmond and left her the lone survivor? Had she been swept up and transplanted, like Dorothy, only to a far less colorful Oz?

She shook her head. *Be logical, for heaven's sake!* But nothing around her made logic easy—or gave her a glimmer of useful information. Pure and simple, she was sitting like a dolt on the hard, damp ground of a strange place.

The dolt part might be permanent, she feared, but at least she could do something about the sitting. Awkwardly, she pushed herself to her feet. Though her knees were weak, she was relieved to find they held her upright.

Good. She was physically intact, but hopelessly confused. And, no denying it, her pulse was racing.

Forcing herself to be practical, she checked the back of her new green calico dress. After brushing away the few sprigs of clinging weeds, she tugged at the skirt to straighten it over her starched petticoats and took another deep steadying breath.

Okay. Now let's get this situation under control. There had to be an explanation.

She reached down for her purse and slung it over her shoulder. With tentative steps at first, then with purposeful strides after determining that her legs worked fine, she walked around the corner of the clapboard building, studying it.

Nondescript was her first thought. *Totally unknown to me,* screamed the overriding second thought. She blocked out the scream, reminding herself firmly that she'd never find answers if she allowed hysteria to take over.

The el-shaped structure had tall, black-shuttered windows. The roof was pitched high, and atop it perched a squat open belfry, complete with bell.

A church? Meredith's brow crinkled.

Moving forward, again commanding her pounding heart to slow down, she went around to what she figured was the front of the building. Its narrow four-paneled oak door was closed, an old-fashioned iron latch where a knob should be.

With some reluctance, she pulled at the latch, but the door was locked. She knocked, but no one answered. Probably just as well, she thought. Whatever had happened, wherever she was, she didn't want to confront anybody. She might start babbling like an idiot.

She backed away from the door. The front of the simple church did look familiar. She had seen it before. Where?

She gnawed at her lip, struggling to remember. And then it came to her. This building looked similar to a drawing she'd seen of an earlier St. John's.

It fronted on the west back then, she remembered. Not that any of that knowledge helped, considering she was standing in front of something she'd only seen in a drawing.

But at least it was something she had seen. Part of her brain's memory store.

Like the blow of a hammer, the truth hit her. *That's it! None of this is real!*

Her sigh of relief collided with her gasp of concern, nearly choking her. She hadn't gone crazy. She was dreaming—or whatever people did when they were unconscious.

Her concern was for her physical condition. Obviously, she had been injured in that storm—stunned by the lightning bolt or struck on the head by something. Even now, she might be on her way to an emergency room.

Just her unconscious mind was wandering around this desolate churchyard; the rest of her—the real her—was being tended to by medics. She was probably in shock. That would explain the cold; and it might explain the lack of aches and pains, too.

Lord, she hoped she hadn't broken anything important. She hoped fervently she wasn't in some kind of coma.

Attempting to calm herself, she tried a few deep breathing exercises. The crisp, fresh air in her lungs convinced her they were operational; for sure, her heart was pumping. Heaven only knew what the emergency squad was discovering, but her vital signs still seemed vital.

Gradually, she relaxed and felt an odd sense of resigned comfort. Since her body was in the control of others for the time being, there wasn't a thing she could do but wait for the return of consciousness.

In the meantime, she might as well check out this fantasy she was having. She'd experiment with those lucid dreaming exercises she'd read about. All she had to keep in mind was that nothing could hurt her (nothing more, she amended), and she could control the events to suit her own needs.

Feeling stronger, she gave the church a challenging reappraisal. So she was imagining an earlier St. John's? While she was at it, why hadn't she conjured up its big event?

Now *that* could be exciting! Why not? Since she was in control, all she had to do was imagine the shutters open, populate the churchyard with spectators, horses and a few carriages, lift the windows, and she could hear the original proceedings of Virginia's Second Convention.

"So be it," she ordered.

But none of those things happened. St. John's remained shuttered and silent. Except for a few lopsided gravestones sticking up out of the weeds, the churchyard was empty. Her imagination was less colorful than she'd thought.

Well, surely she could make the day warmer. Seventy to seventy-five degrees would be perfect, she decided, willing the temperature to rise.

But even that small adjustment was beyond her. Fretfully, she scrunched up her shoulders, longing for a wrap. The lucid dreaming concept had obvious limitations. She wished she'd read that book with more attention.

I must be in an operating room. They keep them at refrigerated levels. Good grief, I hope they're not finding something serious. I hope to heaven they know what they're doing!

She shoved away the thought. Better that she keep moving; better to explore this fantasy world further. Maybe she could discover some important things about herself being in her subconscious this way.

"Beats analysis," she mumbled. Not that she'd ever considered analysis or had reason to consider such a thing. She was the most well-adjusted person she knew.

Oh well, she was far from perfect. Her subconscious might be more interesting than she realized. She should consider this ordeal an opportunity and, meanwhile, pray the ordeal would be a brief one.

Walking beyond the church, she found the steep, windswept hillside provided a clear vantage of what she supposed was her own concept of early Richmond. Again, her imagination disappointed her. The dreary day she'd chosen made everything look like an old sepia photograph. She wished for Technicolor, but couldn't manipulate the transformation.

Way down at the bottom of the hill lay the James River, dull as dishwater under the leaden sky. The scattering of buildings she saw were flimsy gray things—some down by the water, some over where she figured Shockhoe Slip lay, several on the hill itself.

Those below possibly were warehouses, shops or taverns. The structures on the hill looked like small houses, and smoke came from their chimneys. She considered approaching one of them, but decided against it.

She walked slowly, a pace she considered appropriate for someone in a trance. When the toes of her Capezios reached a wide path, she stopped. Was this a rudimentary street? She looked up and down its cleared but unpaved length, noting narrow wheel tracks and hoofprints in the rust-brown dirt.

Glancing back at the church and judging her distance, she guessed she'd arrived at Grace Street—in its earliest form, as produced by Meredith Davis.

Suddenly, she wanted to cry. Blast it all, this whole thing was ridiculous! She didn't care what the street was; she wasn't interested in seeing old Richmond; she didn't want to know what her stupid subconscious mind might reveal.

All she wanted was to wake up and tell somebody, please, to give her a blanket or, for God's sake, to turn up the blamed thermostat!

Meredith hated being out of control of everything in her world. She felt pitiful and lost, and she didn't like that either.

Exasperated, she leaned against the trunk of a gnarled oak and heaved a sigh. What should she do? Go back up to the church and wait till she woke up? No, she'd freeze up there. But she'd freeze here equally fast, she realized, and wandering about like a homeless waif in search of subconscious treasures was no longer the tiniest bit appealing.

Wearily, she pushed herself away from the tree. She might as well head back up the hill.

But as she turned, she nearly collided with a

wild-eyed young woman who had rushed to her side from God knew where.

"You take it," she said, thrusting a bundle into Meredith's arms. "And God help ye and forgive me, but I'll not go to that benighted house! Had ye not by the grace of God been here, I'd have left it alone on the ground."

After her strange outburst, the woman fled, leaving Meredith stupefied and sputtering fervent pleas for her to return. But the cloaked figure disappeared over the crest of the hill.

What on earth? Meredith's brain whirled in confusion. The fur-wrapped bundle she held, though a touch of welcome warmth against her beating chest, compounded the confusion.

Her first instinct was to drop the unwanted thing and run like mad back up to the church. But an impulse of curiosity compelled her to inspect the contents.

Reminding herself that all of this craziness was but a figment of her imagination, she opened a small gap in the fur with trembling fingers.

A baby!

She was standing alone in the middle of nowhere with a sleeping baby in her arms!

Okay, now, enough's enough! It was high time she woke up. Her dratted subconscious wasn't even revealing anything she didn't already know. Of course she'd love to have a baby. But the normal way, thank you, after marriage, should she ever be lucky enough to find Mr. Right.

Anxiety mingled with her impatience to regain consciousness, and consternation quickly set in.

What should she do? What *could* she do?

The fantasy baby, contentedly cocooned in its fox fur wrapping, felt as solid and real as the bag on her shoulder. She was unwilling to rid herself of either burden, though both, she knew, were ephemeral as air.

Even in a dream she wouldn't abandon an infant. The reliable bag, filled with the essentials of her daily organized life, was such a part of her she'd be lost without it. That her subconscious believed the same thing and had kindly brought it along surprised her not at all.

She snuggled the baby closer, relishing the warmth of the fur and feeling a rush of something she might have called contentment under different circumstances.

The sound of hooves and the clatter of wheels shattered the heavy quiet, startling her. She jumped alert and stared to her left with apprehension. A horse pulling a half-covered cart galloped down the road toward her.

She backed against the tree and held her breath. *Go on by, don't see me!* she commanded the vision.

But the horse and two-wheeled buggy stopped directly in front of her.

A tall man stepped from the antique conveyance. As he approached her, she gaped, paralyzed with foreboding. A specter? He was dressed in black from his high leather boots to the top of his tricorn hat. An ascot-like white wrapping around his neck and a narrow strip of white braid on his hat provided the only interruptions to the somber black. Even the wide-lapeled cloak flung over his broad shoulders was black, adding to the spectral quality.

She had conjured up a colonial gentleman! An omnious-looking one at that. He held a whip in his black-gloved hand.

Meredith pressed harder against the tree and clutched the baby tighter, too terrified to blink and forgetting to breathe.

And then he stopped, towering over her. She saw brass buttons, smelled leather and wool, bit her lip and slowly looked up—into a pair of incredible blue eyes. No, not blue. Turquoise. The valued gem variety, set in an angular, stern face that was, without doubt and despite the sternness, the most impossibly handsome face she'd ever seen.

She couldn't think straight. She couldn't think at all.

The specter spoke. "Joshua was to be with you and the babe at the appointed hour, Miss Wetzel. Do you know where he might be?"

DISCOVER THE REAL WORLD OF ROMANCE WITH LEISURE'S LEADING LADY OF LOVE!

Shirl Henke

Winner of 5 *Romantic Times* Awards

RETURN TO PARADISE. Separated at birth and raised in vastly different worlds, the sons of the House of Torres could never know that fate would cast them into a hell of their own making. Yet in the end, the power of love would redeem their sins and destine them for a glorious return to Paradise.

_3263-5 $4.99 US/$5.99 CAN

PARADISE & MORE. Fleeing the persecution of the Inquisition, and the evil of Ferdinand and Isabella's court, Aaron and Magdalena crossed storm-tossed oceans to discover a lush paradise fraught with danger and desire.

_3170-1 $4.99 US/$5.99 CAN

NIGHT WIND'S WOMAN. Proud and untamable as a lioness, Orlena vowed she would never submit to the renegade Apache who had kidnapped her. For a long-ago betrayal had made this man her enemy. But a bond even stronger than love would unite them forever.

_3096-9 $4.50 US/$5.50 CAN

LEISURE BOOKS
ATTN: Order Department
276 5th Avenue, New York, NY 10001

Please add $1.50 for shipping and handling for the first book and $.35 for each book thereafter. N.Y.S. and N.Y.C. residents, please add appropriate sales tax. No cash, stamps, or C.O.D.s. All orders shipped within 6 weeks via postal service book rate. Canadian orders require $2.00 extra postage. It must also be paid in U.S. dollars through a U.S. banking facility.

Name _____
Address _____
City _____ State _____ Zip _____
I have enclosed $_____in payment for the checked book(s).
Payment <u>must</u> accompany all orders.☐ Please send a free catalog.

"Sandra DuBay writes wonderful escapist fiction. It fulfills all her readers' fantasies!"

—*Romantic Times*

GET SWEPT AWAY WITH THESE BREATHTAKING NOVELS BY

SANDRA DUBAY

TEMPEST. Young and achingly beautiful, Dyanna McBride was as impressionable as the heroines of her beloved Gothic novels. So when she heard that Lord Justin Deville had been appointed her guardian, she was sure he would be a ruthless tyrant. One look in his mesmerizing eyes sent a delicious thrill of terror down her spine. But one searing kiss melted her resolve to oppose him at all costs.

_2719-4 $4.50 US/$5.50 CAN

MISTRESS OF THE SUN KING. Abused by her brutal husband, Athenais de Montespan longed for the love of handsome, sensual Louis XIV. But when she thought the monarch's love secure at last, she found her lover's affection threatened by an unexpected rival — a woman she had raised from poverty and introduced to the French Court.

_2990-1 $3.95 US/$4.95 CAN

LEISURE BOOKS
ATTN: Order Department
276 5th Avenue, New York, NY 10001

Please add $1.50 for shipping and handling for the first book and $.35 for each book thereafter. N.Y.S. and N.Y.C. residents, please add appropriate sales tax. No cash, stamps, or C.O.D.s. All orders shipped within 6 weeks via postal service book rate. Canadian orders require $2.00 extra postage. It must also be paid in U.S. dollars through a U.S. banking facility.

Name _____

Address _____

City _____ State _____ Zip _____

I have enclosed $_____ in payment for the checked book(s).
Payment <u>must</u> accompany all orders.☐ Please send a free catalog.

CATHERINE HART

Two-time Winner of *Romantic Times'* Reviewers' Choice Award

"Catherine Hart writes thrilling adventure....beautiful and memorable romance!"   —*Romantic Times*

SATIN AND STEEL. Bound together by a searing passion, violet-eyed Laurel Burke and rugged Brandon Prescott would have to overcome deceit, misunderstanding, and three generations of violent enmity before they could yield to a lifetime of ecstasy.

___2792-5 $4.50 US/$5.50 CAN

FALLEN ANGEL. Called Esperanza because of her sweet face and ethereal beauty, no one guessed that behind her angelic smile burned a hot flame of desire. Only one man could touch that smoldering core and fan it to life with smoldering kisses. His forbidden embrace would send her soaring to the heavens, only to leave her a fallen angel.

___2811-5 $4.50

SWEET FURY. Taught to survive the rigors of the Old West, Samantha Downing could hold her own against the roughest cowhand. Texas Marshal Travis Kinkaid had never known a prisoner as hard to control...or as easy to love. Soon the tables were turned on Travis, and he found himself a willing captive of Sam's earthy charms.

___2947-2 $4.50 US/$5.50 CAN

LEISURE BOOKS
ATTN: Order Department
276 5th Avenue, New York, NY 10001

Please add $1.50 for shipping and handling for the first book and $.35 for each book thereafter. N.Y.S. and N.Y.C. residents, please add appropriate sales tax. No cash, stamps, or C.O.D.s. All orders shipped within 6 weeks via postal service book rate. Canadian orders require $2.00 extra postage. It must also be paid in U.S. dollars through a U.S. banking facility.

Name _____

Address _____

City _____ State _____ Zip _____

I have enclosed $_____ in payment for the checked book(s). Payment <u>must</u> accompany all orders.☐ Please send a free catalog.

BRIMMING WITH PASSION...
BURSTING WITH EXCITEMENT...
HISTORICAL ROMANCE
BY BESTSELLING AUTHOR

KAREN ROBARDS

FORBIDDEN LOVE. After a passion-filled night, Megan knew she had given her body and her heart to the one man in the world whose bride she could never be — her guardian, Justin Brant.
__2920-0 $4.50 US/$5.50 CAN

ISLAND FLAME. Curvaceous Lady Catherine Aldley was furious when pirate captain Jonathan Hale claimed her as his prize, but her burning hatred turned to waves of passion in his muscular arms.
__2960-X $4.50 US/$5.50 CAN

SEA FIRE. Forced out of her marriage to the virile pirate Jonathan Hale and into a marriage to the loathsome Lord Stanhope, Lady Catherine Aldley suddenly became the object of Jon's thwarted passion and jealous fury.
__3121-3 $4.95 US/$5.95 CAN

LEISURE BOOKS
ATTN: Order Department
276 5th Avenue, New York, NY 10001

Please add $1.50 for shipping and handling for the first book and $.35 for each book thereafter. N.Y.S. and N.Y.C. residents, please add appropriate sales tax. No cash, stamps, or C.O.D.s. All orders shipped within 6 weeks via postal service book rate. Canadian orders require $2.00 extra postage. It must also be paid in U.S. dollars through a U.S. banking facility.

Name_____
Address_____
City _____ State _____ Zip_____
I have enclosed $_____in payment for the checked book(s).
Payment <u>must</u> accompany all orders.☐ Please send a free catalog.

SPEND YOUR LEISURE MOMENTS WITH US.

Hundreds of exciting titles to choose from—something for everyone's taste in fine books: breathtaking historical romance, chilling horror, spine-tingling suspense, taut medical thrillers, involving mysteries, action-packed men's adventure and wild Westerns.

SEND FOR A FREE CATALOGUE TODAY!

Leisure Books
Attn: Customer Service Department
276 5th Avenue. New York, NY 10001